PRAISE FOR *THE RABBIT FACTOR*

'Laconic, thrilling and warmly human. In these uncertain times, what better hero than an actuary?' Chris Brookmyre

'A triumph. A joyous, feel-good antidote to troubled times' Kevin Wignall

'Antti Tuomainen turns the clichéd idea of dour, humourless Scandi noir upside down with *The Rabbit Factor*. Dark, gripping and hilarious, Tuomainen is the Carl Hiaasen of the fjords' Martyn Waites

'The funniest writer in Europe, and one of the very finest, Tuomainen is my Antti-hero! There is a beautiful rhythm and poetry to the prose ... original and brilliant story-telling' Helen FitzGerald

'With brilliant characters, a crazy plotline and a setting that adds both apparent danger and great humour, the book made me laugh, smile, and had the adrenaline pumping in all the right places' Jen Med's Book Reviews

'The underlying current of menace, death and criminal activity is brilliantly described, it appeals to the dark side in me ... A must-read' Nordic Noir Buzz

'As comical as the character of Henri is, he is also lovable ... a love letter to mathematics and logical thinking ... *The Rabbit Factor* offers guaranteed entertainment' Amman Lukuhetki, Finland

'The clash between Henri's personality and the adventure park is delightful and creates a hilarious tension' Kirjanurkka, Finland

'Rationality and emotion, death and humour ... Tuomainen handles it all to perfection ... The rhythm is tightly controlled ... This is like listening to the most perfect jazz session' Ruumiin Kulttuuri, Finland

PRAISE FOR ANTTI TUOMAINEN

'Tuomainen is the funniest writer in Europe' Marcel Berlins, *The Times*

'With moral dilemmas, plenty of action, and the author's trademark mixture of humour and melancholy, this is Tuomainen's best yet' *Guardian*

'Finnish criminal chucklemeister Tuomainen is channelling Carl Hiaasen in this hilarious novel' *Sunday Times*

'By no means Nordic noir of the familiar variety, this is eccentric, humorous fare, reminiscent of nothing so much as a Coen Brothers movie' *Financial Times*

'Tuomainen continues to carve out his own niche in the chilly tundra of northern Finland in this poignant, gripping and hilarious tale' *Daily Express*

'While the plots of many Nordic noir writers are turning ever more grim, Finland's Antti Tuomainen opts these days for a wittier, lighter touch … quite the ride' *Observer*

'A gripping thriller whose complications pile to precarious, intoxicating heights' *Foreword Reviews*

'Tuomainen also persuades readers how hard life makes it to do the right thing in a universe that too often feels like a profound personal insult. Fans of Scandinavian noir will relish this one' *Publishers Weekly*

'You don't expect to laugh when you're reading about terrible crimes, but that's what you'll do when you pick up one of Tuomainen's decidedly quirky thrillers' *New York Times*

'Deftly plotted, poignant and perceptive in its wry reflections on mortality, and very funny' *Irish Times*

'A brilliantly inventive and gloriously funny novel from Finland's greatest export' M.J. Arlidge

'The biting cold of northern Finland is only matched by the cutting, dark wit and compelling plot of this must-read crime novel' Denzil Meyrick

'Combines a startlingly clever opening, a neat line in dark humour and a unique Scandinavian sensibility. A fresh and witty read' Chris Ewan

'Brilliant. Absolutely brilliant. I enjoyed every single sentence' Thomas Enger

'Antti Tuomainen is a wonderful writer, whose characters, plots and atmosphere are masterfully drawn' Yrsa Sigurðardóttir

'An original and darkly funny thriller with a Coen brothersesque feel and tremendous style' Eva Dolan

'Deliciously dark, thought-provoking, and gorgeously written. It gave me chills ... I see why Antti is so revered in Finland' Louise Beech

'Both a thriller and a dark, laugh-a-minute journey that will keep you hanging on to the end' Maxim Jakubowski, *Crime Time*

'The off-kilter, black-comedy tone is perfect for such a far-fetched story, guaranteeing plenty of spontaneous bouts of laughter' *Culture Fly*

'Weird but wonderful and utterly addictive with its fast-paced storyline that can be compared to a Finnish *Fargo*' My Chestnut Reading Tree

'The writing is clever, it's electrifying and utterly brilliant' The Quiet Knitter

'Completely unpredictable. It is dark. It is eccentric. It is crime fiction with a zany twist. Hats off Mr Tuomainen' Swirl and Thread

'A tightly written novel – funny, clever, slick. A must' The Literary Shed

ABOUT THE AUTHOR

Finnish Antti Tuomainen was an award-winning copywriter when he made his literary debut in 2007 as a suspense author. In 2011, Tuomainen's third novel, *The Healer*, was awarded the Clue Award for 'Best Finnish Crime Novel' and was shortlisted for the Glass Key Award. In 2013, the Finnish press crowned Tuomainen the 'King of Helsinki Noir' when *Dark as My Heart* was published. With a piercing and evocative style, Tuomainen was one of the first to challenge the Scandinavian crime-genre formula, and his poignant, dark and hilarious *The Man Who Died* became an international bestseller, shortlisting for the Petrona and Last Laugh Awards. *Palm Beach Finland* (2018) was an immense success, with *The Times* calling Tuomainen 'the funniest writer in Europe', and *Little Siberia* (2019) was shortlisted for the Capital Crime/Amazon Publishing Readers Awards, the Last Laugh Award and the CWA International Dagger, and won the Petrona Award for Best Scandinavian Crime Novel. *The Rabbit Factor* is the first book in Antti's first-ever series.

Follow Antti on Twitter @antti_tuomainen, or on Facebook: facebook.com/AnttiTuomainen.

ABOUT THE TRANSLATOR

David Hackston is a British translator of Finnish and Swedish literature and drama. Notable recent publications include Kati Hiekkapelto's Anna Fekete series (published by Orenda Books), Katja Kettu's wartime epic *The Midwife*, Pajtim Statovci's enigmatic debut *My Cat Yugoslavia* and its follow-up, *Crossing*, and Maria Peura's coming-of-age novel *At the Edge of Light*. He has also translated Antti Tuomainen's *The Mine*, *The Man Who Died*, *Palm Beach Finland* and *Little Siberia* (published by Orenda Books). In 2007 he was awarded the Finnish State Prize for Translation. David is also a professional countertenor and a founding member of the English Vocal Consort of Helsinki. Follow David on Twitter *@Countertenorist*.

The Rabbit Factor

ANTTI TUOMAINEN

Translated from the Finnish by David Hackston

**ORENDA
BOOKS**

Orenda Books
16 Carson Road
West Dulwich
London SE21 8HU
www.orendabooks.co.uk

First published in the United Kingdom by Orenda Books, 2021
Originally published in Finland as *Jäniskerroin* by Otava, 2020
Copyright © Antti Tuomainen, 2020
English language translation copyright © David Hackston, 2021

Quotation on pp. 158 from Schopenhauer's *The World as Will and
Representation*, trans. R. B. Haldane & J. Kemp (1844)

A catalogue record for this book is available from the British Library.

Waterstones Special Edition Hardback ISBN 292-8-377071-58-5
Hardback ISBN 978-1-913193-87-4
B-Format Paperback ISBN 978-1-913193-85-0
eISBN 978-1-913193-86-7

Typeset in Garamond by typesetter.org.uk

Printed and bound by CPI Group (UK) Ltd, Croydon CR0 4YY

Nature vector created by renata.s www.freepik.com

Orenda Books is grateful for the financial support of FILI, who provided a
translation grant for this project.

FILI FINNISH
LITERATURE
EXCHANGE

For sales and distribution, please contact *info@orendabooks.co.uk*

To all the friends I know by their first name:
Thank you.

NOW

I'm looking the rabbit in the eye when the lights suddenly go out.

With my left hand I squeeze the tube of industrial-strength glue, with my right I hold the screwdriver, and I listen.

In the half-dark, the rabbit seems to grow. Its head swells, its eyes bulge, the tips of its ears stretch upwards and seem to disappear into the dimness, its front teeth curve like an elephant's tusks. In an instant, the three-metre figure looks twice as tall, twice as wide and considerably more threatening, as though it were guarding the darkness within it. Now it seems to be watching me as if I'm an enticing carrot.

Of course, none of this is the case. The huge, German rabbit is made of hard plastic and metallic reinforcements.

The hall is a large space, tall and empty. YouMeFun. It still smells of children's horseplay and fast food; the saccharine sweetness of the bakery products seems to cling to your clothes.

I'm standing between the Big Dipper and the Komodo Locomotive, and I wait. The ladder beside me casts a long shadow across the floor. Light seeps in from the lamp glowing above the main door and from the various lights, large and small, on the machinery and rides dotted throughout the hall. The result is a misty, soupy light tinged with hues of *EXIT*-sign green, stand-by orange and power-button red.

Only a short while ago, in a situation like this, I would have assumed the reason for the sudden disappearance of the lights was surely a power cut or a technical problem with the lights themselves. But recent events have taught me that what once seemed likely, as per the laws of probability, is more often than not in the realm of the impossible. And vice versa: what once I would have been able to discount through a simple calculation of probability ratios and risk analysis is now in fact the entirety of my life.

Footsteps. I don't know why I didn't hear them sooner.

The final customers left the hall an hour ago. The last member of staff went home thirty minutes ago.

Since then I have been working by myself, checking the rides and machines, and I've even crawled through the Strawberry Fields Labyrinth with rubber gloves on my hands; children leave all sorts of things in the labyrinth, everything from food and clothes to the contents of their nappies. I have climbed up umpteen platforms, terraces and doorways, cleaned the Ghost Tunnel and more than a few of the Turtle Trucks, checked that the vines in Caper Castle aren't twisted round one another but are fully operational, attached to the poles and ready for tomorrow's sticky-fingered little Tarzans. Then I began attending to the broken rabbit. I can't understand how anyone managed to make its right ear fall off. The ear starts growing at a height of two and a half metres. The average height of our clients is around one metre, twenty centimetres, and the median is lower still.

With some degree of exactitude, I identify the footsteps as coming from near the Curly Cake Café. They belong to someone trying to move as quietly as possible but whose sheer bulk makes this impossible.

I move a few metres to the side, then take a number of quick steps back towards Caper Castle. Just then I catch my first glimpse of the new arrival. The stocky man, dressed in dark attire, is walking as cautiously as he can. He seems to be looking for me at the foot of the rabbit, but I've already made it to the protective shadows of the garage housing the Turtle Trucks. I continue moving backwards and head for the gates of Caper Castle. From there, a pathway runs behind the Secret Waterfall. This isn't a real waterfall, of course; it's a climbing wall made of blue ropes. Once inside, getting myself out of Caper Castle will be another matter altogether. That being said, I'm not planning on trying to escape in one of the Turtle Trucks, whose top speed is ten kilometres an hour.

The man has come to a stop in front of the rabbit. I see him in profile, the emergency light above the front door illuminates him from behind, forming a toxic-green halo around his shaven head. He is carrying something in his right hand. Both man and rabbit are standing about twenty metres away, at a diagonal to me. The entrance to Caper Castle is about seven metres to my ten o'clock. I take a few silent steps. I'm halfway there when the man suddenly turns. He sees me and his hand rises into the air.

A knife.

A knife is better than a pistol. Quite simply. But I don't hang around to calculate their respective probability ratios.

I dive inside Caper Castle. I overcome the first section – the wobbly stairs – and hear the man behind me. He isn't shouting for me to stop, isn't bellowing. He's come here to kill me. The room with the slanted floors is equipped with banisters that help guide me through the space. Escaping is harder and much slower than I'd expected. Light drips in through two plastic windows. The man appears at the entrance to the room. He stops, perhaps to gauge the situation. Then he sets off after me. With his free hand, he grabs the banister to give himself momentum, gripping it like he would a barbell. It works, and I'm beginning to doubt my plan.

I reach the door, step into the freely spinning, metre-long Tumble Tunnel and instantly fall onto my right side. The barrel of the tunnel is turning as though it were a unit of its own, independent from everything else. I trip a few times before I'm able to get up on my hands and knees. I crawl towards the opening at the other end. The large man steps into the Tumble Tunnel, and all my equilibrium is gone. Even on all fours, staying upright is impossible. I hear the man slam against the walls and base of the barrel. He doesn't shout. The sound he makes is more a loud snort, almost a roar. We roll around inside the barrel like two drunken, legless friends.

He's gaining on me.

I make it to the other end of the Tumble Tunnel, crawl a metre, another, then clamber to my feet again. The world is spinning and swaying; it's like walking in a squall. I approach what are called simply The Steps. The tips of these columns, designed for feet much smaller than mine, are part of my plan. This is why I've kept hold of the tube of superglue. I open the cap and squeeze glue across the steps behind me. The man's progress is slowed now as he tries to maintain his balance, making the glue more effective on the soles of his shoes.

I hobble onwards, leaving a trail of glue behind me. The Steps seem suspended in the air, somewhere between the first and second floors of the entrance hall. There's more light. It's as though all the individual spotlights in the room have joined together to allow me to walk unhindered. It feels like I'm walking a tightrope through a bright, star-lit night. I take care to stay on The Steps. There's nothing dangerous beneath us, only a soft, deep sea of sponge. But falling now would fatefully slow my journey. I glance over my shoulder and see...

...the knife.

And right then, from the motion of the man's arm, I remember a knife isn't only designed for close combat. You can also...

...throw it.

The knife slices the air. I manage to duck just enough that it doesn't pierce my heart. It grazes my left arm but doesn't actually stab me. I drop the tube of glue. From inside his jacket, the man pulls out another knife. I dash towards the Pinball Parlour. Just then, the man speaks for the first time.

'Stop,' he shouts. 'I'm warning you. I want to show you...'

His argumentation doesn't convince me. I continue on my way into the Pinball Parlour. In the darkness I bump first into one soft rubber pillar, then another. Then my gashed arm hits another of the pillars. Pain erupts through my body, almost knocks me to my knees. I'm a human pinball in a darkened, life-sized pinball machine. The only light in the room comes from the doorways. The middle of the room is pitch-dark. On the plus side, throwing another knife is impossible, as there's no direct line of sight. I keep my right arm outstretched as the flippers shunt me between the pillars and the rubber walls. I make my way towards the light, all the while hearing the man being buffeted back and forth between the flippers and hoping the glue on his shoes will slow him down.

I arrive at the waterfall, slip between the ropes into a space where there is a door leading to the warehouse. I pull the keys from my trouser pocket. The key turns in the lock, but the door won't open. I yank the handle until I realise what has happened. The locks have all been reserialised. But why have they been changed today, and why wasn't I told about it?

I return to the waterfall and walk through it. I see the man on the platform opposite, pulling a piece of carpet from the bottom of his shoe. I do what I can. I run and jump. I'm diving through the air. I crash down onto the tin slide, the pain is so agonising that I let out a yelp. I start sliding. The slide turns and twists. Throughout the slide, the wound on my arm seems only to exaggerate the fluctuations in the force of gravity. The slide and the pain seem such an impossible combination, like a bike without a saddle: you'll get to the end one way or another, but sitting down is out of the question.

I flop off the slide onto the soft mat at the bottom, stand up, and I'm taken aback. I don't hear a sound from the slide. The man can't be inside it. I can't see the upper platform, but I assume he must be back there.

I walk all the way round Caper Castle one more time, then run to get back to the rabbit and the front door behind it. It takes time, but I don't have any other options. My keys won't open the other doors either, only the front door can be opened from the inside without a key. At the final corner I stop, peer round the corner and listen. I can't see or hear anything.

I dash into a sprint, run straight for the rabbit. I run and run, and I'm about to reach the rabbit, when the big, broad-shouldered man steps out from behind it. It takes a split second to understand what I'm seeing. There's a good explanation for the man's quick and silent appearance: either by design or by accident, the soles of his feet are covered in small squares of sponge. He jumped down from the platform, and the padding made his steps silent.

Anger boils inside me.

I play by the rules. Again.

I carry on running. All I can think of is the rabbit. I slam into it and it topples over on top of the man. We all fall down, all end up on the concrete floor. The man sees me beside him, and at the same moment I see him too. He is the first to act. I only manage to free part of myself before he lashes out with the knife. The blade cuts my thigh and strikes the laminate flooring beneath us. In doing so it pins my trousers to the floor. I'm stuck. I shout out, and, with my arms flailing, I grip the first thing I can reach.

The rabbit's ear.

It's come loose again.

I grab the giant ear and hit out in the man's direction. I strike something. I stand up, my trousers rip. The man reaches into his jacket pocket. A third knife, I wonder? No, that would be too much. I act before he has the chance to throw it or stab me. I hit, hit, hit again.

Then I let go of the ear. The entrance hall is empty and silent. All I can hear is my own panting. I peer around.

The hall looks different.

An adventure park for all the family.

Suddenly it's hard to remember everything that has led to all this being my responsibility. This and much more besides – everything is suddenly uncontrollable, unpredictable.

I am an actuary.

As a rule, I don't run adventure parks, and I certainly don't batter people to death with giant, plastic rabbit ears.

But as I said, my life hasn't been following the probability calculus for some time now.

Kannelmäki in September. I knew nothing more beautiful. Radiant, crimson leaves and the most competitive house prices in Helsinki.

The smell of autumn hung in the early-morning suburban air – air that had been scientifically shown to be the crispest in the city. From the surfaces of large leaves in shades of red and yellow hung beads of dew, the rising sun making them sparkle like feather-light mirrors. I stood on my fourth-floor balcony and realised once again that I was in exactly the right place, and nothing could ever make me change my mind.

The area around Kannelmäki train station was the most effective piece of town planning in Helsinki. From my door, it was a brisk two-and-a-half-minute walk to the station. The train took me to my workplace in Pasila in nine minutes and, once a month, to the cinema downtown in thirteen. Given their proximity to the city centre, apartments in Kannelmäki were very good value for money, and they were well designed with excellent functionality and no wasted floor space. There was nothing decorative, nothing superfluous.

The houses were built in the mid-1980s, a time of optimal rational thinking. Some people called this area of the city bland, depressing even, but perhaps that was because they only saw the façade, the cubic repetitiveness and general greyness of the neighbourhood, in itself a feat of astonishing uniformity. They made a mistake that people often make. They didn't make detailed calculations.

For, as I know from experience, it is calculations that tell us what is beautiful and what is not.

Kannelmäki was beautiful.

I took another deep breath and stepped back inside. I walked into the hallway, pulled on my shoes and jacket. I did up the zip, leaving it slightly open at the top. My tie gleamed, its knot balanced and orderly. I looked at myself in the mirror and recognised the man looking back at me. And at the age of forty-two, I had only one deep-held wish.

I wanted everything to be sensible.

🐇

Actuarial mathematics is a discipline that combines mathematics and statistical analysis to assess the likelihood – or risk – of any eventuality, in order to define an insurance premium that from the insurer's perspective is financially viable. This is the official definition. Like many other official-sounding, and therefore potentially boring, definitions, this is one that goes over the heads of most people. And even when it doesn't go over their heads, few people pay attention to the final two words of that definition, let alone ask what, in this context, the words 'financially viable' actually mean.

Insurance companies exist to make a profit; in the case of insurance against accidents, to the tune of almost thirty percent. Few companies ever reach such revenue figures with a single product. But insurance companies do, because they know that people don't have any other options. You can choose not to take out insurance – everyone can make their own decisions – but on balance most people decide to insure at least their home. Insurance companies also know that people are fragile and that human beings' capacity to get themselves into trouble vastly exceeds that of all other living species. And so, right now insurance companies everywhere are calculating how often people will slip and fall over in their own gardens, how often they will stick objects of varying shapes and sizes into various orifices, how often they will tip smouldering barbecue coals into the rubbish bin, crash into one another on brand-new jet skis, reach up to the top shelf to find something behind a row of glass vases, drunkenly lean on a sushi knife, and how often they will send fireworks flying into their own and other people's eyes ... next year.

Insurance companies, therefore, know two things: one, that people essentially have to take out insurance policies; and two, that a certain number of people, despite advice to the contrary, will inevitably set themselves on fire. And it is between these two factors – shall we say, between the pen and the matchstick – that actuaries operate. Their job is to ensure that while the self-immolator will be reimbursed for his troubles, the insurance company still makes its predefined profit margin by insuring him and many others besides.

And there, right between the sharpened pencil and the burning flame, was I.

My workplace was in the district of Vallila. The new office block on Teollisuuskatu was completed last spring, and our company moved in while the paint was still fresh. Now, when I arrived at our open-plan office every morning, I always felt the same annoyance and disappointment, like a chunk of black ice inside me that refused to melt: I had lost my office. Instead of an office of my own, I now had a workstation.

The word 'station' told me everything I needed to know. My 'station' was nothing but a narrow, cramped slice at the end of a long desk facing the window. In front of our long desk was another, identical communal desk. Opposite me sat Miikka Lehikoinen, a junior mathematician who regularly regaled me with endless barbecuing anecdotes. On my left sat Kari Halikko, a junior risk analyst with a habit of chuckling to himself for no obvious reason. Apparently, they represented a new generation of actuarial professionals.

I didn't like them and I didn't like our open-plan office. It was noisy, full of distractions, interruptions, banalities. But more than anything, it was full of people. I didn't like the things that so many others seemed to like: spontaneous conversations, the continual asking for and giving of advice, the constant cheap banter. I didn't see what it had to do with demanding probability calculations. Before moving into our new premises, I tried to explain that our office was a risk-control department, not Disneyland, but this didn't seem to have any impact on those making the decisions.

My productivity levels had dropped. I still never made mistakes – unlike almost everybody else. But my work was significantly hampered by the constant stream of meaningless chatter concentrated around Halikko's workstation.

Halikko laughed at everything and seemed to spend most of his time watching videos of high-jumpers' backsides, ridiculous singing competitions or people with strange pets. Everybody laughed, and one video led to another. Halikko sniggered and guffawed. I thought it unbecoming behaviour for a risk analyst.

The other cause of disturbance was Lehikoinen, who talked non-stop. On Mondays, he told us what had happened over the weekend, in the autumn he told us about his summer holiday, in January I learned all about his Christmas. Things seemed to happen to Lehikoinen. On top of this, he had already been married and divorced twice, which to my mind demonstrated a weak, unpromising grasp of the notion of cause and effect. A junior mathematician ought to know better.

On this particular morning, they were both sitting at their workstations before me. Halikko was scratching the short, shaven hair on his head, while Lehikoinen was pursing his lips, staring at something on the screen that made him drum his fingertips against the arm of his chair. They both looked as though they were concentrating solely on their work, which in itself was surprising. I looked at the clock on the table. It was nine o'clock exactly, the end of our flexible start time.

Since moving into the new premises, I had delayed my departure from home by approximately thirty seconds every morning in order to avoid the daily exchange of meaningless chit-chat before work, and this was the result: arriving only barely in time. This was out of character for me. I placed my briefcase next to my chair and pulled the chair out from beneath the desk. This was the first time I'd heard the sound of its hard, plastic wheels rolling against the carpet. There was something about the sound that made me shiver, like cold fingernails running along my spine.

I booted up my computer and made sure I had everything on the desk for the day's work. I had been conducting my own research into the influence of shifts in interest frequency on pay-out optimisation in an ever-changing economical world, and I was hoping to conclude my two-week investigation today.

The silence was like water in a glass, transparent but still concrete, tangible.

I typed in my username and password to sign into the system. The boxes on the screen shuddered. A red text beneath the box told me that my username and password were invalid. I typed them again, more slowly this time, making sure the capitals were capitals, the lower-case letters were lower case, and that every letter was as it should be. Again the boxes shuddered. Beneath the box there were now two lines of red text. My username and password were invalid. Additionally – and this was written in BLOCK CAPITALS – I had only one (1) attempt left to enter them correctly. I glanced over the screen at Lehikoinen. He was still drumming the arm of his chair, gazing out of the window at the McDonald's across the street. I stared at him as I thought through my username and password one more time. I knew them both, naturally, and I knew I'd entered them correctly on both attempts.

Lehikoinen turned his head suddenly, our eyes met. Then just as quickly he looked down at his screen again. The drumming had stopped. The office space hummed. I knew it was the air conditioning and that I could hear it because nobody was talking, but suddenly there was something about the hum that got inside my head. Maybe it was this that stopped me turning around and asking Halikko if he'd had trouble signing into the system this morning.

If there had been problems earlier on, they were long gone: Halikko was tapping his mouse as though he were giving it a thousand tiny fillips one after the other. I placed my hands on the keyboard, and the cold fingernails started scratching my back again. I moved my fingers carefully, concentrating on every key I pressed. Finally, I pressed 'Enter', making sure I only pressed it once and that I pressed it with an appropriate dose of briskness and determination.

I didn't even blink, let alone close my eyes. But the pressing of that button felt significant, as though one moment I was looking at one kind of day, and the next moment I had fallen asleep or otherwise lost consciousness, and when I woke up the landscape in front of me had changed beyond recognition. The day had lost its brightness and colour, the fulcrum of the entire world had shifted. The box in the middle of the screen shuddered a third time. A blink of an eye later, it disappeared altogether.

I heard a familiar voice.

'Koskinen, my office for a moment?'

2

'Let's have a little chat,' my department manager, Tuomo Perttilä, said. 'Bounce some ideas around.'

We were sitting in Perttilä's office, a glass-walled cube whose unpleasant attributes included, alongside the lack of privacy, the fact that there was no table between the people sitting there. To me this was unnatural. We sat opposite each other as though we were in a doctor's reception – I didn't want to think which of us would be considered the patient and which the healer. The chairs had hard, uncomfortable metal frames with nowhere for me to put my hands. I placed them in my lap.

'I want to listen,' said Perttilä. 'I want to hear you.'

Physical discomfort was one thing, but I found Perttilä's new role far more difficult to swallow. I had applied for the position of department manager. I was the more suitable and experienced candidate. I didn't know how or with what Perttilä – a former sales chief – had convinced the board of directors.

'This way, I think we'll understand each other better,' he continued. 'I believe if we open up to each other, we'll find something we share, reach a decision. And a shared decision is the right decision. It'll only happen once we realise that we're just two people having a discussion, two people stripped of all excess, with no hierarchy, no forced agenda. Two people sitting round a campfire, coming together, opening up, on an emotional level, moving forward.'

I knew it was fashionable to talk like this, I knew Perttilä had taken countless courses on the subject. Naturally, I couldn't imagine the two of us naked in the middle of the woods. But there was a bigger, more fundamental problem with his manner of speech: it didn't impart information, it didn't resolve anything.

'I don't follow,' I said. 'And I don't understand why the system wouldn't...'

Perttilä gave a friendly chuckle. His head and face were one and the same thing: he shaved all his hair off so he was completely bald, and when he smiled you could see it at the back of his head.

'Hey, sorry, sometimes I get a bit carried away, I'm so used to opening up, I forget to give people space,' he said in a voice that even a year ago he didn't have. A year ago he spoke like everybody else, but after attending all those courses his tone was somewhere between reading a bedtime story and negotiating a hostage situation. It didn't fit with what I knew about him. 'Don't get me wrong, I want to give you space. You talk, I listen. But before we get started, there's something I'd like to ask you.'

I waited. Perttilä rested his elbows on his knees, leaned forwards.

'How have you been finding our new set-up here, the teamwork, the openness, doing things together, sharing knowledge in real time, the whole community vibe?'

'As I've already said, I find it slows down our work and makes it more difficult to—'

'You know, the way we're all in this together, we get to know one another, we can feel each other's presence, learn from one another, bring our sleeping potential to life?'

'Well—'

'People say they've found their true selves,' Perttilä continued. 'They tell me they've reached a new level of awareness, not just as mathematicians and analysts but as human beings. And it's all because we've made a point of breaking down boundaries. All boundaries, internal and external. We've risen to a new level.'

Perttilä's eyes were deep-set, the dark eyebrows above them made it hard to read his expression. But I could imagine that, deep behind his eyes, a fire roared fervently. Uncertainty scratched its nails down my back again.

'I don't know about that,' I said. 'I find it hard to assess these ... levels.'

'Hard to assess...' Perttilä repeated and leaned back in his chair. 'Okay. What kinds of tasks do you feel ready to take on?'

The question blindsided me. I could hardly keep my hands in my lap.

'The tasks I already have,' I said. 'I am a mathematician and—'

'How do you see yourself fitting into the team?' Perttilä interrupted. 'What do you bring to the team, the community, the family? What's your gift to us?'

Was this a trick question? I opted for full honesty.

'A mathematical—'

'Let's forget the maths for a minute,' he said and raised his right hand as if to stop an invisible current running through the room.

'Forget mathematics?' I asked, dumbfounded. 'This job is based on the principles of—'

'I know what it's based on,' Perttilä nodded. 'But we need a shared path that we all walk along together, whether it's with maths in our arms or something else.'

'Our arms? That's the wrong body part, I'm afraid,' I said. 'This is about logic. We need a clear head.'

Again Perttilä inched forwards, placed his elbows on his knees, leaned first to the side, then struck a pose. He held a long pause, then finally spoke.

'This department was stuck in the mud when I took the helm. You remember, everyone shut away in their own little rooms, working on whatever, and nobody knew what anybody else was doing. It wasn't productive, and there was no sense of community. I wanted to bring this group of pen-pushers and astrophysicists into the twenty-first century. Now it's happened. We're flying, flying up towards the sun.'

'That's inadvisable,' I said. 'Under any circumstances. Besides, even metaphorically speaking, it's—'

'You see? That's exactly what I mean. There's one guy always pushing back against everything we do. One guy still sitting in his own little corner calculating away like fucking Einstein's long-lost cousin. Guess who?'

'I just want things to be rational, sensible,' I said. 'And that's what mathematics gives us. It's concrete, it's knowledge. I don't know why we need all these internal children, these ... mood charts. As far as I can see, we don't. We need reason and logic. That's what I bring.'

'Brought.'

That one word hurt me more than the thousand previous words. I knew my professional calibre. I could feel my pulse rising, my heart racing. This was wholly inappropriate. The uncertainty passed and was now replaced with irritation and annoyance.

'My professional skills are second to none, and they have improved with experience...'

'Not all of them, apparently.'

'What we need nowadays—'

'What we need nowadays is something different from what people needed in the seventies,' said Perttilä, now agitated. 'And I mean the *nineteen*-seventies. Or shall we go even further back?'

I realised that the shuddering of the password box was only the beginning. And I knew this side of Perttilä. This was his real voice now.

'Now listen up. As senior actuary, you can have exactly what you want,' he said. 'You don't have to be a team player. You don't have to use the intranet. You can sit and calculate things all by yourself. You can have your own room too.'

Perttilä sat up straight. He was sitting right on the edge of his seat.

'Everything's been taken care of,' he continued. 'Your office is on the ground floor, the little room behind the janitors' desk. You can even shut the door. There's a notebook and a calculator. You don't need the intranet. Your task is to assess the impact of inflation from 2011 on insurance premiums in 2012. The material is all on your desk. If I remember, there are about sixty folders.'

'That's not at all sensible,' I said. 'It's 2020. Besides, that was already calculated when we defined the insurance premiums for that year...'

'Then calculate it again, check everything was as it should be. You like that kind of thing. You like mathematics.'

'Of course I like mathematics...'

'But you don't like our team, our openness, our dialogue, the way we communicate, open ourselves up, explore our emotions. You don't want to let go of yourself, you don't trust the moment, you don't trust us. You don't like what I'm offering.'

'I don't...'

'Exactly. You don't. So...' Perttilä reached over to his desk '...there is another option.'

He handed me a piece of paper. I quickly read it. Now I was no longer irritated or annoyed. I was flabbergasted. I was furious. I looked up at Perttilä.

'You want me to hand in my notice?'

He smiled again. The smile was almost the same as at the beginning of our conversation, only now it lacked even the faint, distant warmth I might have detected only moments ago.

'It's a question of what *you* want,' he said. 'I want to help offer you different paths.'

'So, either I conduct meaningless calculations or I take part in amateurish therapy sessions that jeopardise our attention to serious mathematical thinking of the highest order? The former is pointless, the latter leads only to disorganisation, chaos and perdition.'

'There's always the third option,' said Perttilä and nodded in the direction of the sheet of paper.

'Precision requires precision,' I said, and I could hear my voice quavering, the blood bubbling inside me. 'You can't achieve inscrutable exactitude in correlation matrices with the KonMari

Method. I cannot be part of a team whose highest ambition is going on a sushi-making weekend.'

'There's a small room for you downstairs...'

I shook my head.

'No,' I said. 'It's just not sensible. I want things to be sensible, I want to act sensibly. This agreement is ... More to the point, it says I would have to give up the six-month severance pay to which I am entitled and that my resignation would be effective immediately.'

'That's because this would be a voluntary decision,' said Perttilä, now in that soft voice again, as though he very much enjoyed the sound of it. 'If you want to stay with us on this floor, tomorrow morning there's a compulsory, three-hour seminar on transcendental meditation, which will be led by a really excellent—'

'Can I have a pen, please?'

🐰

From their faces, I could tell the others already knew. I had just one personal belonging at my workstation: a picture of my cat, Schopenhauer. I emptied my leather briefcase of work-related papers and dropped Schopenhauer's picture into the now-empty case. I took the lift down to the ground floor and didn't so much as glance at the janitors or the door behind them. I stepped out into the street and stopped as though I had walked right into something, as though my feet had stuck to the ground.

I was unemployed.

The thought seemed impossible – impossible for me at least. I'd never imagined I could be in the situation of not knowing where to go first thing in the morning. It felt as though a great mechanism keeping the world in order had suddenly broken. I glanced at the watch on my wrist, but it was just as useless as I'd imagined it to be. It told me the time, but all of a sudden time didn't have any meaning. It was 10:18 a.m.

It seemed only a moment ago that I was pondering the difference between conditional probability and original probability and was trying to find a way to define mathematical independence in complementary events.

Now I was standing by the side of a busy road, unemployed, with nothing but a picture of my cat in my briefcase.

I forced myself into motion. The sunshine warmed my back, and I began to feel slightly better. As Pasila train station came into view, I was able to see my situation more pragmatically, applying logic and reason. I was an experienced mathematician and I knew more about the insurance industry than Perttilä's team of functionally innumerate psychobabblers combined. I began to relax. Before long I would be calculating for his competitors.

How difficult could it be to find an insurance company that took both itself and mathematics seriously?

It can't be that hard, I thought. Soon everything will look much clearer.

Quite simply, everything would be better.

3

'Your brother has died.'

The light-blue shirt and dark-blue jacket only enhanced the third shade of blue in the man's eyes. His thinning, wheat-blond hair combed over to the left looked tired too, somehow wilted. The man's face was pale, all except for the bright red of his cheeks. He had introduced himself and told me he was a lawyer, but his name seemed to have disappeared with the news.

'I don't understand,' I said in all honesty.

The taste of the morning's first cup of coffee still lingered in my mouth, and now it took on something new, a tinny, almost rusty aftertaste.

'Your brother has died,' the lawyer repeated, trying perhaps to find a more comfortable sitting position on my couch. At least, that's what his movements seemed to suggest. The autumnal morning behind the windows was cool and sunny. I knew this because I'd let Schopenhauer out to sit in his favourite observation spot right after breakfast and walked straight to the door as soon as the bell rang. Eventually the lawyer leaned forwards slightly, propped his elbows on his knees. His jacket tightened around the shoulders, its fabric gleaming.

'He left you his amusement park.'

I spoke without even thinking. 'Adventure park,' I corrected him.

'Excuse me?'

'An amusement park is like Linnanmäki, like Alton Towers. Rollercoasters and carousels, machines that you sit in and let them toss you around. An adventure park, on the other hand, is a place where people have to move by themselves. They climb and run, jump and slide. There are climbing walls, ropes, slides, labyrinths, that kind of thing.'

'I think I understand,' said the man. 'Amusement parks have that catapult with bright flashing lights that throws people into the air, but an adventure park has ... I can't think of anything...'

'A Caper Castle,' I remembered.

'A Caper Castle, right,' the lawyer nodded again. He was about to continue but looked suddenly pensive. 'Well, an amusement park could have a Caper Castle too, I suppose. Like the old Vekkula in Linnanmäki. You had to climb in and keep your balance, and by the time you came out at the other end you were drenched in sweat. But it's hard to imagine a simple catapult in an adventure park, all you do is sit down and experience a momentary shift in gravity ... I think I understand the difference, but it's hard to find a clear dividing line...'

'My brother is dead,' I said.

The lawyer looked down at his hands, quickly clasped them together.

'Yes,' he said. 'My condolences.'

'How did he die?'

'In his car,' said the lawyer. 'A Volvo V70.'

'I mean, what was the cause of death?'

'Right, yes,' the lawyer stammered. 'A heart attack.'

'A heart attack in his car?'

'At the traffic lights on Munkkiniemi Boulevard. The traffic wasn't moving, someone knocked on the driver's window. He was adjusting the radio.'

'Dead?'

'No, of course not.' The lawyer shook his head. 'He died while he was adjusting it. A classical channel, I believe.'

'And he'd made a will?' I asked.

To put it nicely, Juhani was a spontaneous, impulsive person. He lived in the moment. The kind of forward-planning required to draw up a will didn't sound like him at all. He used to joke, saying I would die of stiffness. I told him I was very much alive and not at all stiff, I just wanted things to occur in a good, logical order and that I based all my actions on rational thinking. For some reason, he found this amusing. Still, it should be said that though we were the diametric opposite of each other, we were also brothers, and I didn't quite know how to take the news of his passing.

The lawyer reached for his light-brown leather briefcase, pulled out a thin black folder and flicked open the bands at the corners. There didn't seem to be very many papers inside. The lawyer examined the uppermost document for a long while before speaking again.

'This will was drawn up six months ago. That's when your brother became my client. His final wish was very clear: you are to receive everything. The only other person mentioned by name is your brother's former wife, whom he explicitly disinherits. There are no other relatives; at least, he doesn't mention any.'

'There are no others.'

'Then everything is yours.'

'Everything?' I asked.

Again the lawyer consulted his paperwork.

'The amusement park,' he stated again.

'Adventure park,' I corrected him.

'I'm still having difficulty appreciating the difference.'

'So there's nothing in there except the adventure park?' I asked.

'The will doesn't mention anything else,' said the lawyer. 'After a brief investigation, it seems your brother didn't own anything else.'

I had to repeat his last statement in my head to fully grasp its contents.

'To my knowledge, he was a wealthy and successful entrepreneur,' I said.

'According to the information here, he was living in a rented apartment and drove a part-owned car – both of which have been in arrears for several months. And he ran this ... park.'

My first thought, of course, was that none of this made any sense – because it simply didn't. Juhani was dead and essentially penniless. Both statements seemed like misunderstandings of the highest order. Besides...

'Why am I only hearing about his death now?'

'Because he wanted it that way. He wanted me to be informed if anything happened, then I was only to tell the next of kin once everything was sorted out. That goes for the will too, once the assessment and inventory of his estate was complete.'

'Was he ill? I mean, did Juhani know that he...?'

The lawyer leaned forwards an inch or two. He no longer looked tired; he almost seemed a touch enthusiastic.

'Do you mean, are there grounds to believe someone might have ... murdered him?'

The lawyer looked at me as though we were doing something terribly exciting together, solving a mystery or competing to win a quiz.

'Yes, or rather—'

'No,' he said, shaking his head, and no longer looked at all enthusiastic. 'Nothing like that, I'm afraid. Heart problems. Something inoperable. He explained it all to me. There was always a risk it could happen, then one day it happened. His heart just gave up. The death of a middle-aged man is generally pretty uneventful stuff. No material for a blockbuster, I'm afraid.'

I turned and looked out at the autumnal morning. Two crows darted past the window.

'But look at it this way,' I heard the lawyer saying. 'This is a great business opportunity. Your brother's ... park.'

'No,' I said. 'I'm not an adventure-park kind of man. I am an actuary.'

'Where do you work?'

The blue of the lawyer's eyes was so exactly between that of his shirt and his jacket that there was an almost mathematical symmetry to it. In other circumstances it might have felt like an interesting feature. Now it didn't. This morning at 7:32 a.m., after only a week and a half of diligent job searching, the final actuarial door had slammed shut in my face. Without delay, I had sent my CV and an application to every respected insurance company and stressed that I took traditional mathematics very seriously indeed and said upfront that I had no time for buzzwords and parlour games. When I heard nothing from these companies, I contacted them myself and listened to their banalities in stunned silence. One wanted to create a soft-flowing team dynamic, another wanted to shift towards a newer form of algorithm-based calculation. Each of them took pains to explain that there were no current vacancies. This I was able to correct. I told them I knew their companies had been recruiting. Time and again, this led to a hum of silence at the other end of the phone before the call was abruptly rounded off by wishing me a pleasant autumn.

'I'm looking around at the moment,' I said.

'And how's that going?'

It was a good question. How *were* things going? This morning's balance sheet was clearly in the red. I wasn't going to find work in my own field, my brother had died, and it seemed I now owned an adventure park.

'I'm sure things will work out sensibly,' I said.

The answer seemed to satisfy the lawyer. An expression crossed his face that seemed to suggest he had just remembered something important. Again he leafed through the folder. An envelope.

'Your brother left you a message. A letter, just in case. It was my idea. I told him that once the will was ready, due to his diagnosis there were two things he should take care of right away: my bill and this greeting to you.'

'Greeting?'

'That's what he called it. I don't know what's in it. As you can see, the envelope is still sealed.'

This was true. My full name was written across the C5-sized

envelope: Henri Pekka Olavi Koskinen. It was Juhani's
handwriting. When was the last time I'd seen him?

We'd had a quick lunch together in Vallila about three
months ago. I paid for the pepperoni pizzas because Juhani had
left his wallet in the car. Of course, now I wondered whether
there were more problems with his wallet than its simply being
left behind. What did we talk about? Juhani told me about some
new acquisitions at the adventure park, I mentioned
Kolmogorov's foundational principles of probability theory in
explaining why he should make big investments one at a time,
once he'd been able to see and assess how many people each new
acquisition brought to the park. Juhani didn't look as though
he was about to drop dead any second. And he didn't look like
he had just drawn up a will either. What do people usually look
like after writing a will? I'm sure there's no quintessential mien,
though such people are on the cusp of the impossible: trying to
influence life after death.

I opened the envelope, slid out the folded sheet of paper inside.

HI HENRI
I'm not dead after all! Hahaha – I know you're not laughing,
but I want to laugh. I can't think of anything else. No,
seriously, if you're reading this, I probably am dead. The
doctors told me this heart defect was so bad that my time might
be up much sooner than planned. Anyway, I guess by now
you'll have heard what's going on. I'm dead and the adventure
park is all yours. I've got one last wish for the place. I've never
had much luck with money, and the park's finances aren't in
very good shape, not to mention my own finances. I've never
had the patience to count things properly, dot the Is, cross the
Ts, that sort of thing. But you're a mathematical genius! Do
you think you could keep things ticking over for me? That's my
final wish. In fact, it's my only wish. I don't think I've ever said
this out loud, but of all my business ventures – and you know

there have been plenty of them over the years – the park is the most important. I want it to be a success. I suppose you're asking yourself why. There are as many reasons as there are debtors, I'm afraid. I want to be good at something, to leave something behind. And there's another reason you'll discover once you've successfully completed your mission. Remember how we used to spend the summers at Grandma's place, and how we were allowed to be away from home, where everything was always screwed up? I think of those summers now. You would always sit inside counting things, and I was outside playing. But we always went fishing together. If I'm dead, sit inside for a while, count things up and save the park, then go fishing. I'll bring the worms. (Compulsory joke, sorry, couldn't resist. Everything else is deadly serious.)
JUHANI

I felt annoyance verging on rage. This was typical of Juhani, a complete and utter lack of responsibility. The letter was clearly written in haste, drawn up on the spur of the moment. It lacked all rational thought and argumentation. Detailed analysis and clear conclusions were conspicuous by their absence. For the thousandth time in my life, I wanted to tell him there simply wasn't any sense to this.

But Juhani was dead.

And I was sad, angry, confused, frustrated and, in a peculiarly intangible way, exhausted. Combined, these emotions burned my lungs, clawed at my chest. Everything pointed to the fact that I did, indeed, now own an adventure park.

'So, this is everything?' I sighed.

'Not quite,' the lawyer responded, quickly rummaged in his briefcase and, in a considerably more practised gesture, produced a slightly larger envelope. 'My bill.'

He placed the envelope with his bill next to the envelope with Juhani's letter. I noted that both of them bore my name. The lawyer checked the papers one last time, then slid the folder to my side of the table.

'Congratulations,' he said. 'My condolences.'

4

YouMeFun sprawled through the autumnal landscape in technicolour, almost genetically modified splendour. A box of tin and steel, painted in garish red, orange and yellow, and almost 200 metres across, it was an eyesore, no matter which colour of tinted spectacles you used to look at it. Presumably the point of the brash colours and enormous lettering was to spread the joyous gospel of sweaty fun and games for all the family to everyone who entered its gates. It was hard to gauge the height of the adventure-park box, fifteen metres maybe. There was enough space inside for a sports ground and an air hangar, a few schools and a truck park. YouMeFun was situated just beyond the Helsinki city limits.

Two days and two rather sleepless nights had passed since the lawyer's visit.

I accidentally got off the bus one stop too soon. The closer I got, the harder walking became. It wasn't because of the slight incline or the faint headwind, or the fact that I wanted to enjoy the cobalt-blue sky and almost white afternoon sun. It was more a question of disbelief, disgust and despair that I felt welling within me the closer I got to the park. As though something was forcing me to turn around, walk in the opposite direction and never look back. This must have been the voice of reason, I thought. But at the same time, I heard Juhani's voice: *It's my only wish*.

I knew very little about the adventure park's operations. I knew that Juhani had nothing to do with its day-to-day running. The doors opened and closed without him. He had an office in the building, but he was away a lot, vaguely 'on business', as they say. As to who did take care of the day-to-day running of the park, I knew nothing at all. The car park, a field of concrete the size of three football pitches, was half full. Most cars were family-sized, most of them a few years old. I looked at the lettering on the roof of the building.

YouMeFun

The letters looked bigger than on my previous visit – which was also my only visit to date. To my surprise, they looked almost threatening. I found myself thinking I'd need to be careful not to be struck by the sharp prongs of the Y or caught in the fluttering flag of the F. Where had the thought come from? I could only assume that recent events had been more than enough to foster such irrational trains of thought. I walked towards the entrance and glanced up at the roof one more time.

Once inside, I queued at the ticket desk. The foyer seemed to give a clue as to what was in store: children bursting with energy, wild cries and high-pitched shrieks, and the lower, rather less enthusiastic conversation of the mums and dads. The semi-circular counter, around ten metres in length, was painted in the same colours as the rest of the park. Along the length of the red-orange-and-yellow counter, a large dome curved through the air. Between the counter and the dome, as though caught inside an enormous, psychedelic space helmet, stood a man in an adventure-park uniform.

The man was young, twenty-five perhaps, and had a name badge on his shirt. In large white letters was the word 'YouMeFun' and in smaller black letters the word 'Kristian'. Kristian was brown-eyed and muscular. Judging by the toolkit hanging from his belt, I assumed he was responsible for park maintenance. Standing behind the counter he looked half at home and half very out of place.

When it was my turn, I stopped.

Why was I here? My original idea had been to inform the staff of Juhani's passing and the park's transferring into my ownership, but now that felt terribly insufficient. I hadn't considered Kristian or the other members of staff. And I hadn't considered the customers at all, crowds of whom seemed to be gathering, even at this hour of the morning.

It looked very much as though there was literally nothing in the world that could prepare a person to inherit an adventure park.

I told Kristian who I was and asked to speak to someone responsible for the park's operations. He asked why I didn't just talk to my brother. I told him I couldn't do that because Juhani had died unexpectedly and now I owned the park. Kristian's smile disappeared, and he told me a woman by the name of Laura Helanto was in charge of things. I asked if I could meet Laura Helanto. Kristian held the phone against his ear and turned away from me before I managed to say I'd rather tell Helanto the news in person. Right then I heard Kristian saying into the phone that Juhani is dead and there's someone here who says he's his brother, he doesn't look like Juhani, should I check his ID to make sure this isn't some kind of Nigerian inheritance scam ... Baltic, then ... well ... okay, bye. Kristian ended the call and turned to face me again. We stood silently on either side of the counter and waited. Eventually he spoke.

'Juhani was a really good boss, gave us free rein. He was chilled out, he wasn't always looking over your shoulder and counting every penny.'

You're not wrong, I thought. Then I remembered why I'd thought there was something strange about the sight of Kristian behind the counter.

'Why exactly are you in the ticket office?' I asked and nodded at the tools dangling from his belt. 'It looks like you do a rather different job here.'

'Venla hasn't come in today.'

'Hasn't come in? Why not?'

'She can't get up.'

'Is she ill?'

'What do you mean?' asked Kristian, and this time he sounded genuinely worried. 'Have you heard something about her?'

I was about to open my mouth, but just then I heard a woman's voice behind me. The voice said hello. I turned and gripped her outstretched hand.

Laura Helanto had dark-rimmed glasses and brown hair that curled and spread out like a bush until it touched her shoulders. Her eyes were blue-green and had an inquisitive alertness about them. She was around forty, perhaps a year or two over, just like me. She was approximately twenty-five centimetres shorter than me, about average height for a Finnish woman. I was rather adept at estimating people's height because I was a tall man myself, one hundred and ninety-two centimetres, so I was used to continuous, meaningless questions on the subject.

Laura Helanto gave me a quick glance, quite literally looked me up and down from head to toe, and gave me her condolences. I wasn't sure how it was customary to respond to this, and from her expression it was hard to tell whether she was genuinely sorry or just simply continuing to scrutinise my appearance.

Then we marched off apace.

🐇

'The Doughnut,' said Laura Helanto and pointed at an enormous, transparent plastic tube where a few children were bumping into one another and knocking against the padded walls. 'Our first acquisition, still one of the park's firm favourites. You can run in a circle and defy the force of gravity. Just say if you've heard all this before.'

'I haven't heard anything at all,' I said. It was the truth.

The air was heavy with an indistinctly sweet smell, a combination of the aroma of the cafeteria, disinfectant and something human. There were shrieks, squeals and high-pitched cries on all sides. I kept a constant watch on my feet and realised I was worried I might accidentally step on one of the shorter clients.

'Just ask anything that comes to mind,' said Laura Helanto. As we took a sharp turn to the right, she glanced at me. There was something about that glance; it had the same curious, inquisitive shimmer as before. As her head turned, her bushy hair bounced as though caught in the wind. 'It's your park now. That over there is Caper Castle, one enormous climbing frame. There are a couple of alternative routes through it. In each area of the castle, you have to climb a little differently and the obstacles are different too. From a maintenance perspective, this is one of the most critical places in the park. There's always something broken. Caper Castle is affectionately known as Spare Part Castle. There's a lot of wear and tear. You wouldn't think a child weighing only thirty kilos could be such a terminator, but that's how it is.'

'Indeed,' I said, feeling a growing sense of horror. 'And the repairs are carried out by...?'

'Kristian,' Laura nodded. 'Who you've already met. He's a good kid, skilled, but...' Laura seemed to be looking for the right words. 'Sometimes getting information through to him can be a bit of a challenge, but he's conscientious and hard-working. Unlike...'

'Venla,' I said.

Laura looked surprised. Just then our pace slowed slightly, giving me a chance to look somewhere other than at my feet.

'Kristian informed me that Venla was having difficulty getting out of bed this morning.'

'This morning,' Laura scoffed and sounded as though she meant something else altogether. She brushed the hair away from her glasses. 'Right. This is where the Turtle Trucks set off. We have thirty trucks in total. The route runs almost right the way round the building. As the name suggests, this isn't exactly Formula One. This ride is a good way to calm down the rowdier kids. You sit them in the cart, let them career round the hall a few times, and gradually things cool off. As you know, I'm sure. Do you have children? A child? Sorry, it's none of my—'

'None at all,' I interrupted her. 'I live by myself, alone. Given all the stochastic variables, it's by far the most sensible option. Do you mean Venla has difficulty getting out of bed on other mornings too? Why does she work here then? What exactly is she paid for?'

We had come to a stop. One of the dark-green Turtle Trucks jolted into motion, the number 13 on its bonnet. Sitting in the truck was a driver about three years of age, who was looking at us instead of at the course ahead. In the truck behind sat the child's father, who looked as though he might nod off at the next chicane. Nothing terrible would happen: the trucks were travelling slower than average walking speed.

'Did you and Juhani ever speak about...' Laura hesitated. 'About our ... I mean, the park's business affairs?'

'Not in so many words,' I said. 'He sometimes told me about new acquisitions, the Trombone Cannons, the Komodo Locomotive, maybe the Doughnut, perhaps some other investments. But otherwise...' I shook my head. 'No, we didn't.'

'Okay,' said Laura. 'I'm sorry. I assumed you'd be up to speed on things – at least vaguely. I suppose I'd better start by explaining who I am and what I do. My official title is park manager. That means I'm responsible for the day-to-day running of operations in the park, making sure everything is working and that our staff are in the right place at the right time. I've been park manager for two and a half years now. I'll admit straight away, I wasn't planning on a career in adventure-park management. I'm an artist by profession, a painter, but then ... life got in the way. You know how it is.'

'I'm not at all sure I do,' I replied honestly. 'In my experience, automatic assumptions regarding the proportionality of things often lead us astray.'

Now Laura Helanto was openly looking me up and down. Her gaze was studious, her expression somewhat concerned. Perhaps not so much concerned as suspicious.

'A messy divorce ... and I have a daughter, Tuuli, who needs very expensive treatments for her allergies,' Laura said eventually. 'But you asked about Venla. Juhani hired her.'

Both the subject and her tone of voice seemed to have changed in a flash. I assumed the vaguely defined concept of life getting in the way had now been dealt with. That suited me.

'Given what I've learned about her behaviour, it doesn't seem a very sensible appointment,' I said.

Laura looked over at the gleaming steel of the slides.

'Your brother always wanted to give people a chance.'

A group of little people scurried past us. The decibel levels reached rock-concert proportions. Once the shouting had died down a little, I dared to speak again.

'I understand,' I said, though I didn't fully understand. 'How many members of staff are there in total?'

We were on the move again. Laura Helanto led the way; I was following her though we were walking side by side. She was wearing a pair of running shoes, colourful and with thick soles. Her gait was that of someone used to walking. Her hair gave off a most pleasant fragrance. But my attention was drawn to the way her eyes moved. She had a unique way of scrutinising me while avoiding eye contact altogether.

'We have seven full-time members of staff,' she said. 'I'll introduce you to the others shortly. Then there are the seasonal workers. Mostly in the café, the Curly Cake. The number of seasonal workers is constantly changing, depending on the day or week it can be anything from zero to fifteen. The half-term holidays in September and February are our peak season. Summer holidays aren't quite as full, though they certainly keep us busy. Each and every one of us. Sometimes I bring Tuuli along with me. She quickly makes friends – like most kids. I'm sure you remember.'

I remembered, but in the opposite way. As a child, I always enjoyed my own company. My early experiences reinforced the fundamental truth that the more people there are, the more problems there are – and the bigger the problems are too.

'Was Juhani often on site?'

'No, to be honest. In the time I've worked here, he visited less and less. He seemed content with the way I run the park – if I say so myself. He said there was no use for him here, seeing as I take care of everything.'

'Did he ever talk to you about the park's financial situation?'

'Yes,' Laura replied quickly. 'Our visitor numbers have been steadily increasingly. Juhani kept saying things are great, just great. Recently, in particular. He would clap his hands and shout funny words of encouragement. A while ago he said he would pay us all a bonus.'

'A bonus?'

Her hair bounced again, her head turned towards me. Now there was something more than just caution in those blue-green eyes.

'Once we meet our footfall target and the results of the customer-satisfaction surveys are up to scratch. Things are looking quite promising. The bonus will be paid at the end of the year, as a Christmas present.'

'This Christmas?'

'It's only eighty-seven days till Christmas,' said Laura. 'I know this because I have a Facebook friend who posts every week about how many days it is till Christmas. God knows, I need that bonus, otherwise it'll be a grim festive season for me and Tuuli.'

In my mind's eye, I could see and hear the side of Juhani that lived in a completely different reality and who said and did whatever popped into his mind. We stopped. Laura pointed at various activities and explained what they were, she spoke quickly and enthusiastically. The size and scale of the park caused me physical sensations – and they were far from pleasant. Laura pointed at the slides.

'Do you want to try?'

I looked at her. She smiled.

'Just joking,' she said, now serious. 'Sorry. You're not in the right frame of mind. When someone close suddenly...'

'It seems we weren't all that close after all,' I said before I'd even noticed I'd opened my mouth. 'There's so much I didn't know about Juhani. Well, everything, it seems. I knew he had this...' I said and swirled my right hand through the air, like stirring an upside-down porridge pot. 'But I must admit, it turns out I didn't know the first thing about the place. It is a ... surprise. In so many ways.'

Laura Helanto looked at me, now somewhat tense and expectant. At least, that's how I read her expression. I heard the clatter of dishes from the café. A child cried out for its mother. And didn't stop.

'How does this feel?'

'How does what feel?' I asked. It was a genuine question.

'YouMeFun,' said Laura. There was almost a hint of pride in her voice.

I quickly looked around. What could I say? That every single detail I had seen and heard here was each perhaps the most grotesque thing I had ever encountered? Pygmies dashing here and there, an unbearable lack of organisation, staggering maintenance bills, unproductive use of man hours, economical recklessness, promises nobody could keep, carts that quite literally moved at tortoise speed? I raised my fingers to my throat and checked the position of my tie. It was impeccable.

'Okay,' said Laura. 'This must be a lot to take in, bringing so much happiness to so many people. Let's go and meet the others, shall we?'

Samppa was a thirty-something former nursery teacher. He had earrings in both ears, an eclectic collection of tattoos across his arms and a thick red scarf round his neck. A group of children was beating a set of jungle drums as Laura told Samppa who I was and why I'd come. Samppa raised a hand across his mouth, perhaps to smother the gasp the news had elicited. He spoke for a moment about the healing, holistic impact of play. We left him and moved on to the café.

Johanna was in charge of the Curly Cake Café: red hair, slightly older than me, and she was extremely thin – she looked like she was preparing for an Ironman competition or had recently completed one. There was something steely about her face, something endlessly resilient. She offered to mix me a smoothie that would boost my ferritin levels, because apparently I looked exhausted. I told her I'd just lost my job and my brother, and inherited an adventure park. The explanation didn't seem to convince her.

We headed towards a metallic door between the Trombone Cannons and the Ghost Tunnel. On the door was a plastic yellow sticker bearing the text *CONTROL ROOM*. Laura opened the door with her master key, and at the end of a short corridor we arrived at a small room with two more doors. The first room looked like it contained the electrical switchboard. In the second room, a broad-shouldered man in his fifties sat in an office chair with an adjustable head rest. In front of him was a wall full of monitors, which revealed that the adventure park had many more security cameras than I'd noticed during our walk around. The man's name was Esa. He was the park's head of security. His college sweater bore the text *US Marine – and Proud*. I found it hard to believe that he really was a trained soldier in the US army. Still, if I was now the owner of an adventure park, who knows what Esa had done before ending up in the control room. Around his mouth was a thin, black square of beard, trimmed with millimetre precision. He had a broad, short nose and blue eyes, red round the edges. We introduced ourselves. That was the extent of our conversation.

The last person I was due to meet was located – yet again – at the other side of the complex. Minttu K was sitting in her office, the Venetian blinds on the windows tightly shut. She was the marketing and sales manager. At least, that's how she introduced herself.

Minttu K was slightly younger than me, she had cropped fair hair, a heavy tan, and she was wearing a dark-blue blazer at least one or two sizes too small for her. She gave me a very friendly smile and boasted that she could sell anything to anybody. By the end of our fifteen-second acquaintance, I believed this was highly probable. I was also almost certain I caught a faint hint of grapefruit and alcohol in the air. Minttu K made her apologies and said she had to make a phone call. She winked at me, pulled a cigarette from the pack of menthol Pall Malls on the table and placed it between her fingers. 'Just some little prick that needs his arse handed to him,' she said, then in a gentler voice: 'Hey, sorry about your bruv.'

We walked back into the corridor, turned right and arrived at Juhani's office. On the door was a plaque bearing his name. Seeing it elicited the same sense of confusion I'd experienced during the lawyer's visit. The name was left hanging in the air, as if waiting for someone to appear and bring it to life.

The office looked like it belonged to a man with more than simply running an adventure park on his mind: the desk sagged under piles of papers, the coffee table was covered in illustrated leaflets and a colourful miniature model showing some kind of play castle complete with towers. From one of the towers, a springboard extended into the air. Without a swimming pool underneath, I thought, the design might soon run into problems.

'I just realised I haven't asked what you do for a living.'

Laura's words brought me back to the office.

'I am an actuary,' I said. 'Well, I gave my notice two weeks ago.'

'Because of YouMeFun?'

I shook my head. 'I didn't know about this park at the time. I resigned because I couldn't stand watching my workplace turn into a playground. Then I inherited one.'

Was Laura Helanto smiling? I didn't think I'd said anything amusing. She had raised a hand in front of her mouth. When she lowered it again, her expression was neutral.

'You probably want to take your time to explore everything.'

I certainly did not. But again I heard Juhani's words in my ears: *my only wish*. I looked at the desk, the towering piles of papers.

Just then, the phone in Laura's hand started to ring. I noted that the ringtone was that of a normal telephone, not an inane jingle or the sound of a flushing toilet that was supposed to titillate everyone around her. An eminently sensible choice, I thought. She looked at the phone.

'Esa,' she said before answering.

Then she turned, and after saying her name into the phone she disappeared round the corner. Her scent lingered in the air.

Herbs and meadow flowers.

5

Minus sixty-three thousand, five hundred and forty-one euros and eighty cents.

The sun had set. I'd only waded through a fraction of the papers, but already there was a pile of unpaid bills and final demands as thick as my forefinger. It was a considerable sum of money.

At some point I'd switched on Juhani's computer, but without the password I hadn't got very far. The machine was nothing but a gently humming box of light metallic components and a plastic shell. I'd switched it off and continued clearing the desk.

I was sitting in the office chair Juhani had left me, trying to decide whether to set everything alight or sink with the park like the captain on the *Titanic*.

At first I'd thought this would be the last time I would ever be in this room, this chair. I had done my duty. I had assessed the situation, accepted the facts, and been forced to draw a painful but unavoidable decision. At least, that's what I tried to think. But I couldn't keep my thoughts in check. They were restlessly ricocheting from one place and time to another.

At times I was engaged in renewed discussion with Perttilä over my resignation, at others trying to talk sense to Juhani. The former was an idiot, the latter dead.

Juhani – did you really know what you were doing when you decided to adjust the car radio? Was the road you took, at least to some extent, your own choice? The intense greenery of the park boulevard in August, perhaps some Brahms coming from the speakers? It was certainly a more appealing proposition than trying to make sense of the wholesale orders for the Curly Cake

Café or sourcing a new, even bendier replacement for the broken Banana Mirror.

Death.

I knew a lot about death.

Not from first-hand experience, but from my work as an actuary. Insurance companies and their feel-good advertising never tell you this, but they know that some of the people they insure will stop their monthly payments in a heartbeat, as it were, and take a one-way trip somewhere their insurance payout will never reach them. I could have tried doing the same: running out of the office and throwing myself under the Komodo Locomotive.

But no.

I wasn't that kind of man. I was more of the belief that we don't have to go out of our way to find difficulties in this life; before long, they will find us.

My hand reached up to loosen my tie, but I'd already loosened it hours ago. The sense of claustrophobia was coming from somewhere else. While looking at the figures, it had dawned on me that with the park came every last object in this building. It was a terrifying, overwhelming thought. The chair beneath me, the pen on the desk, the trapeze swings, the slowest go-carts in the known universe, the jacket with the chocolate-bar sponsor logo hanging in the doorway.

Everything.

Juhani was dead, so his belongings were now my belongings. Death wasn't abstract, empty and silent; it was a thousand and one objects of different shapes and sizes, each of which took up space and made a noise when it was thrown in the bin or placed in apparently temporary storage boxes.

I wasn't planning on setting everything ablaze. Again, I wasn't that kind of man. I knew there were men who set buildings alight then masturbated in the nearby woods as they admired the flames, but I didn't imagine such actions would achieve the results I needed.

More importantly, there was another pile of papers too, this one almost a centimetre thick. And this pile disconcerted me far more than the pile of bills and final demands.

The park's business activities were sustainable, almost profitable.

But still Juhani had neglected to pay almost all the bills and taken out an extra loan in the park's name.

I didn't understand the equation.

Through the course of my studies, I'd learned the basics of accounting. So far, I hadn't needed these skills for my own work, but accounting employed the same principles that I so loved in mathematics. The pursuit of perfect clarity, precision, impeccable balance, water-tight presentation, flawlessness. I liked that. Of course, the material in front of me was wholly inadequate and full of errors, but it gave the impression of a park whose business operations were satisfactory or even rather good. I located the financial statement drawn up by the park's accountant, but in the other pile was the same accountant's notification of termination of contract and a bill, dated earlier this year, which had already been forwarded to a debt-collection agency. I couldn't find anything to suggest a new accountancy firm had been hired. Perhaps there was no new accountancy firm.

If the park's operations were indeed profitable, why had Juhani taken out another loan to keep it running? What was the extra money for? It can't have been for the park's latest acquisition, the Crazy Coil, a twisting, turning slide, shaped like a corkscrew, attached to the Big Dipper. For this Juhani had only paid the initial down payment – in cash – and the first instalment. Looking at the timeline, the bills had started to pile up around the same time the accountancy firm had terminated its contract. After that, almost everything was in arrears. Something had happened. With one exception, all the bank loans had been taken out after that point in time. Adding up the loans and unpaid bills on the table, it seemed that just shy of two hundred thousand euros had disappeared into thin air.

Two hundred thousand euros. In just under a year. One would expect there to be evidence of the existence of such a sum of money. But where was it?

Juhani had been driving an old, part-owned Volvo for the better part of two years and was living in the same one-bedroom apartment, fitted out with MDF furniture, where he had been living since his divorce. His clothes were from Dressmann and he ate at a cheap local Chinese buffet. The Juhani I knew – badly, I admit – barely knew what Versace and the Savoy meant. I couldn't imagine the money being squandered on skin treatments, manicures or extravagant trips abroad. Juhani had visited Tallinn, spent one night at the Viru Hotel, then returned to Finland. On the surface, he looked like a very average middle-aged Finnish man who didn't like anything excessively, didn't have any particular hobbies, and certainly nothing for which you might say he had a passion. Men like that got by with less money than most sparrows. But all that money had to have gone somewhere.

I was again about to ask myself where, when there was a knock at the door.

6

I hadn't closed the door at any point. Then I remembered the steps I'd heard first getting closer, then moving away again. Someone else had closed the door. Why? Another knock. I had to say something.

'I'm here,' I said, then, 'Come in.'

The handle turned, the door cautiously swung open. Had the park already closed for the day? I looked at my watch. Yes, half an hour ago. I could have been alone in the building – well, of course I wasn't alone because someone had knocked at the door. Still nobody ventured into the office. Then I caught a glimpse of a shoulder, a shirt, then half a face.

'What?' asked Kristian.

'Yes, I'm ... here. I tried to say so.'

'I didn't hear,' he said, still in the doorway. Kristian didn't move.

'Come in,' I said, this time almost a shout.

'Okay,' said Kristian and stepped into the room.

He stopped across the desk from me. I gestured to the chair and he sat down, the tools on his belt rattling against the plastic seat. His brown eyes were like almonds. His pectoral muscles tested the seams of his YouMeFun shirt.

'Were you at the ticket office all day?' I asked.

Kristian nodded. 'Brilliant sales today,' he said. 'I sold loads of Newt Bracelets.'

'I take it Venla didn't come to work.'

Kristian lowered his eyes. 'No, she's probably still ill.'

I thought of the missing two hundred thousand euros and what Laura had told me: Juhani had taken on Venla at least in part for reasons that had nothing to do with her ability to sell Newt Bracelets.

Was there a connection between the two? I had to talk to this Venla
– assuming she ever turned up for the full-time job for which we paid
her wages. The thought was both absurd and infuriating.

'Did she call you?' I asked. 'Do you talk to her often?'

Kristian looked even more confused, then I saw the blood
rushing to his cheeks.

'Yes. I mean, no.'

I waited.

'Not really,' he corrected himself. He was bright red. 'Well, not
at all.'

'So the two of you don't talk?'

'No.'

'But you're filling in for her.'

'Yes.'

'And yet you're the maintenance man.'

'Yes.'

'Shouldn't Venla take care of her own job?'

Kristian looked as though he'd swallowed something he
couldn't get down but was either unable or unwilling to show it.

'It's no trouble.'

'Why don't you do the others' jobs too?'

'Why?'

'If it's no trouble.'

'Everyone else's jobs? Where are they going?'

'I don't know,' I said. 'Maybe the same place as Venla.'

Kristian's expression showed that, at least to some extent, the
thought was excruciating.

'Has someone suggested that?'

'No,' I sighed. 'Not that I know of. The original question was
rhetorical. My intention was to demonstrate that your chosen
course of action is profoundly illogical.'

Kristian looked like he was scaling a particularly steep hill.

'You had something on your mind,' I said eventually. 'When
you knocked at the door.'

'Right, yes,' he said, visibly relieved at the change of subject. 'I know this is your first day and everything. But out there we were talking – I mean, the others were talking and I was listening. Anyway, since there's a new owner here now, you're the new owner and you're responsible for...'

'It certainly looks that way,' I nodded.

'The thing is, about a month ago me and Juhani were talking. We had an agreement, and Juhani is ... well, he's not in that chair, which I'm really sorry about, but seeing as we had an agreement and everything, I was wondering what kind of timetable we might be looking at...'

I waited for a moment. 'What agreement?'

'Well, we talked about...' Kristian's eyes roamed the room to find something to focus on, seemingly without success. 'You see, I was supposed to become ... or be made ... become ... whichever way you look at it...'

'You were supposed to become something...' I tried to prompt him.

'The general manager,' he finally blurted out.

I was sure I'd misheard.

'Excuse me?'

'The boss. The CEO. The big cheese.'

I finally understood. Of course. Juhani had been planning to make Kristian the general manager, the kind of general manager who ... might not pay attention to every detail, every signature. Someone who would be a general manager only on paper. Of course, it was always possible that Kristian had a vast array of hidden managerial talents. I looked at him and thought about what I'd just heard. I couldn't help thinking that, if he did possess hidden managerial talents, they were hidden with the precision of a stealth bomber.

'Kristian,' I said. 'That isn't ... going to happen.'

Kristian's brown eyes suddenly stopped roaming. He looked directly ahead.

'Yes, it is.'

'No. You—'

'Yes. Me. Manager.'

'You know, Kristian—'

'I don't want to know anything,' he said emphatically. 'I want to be the general manager.'

We sat in silence for a moment.

'We have an agreement,' said Kristian. His voice had lowered an octave.

I glanced at the piles of papers on the desk, the ones I had already gone through. It now looked as though Juhani was caught up in the middle of something – something besides an economic catastrophe. If what Kristian said was true – and I had no reason to doubt him, he seemed very sincere indeed – then only a month ago, Juhani had found himself in a situation in which he needed to erase himself from the company's board.

'Kristian,' I said cautiously. 'Let's talk about this later.'

Kristian bolted up from his chair and reached a firm hand across the desk. I stood up and took it. Kristian shook my hand – literally. I could feel the force of his grip. The power seemed to flow through his whole body, as though even the tectonic pectoral muscles rippling across his chest had played their part in sealing our conversation.

'It's a deal,' he said.

I was about to open my mouth but stopped myself at the last moment. I repeated what I'd said: we'd talk about it later. This seemed to satisfy Kristian and he released my hand. He turned, stepped towards the open door. Just before reaching the doorway he stopped, turned again and stretched out his arm. He raised his thumb and forefinger like a pistol going off, then tried to wink at me, but succeeded in blinking both his eyes.

'Cool,' he said.

7

The man was waving a handful of documents in my face. *Lalla-lalla-laa*, he taunted me. He walked backwards, and I pursued him. I tried to grab the bundle of papers, but my arms felt heavy and my movements hopelessly slow. The man continued tormenting me. I couldn't make out his features. The parts of his face – the mouth, nose, cheeks, forehead – all kept changing place, never settling in one position. Those documents contained the information I needed, they explained where the money had gone. Finally I wrenched myself into motion, dived and grabbed the…

I woke up just before I hit the ground, but nonetheless hit it I did, with a thump. I fell on my left side, bashed my right fist against the bedside rug as I reached for the papers. The pain from the fall arrived with a slight delay. I was already staggering to my feet when I realised I'd hit my head too. It had struck the laminate floor beside the rug. The left side of my forehead started to throb. I managed to stand up and assess the situation.

The digital clock on the bedside table showed the time in blood-red numbers: 03:58.

The commotion had woken Schopenhauer, and he watched my movements from the end of the bed. I didn't say anything, I didn't want to argue over his night-time snacks. I pulled on my dressing gown and a pair of woolly socks. I walked into the kitchen, drank a glass of water and opened the balcony door. The concrete floor felt cold under my feet, but the air was fresh and light. The silence was absolute.

I had arrived home exhausted. I'd eaten quickly – a few cold sausages and a tart apple – and gone straight to bed. My first day at the adventure park had had the same effect on me as it did on all our visitors. At least, that's what Laura Helanto said. When you've been running around the park all day, come the evening you're out like a light. There was no arguing with that.

The cold no longer felt bad. My forehead was still throbbing, the dull sensation beginning to subside. Many things Laura Helanto had said kept popping into my mind, like someone casting a stone at regular intervals into a still, nocturnal pond. She had expressed surprise at how soon I'd visited the park after my brother's death. I hadn't understood the question. She said I needed time to grieve properly. Wasn't I planning on taking some time for myself? At this point, we had just arrived at the broken Banana Mirror when something urgent came up, so I never got to answer her. But right now, just like every day in the early hours, I was having conversations with people who weren't there.

I mentally answered her, saying I didn't see how the situation would change or get any easier were I to sit on the sofa for a while, pondering future plans and the nature of death. My musings on the subject were neither here nor there.

And the funeral had been taken care of too. The lawyer said he would arrange everything according to Juhani's instructions. I would choose the casket and it would be duly incinerated. After that, I would be informed when it was time to bury the urn. There wouldn't be any formal memorial service. There was no one to invite; nobody wanted to eat dry meatballs, warm potato salad and stale cinnamon buns from a catering company. No one wanted to hear a priest giving a eulogy for the deceased, a speech full of second-hand information but without any first-hand corroboration. I assumed I would be told where to bury the urn. I assumed I would be able to borrow a rope too – to bury the urn, not to follow Juhani into the bosom of the earth. More importantly, what was a suitable period of grief for such a loss?

Juhani was my brother.

Our childhood was chaotic.

Our parents took turns losing their grip on various aspects of everyday life. The expression 'out of the frying pan, into the fire' suited them to a tee. When they'd brought their Bohemian alcohol problems at least temporarily under control, before the week was out they would start buying things that we didn't need and that they couldn't afford. When the situation had reached almost catastrophic levels, they managed to stem their compulsive hoarding by moving house and starting over in a smelly commune led by a bearded man in a dirty woolly jumper that was too short for him, and who even a child could see was hopping in and out of bed with all the women in the house. When our impulsive father finally uncovered the truth, we were on the move again and, apparently in revenge for Mr Utopia, heading right into a world of capitalism: my parents became Tupperware agents for a while, until our over-priced rented apartment became filled with plastic dishes and boxes of all shapes and sizes and which my parents decided to pay for by starting up a puppet theatre. Which, even at the age of thirteen, I realised would only lead to another catastrophe of a slightly different complexion.

And so on.

There was never any sense to anything.

When I was young, I swore my life would be based on recognising facts, on reason, forward planning, control, assessing what was advantageous and what was not. Even as a child I saw mathematics as the key. People betrayed us, numbers did not. I was surrounded by chaos, but numbers represented order. After finishing my homework, I would calculate all kinds of things for pleasure. In mathematics, I was two years ahead of everyone in my class.

Our parents died when Juhani and I were in our early twenties. Their deaths weren't at all dramatic. In a way, my parents died of old age, though they were relatively young, just shy of sixty. I assumed the reckless lifestyle must have eventually taken its toll on them, aged them; that their unfathomable antics had quite simply worn them out. At the time of their death the latest hairbrained scheme was a Bulgarian-yoghurt festival that they had, yet again, organised completely the wrong way round: by importing vast quantities of yoghurt first and storing it in the house while they waited for the festival to begin.

But what did this have to do with Juhani and grieving his death?

I supposed, as I leaned against the metal railings of my balcony, that in a way I had already grieved for him long ago, when I grieved for my parents. Juhani and our parents were very much of a kind. This didn't seem to bother him. He had similarly slid from one desperate situation to the next, inevitably leaving smouldering ruins behind him, time and again fleeing the scenes of devastation he had caused, laughing as he went. I think this was why I was so angry at him. And, of course, the fact that he had left me an adventure park with mysterious debts to the tune of hundreds of thousands of euros.

For now I finally realised, as I gripped the cold, square railing in my hands and filled my lungs with night-chilled air, that this was the story of my family.

YouMeFun was Juhani – it was my mother and father.

YouMeFun was our family.

And that was precisely what made all this so difficult.

I hadn't forgotten all those conversations with my family members. I'd tried to make each of them see the inconsistency of a given course of action and point out the pitfalls of the rose-tinted, *laissez-faire* attitude that infused everything they did. In each instance I explained the facts, how much everything was likely to cost – in contrast to what they thought things would cost – how one decision affected the next, and explained what the most probable outcome might be. These conversations always ended the same way: arguments, insults, offence, silent treatment, tensions – and fresh arguments.

Until they were all dead.

The concrete floor radiated cold, and the soles of my feet were starting to ache. The stars were like pinheads lit with bright LEDs.

The thought was like a wave born long ago, like a train gathering speed, and I knew it was heading right towards me. I knew its content long before I was able to put it into words. I knew what decision I would eventually reach, though for a fraction of a second I wanted to avoid it all: the thought, the conclusions, the implications, the responsibility I would have to bear.

8

Laura Helanto was sitting alone, eating her lunch in the yard behind the adventure park, in the delivery area, where a set of garden furniture had been laid out for the staff. I walked down the clanging metallic steps from the loading bay and headed towards her, the table and chair. Given the time of year, the day was calm and warm, the cloudless sky a deep blue. The world was bright and open and as motionless as could be.

I took a deep breath.

I had spent the previous evening and the early hours of this morning with Juhani's paperwork. My sense of despair had, if anything, only deepened. That said, I thought I might have found a small glimmer of financial hope amid the chaos.

Laura was holding a fork in her right hand while flicking through her phone with her left. She only looked up once I was three steps away from the table. Her glasses reflected the sunshine, but I caught a fleeting look of bafflement in her eyes before a smile spread across her face.

'Oh, hi,' she said.

'I see the accounting for the petty-cash register lives a life of its own,' I said and sat down across the table from her. 'Whose responsibility is that?'

Laura said nothing at first, instead skewering cubes of cucumber from a plastic box with her fork. Her smile had gone.

'Juhani made it my responsibility,' she said.

'Why?'

'Is there a problem with the accounting? I always submitted the previous day's sales report to him, every morning, just as we agreed. And a weekly report every Monday and a monthly report at the end of the month. Hard, printed copies. On his desk. Just as he asked.'

'Right,' I said. 'It looks strong – the petty-cash register, I mean. I found the most recent report on the desk, and a few dozen previous reports too. But why...? Did Juhani say...? Or were things done a different way in the past?'

The cucumber cubes remained suspended in mid-air. The fork was almost diametrically halfway between her mouth and the box.

'If I've understood right, everything used to go straight to the accountant in one attachment, directly from the computer,' she said. 'But Juhani told me he'd sacked the accountant and that he was looking for a new one, so in the meantime he asked me to look after the cash register and deliver the reports to him directly.'

Just then there was a hint of hesitation, of uncertainty, in Laura's expression. She lowered the fork back towards the box.

'Is there a problem?' she asked.

The short answer was: yes. The fact was that quite a lot of money came into the accounts, but a far greater amount was flowing out again. And the more I put everything together – the lawyer who'd visited my apartment; Kristian with his dreams of becoming general manager; the two accounting reports, one of which was drawn up by a painter; Juhani's recent loans; the park's other debts – the more peculiar everything started to look. I hadn't yet answered when Laura Helanto spoke again.

'All I know is, the park is doing quite well and I have taken care of everything, as we agreed.'

Laura Helanto sounded genuine. This too was a problem. Kristian seemed genuine; so did the lawyer, in his own way. Everyone was genuine, but that still didn't explain why a large sum of money was now nowhere to be found.

'Do you have any previous experience of these matters?' I asked.

'What kind of matters?'

Her answer was quick, and it came with a flash, another reflection from her glasses.

'Experience with corporate finance,' I said. 'YouMeFun is more a mid-sized company than a small start-up, so...'

'Do you?' she began. 'Do you have that sort of experience?'

The question took me by surprise, though it was a perfectly reasonable one. Perhaps Laura noticed this.

'No,' I replied honestly. 'None whatsoever.'

We looked at each other. Laura Helanto said nothing. I had nothing to add either, and I didn't want to express any incomplete, half-baked conclusions on the subject. It befitted neither me nor the situation at hand.

'I'm just trying to establish how everything works round here,' I said eventually, and it was true. 'This is all new to me. There are plenty of customers, that's a positive. As you said, the park is doing well...'

Again, I left the end of the thought unspoken: the park is doing well *all things considered*. Laura looked at me for a moment, she seemed to relax. She raised her fork again, was about to pop it in her mouth.

'Have you already had lunch?' she asked.

'No,' I said, and realised I hadn't made plans for lunch or any kind of meal. By now I was hungry. 'And I haven't ... Maybe I'll pick up something at the Curly Cake...'

'Here's some falafel and hummus,' she said, moving little plastic boxes across the table one at a time. 'I've already eaten. I'll have some more cucumber – I've brought so much of it.'

I looked at the boxes. They contained food, but it looked as though someone else had eaten from them. Despite my hunger, I had no desire to eat leftovers from someone I might later come to suspect of embezzlement.

'No, thank you,' I said.

Laura continued eating her cucumber. Her phone rang. She glanced at it, flicked it open. A colourful image appeared on the screen, and despite the reflection I realised it was a painting. Laura sighed then looked up at me.

'Sorry,' she said. 'This guy wants to buy a painting, but he's offering less than I spent on the materials. That's how it is these days. People want everything for free. Nobody wants to pay for an artist's work. Everybody thinks if they had the time and inclination, they could have painted something similar. Not even similar, but better.'

'Can I see the painting?' I asked before thinking the matter through.

It was the second time this had happened. The day before, I had, to my own surprise, begun telling Laura Helanto about my relationship with my brother. I didn't know quite what was going on.

'Sure,' she said and angled the phone towards me.

The screen was filled with powerful reds and white. The painting must have been quite large. It didn't seem to represent anything in particular, but I soon began to make out figures and movement in the swirls. After a while, I realised I was almost transfixed. I almost had to wrench my eyes free.

'Impressive,' I said instinctively and instantly felt that I'd stepped into dangerous territory. I couldn't understand why I carried on talking. 'Powerful. It grows on you. You can see motion, it's alive, you're always finding something new.'

'Thanks,' said Laura, took the phone and locked the screen. 'That's nice to hear.'

I wanted to extract myself from the situation, but I was still sitting there. I had started the conversation with purely accounting-related matters and ended up talking in blurred, spontaneous artistic metaphors. This wasn't like me at all. I stood up, trying to avoid making eye contact with Laura Helanto.

'So you *do* have an artistic side,' she said.

'A what?' The question blurted out of its own volition.

'What you said about my painting. That was very kind of you.'

What was I supposed to say: that I didn't know where the words had come from?

'It's nice to hear, seeing as painting has been so difficult for me recently,' she said. 'Thanks for the encouragement.'

'You're welcome,' I said.

Perhaps I heard another humming sound, something on a different frequency from the roar of traffic on the nearby highway. Laura leaned against the table, her shoulders rising like waves.

'But when you arrived, you went straight to the point, no small talk, you didn't say hello, didn't ask how I'm doing.'

'I never ask things like that,' I said, and instantly felt myself relax. This was an easier subject: I knew what I was talking about.

'Okay,' Laura nodded.

'I don't need to know how other people are doing. I don't want to know what they're thinking, what they've done or how they experience things. I don't want to know what they are planning, their hopes and aspirations. So I don't ask.'

'Okay.'

'Except in extreme situations.'

'Okay.'

I was still standing on the spot. Was Laura Helanto smiling? Her reaction was just as unexpected as mine. I hadn't planned to say what I was thinking; it just happened. I felt a growing sense of unease. The accounting and financial discrepancies were foremost in my mind, getting to the bottom of them was my top priority. Not this kind of ... what exactly? I didn't know, specifically, generally or even vaguely. And why was I still standing there, still looking at Laura Helanto's eyes? Again I was about to say something I had no intention of saying out loud when salvation blared out behind me.

'Hey, Harry,' Kristian shouted from the loading bay, waving his hand. 'There are two guys here, said they've come to see you. They're in your office. They said they know you and know where you sit.'

I took a step towards Kristian, then turned back to look at Laura.

'Nobody calls me Harry,' I said. 'I don't like it.'
'Okay,' said Laura Helanto, then added, 'Henri it is.'
And yes, she was smiling.

9

The first impression was that these two men were such an odd couple that they must represent two separate, one-man outfits.

The older of the two, who was around my age, was dressed in a blue shirt and black blazer, light jeans and a pair of light-brown deck shoes. He appeared to know who I was as soon as I walked into the room. Or, more specifically, it seemed as though he had known long before I arrived.

'I'm sorry,' he said. 'Your brother was an interesting man.'

His face was round, his skin pock-marked, his eyes blue and small. His short, light, neatly trimmed hair was combed with a left-side parting. He was of average build, apart from the half-football protruding from his stomach. Our handshake was short and perfunctory. I gave him my name, though he already knew it. I expected to hear his.

'Let's have a little chat,' he said instead. That was it.

I glanced at the other man, leaning against the wall at the other side of the room. Young, bald, broad-shouldered, his jaw munching on chewing gum. A black, XXL Adidas tracksuit. A large smartphone in his right hand, a set of white headphones over his ears. The impression was of a giant, mutant teenybopper.

'What is this about?'

The older man closed the office door as though he were at home. Then he gestured me to my own chair behind my own desk and took a chair from the conference table for himself. I walked round to my place and sat down. The mutant stood in the corner like a statue, the headphones clamped over his ears.

'I hear you're a mathematician,' the man said once he had sat down.

'I'm an actuary. And what's your business here today?'

The man looked at me for a moment before answering.

'It's your brother's business, actually. Which, of course, is now your business.'

Of course, I thought. I leaned forwards, gripped the pile of unpaid bills and placed them on the desk in front of me.

'What company do you represent?' I asked.

The man's small blue eyes slowly opened and closed. I didn't want to think of a lizard, but I did. A reptile, an iguana.

'When he died, Juhani's debt was two hundred thousand euros,' the man said. 'Now it's two hundred and twenty thousand. You know why?'

'Which debt are we talking about?' I asked.

'Do you know why?' he repeated.

'First I have to know which—'

'Because now there's interest to pay,' he said. 'And the interest rate is ten percent.'

'Over what period of time?'

'The time since he popped his clogs. Your brother, that is.'

'Two weeks and four days? Ten percent interest? Where did he agree to that?'

'Right here in this room,' the man said, opening out his arms as if to bequeath me the office I already owned. 'We shook on it.'

'You shook on it? Two hundred thousand?'

Now the man clasped his hands in front of him, showed them to me and nodded slowly. This bizarre performance of his had gone on long enough.

'This is absurd,' I said. 'I'll have to ask you to leave. I don't know who you are, and you won't tell me. And you don't have a formal agreement or contract. There's no sense in this. Please leave.'

The man did not move. The mutant hadn't moved throughout the whole conversation. The older man's small, piercing eyes closed, then slowly opened again.

'I can increase the interest rate, if necessary,' he said.

I shook my head. 'You come here demanding two hundred thousand euros—'

'Two hundred and twenty thousand,' he corrected me.

'And as for that interest rate,' I said. 'Ten percent in two weeks and four days. That's nearly six hundred percent per annum.'

'Did you just work that out in your head?'

'Of course. It's a simple enough calculation:

$\left(\frac{220000}{200000}\right)^{365/18} \times 100\% - 100\% = 590.799\%.$'

'Impressive,' the man said.

'What is?'

'You worked that out pretty quickly. I wouldn't have been able to tell you anything about the annual interest rate.'

'I calculated it so that you'd see what nonsense you're talking. The next time you try to swindle someone, at least try to make the numbers sound credible.'

'Credible?'

'The way Wertheimer almost conned Einstein himself, for instance. Wertheimer presented him with the following conundrum: an old car drives for two kilometres, first uphill then downhill. Because the car is old, it can't drive the first kilometre faster than an average of fifteen kilometres per hour. The question is: how fast must the old banger drive the second kilometre – going downhill, where it can drive faster – so that the average speed for the entire journey is thirty kilometres per hour?'

The man pursed his lips a few times, then reached a conclusion.

'That's an easy one,' he said. 'Two kilometres. The first kilometre at fifteen km/h. Fine. The second has to be at forty-five. Because forty-five plus fifteen is sixty. Sixty divided by two is thirty. So forty-five on the way down and Bob's your uncle.'

'So one would think,' I said. 'But it's a trick question. The right answer is, it's impossible. Not even if the car shot down the hill like a space shuttle.'

The man said nothing.

'At a speed of fifteen kilometres per hour, it takes the old car four minutes to reach the top of the hill, a journey of one kilometre,' I said. 'But how long does it take to drive up the hill and back again at an average speed of thirty kilometres per hour? The journey up and down is two kilometres in total. At thirty kilometres per hour, two kilometres will take four minutes. Thus, the car needs only four minutes to cover the whole journey at the faster speed. But these minutes have already been used up by the time it reaches the top of the hill.'

Again, those iguana eyes. The eyelids lowered, then rose again.

'Einstein only realised this once he started looking at the problem in greater detail,' I continued. 'But not everyone is like Einstein. Not even you. No offence. I'm just saying you should look a bit more closely at things, like Wertheimer.'

'What about you?'

'What about me?'

'Did you fall for it?'

'At first,' I replied honestly. 'But because I calculate everything carefully and think methodically through everything I do, I noticed almost straight away what was going on. You can't trick me. I don't leave anything to chance that doesn't need to be left to chance. I believe in the calculus of probability.'

'Sounds promising.'

'In what way?' I asked, without really knowing why. I just wanted the men to leave.

'With a view to understanding our situation here,' he said and turned his head. 'Let's add another level of understanding, shall we? Ay-Kay.'

The last, confusing word was seemingly aimed at the mutant. He didn't react at all, perhaps there was something more interesting coming from his headphones.

'AY-KAY!'

The mutant flinched, removed the headphone from his right

ear. I could hear a low-pitched thumping. The mutant, who I now realised answered to the initials AK, looked at the older man with renewed interest.

'AK,' said the older man. 'If you would.'

After this brief instruction, everything happened very quickly.

AK replaced the headphones over his ears, slid his phone into his tracksuit pocket, took a few brisk steps that, with surprising speed and agility, brought him round the desk and right next to me. In the same series of movements, he gripped my right hand as though it were part of his own body.

I was wrenched out of the chair and under AK's arm. I caught the thick smell of aftershave and deodorant. The pain felt like an explosion whose pressure waves rippled through my body. AK twisted my little finger upwards. With my free hand, I grabbed AK's hands and tried to prise them from round my own. It was like trying to stop a dam bursting with your bare hands. AK twisted again. I was paralysed with pain, couldn't breathe.

'Right, Einstein, or whoever the fuck his friend was. AK here could pull your finger right off. I've seen him do it. He just yanks it off in one go. It's impressive. I like the sound. Like pulling a leg off a roast chicken. It's a meaty, juicy sound, only much, much louder. I don't know if that's what's going to happen right now. He can't hear me. Can you hear me, Henri?'

I nodded once, twice.

'Good,' said the man.

AK twisted again.

'It looks like this has all come as a bit of a surprise to you. You see, your brother Juhani liked playing poker. He liked it a lot. We lent him money so he could keep on playing. Everything was going well. He kept playing, we lent him more money. He paid his debts, then borrowed some more. Where's the problem? We were all happy bunnies. Then suddenly he stopped paying but carried on playing. Not such happy bunnies now. Do you follow?'

I nodded twice, this time in much quicker succession. The older man waved his hand like a football referee disallowing a goal. AK let go. My hand was on fire. AK returned to his spot near the wall, as if he had never left it. I felt my right hand with my left. I couldn't tell if anything was broken.

'Looks like your finger's still attached,' said the man, then paused. 'Two hundred and twenty thousand euros.'

'I don't have—'

'You do, and I know you do,' he said. 'The petty-cash register is in good shape.'

I heard these last words twice, first when he uttered them, then as I mentally repeated them to myself. He knew.

'In case you're thinking of calling the police,' he continued, 'think twice about that. In the worse scenario, the amusement park will close down and you'll still owe us the money. Then how will you pay your debts?'

The man paused. For a few seconds, the lizard reappeared. He continued.

'But there is an upside to all this. We are prepared to extend the repayment schedule. Naturally, the debt will accrue more interest, but what's most important is to get things rolling, as it were. The amusement park is ticking over nicely and...'

Pain was throbbing the length of my finger. I had reached a decision.

'No,' I said, then added, 'This is an adventure park.'

'What?'

'This is an adventure park, not an amusement park.'

I explained the difference just as I'd explained it to the lawyer: an amusement park hurls people around, but in an adventure park people hurl themselves around. And so on. I added that though both parks might feature places like Caper Castle, the difference was still important and should be duly noted. For a moment the man was silent.

'No?'

'That's right,' I nodded. 'I am not responsible for my brother's debts. I don't see how I possibly could be. I won't pay.'

For the first time, the man showed a flicker of irritation.

'AK could have torn your finger off,' he said. 'I told him to stop. I did you a favour.'

I glanced up at AK; he wasn't listening to us.

'Now please leave.'

The lizard reappeared, and this time it remained in the man's eyes. He slowly turned his head towards AK and was about to say something when there came a knock at the door. I said 'come in' before anyone had the chance to open their mouth. A second later and Laura was in the room.

'We need to talk about the maintenance to the Turtle Trucks...'

Laura stopped. Her eyes moved from me to the older man, then to AK, and finally back to me.

'Sorry, I didn't realise...' she began, but didn't continue. From her expression, I could tell she knew she'd walked in on something very unexpected. Her gaze moved from the men to me, then to the middle of the room.

'I didn't realise either,' said the older man, now more reptilian than human. 'But if AK over here were to expand his activities, as it were, maybe we'd all realise something, yes?'

The older man shifted his lizard gaze from me to Laura. No, I thought instantly and automatically, no, no, no. You can break all the bones in my body and I still won't pay, I was about to say, but so much as touch Laura and...

Right then I heard the sound of high heels against the laminate floor.

'About the marketing budget,' Minttu K said as she strode into the office. 'Can we have a word, honey?'

Then she too came to a halt. There were now five of us in the small room.

For a moment, maybe as much as ten throbbing seconds, the office was like a wax museum where realistic dolls of living people stood frozen in position. Then the numbers, the facts, did their job. There were three of us. Even AK wouldn't be able to snap all thirty of our fingers before the situation descended into chaos.

The wax dolls came to life.

The older man stood up from his chair, Laura stepped closer to my desk, Minttu K glanced inquisitively at both the men, particularly AK, corrected her posture and tugged down the hem of her all-too-short blazer. AK moved, following the older man towards the door. Once at the door, the older man stopped, and AK stopped too.

Laura took half a step closer to the desk, and I don't know why noticing this seemed to warm me so much amid all the agitation. The older man turned, noticed AK in front of him, moved beside him and spoke in the friendliest voice he had used thus far.

'Thanks again, Henri,' said the iguana. 'We love amusement parks. We'll certainly be coming again.'

AK said nothing at all.

10

The following three days – Thursday, Friday, Saturday – I spent almost entirely in the adventure park. I was woken in the mornings by the gentle nudge of Schopenhauer's paws. He sat purring beside my face, and prodding me beneath the nose. I got up and gave him some food. This always happened between five and a quarter past five in the morning. I shaved, had breakfast, tied my tie and headed to the adventure park.

I first took the commuter train, then changed to the bus. The journey took an average of forty-seven minutes, and I needed a two-zone ticket. I used the journey to calculate everything. Well, not quite everything. I didn't take Juhani's alleged gambling debts into account. The whole matter seemed more absurd with every day that passed: the visit of the two men, their claims and demands. My little finger was swollen and still sore to the touch, which reminded me that all this really had happened, but other than that...

What I said was exactly what I thought.

Even if Juhani had been playing poker more than he could afford, it was none of my concern, except for the fact that it had left the adventure park in something of a financial quandary. It was perfectly possible that Juhani had gambled a lot. In fact, it was highly probable, given everything that had come to light. A fanciful and unrealistic approach to the laws of probability makes people try their luck in situations that have nothing to do with luck – be it personal relationships or making a quick buck. For this reason, I didn't gamble in any way, shape or form. To me it was like swimming in a pool half filled with sharks: though the sharks only took up half the pool, it was still their pool.

Once the man with the reptilian eyes and his not-so-little helper
who only answered to the name AK had left my office, I asked
Laura Helanto to show me how everything worked. Everything?
she had asked. Yes, I replied, I want to know how my park
functions, what goes on where, I want to master every aspect of
this. I didn't tell her I had no choice in the matter. I didn't offer
any explanations for this or for what had just happened. And I
didn't tell her about the park's catastrophic financial situation or
Juhani's alleged gambling problems.

The next few days were packed.

I learned how to do everything in the park.

With a screwdriver in my hand, I tightened the structures beneath
the slides. I acquainted myself with the most critical aspects of the
park's cleaning operation, sat with Minttu K – in the afternoons the
smell of alcohol, specifically gin *lonkero*, was overpowering – as we
went through the marketing budget, negotiated with the stony-faced
Johanna about reducing the cafeteria's acquisition budget (the answer
was no), tried to coax Esa away from his screens and to expand his job
description to include live interaction with the customers (this
apparently wasn't possible if maximum customer safety was to be
ensured at all times), wondered when Venla might turn up for work
(I still hadn't actually met her), and, of course, all the while trying to
avoid Kristian, who at every opportunity whispered various ideas
about the general managership and the transition strategy, as well as
asking when he could break the news to the others.

On Sunday morning I was sitting on the train once again.

The sun was rising. The streets, fields, parks and cycle paths
were empty, as though they too were resting. As autumn had
progressed, the gold and crimson of the trees seemed to have lost
part of their previous splendour, but with each stop, as the sun
slowly rose, their glow intensified, and when I arrived in Vantaa I
stepped off the bus into an ocean of colour.

According to Laura Helanto, Sundays were almost as good as Saturdays in terms of footfall. I told myself that Sunday would be my last day as a trainee at the adventure park and that the last few days could be considered my induction week. As the new, full week began, I would be ready. Ready to introduce the staff to my list of changes, to our new ways of working, and especially to the new budgets for each department.

I noticed I was smiling.

'Are you alright?' Laura Helanto asked when we met at midday.

'What do you mean?'

'You look a bit ... No offence, but you look a bit ill. You're different somehow.'

I realised that this misunderstanding was probably due to my expression. I stopped smiling, and Laura didn't ask anything else. She explained that the giant rabbit, which greeted everybody as they arrived, suffered from a loose, flapping ear. Just then, she turned and pointed at the rabbit.

'Its ears aren't supposed to flap around,' she added, and now she was smiling too. I was unsure whether the smile was intended for me or the rabbit.

'I'll fix it myself,' I said because I knew Kristian was currently at the entrance counter, standing in for Venla. Again. Then I remembered the other pressing matters on today's schedule and added: 'Once we've closed for the day.'

Laura looked at me again. I'd noticed that I liked her eyes. There was something about their brightness, their inquisitiveness, something that made even me realise it is possible to look at certain things and experience joy and excitement. Perhaps. And I noticed I liked her wild hair too. Its bushiness was both fun and attractive, all at once. But I didn't want to prolong our meeting. All week Laura had been asking awkward questions about the men's visit and why I wanted to pay greater attention to the petty-cash register and all other financial transactions.

'Is it alright if I leave a bit early today?' she asked.

The question took me aback. Then I realised that, naturally, I was the one who made these kinds of decisions now.

'If everything is in order,' I said.

Laura glanced quickly to her side.

'I think everything is in order.'

Had her tone of voice changed?

'Of course, I'll go around the park once more,' she continued, 'and I'll tell the others I'm leaving. And I'll remind people to make sure they don't accidentally do any overtime.'

Excellent, I thought. Sunday overtime pay was poison to the park's finances and might upset our new-found financial equilibrium. If we could put Sunday overtime behind us, so much the better. And if some chores were left unfinished, they could be done on Monday, the quietest day of the week.

'That's fine,' I said. 'I can close up.'

Another quick glance to the side.

'So I can tell everyone they can leave as and when they are done?'

'That will be fine too,' I replied. 'I can glue the rabbit's ear by myself.'

Laura Helanto looked first at me, then the rabbit.

'It can be quite an unpredictable rabbit,' she said. 'Be careful.'

NOW

1

The German rabbit's large ear looks like it is growing right out of the dead man's forehead.

I manage to raise my eyes and spin around. My legs are trembling, my heart is thundering like an icebreaker pushing through the frozen sea. I am standing in the middle of the adventure park, in the area between the Komodo Locomotive and the Trombone Cannons with the giant rabbit behind me, a dead man at my feet, and I'm bleeding. At times I can almost fathom all this, at others it threatens to hurtle out of my control, turn to panic and terror. Instinctively, I know that the wisest thing to do is to stay still, to try and stand on the spot and wait.

Time passes slowly.

I can feel the seconds ticking within me, like someone knocking the wind out of me over and over. Gradually I start sensing things outside my own body again. The smells of the adventure park, the permeating sweetness wafting out of the cafeteria, the building materials around me: veneer, metal, plastic. Small, brightly coloured spots of light. The sheer motionlessness. The silence. My breathing slowly steadies, my sweaty clothes start to feel cold and tacky against my skin. My left shoulder is pulsing, blood is pumping into my adventure-park T-shirt and seeping through the fabric. The lactic acid gradually fades from my limbs, and I can sense the feeling and mobility returning to my thighs and calves. I realise I must be in shock, in a state of post-adrenaline rush, and maybe I'm not entirely myself. But to some extent, I am.

Therefore, I count.

Three days ago, two men visited me, one of them twisted my

fingers, the other demanded money. I refused to pay, and they said they would be back. It's not a very complicated equation – despite the indisputable fact that the man lying on the floor is neither of the men that visited me. Still, I don't need to know who he is to know that he represents the same organisation. And this organisation doesn't appear to operate the way banks usually do. Though banks have a habit of continuously and systematically making their customer service worse, they haven't quite reached the point where they send knife-throwers after their debtors in the dead of night. I can hear the man's cries as though they are still echoing around the hall.

This is your final warning.

If the knife that struck my shoulder was my final warning, what will the next step be? Again, it's a simple calculation. It also tells me who – or rather what – I'm dealing with.

Juhani was in debt to a bunch of criminals. Either they will get their money or...

I am beginning to appreciate both the scope and the true nature of my problem.

Only a few seconds, a few blinks of an eye ago I was about to call the police, an ambulance.

But if I were to do that, what would happen next? The chain of events is obvious: the park would be closed indefinitely, its reputation would be gone, its finances would collapse for good, I would still be in debt to the crooks and I wouldn't have a park to help me clear that debt, which was accruing interest with every passing day. If I sold my one-bedroom flat, I might be able to survive for a short while, but then I would be in an even worse situation: homeless, park-less and penniless – and what would these men do to somebody like that?

No, absolutely not. The solution must be elsewhere. And what was it I was thinking only a moment ago? How I am sick to the back teeth that I am continually – and unjustly – placed in situations for which I am not in any way responsible, I am sick of being snubbed with a mixture of cunning, plotting, lying – and now crime.

But first things first...

I need some distance, some time to think. Time to draw up a plan, to make the necessary calculations, to see things more clearly. To know how best to proceed. I need...

That's right.

I spin round again. My first steps are unsure, my legs are still stiff with exertion. They start to work again as I walk towards the doors and look outside. The car park is like the surface of the moon, cold, motionless and devoid of people. I might just have survived the first test. I return to the hall, walk up to the man and kneel down in front of him. I look somewhere else. I don't like doing it one bit, but I pat the man's pockets. The feeling is extremely unpleasant. The man is still lukewarm, gradually cooling, his body strangely broader than one might expect. The zip pockets in his coat are far away from each other, like two little bags of assorted belongings dropped at two different sides of the park. Finally I find what I'm looking for.

A set of car keys.

This is the second piece of good news. If there is a set of car keys in his pocket, in all probability he must have come here alone. I must admit, this conclusion isn't based on rigorous logical probability, but on so-called gut feeling – something for which, as a mathematician who is serious about statistical analysis, I cannot say I have much time. But this is an exceptional situation, and there isn't nearly enough observable evidence to reach a more thorough conclusion. I'm not sure which I'm trying to convince myself of more: what I have to do next or the fact that I can so easily dismiss serious probability equations for the nth time in the same week.

I stand up, the car keys in my hand, and push them into my own pocket. I listen for a moment longer, just to be on the safe side – nothing but the gaping, empty adventure park around me

and the Komodo Locomotive stopped in the night in front of me
– and begin walking off towards what the park's staff call the
workshop.

When I've found what I'm looking for, I return to the rabbit,
place the tools on the floor and try to prepare myself for
something I could never have imagined myself doing. Very few
people can imagine it. You don't need an analyst to tell you that.

Namely:

Removing the ear from the man's head is easier said than done.
The metallic parts inside the ear have moved, the steel meshing
has begun to unravel, individual strands have snapped and are now
poking out of the ear like dogged, determined hairs. I tease the
individual metallic hairs from the man's head, and eventually the
ear comes loose and I hold it in my hand again. I place it on the
floor and pick up the roll of plastic wrap. I position the roll on
one side of the man and step backwards, pulling the roll open as
I go. Once I have pulled it about five metres back, I return to the
man and roll him on top of the plastic. Then I grip the plastic
firmly and wrap the man once, twice, thrice. I wrap him in plastic
until the pain in my shoulder forces me to stop. He's wrapped well
enough. I fasten the plastic with a stapler. The package is tight and
– as was my original intention – transportable.

The wheelbarrow is propped next to the door of the loading
bay. I manage to heave the package diagonally across the barrow
and begin hauling the load towards the Curly Cake Café. I can
only pull the barrow with one hand, which means leaning
forwards and straining myself with every step. Needless to say, this
isn't a very satisfactory plan, let alone perfect, but what's most
important is that if I succeed, I win.

Only yesterday, I tried to suggest to Johanna that she keep less
surplus stock in the café. Now, I think, thank goodness she flat-
out refused.

I pull the barrow and its load through the café. Johanna has left
on the stand-by lighting. Hanging above the counter, the price list

and pictures of the café's various dishes glow in the pale light. Mighty Meatballs and Silly Spaghetti, Cinnamon Gigglebuns and the Boisterous Breakfast. The prices are more than reasonable.

I reach the kitchen and push my way through the swing doors. Then I stagger through the kitchen until finally reaching my destination.

There are two enormous freezers in total. I choose the one on the left. I lift the lid and get to work. I empty the contents of the freezer onto the floor and a nearby table, careful to remember the order in which everything is packed. Though at times my attention is drawn to how wasteful and imprecise Johanna's acquisition methods are, how much room there is for improvement, I don't waste time thinking about that now. I don't want the products to thaw. This would be problematic on a number of levels: the food would go off, which would cause waste, and someone would ask why it had happened. I try to take into account both the ecological and criminological dimensions of what I'm doing by placing the products in neat piles, to make sure they thaw as little as possible. The large black-and-white clockface attached to the wall tells me that time is marching on more briskly than at any time in my life thus far.

Once the freezer is completely empty – this operation takes longer than I had anticipated because my left shoulder is getting sorer by the minute and because there are more products in the freezer than one might imagine could ever fit inside – I begin lifting. I hold the barrow's handles as high as I can, which lifts the plastic-wrapped knife-thrower almost exactly halfway between the mouth of the freezer and the concrete floor. That's enough. I bend my knees, assume a firm squatting position, place my hands beneath the man and push.

The performance isn't flawless. But after some creaking and groaning, and one large, convoluted hoisting motion, the man is lying in the freezer. He fits perfectly. I pick up the polystyrene panels I found in the workshop and cut them into pieces big enough to cover the swaddled body at the bottom. This double bottom works better than I'd imagined: the polystyrene panels fit tightly and look almost like the bottom of the freezer, particularly once I pack a layer of raw dough and chicken wings on top of it.

I clean up the kitchen and leave. At the swing doors, I stop. I return to the fridge, open a half-litre bottle of yellow Jaffa and down the fizzy orange in a single gulp. From the cardboard box on the counter, I take two Mars bars and eat them both. Then I glance at the time again.

Sweeping the floor in the hall is a relatively quick operation. I return the wheelbarrow to the warehouse and take the ear with me into the workshop. I almost have to take the whole ear apart, then rebuild it from scratch. The paint is still tacky as I finally take the ladder back into the hall, climb up the steps and reattach the ear to the rabbit's head with glue and a few screws. I come back down the ladder, take a few steps back and look at the rabbit. If my shoulder wasn't throbbing with pain, if my thoughts weren't dashing here, there and everywhere, flashing terrifying images through my mind, if I wasn't so utterly exhausted, I might behold the enormous animal with its slender ears and think, it's alright for you, standing there with your twenty-five-centimetre buck teeth; everything is fine, just as it used to be, as the giant German-Finnish rabbit smiles back at me and pricks up its friendly ears.

I clench the car keys in my hand and remind myself why I started doing this in the first place: one way or another, I'm going to save this adventure park.

The night outside is dark and cold. I zip up my coat, pull the baseball cap further down my head. I wait and listen, then I set off. After flicking the button on the keyring to open and shut the doors a few times, I easily locate the right car. The lights of a Hyundai start flashing against the eastern wall of the building. In addition to all his other unbusinesslike behaviour, the man has parked in one of the parking spaces reserved for staff members only. These spaces are clearly marked, and the relevant registration

number is on the wall in front. I don't know all the staff registration numbers off by heart, but I don't think it matters right
now. I doubt anyone told the man, just park in my space when
you turn up to throw a knife at the new boss.

The car is messy and smells of McDonald's. The source of the
smell is a paper bag of fast food in the legroom on the passenger
side. A few French fries protrude from the opening of the bag. I
start the car, open the window slightly and pull away. I drive slowly
and carefully, looking calmly around me and regularly checking
the rear-view mirror. But this is all unnecessary. Nobody is
following me, let alone paying me any attention. There is no
traffic. I look at the clock above the speedometer; I am on
schedule.

On arrival in Myyrmäki, I park the car beside a driveway
between two blocks of flats, a place where security cameras are
unlikely and which is at the intersection of several possible
footpaths. I leave the car's door unlocked, the keys on the
dashboard. I walk half a kilometre to the train station and get the
first train of the morning heading towards the airport. Once
inside the train, I sit by the window and for a few stops I watch
the landscape passing by, the night-time streets, the few
illuminated windows.

I walk home from the station, and as I have correctly predicted,
Schopenhauer is not amused. He hasn't been fed, he's hungry and
now he's been abruptly woken up. I tell him I'm sorry, I open a
can of cat delicacies and pour a drop of cream into his cup for
dessert. Schopenhauer eats. As always, I tell him about the events
of my day – or, in this case, my evening and night too. Twice he
looks up from his bowl. I then take off my shirt and look at my
shoulder. The bleeding has stopped, and I've already become used
to the pain. I should get up and have a shower, but I'll do it in a
minute. I sit in the kitchen with Schopenhauer and gaze out of
the window, as though looking at this view for the first time.

2

'Dead.'

I've only slept an hour and a half, and I'm not at all prepared for what Minttu K is telling me. Her voice is hoarse, and she has brought into the room both a hint of morning-fresh perfume and something nocturnal, a heavier note that makes me think of nightclubs and popping bottles of prosecco. It's a minute past nine, and I have just arrived at the adventure park and sat down at my desk.

'*Kaput*,' she continues, and beneath all that tan she looks as though she might be blushing ever so slightly. 'End of. What are you trying to do to me?'

I don't quite understand what she means. My bewilderment is, naturally, compounded because I'm confusing two things. At first, I imagine someone must have found something in the hall or the cafeteria freezer that doesn't strictly belong there and now Minttu K has turned up to ask me about it. Then, in her hand I see the piece of paper I left on her desk yesterday.

'We all have to tighten our belts,' I explain.

'You're killing me here.'

'Not just you,' I say. I realise this must have sounded rather rude, so I continue. 'Not you personally. I mean, neither you nor the marketing, nor anyone else or any other particular sector. I'm just trying to save money where it's possible to do so.'

Minttu K sits down and crosses her left leg over her right. Her trousers are excruciatingly tight.

'Listen,' she says. 'I get that this is all new to you and you're finding it hard. What with your brother and ... all that. This must have taken you a bit by surprise.'

'You could say that.'

'But I can assure you, I've been in tighter situations that this. I'll tell you about it one day. You wouldn't believe—'

'Probably not.'

Minttu K seems to stop in her tracks. She casts a somewhat longer glance at me.

'You look kind of ... different,' she says.

'I didn't get much sleep.'

'Honey, I haven't slept since the nineties,' she nods. 'Listen, my point is, reputation is how you sell things. And how do you build a reputation? By doing things and telling people about them.'

Minttu K speaks almost as much with her hands as with her red-painted lips. Her silver rings twinkle in the air.

'You need to have balls,' she says and grabs her crotch. I quickly avert my eyes. 'This piece of paper doesn't have balls.'

'It's a budget proposal.'

'Exactly,' she says, now rather animated. 'I need money, dough, wonga.'

The last sentence seems to fly out of her mouth involuntarily. The words have a different quality to everything else she has said, particularly her incessant saccharine 'honey'. Her voice sounds more emphatic now, almost with a hint of genuine panic.

'You?' I ask.

Minttu K looks away, first at the floor, then at me again.

'The marketing needs money,' she says quickly. 'And I ... am the marketing.'

I think of all the missing money. Who ultimately scrutinises the way Minttu K uses her marketing budget? What was I thinking about nightclubs and prosecco bottles a moment ago? These aren't my only questions. All night and all morning I've been asking – thus far only asking myself – how the knife thrower got into the building in the first place. How did he know I was doing overtime, alone? Before I manage to formulate a question, my attention is drawn to the door. I see Laura Helanto before she sees us. She is walking past the open door, but as she notices us she seems to flinch slightly and stops as though she has bumped into something soft.

'Well, good morning,' she says eventually.

Minttu K glances at the door, then turns her head away without wishing Laura good morning back. I'm reminded of the change in atmosphere during my introductory tour when we stepped into Minttu K's office. Laura and Minttu K didn't greet each other then, either. If I remember right, I haven't seen them speak to each other once since my arrival.

'Morning,' I say and wait.

'Just on my way to the office-equipment room,' says Laura and waves a hand towards the end of the corridor. 'I didn't realise you were already here, Henri.'

Again, Laura addresses her words only to me. She only sees one person in the room. It's not all that out of the ordinary. One can't always get on with everybody – as I know from experience. Perttilä would doubtless send Laura and Minttu K on a confrontation-therapy course with a mentor to guide them in the right direction; it might take place in a yoga room, maybe even by candlelight. But right now, this isn't at the top of my list of priorities.

'Why wouldn't I be here?' I ask Laura.

She thinks about this for two seconds.

'You stayed on after closing last night. I thought you might want to rest this morning. Monday is the quietest day of the week, especially before lunch.'

'Have you seen the rabbit?' I ask.

It can be an unpredictable rabbit. That's what Laura Helanto had said only a few hours ago. She looks behind her. The rabbit isn't behind her.

'Not yet,' she says. 'I haven't been into the hall yet, I thought I'd just ... sort out ... one ... little thing...'

Her phone rings. Laura steps out of the doorway. I can hear her answering. Minttu K shifts position in her chair, crosses her right leg over her left.

'Honey,' she says, her voice syrupy once more. 'Let's not cut the marketing budget, okay?'

My thoughts are still with the rabbit, and I'm trying to move them back to Minttu K when Laura appears at the door again.

'Bit of a situation, I'm afraid,' she says.

🐰

The situation, as she describes it, is out in the forecourt. Someone has knocked over our flagpole – either driven into it or pushed it over. It is a bright, beautiful morning, the wind is cool and autumnal. The light-blue sky is clear and cloudless. We meet at the foot of the flagpole. The yellow-green-red YouMeFun flag is lying on the dry, grey concrete about twenty metres away. To be more precise, we meet at the stump of the flagpole. I look at Kristian, who has called Laura, and it looks as though he is about to cry. Then I realise it's because he is livid.

'Fucking amateurs,' he seethes. 'Fucking learner drivers.'

'Who?' I ask.

Kristian turns to look at me, his eyes glistening and agitated. 'The people that knocked into the flagpole.'

I look around, turn a full 360 degrees. There is at least thirty metres of space on all sides. Nobody knocks into a flagpole by accident. You have to aim for it over a considerable distance, in fact you have to start heading towards it from the turning that leads down to the car park. That's 150 metres away. Whoever knocked into the flagpole really put their mind to it.

'I doubt the problem is with the driving instructor,' I say eventually. 'Kristian, take care of this, please.'

'But who will man the customer-service desk?' he asks.

'Isn't Venla there?'

Kristian stares at the ground in front of him.

'Ill.'

'Again?'

'Yes.'

The flagpole lying on the ground looks more woeful with every passing minute. There's something metaphorical about it. Something about which I don't need to be reminded. Kristian and I are alone in the forecourt. The wind is penetrating my shirt, whipping my tie over my shoulder. Inside, Laura Helanto is holding a course for children that seems like a combination of art and aerobics.

'Take care of the flag and the pole,' I tell him. 'And do it today. I'll go to the customer-service desk.'

I have already turned and am about to take my first step towards the front doors when I hear Kristian behind me, cursing again.

'Think they can come into my park for a fucking joyride. This is my park. Mine.'

I don't stop, don't look behind me as I stride off towards the entrance. My mind is ablaze with questions burning like an iron poker against the skin. My shoulder aches as though someone were pressing a hundred needles into it at once. It feels as though the whole confounded adventure park has collapsed on my back, as though its weight were driving me into the ground, winding me, zapping my energy. I can see people filing through the gates. Mostly mothers and small children, a few fathers among them too. I've never worked at the front desk before, but I know the park and how it works perfectly well.

Besides, how difficult can customer service possibly be?

🐇

It turns out customer service is very difficult. And it's because of the customers.

It has never occurred to me that so many people might ask for things that clearly aren't on offer or ask for changes to what they have already bought, or that they might want to ask endless questions about different options only to settle for the only option that was originally on offer or, with the queue growing behind them, to engage in lengthy negotiations with the three-foot person next to them who simply cannot have all the facts or critical faculties necessary for rational decision-making. I hear that apparently the weather outside is so beautiful that it would be a shame to spend time indoors. I reply that visiting our facility is by no means compulsory and that the weather is in fact set to cool as the wind from the north strengthens, that in an hour's time the winds will be blowing at eight metres per second and that a cloudy area of low pressure is forecast to bring heavy local showers, so the idea of beauty is, at least to some extent, a matter of interpretation.

The father, who mentioned the weather in the first place, is silent.

I manage to clear the morning queues. For a moment the entrance hall is empty. I walk around the counter and look outside.

Kristian is pacing the length of the fallen flagpole, speaking on the phone. Hopefully he is either asking someone to take the old pole away or ordering a new one. I don't understand what this obvious case of sabotage is supposed to tell me. I can't think what impact it's supposed to have; all I know is it's yet another little inconvenience. As if there weren't enough of the larger inconveniences.

There is no money. I have thought through several options, everything from increasing the entrance fee to cutting back the staffing budget, but we have already exhausted these options as far as possible. Crucially, our entrance fee is a full euro cheaper than our nearest competitor, the largest adventure-park franchise in the country. We already operate on the lowest staffing costs around. (We don't go out of our way to publicise this fact. We don't want the parents to think their little ones' development will be adversely affected just because we don't have an on-duty ballet dancer or puppet-therapy classes.)

And after their last visit, I'm not naïve enough to imagine I could intimidate Lizard Man and his finger-snapping friend with the headphones. They'll soon be back. Their colleague is in my freezer.

My actions last night were optimal given the pervading circumstances. I know that. From what I've read, I know that in almost one hundred percent of suspicious deaths, the body itself does most of the detective work. In an intermediary sense, that is. Who has died? How, where and when did they die? The body tells us everything. But if there is no body, getting to the bottom of things is a bit harder. I'm not especially proud or happy about what I've done, but I did it to save my life and to defend my adventure park, my brother's estate and my parents' memory. I had no other options. I did what I had to do. But after all this, I must admit that, at most, all I have done is postpone the inevitable. When the men return, I will need to have some answers.

I need money.

YouMeFun needs money.

Lots, quickly, somewhere, somehow.

In the car park, Kristian kneels down next to the fallen flag. He begins folding it slowly, respectfully, with a sense of ceremony. The moment is clearly important to him. The wind, however, doesn't agree. The corners of the flags are whipped into the air whenever his hands aren't touching them. He tries in vain to hold down all the fluttering corners at once. But there are four corners, and he only has two hands. Before long he is flailing here and there. A moment later and it looks like he is engaged in a ferocious wrestling match with an invisible opponent, the adventure-park flag as his arena. I don't know how to break it to him that he will never be the general manager.

An ancient, turquoise Opel Vectra parks near the door. The driver's door opens, and a man in his thirties steps out of the car.

Black hoodie, light jeans, white trainers with three stripes on the sides. He is walking around the car as the passenger door starts to open, little by little, with a shove, the way small children open car doors. Dad helps the child out of the car. The girl must be about six years old. She is wearing a bright-yellow T-shirt with a picture of a violet unicorn on the front. She is visibly excited when she realises where she is. I turn from the doors, return to the service desk and wait. Father and daughter step inside. The girl is nattering the way children natter, her words have nothing to do with what is going on around her. Wait a minute, darling, Dad says eventually.

Dad has short, light-brown hair without any form of parting or other discernible style. His slender face is serious, his eyes blue. He tells me he would like one adult ticket and one children's ticket. I type the price into the cash register and hand him the card reader. The man keys in his PIN, the machine thinks about this for a moment before informing us the transaction is rejected. We try again, and again. The card doesn't work. I apologise to the man and explain that we also take cash, and that if he doesn't have any cash, the nearest ATM is in the business park on the other side of the narrow strip of spruce trees and that—

'Daddy, can I go and play yet?'

The girl has already walked through the adventure-park barriers and hollers back towards us. Dad glances up at the girl, then looks at me.

'How about she goes in and I wait in the car?'

I explain that children must be accompanied by an adult at all times, that this is a regulation we cannot circumvent. The girl shouts at Dad again, eager to run off and play. Dad stares outside, and my eyes follow his. Perhaps both of us can see his car, the old Opel riddled with rust, its hubcaps missing.

'Do you want to buy a car?'

'Owning a car doesn't make financial sense for me at the moment,' I reply. 'I've calculated it many times.'

Again the girl shouts in our direction. From the hall comes the clamour of other children's squeals of high-pitched excitement. The last glimmer of life seems to have drained from the man's face. What was serious is now deathly serious. He looks so disappointed, he'll soon be unfit to drive – another reason he won't be needing his car.

Overall, the situation looks perfectly clear. He has promised his daughter a day at the adventure park, but he can't afford it.

And here he is – faced with rolling back on that promise.

I don't know where the idea comes from, but it appears in a flash, instantly causing a chain of further thoughts, all linked to one another, growing and ... accruing interest. Quite literally. I have found a solution. It's standing right in front of me, and last night it tried to kill me. A combination of the two. It sounds insane, but it isn't. It is logical, rational, the straightest line from A to B.

'May I ask you something?'

The man turns to look at me. He says nothing. The girl shouts at him for the umpteenth time. This time the voice sounds further away. Soon the park will swallow her up altogether.

'What would you say to an adventure-park loan?'

'What's that?'

'It's a loan that you can take out as soon as you step into the adventure park.'

'Really?'

'Not quite yet,' I say, trying to contain the flood of ideas rushing through my mind. 'But let's assume the adventure park did offer such loans, and let's assume the interest on that loan was several percentage points cheaper than for the next-cheapest loan of its kind. Would you take out a loan like that?'

The girl's voice has disappeared. She has already dived into the depths of the park. The man and I notice this simultaneously and both look towards the hall.

'What options have I got?' he asks.

I ask him a few follow-up questions, and he answers. Then I offer him and his daughter free tickets to the park. The man stands in front of me, the tickets in his hand.

'Thank you,' I say and tear two tickets from another batch. 'These are for the Curly Cake Café. Parrot Pancakes with cream and strawberry jam are on special offer today.'

I hand the man the tickets. He seems to be thinking things through.

'When can I take out that loan?' he asks.

'Very soon, I believe,' I say. 'I'll be meeting the investors again any day.'

3

The car park is an empty field, and above the field a full moon glows. The door of the adventure park slides and clicks shut behind me as I walk towards the bus stop and the last bus that will take me to the train station, then home. The moon looks about as much like creamy Finnish cheese as it possibly can: it is yellow and hangs heavily in the sky, almost within reach. I imagine Schopenhauer sitting on the windowsill, staring hungrily into space. I hear my own footsteps, the hum of traffic along the highway up ahead. More precisely, my ears are still ringing with the ratcheting of a large calculator. I've been counting all afternoon and all evening. This is the first time since leaving the insurance company that I have felt so much satisfaction in my work. I realise that this is happiness.

I feel almost lighter. Besides the fact that I'm hiding a man in the freezer, I'm in debt to numerous companies, the state and a gang of criminals who knocked over my flagpole (both flag and pole have now been taken away, leaving only a concrete plinth with a short stump jutting up in the middle), and the pain in my shoulder is more acute than at any time thus far. My steps are quick, it feels as though my feet barely touch the ground. Numbers race through my mind. This is what the real, serious application of mathematics can give us. Happiness, comfort, hope. Sense and logic. And above all: solutions.

Mathematics wins. Mathematics helps. Mathematics—

A car appears behind me. I haven't heard it approach because it must have started accelerating from behind the building and, initially, the sound of its engine merged with the general roar of traffic coming from the highway. It only stands out from the background noise once it has turned the corner and begins heading for the middle of the car park, where I am walking. The car is tall, and it's heading right towards me. I don't recognise the car, but I don't stand around thinking about it, waiting to get a better view of the insignia on the bumper. It's an SUV, large and heavy.

I turn and break into a sprint. All I can think of is the ditch running between the car park and the road. You can't drive across it and keep all four tyres on the ground. Few people would be able to jump across it either. You have to go down one steep side of the ditch then climb up the steep incline on the other side. Suddenly the edge of the car park feels kilometres away. I run and run, and for some reason it no longer feels like I'm almost walking on air. On the contrary, it feels as though my feet are glued to the tarmac. I hear the car's tyres. I hear its motor. I suddenly change direction and hope it confuses the driver.

My diversionary tactic works. But only for half a fleeting second. The tyres screech against the asphalt. The car turns. I hear the tyres turning, the motor roaring, as the driver first slams on the brake, then hits the accelerator again. It's as though I'm being chased by an exceptionally agile tank. I change direction again, making my own journey longer in the process, but the driver doesn't fall for the same trick twice. I'm beginning to doubt I'll be able to reach the ditch. It's quite simply too far away and the SUV is quite simply too close. Still, I continue running. The sound of the engine drowns out everything else. The noise grows louder, the engine revs, moves up a gear. Before long the bumper is right at my back. A moment more and I'll be under the car. Another moment and...

The car passes me. The mirror on the passenger side clips my left shoulder, the one with the knife wound. I stagger from the impact and see the SUV making a quick, tight turn. And that's all I see.

I fall to the ground, roll over a few times, the asphalt grazes my knees, my palms, my elbows. I hear the tyres screech again, then the SUV's door opens. I hear footsteps and realise I should start running again, because this time I haven't got a rabbit's ear to help me. But just as I'm trying to clamber to my feet, AK yanks my hands behind my back and hauls me upright.

The pain is dizzying. I try to wriggle free of his grip, but it's no easier than last time. For us to be equal wrestling partners, I would have to be twenty years younger and seventy kilos heavier. That's not going to happen tonight.

We take a few steps towards the SUV. The back-seat door is open. For some reason, it occurs to me how much my life has changed since, only a few weeks earlier, I was taking part in Perttilä's Positive Impact seminar. Then I see Lizard Man in the driver's seat, his expression every bit as cold as his eyes.

🐇

The SUV heads out of the city. AK is sitting next to me on the back seat, his headphones over his ears. I'm sure I can hear the constant, low-pitched thump of his music. AK holds me by the wrist. No handcuffs, no tape, no cable ties. Only his palm, the width of a chopping board, and his fingers clamped like steel cables around my mathematician's wrist. We're still no match for each other, but at least this time he's not twisting. On the one hand, I'm relieved that the person who tried to scare me by nearly running me over is someone familiar, but on the other I realise there's no time to lose. We are not on our way to the cinema or to grab a hot dog.

'I was expecting you sooner,' I say. 'I've been doing some calculations. I have a suggestion.'

'I've got a suggestion too,' Lizard Man replies immediately but doesn't continue, so the nature of his suggestion remains unclear.

'It's just, I wasn't sure how to contact you,' I say and try to stretch my legs. My knees are still sore from the fall. 'I don't even know your names. Well, I know his. Sort of. I assume the letters denote his first and last name. There are about fifty men's names beginning with A in common use in Finland, but about five hundred surnames beginning with K. But if we look at the distribution of these names across different age demographics, and assuming I can more or less correctly guess his age, it's much more likely that he is Antero Korhonen than Abraham Keräsaari. I trust in the laws of probability, and this would have been a good start if only I'd—'

'AK is a first name and another first name,' says Lizard Man. 'Both are nicknames, both made up by me. Nobody else knows them but me. Not even AK.'

'That makes finding the exact number rather difficult,' I admit and glance to the side. AK looks as though he cares neither for our discussion nor for the origins of his name. 'As I was saying, I've been doing some calculations and—'

'Why didn't you mention these calculations earlier?'

'I only calculated them today. I had an idea today. This morning, to be precise.'

'Right,' Lizard Man says in that icy voice of his. 'You suddenly had an idea when an SUV nearly ran you over, AK took you in a headlock and threw you in the back of the car. That'll give people ideas. I've usually heard quite a few ideas by this point in proceedings. I don't suppose you've seen a broad-shouldered man who was supposed to pay you a visit?'

The car arrives at an intersection, then turns onto a smaller, winding road. The streetlamps quickly disappear behind us. Then we continue through the autumnal night.

'To pay me a visit?' I ask.

Lizard Man's eyes leave the surface of the road and glance in the mirror for a second.

'To remind you of the loan,' he says. 'It's a funny thing. I told the guy to pop round and tell you the same thing we told you at our last meeting, only in a slightly different way. So that you'd really understand. The guy left, then called us on the way, said he wasn't sure whether it was an amusement park or an adventure park.'

I'm about to tell him it is an adventure park, that the difference is significant and that it is based on this, that and the other, but at the same time I realise this is one conversation I'd rather not prolong. I bite my lip.

'But since then,' Lizard Man continues. 'We haven't heard a peep out of him. We drove around the park, his car is nowhere to be seen. It seems he's completely disappeared. So you haven't seen him either?'

I can see those reptilian eyes in the driver's mirror, the road ahead lit in the faint moonlight.

'I don't remember any particularly broad-shouldered customers,' is my honest answer. Most of the park's clientele are distinctly slender.

Lizard Man doesn't say anything at first. The houses are now fewer and further between.

'I've tried calling him,' he continues. 'But it doesn't connect to his phone. Which makes me a little worried, if you get my drift. Worried something might have happened to him.'

The phone. Of course. It's at the bottom of the freezer, probably in one of the man's pockets. I only took his car keys.

'So I thought I'd better ask you too, ask whether you'd spoken to him, and how that conversation went.'

'I haven't spoken to anyone broad-shouldered,' I tell him, and that too is true. We did not speak at any point.

Lizard Man is silent. He indicates in good time before turning and drives exactly at the speed limit. Our arrival at the turning is exemplary driving. He would be a dream student for any driving instructor. Gravel patters against the bottom of the car. The night is both dark and faintly lit; the moon is like a dimmed projector light. Little by little the car slows. The gravel turns to dirt. The car begins to rock from side to side as the tyres sink into little potholes.

'I'm offering ten thousand euros,' I say.

'The debt is two hundred and twenty thousand.'

'But that money isn't for you.'

He says nothing.

'I'll pay you, personally, ten thousand euros if you'll set up a meeting,' I say.

'A meeting?'

'The last time we met, you told me you represent someone.'

'I did not. I never say things like that.'

'You used the first-person plural. That provided the parameters for my hypothesis.'

'What's that supposed to mean?'

His cold eyes gleam in the mirror. The car is moving very slowly now. We leave the cover of the trees and arrive at the shore of a pond or lake. How long did the drive take? I estimate between thirty and thirty-five minutes. I can't see a house or cottage on either side of the car. This is nothing but an overgrown shore. The motor is switched off. I've read about how challenging it is for start-up companies, how hard it is to get investors fired up over a new idea, how quickly you have to make an impression. But I doubt many people have to pitch their business ideas in the middle of the night by a lake where they will be drowned if the idea doesn't find the necessary traction. Because now I realise that is precisely what is happening. The clock is ticking.

'In this context, it means ten thousand euros,' I say. 'In cash or as a bank transfer. To your personal account. In exchange for organising a meeting with whoever you're working for, someone who has the kind of money at his disposal that my brother borrowed from you. I repeat, for organising this meeting, I'll give you ten thousand euros.'

AK tightens his hold on my wrist. I feel his pincer-like grip, but at the same time my fingers have lost all sensation. That bass is still booming from his headphones. It must be one of the longest songs ever uploaded.

'First you didn't have any money,' says Lizard Man. He sounds less than convinced. 'Now you want to cough up ten grand just for me to make a phone call.'

'This is very simple mathematics,' I explain. 'I have ten thousand, but I don't have, say, three hundred thousand. In order to obtain the larger sum, I'm prepared to pay a smaller sum first. And once I have acquired this theoretical three hundred thousand, you'll have even more.'

'How much more?'

'That depends what we decide at the meeting.'

'Meaning?'

'The ten thousand requires a certain amount of patience. I'll tell you at the meeting.'

'How do I know you're good for it?'

'I am an actuary. I don't make unfounded promises.'

For a moment, everything is motionless. Then Lizard Man raises his hand, points straight ahead. The still water gleams in the moonlight like ice.

'Do you see that?'

I answer in the affirmative.

'There's plenty of room at the bottom for a skinny man like you.'

'I understand,' I say but decide against considering out loud the human to cubic-volume ratio or criminological dimensions of the matter.

Again Lizard Man glances in the mirror, then he opens the door and slides himself out of the car. He walks a short distance, and I see him raising a phone to his ear. Then he disappears behind the trees.

I am sitting in a relatively new, high-end, Sino-Swedish vehicle.

AK, a man the size of a mountain, is holding my hand.

In other circumstances, this would be statistically speaking one of the safest ways of travelling anywhere. Tonight it is one of the most perilous. When you turn the equation around, everything changes. At the same time, I think of my surprising calm. This is partly explained by the fact that I'm utterly exhausted and in some form of shock. I can feel it almost like a fever in my muscles, in the agitation of my mind, which must surely have achieved critical mass, crossed a final frontier. As though I have reached the top of a tall mountain: on the one hand, I am being whipped by the wind in all directions, but on the other, at least I can still breathe.

Lizard Man appears from somewhere. He is no longer speaking on the phone, but now his arms swing freely at his sides as he walks. His expression is impossible to read. He gets into the car, closes the door and makes himself comfortable in his seat. This takes a minute. Then he sits there in silence.

I realise his next words will determine whether I will be heading to the nearest cash point or for an extended walk off a very short pier. His iguana eyes appear in the rear-view mirror. I haven't felt my fingers for some time, and now I can't feel my other limbs either. I am in mid-air, a single, cold, almighty heartbeat.

'I'll take the ten grand in cash,' he says.

4

The phone has been ringing for some time, I realise that immediately. Schopenhauer is lying at the foot of the bed, out for the count. I haven't the faintest idea what the time is. Naturally, this isn't like me. Neither is it like me to set up meetings with gangsters and take my savings out of the cash machine in the early hours. But that's what has happened. Schopenhauer raises his head and squints at me as the phone continues to ring. He isn't looking at the phone but at me, as though I were the one responsible for disturbing his sleep. Which, of course, I am. I sit up and fumble on the bedside table for the phone, but it isn't there.

I walk into the hallway. My phone is on the table next to the coat rack. I don't recognise the number. I answer with a simple 'hello', and Laura Helanto asks if it's me speaking. Her voice has that familiar bright, perky quality to it, and my mood changes instantly upon hearing it. I can't say how or in what way – but something happens every time I see her, every time I hear her voice. It is me, I say. Then I catch sight of myself in the hall mirror and wonder if it might not be me after all. I've slept in my dress shirt. Such a thing has never happened before. I turn away from the mirror and try to concentrate on what Laura Helanto is saying.

'I'm sorry,' I interrupt her. 'I've just woken up. Is something wrong?'

'No,' she says. 'It's just, I'm in Pitäjänmäki and wondered if you'd like a lift to the park. I can pick you up on the way.'

'A lift? In Pitäjänmäki? But how...'

'At the industrial park,' she says, as though she hasn't heard me properly, which might well be the case as she is clearly calling from her car. There's a rushing, humming sound in the background, and at times her voice sounds as though she is speaking underwater. 'I went there to pick out a new flagpole. You live in Kannelmäki, right? It's nearby and basically on my way back to the park.'

'How did you know that...?'

'That you're at home? It's half past ten. And you weren't at work when I left a short while ago.'

I turn again and look at the clock above the front door. I haven't slept this late since ... ever, actually. Schopenhauer appears in the hallway. He stretches and yawns, then looks around as though it is the very first time he has been in this apartment. In a curious way, I can feel Laura Helanto's presence at the other end of the phone, though she isn't saying anything.

'I still haven't...'

All at once I feel as though life and the world have somehow taken me and Schopenhauer by surprise, that we have awoken to something so strange and unfamiliar that we no longer know who we are.

'I can wait,' she says. 'Actually, there's something I'd like to talk to you about. If I offer you a lift, you can make the coffee. I'll pick up some cinnamon buns and see you in fifteen minutes. Deal?'

I look at Schopenhauer. He looks at me.

'I suppose I can manage that,' I hear myself saying.

Exactly fifteen minutes after the end of the call, the doorbell rings.

🐇

The dual scent of Laura Helanto and the cinnamon buns. Laura with her bushy hair and large, dark-rimmed glasses on the other side of the table, the cinnamon buns the size of dinner plates in the middle. The coffee maker is gurgling away, and I've got my work cut out trying to control myself. For some reason, I feel the need to explain why I have slept this late, that this wasn't a trivial matter of oversleeping. That the real reason is that I saved my skin by the shores of a dark pond with ten thousand euros, half of which – a down payment – I took from an ATM in the wall of a large hypermarket I'd never seen before, and that I was already tired from lack of sleep the night before when, in self-defence, I killed a man with the enormous rabbit's ear, which you described as especially 'unpredictable', and because dragging the man's body into the freezer in the café's kitchen was a two-hour operation requiring raw physical exertion. Instead, I remain quiet, raise a hand to check my tie is straight and notice that my hand is trembling.

'Sorry,' Laura says for the second time. She first apologised the minute she stepped into the hallway, as she placed a large case on the floor and handed me the bag of buns. 'But this is something I've been thinking about for so long, and now all my regular work is done and dusted and all I need is ... But this, well, inviting myself and turning up like this...'

'I only let in the people I want to let in,' I say, and it's the truth.

Laura Helanto looks at me with those blue-green eyes and gives something approaching a smile.

'Well, that's good to know,' she says.

'It is,' I nod because I can't think of anything else to say, and I'm starting to feel distinctly uncomfortable. I haven't forgotten some of our encounters, the things she has said, her look of surprise at the door of my office yesterday. These things bother me, but in a way I can't put my finger on.

'The new flagpole is going to look great,' she says suddenly, as though she was about to say something else but ended up with this. She takes one of the buns and places it on her plate. 'And it's much sturdier than the last one. At the store, they assured me it would survive someone accidentally reversing into it.'

I decide not to mention that the probability of this being an accident is more or less zero. I eat my bun and take a sip of coffee. Laura Helanto eats too and looks around, paying, it seems, particular attention to the living room. We are sitting between the kitchen and the living room, almost. This was the most practical solution. The oblong kitchen is too narrow to fit my parents' old dining table, while the living room is too far from the essential elements of dining, like the fridge, the cooker, the microwave and now the coffee maker.

'I see you're a fan of minimalism,' she says, and now I look towards the living room too.

In the bright morning light, things appear to be slightly further away from one another than they do normally. The room contains one long sofa, upholstered in light blue, with a matching armchair, and standing beside the armchair is a metallic floor lamp. Between the sofa and the armchair is a low coffee table. On one of the longer walls is a bookcase, on the wall opposite a large painting, a reproduction of papers by Gauss, covered in handwritten equations and formulae. A light-grey rug covers the floor and a rice-paper lampshade hangs from the ceiling. Nothing is new, I have to admit, but I doubt that's what Laura Helanto's comments were referring to. I decide the matter probably warrants something by way of an explanation.

'I once calculated how much I use each individual item of furniture,' I begin once I've swallowed my mouthful of bun. 'Based on these calculations, I drew up a template both for the probability and the cost-benefit ratios of any potential new acquisitions. The results were clear. The probability of sitting on yet another chair or placing a book on yet another coffee table in the course of a randomly selected week was so infinitely small, and the time spent sitting in the chair so microscopic, that I couldn't possibly defend the acquisition with any logical or reasoned economic arguments.'

I paused, then added:

'Not that I was looking to buy any new furniture. I already have furniture, as you can see.'

As I speak, Laura Helanto turns from the living room to look at me. Is that the twitch of a smile at the corners of her mouth?

Initially I thought Laura's arrival was first and foremost surprising, but now I realise I find it exciting in an entirely new way. Then I remember something.

'You said there was something you wanted to talk about.'

Laura Helanto seems to remember this too. Alongside her usual cheerfulness, there is now a sense of doubt.

'Right, I'm just not sure it's all that sensible,' she begins, stressing the final word so that it's almost all I hear. 'It's more of an ... emotional suggestion. At least, I hope it is. Perhaps if I show you...?'

By all means, I indicate. Laura gets up and fetches her A3-sized portfolio from the hallway. On the way back, she seems to stop briefly to look at Gauss's calculations. I find myself hoping she'll ask me something about them. She doesn't. She moves the dishes to make space in the middle of the table and asks me to stand up. We both stand beside the table. Laura unzips the portfolio, opens up the folder inside and shows me an A3-sized photograph of the adventure park. Except it isn't a photograph. Things have been added to the image: wild patterns, fantastic colours.

'These are murals, wall paintings,' Laura explains as she turns the pages. 'I'd like to paint the walls at the adventure park. These are just sketches from which I'll design the eventual murals. I've been trying to combine the tradition of graffiti with the influence of various artists I admire. These are very different from the canvasses I usually paint, but that's because I really want them to suit the character of the adventure park, the rhythm, the childish sense of play and adventure, as the name YouMeFun suggests, and they'll really fit the different spaces too. It's a form of installation, I suppose, though that term normally has a rather different meaning.'

I can hear from her voice that Laura is her usual, enthusiastic self again. I look at the images. To me, what I see doesn't make any sense, but I can't stop looking at them, all the same.

'Here,' she says and taps the upper left-hand corner of the third picture with the tip of her finger. 'You can certainly see the influence of Lee Krasner, though the reference is maybe a bit oblique, whereas in the next picture we're clearly in the world of Dorothea Tanning. I have named each wall accordingly, so this one is *Krasner Goes Adventure Park* and this one is *Tanning Takes the Train*, because the wall will be right behind the Komodo Locomotive. Essentially, one way or another, each wall comments upon its surroundings. There are six of them in total: Krasner, Tanning, de Lempicka, Frankenthaler, O'Keeffe and Jansson. The murals are all between four and twelve metres in length, and they are all four metres tall. I'll have to hire someone to help me during the work phase, but I'm sure it could all be done in a month. Alongside my own work, that is. I'll paint all night, if need be – with your permission. The costs are very reasonable too, because I'll be working with normal wall paint, except in a very few places, where I'll have to mix something special. I estimate that we can keep the costs within the standard renovation budget. I just love the walls in that big hall. I've been looking at them right from the start, but without really knowing what I'd like to do with them. Now I know. That's why I wanted to come and present my ideas to you. Directly.'

I am still looking at one of the images when I realise Laura has already stopped speaking. What's more, I realise I'm smiling. Just as I did when I looked at the small photograph on her phone, I feel an almost irresistible desire to continue looking at it, because with each passing moment I see more. Not to mention the fact that Laura Helanto's paintings, her swirls and patterns, quite simply delight me and please me without any useful or practical reason, and I can't explain why in this context it feels so acceptable, so right, though in everything else I reject such illogical and irrational behaviour. Neither can I help picking up the sheets of paper and flicking through them.

'I like this one most,' I hear myself saying. 'No, it's definitely this one.'

And so on. Though it's hard, I eventually manage to close the folder. I see that Laura Helanto is trying to respond to my smile. But she is clearly tense, nervous. That makes two of us: I am constantly tense and nervous whenever I'm around her. Then I say something I could never have imagined hearing myself say.

'This doesn't make any sense. But it has to be done.'

What happens next is even more radical. Laura Helanto shouts – a cry of victory, perhaps, a universal, international *yes* – and throws her arms around me, pulls me towards her and squeezes tight. The squeeze is forceful, we collide against each other. There's warmth, a sense of nearness in so many parts of my body that the word 'holistic' wouldn't be entirely unwarranted. I can smell her, feel her, her arms, her body. I hear her triumphant whoop so close to my ear that I'm certain I can feel the warmth of her breath against my eardrum. The scent of her hair, of her body, her clothes, all discernible as individual fragrances, because she is so close and she remains there for a good few seconds, and those seconds echo like chimes from a belfry. Then she releases me, steps back and shakes her arms and apologises for the third time in the course of this visit.

'I was so overcome,' she says. 'I'm so happy. You're so different from other people ... You are...'

'I am an actuary.' The words come out of their own volition.

'Exactly,' she says, almost a shout. 'You're matter-of-fact, a bit edgy and strictly businesslike, and yet so fair and nice and ... reliable. Do you know how rare that is? Do you really like my paintings?'

'No,' I say and instantly realise I was replying to the first question. I try to rectify the situation, and in doing so I say something extremely out of character for me. 'I love your paintings.'

I know I am standing in the middle of my very own living room, my tie neat, but still it feels as though I have stepped into a new world, completely naked, without any form of protection.

5

This time they cover my eyes. AK is holding me by the hand again. I'm used to it by now, which in itself feels quite bizarre. But here we are, on the road again. The air inside the car is cool and pungent. I catch the smell of expensive aftershave and pine-forest Wunderbaum. I can feel the SUV's acceleration in my body, the brakes, the turns. Covering my eyes has nothing to do with the time of day, that much was clear when I received instructions to stand in the staff car park situated behind the adventure park at ten-thirty at night. Nobody says anything.

It's been a normal day, as normal as my days get at present.

I spent the morning learning about art: I'd agreed to the transformation of the adventure park and listened to a more detailed explanation of how it would happen. Laura Helanto drove us to the park. In retrospect, it feels as though I was walking on air and spent all morning living someone else's life. In the afternoon, I tried to find a moment in Johanna's diary when she would be away from the café and the kitchen, so that I could check the phone situation at the bottom of the freezer, but no such opportunity was forthcoming. Johanna is very dedicated and hard-working. I also visited Esa in the control room.

The air in his room was fusty. I learned a few important things. Firstly, of all the cameras on the outside of the building, only one is currently in operation. Secondly, unless there is a particular reason, Esa doesn't routinely check the night-time security tapes, which in any case automatically delete themselves after a week. I didn't ask a single direct question; I just let him talk. People talk when you ask them whether they think they need a rise in their annual budget. All I had to do was sit there breathing through my mouth. The air in the small room contained large quantities of sulphur, which caused a wave of nausea when inhaled through the nose.

We drive along a quiet, winding paved road. I can't hear the whoosh of any passing cars; my bodyweight shifts from one side to the other, and we move through the night almost silently. I feel our speed slowing, gravel starts to crunch beneath the tyres. Shortly afterwards we stop, and the motor is switched off. AK lets go of my hand. His grip was so comprehensive that it feels like I'm finally getting my arm back after lending it to someone else for a while. Car doors open and close, then someone opens the door on my left.

'Out,' says Lizard Man.

I step out of the SUV. AK pulls me out, gripping me by the shoulder. For a while there is gravel under my shoes, then something firm. We take a few sharp turns then come to a halt. I'm not sure what it is I can smell. AK tears the blindfold from my eyes.

We are in an old barn.

I open and close my eyes as they adjust to the light. Both Lizard Man and AK are now standing behind me. The building is large and tall; there is a concrete floor under our feet and walls made of wooden slats around us. The lights are attached to long, sturdy beams across the ceiling. There is an array of machinery, everything from tractors to snow ploughs. There is lots of assorted junk too, but the contours of the objects fade into the dim, making any closer examination impossible. My attention is drawn to my nine o'clock and a man making a series of choked, sputtering sounds.

The rope looks tight. It runs from the man's neck right up to one of the beams, then descends, taut as a violin string, at a diagonal, where it is attached to the back of a quadbike parked about ten metres away. The man is balancing on top of a rickety log propped on end. Keeping his balance is visibly difficult, for which there are at least three reasons. The noose is tightening around his neck, the floor and the thin end of the log are not properly aligned, and the man's hands are tied behind his back. He looks older than me, average build, blond hair. He is wearing a light-blue piqué polo shirt, light-brown trousers and a pair of brown leather shoes. Understandably, his face is bright red. To say the situation doesn't look good for him is something of an understatement.

And it dawns on me that I'm not sure how advantageous it is for me either. I'm the one who asked for this meeting, and I realised from the start that we would be meeting on their terms – whoever *they* are. But if these are the terms…

I hear footsteps. A moment later I see through the dim a large pair of dark-green Wellington boots moving towards us with heavy, purposeful strides. A figure appears out of the dark at the other end of the barn. The boots must be at least a size fifty. Then I see a pair of black overalls and an enormous red-and-black flannel shirt. Then the face. Even and angular at the top and sharp at the bottom, like a good old-fashioned spade with skin stretched across it. On the surface of the spade is a set of eyes. The face doesn't look especially happy. And the face doesn't so much as glance at the man balancing on the log as he walks past. As the big man comes to a stop in front of me, I find myself thinking that he makes even me feel short. The man teetering on the log gives another muffled cry, making the big man turn his big head. But only a little. Then he turns his attention to me.

'We were in the middle of a negotiation,' he says. His voice is low and calm.

'Right,' I say.

'Don't let him bother you.'

'I won't.'

'You have a proposal.'

'Yes,' I say. 'I've been doing some calculations…'

Just then I hear the log creak ominously against the concrete floor.

'How long do I have?' I ask. 'This matter requires a certain amount of background.'

The big man is listening. At least, that's how I interpret his expressionless face.

'Good,' I say. 'It appears I have inherited not only a very indebted company but all my brother's debts to you too. And it also appears that you largely operate within a cash-only economy, yet you still expect interest on your deposits. These four matters – the adventure park's debts and tax arrears; my brother's unofficial debts; the problems of cash; and your growth expectation on that money – can all be solved by combining them into one.'

It seems the big man is still listening. I look at him, but the whimpering, wobbling man to the left of his head makes me want to look somewhere else, anywhere else instead. I note that I can't hear any sounds from outside. Any sounds would surely penetrate the slatted walls. We are far away from any traffic, any houses. We are isolated.

'YouMeFun is the solution,' I say.

The big man turns to look at Lizard Man. Then he turns his attention to me again.

'Money laundering?'

'I don't like to think of it in those terms,' I say. 'Besides, Mr, erm … what you might consider money laundering—'

'No need to stand on ceremony,' he interrupts. 'Call me Jouni.'

'I'm Henri.'

'I know.'

Of course he knows.

'What you, Jouni, think of as money laundering is, in my proposal, just a matter of sales. And that's just the start. The first stage is, I sell you tickets.'

'Tickets?'

'Entrance tickets, to the adventure park. Initially fifty thousand of them.'

I hear Lizard Man laugh. His laugh is curt, scornful, disdainful. A laugh like that only has one purpose: to show up someone else's stupidity. I note that the big man isn't laughing.

'This one's a real fucking joker...' I hear Lizard Man begin, but the big man, Jouni – if that really is his name – glares at him, and I don't hear another peep out of him.

'I will sell you entrance tickets at a substantial discount, ten euros each. That includes the Doughnut of the Day at our cafeteria.'

I intend this to lighten the mood, but nobody seems remotely amused. I continue.

'In any case, these tickets represent a cash injection of five hundred thousand euros into the park's balance sheet. This means the park will be able to pay off its debts, which in turn means financial solvency, which will enable the park to take out a new loan because it will be operationally viable and profitable. Interest rates – the official ones, that is – are very low at the moment; money is essentially free. We will use this new loan to set up a subsidiary company; we will establish a company that will operate within the adventure park and—'

'The money will go to the bank?'

'In the first phase, yes,' I say. 'Obviously.'

'That's your proposal?' asks the big man.

'No,' I say. 'My proposal is that money will come out of the bank.'

The big man looks at me. His spade face is pure, cold steel. I say what I have come here to say, what I think will save not only my brother's estate but my own life too.

'We will become a bank.'

The sound of wood cracking. The man with the noose round his neck loses his balance. Either he falls or the log falls. He lets out a sound, somewhere between a dog's yelp and the cry of an Arctic loon, but it is abruptly cut short. The man twitches as though a bolt of lightning were striking him over and over again.

The quadbike does not move, the rope does not slacken; it creaks against the ceiling beam.

I turn my eyes away.

My heart is racing, I can't breathe. The seconds pass heavily, each one requiring momentum of its own to pass to the next. At this point, I can say the evening hasn't gone quite as I'd planned. Naturally, I don't know everything there is to know about starting a company, but I can't believe that all this is an elaborate overture to something else. An unbearably long time passes. Eventually silence descends on the barn.

'Who's "we"?' asks the big man.

I turn to my left. The man is swinging calmly at the end of the rope. I look at the big man. Perhaps it's best not to say that 'we' means those of us who are still alive.

'You,' I reply. 'You and ... me. We will lend people money.'

'I already lend people money,' he says.

'And that's precisely the problem,' I say. 'These loans have no legal protection. And cash has the same problem, no matter which direction you move it in. The solution to this is a bank that offers payday loans.'

Lizard Man laughs again, again the laugh is short, scornful. The big man doesn't pay him any attention.

'In fact, he gave me the idea in the first place,' I say and glance over at Lizard Man, his expression now more hostile than ever. It occurs to me that I am somehow about to step on his toes. 'And everything became clear to me when I was selling tickets at the park. Initially, it was the matter of the interest on my brother's original loan from you. I couldn't help thinking that the interest rate seemed very ... loan-sharkish. In a nutshell: we set up a payday loan company with the capital that the park will accrue through the increased volume of ticket sales. We will offer our customers small loans, which they can receive immediately. The body of loan customers will grow, as will, I believe, footfall at the park in general, because people will instantly have more money at their disposal. As sales figures rise, we can either grant more loans or I can pay back my brother's debt to you. That way, you will receive not only the original sum of the loan, but the interest on all the smaller loans too. And what's more, so far all that money is legal and above board.'

'You've clearly given this some thought,' says the big man.

There's no need to look at the hanged man. I recall one of Perttilä's favourite buzzwords.

'I'm highly motivated,' I say.

'But now that everything is sorted out, what do I need you for?'

For this question, I always have an answer at the ready.

'I am an actuary.'

Lizard Man laughs for a third time, but this time the laughter is forced, the scorn a little unsure of itself.

'By that, I mean that my arithmetic skills are of the highest calibre and, as such, they are invaluable to you: I am one hundred percent reliable,' I continue. 'And I presume, based on what I have, shall we say, seen and personally experienced in recent weeks ... I presume I am the only person in this room without a criminal record.'

This time nobody laughs. Nobody pipes up to defend their honour or reputation. Perhaps I have struck a nerve. I might just have saved my life.

'I am the only one of us who can establish a money-lending service like this and I am the only one who can count everything,' I add.

The barn is silent.

'We might have use for a man like that in certain circumstances. If the proposal is legit.'

And what if it isn't? Will my noose be tied to the same quadbike or a different one?

The big man holds a short pause.

'How soon?' he asks eventually.

'How soon, what?'

'How soon will we see if this works or not?'

'Two weeks from when the bank commences operations,' I say, though my original calculations were based on an initial phase of a month. Right now that feels too long.

'And what happens if everything falls through?' he asks.

'I've taken that into consideration too,' I say. 'It won't fall through. If nobody takes out a loan, you will still have legal, clean money to the sum of the original investment. That, at least, is a win. If, meanwhile, people don't pay back their loans and the bank goes bust, which I don't think is at all likely, then the adventure park acts as a guarantee, which again means that you will get at least the original investment back. And, again, this money is all above board.'

I quickly glance at Lizard Man. He doesn't look remotely satisfied. He looks as though a storm is raging within him.

'And what happens if the profit levels aren't high enough?' asks the big man.

Involuntarily, I catch a glimpse of the hanged man. I say what I have to say.

'This is the crux of my idea,' I say. 'I believe we'll be able to find that elusive happy medium...'

'What's happy about that?'

I haven't forgotten the father who arrived in his Opel with his little girl, desperate to play in the adventure park. My idea is to set an interest rate that makes the act of lending money sensible for all concerned. But now, for the first time, I see a hint of an expression on the big man's face. On closer inspection, this isn't an expression either. He simply opens and closes his eyes a few times.

'I thought you were an actuary. Now you want to be a money lender,' he says.

His tone of voice seems to have lowered the temperature in the barn by at least ten degrees. I decide this probably isn't the best time to talk about the importance of the principles of mutually beneficial banking.

'That's the point: I can be both,' I say. '*Precision*. Everything will be calculated with the utmost precision.'

The big man looks at me again. Several seconds pass, during which a decision is reached about my fate. I know this. We are in an isolated location, and besides the dead man and me, there are only criminals present. Not exactly the optimal circumstances for a spontaneous outburst of positivity, as Perttilä would say. Eventually, the big man turns his head and nods in Lizard Man's direction. I can't help it, but I turn my head to look behind me. At first Lizard Man shakes his head a few times, then he sighs and eventually nods. Whatever he has agreed to, he does so very, very reluctantly.

'Actuary or no actuary,' says the big man. 'We'll be keeping a close eye on you.'

Then for the first time he looks at the man hanging from the roof beam. When he eventually speaks, his voice is pensive.

'Money doesn't grow on trees, you know.'

🐰

The return journey is a repeat of my arrival. My eyes are blindfolded. We first drive along smaller roads; the car still smells of aftershave and pine-forest Wunderbaum. The air conditioning blows chilled, frigid air against my thighs and face. AK holds me by the hand. Nobody speaks. Nobody except me, once we reach one of the larger roads, which I deduce from the hum of traffic and passing cars.

'Who was that man?' I ask.

Lizard Man answers almost immediately:

'The last mathematician.'

6

When I break the news, Esa looks disappointed, as though he is trying to swallow something angular and foul-tasting. But his voice remains calm.

'It's a question of the park's security,' he says. 'And security is, in many ways, like a long, drawn-out defensive battle. The line of defence is only as strong as its weakest link. I've been dealing with the cash deliveries for a long time. It's part of the park's overall defence strategy.'

'Defence strategy?' I ask.

'I drew up a strategy a while ago, and Juhani signed off on it,' Esa nods. 'The strategy is based on the best military practices from around the world.'

It's been three days since I pitched my proposal in the nocturnal barn.

Now Esa and I are in the control room, lit only by the electric glow from the array of screens in front of us. Working as a money courier was never part of Esa's official job description, and he has been using his own SUV to do the job without receiving any compensation for mileage or petrol or anything else for that matter. I'd assumed he would be only too happy to give up this extra task. I assumed wrong. Yet the cash remains a problem (not to mention the body in the freezer at the Curly Cake Café or the fact that, at any moment, I might end up hanging from the rafters in an isolated barn). I have two grey sports bags full of cash. More to the point, the problem isn't so much the cash as the people that this cash will encounter along the way.

At the ticket office, Kristian – Venla is still on sick leave – receives the money when he sells tickets; park manager Laura counts the money in the till and hands it over to the cash-security manager, Esa, who deposits it in the bank. I'm now forced to relieve the latter two of these tasks – if nothing else, for their own safety. And the fact that I want to save both the park and my own life.

'Esa,' I begin, and realise I will have to resort to a form of détente diplomacy. 'I respect your work. And I don't want to undermine your ... overall strategy. This small shift in defensive priorities will—'

'The adventure park isn't on the offensive, is it?'

'Excuse me?'

'We defend our own turf convincingly, that's enough.'

The last three days have been full to the brim. I have been managing the adventure park, crunching the numbers, filling in forms, I have made various fiscal declarations, provided necessary documentation. And generally worked round the clock. I have created a new, temporary book-keeping for the adventure park in Excel, the aim of which is to spread out future increased sales revenue as seamlessly as possible over a sustained period of time, then, once the situation is over, to make the excess money disappear altogether. In doing so, I have reminded myself that the intention is simply to survive our current debts, to evade a possible death sentence and keep the adventure park afloat. I have also paid a visit to a lawyer named Heiskanen – that is his real name, according to the business card and bill he gave me – in his office in Kallio and given him a number of tasks. I need his knowledge of the law and some very quick action.

Everything needs to be ready in just a few days. In theory. But first I have to sort out...

'The adventure park will always strive to be a peaceful operator,' I say and look Esa in the eye. 'You have my word. Our strategy of neutrality and non-aggression remains in place.'

The feverish glare of the monitors makes his eyes gleam in his shadow-covered face. I fear the same must be true of me too. We stare at each other for a while. Eventually Esa gives me a quick, military nod.

'Fine, you take care of the cash deliveries, and I'll move to the reserves for a while,' he says. 'But remember, if the situation escalates, I'm always at the ready.'

'Thank you, Esa.'

We sit in silence for a moment longer. Naturally, my mind is aflutter with a thousand questions that our conversation has thrown up, but in a very short time I have learned something fundamental: I don't want to know about everything or to find out about everything. If Esa has drawn up a strategy to defend YouMeFun in the eventuality of a guerrilla attack, good. I doubt Juhani will have given the matter much thought. I can almost hear his voice – *sounds great, man, good job* – as he gives Esa the thumbs up without having listened to a single word. I stand up.

'*Semper fi*,' Esa says.

I recognise the phrase. 'Always faithful', the motto of the US Marine Corps. It's unlikely that either one of us has ever served in an elite North American military unit, and I decide against speculating out loud about the statistical probability of the matter. I thank Esa for his dedication, leave the control room and step out into the hullabaloo of the park.

In the afternoons the hall is filled with sound and movement. By now, some of the children are beginning to tire: there are considerably more tears and tantrums than in the mornings. Some of the children, meanwhile, become even more excited, slipping off the final shackles of restraint as closing time approaches. By this time, the parents who arrived at the park in the morning already look as though they are planning to do something criminal then quickly leave the country.

It doesn't take long to find Laura Helanto. In her right hand she is holding a professional-looking measuring tape and in her left a folder. The folder is familiar; the last time I saw it, it was on my kitchen table when she was showing me her sketches. Laura is standing with her back to me, and I am about to say hello to her but begin to doubt myself. What if she is particularly attached to her role in the park's finances? I take a deep breath, prepare myself and say hello.

Laura Helanto spins around and gives me the quickest smile I have seen in a long time. The smile has the same hazy, stupefying effect as before: I have to remind myself exactly what I'm about to say.

'Frankenthaler,' she says and points her measuring tape at the concrete wall. We turn our heads in sync. The wall bears different-shaped curves and markings in white chalk.

'We need to make a few organisational changes,' I begin, and tell her that I will take responsibility for all transportation of cash from now on and that I hope this isn't a problem.

'Of course not,' says Laura, her eyes fixed on the wall. 'On the contrary.'

Then she turns to me. And smiles. 'Every extra minute I can spend on this is invaluable. Thank you so much.'

I am about to say something, though again I'm not entirely sure what, but I miss my chance. Laura's phone rings. She takes it from her pocket and looks at the screen.

'One minute,' she says and answers.

We stand on the spot. Laura says a few words then ends the call. She shakes her head.

'It's Tuuli, my daughter,' she says. 'I've been trying to find her a physiotherapist who specialises in working with children with asthmatic complications. But it's not cheap, and the bank still won't sign off on a loan.'

We look at the wall, the grey concrete, the white chalk markings.

'There's a Monet exhibition on at the Ateneum at the moment. It's open till eight this evening. What do you say?'

My first reaction is akin to both the excitement and the slowing effect that seeing Laura's smile arouses in me. And my next reaction too is completely automatic.

'Six o'clock suits me fine,' I say without giving it a second thought.

I'm not sure if I've said something amusing or not, but Laura smiles all the same.

'Great,' she says. 'See you there. Is it okay if I move on to de Lempicka now?'

I nod, say goodbye, see you at the museum. I only manage to utter these last words once Laura has already started walking away and is allowing the measuring tape to wind itself back inside its case.

I have almost made it to the other side of the hall when I hear someone call my name.

The Komodo Locomotive has come off its rails. Despite what one might think, this is not a large-scale catastrophe. No human casualties were sustained: the kids were simply lifted out of the train's carriages. I position myself next to Kristian, and together we shunt the engine back into place on the tracks.

'I don't understand this,' I say to him when we have assured ourselves that the engine can once again pull the chain of carriages without any hiccups. 'How can a train that you have to pedal come off its rails? At the corners, the maximum speed can't be more than ten kilometres an hour.'

Kristian runs his eyes first along the tracks, then the entire length of the train.

'Sabotage,' he says, so quietly that I have to put the word together in my mind. Then I too look at the miniature train set made of wood and metal. Kristian's words don't make sense at all.

'I don't think so,' I say, and perhaps I'm about to say something else too, but Kristian shakes his head as if to forbid me.

'Do you know all the staff at the park? All the customers? Do you have years of experience with the technical side of running an adventure park?'

I quickly glance around. 'If it is sabotage,' I ask, my voice hushed, 'is there any reason why you shouldn't be first on my list of suspects?'

Something flashes in Kristian's brown eyes. He assumes a sturdier stance, his legs further apart, and even his shoulders seem to broaden. There he stands in front of me like a wall of muscle.

'For your information,' he says, his fricatives hissing, 'I built this Komodo Locomotive myself. I screwed those red lamps into the engine's eyes. They weren't on the original. That was my idea. I told Juhani it would bring the train a sense of speed and danger, in a good way. Juhani agreed. Juhani thought it was a good idea.'

Kristian looks serious. Again, he seems completely sincere. I must admit, he doesn't look like a man who would derail his own train.

'Why did you say it must be sabotage?' I ask.

Kristian stares at me for a moment longer, then gestures towards the beginning of the bend in the track. I turn and hear him behind my back.

'Someone left a thawed-out chicken leg on the track,' he says. 'From that point, the engine was destabilised, then as the curve became tighter, it came off the rails completely. This could have caused a very serious incident.'

I respectfully disagree about the possibility of large-scale carnage. The thawed chicken leg, however, sounds like a far more acute cause for concern. The only place there should be any chicken legs is in the freezer in the café.

'I'll look into it,' I say quickly, before Kristian has the chance to speculate any further. 'Everything is in order now. The train is up and running again and—'

'When are we going to make the announcement?'

It takes a blink of the eye for me to realise quite what he means, then another blink of the eye to come up with something suitable to say. Kristian notices my hesitation.

'We agreed on this,' he says.

'In actual fact…'

'I've already told people I'm going to be the new general manager.'

The last sentence spills out of Kristian's mouth so quickly that even he seems taken by surprise. In a fraction of a second, he blushes, his eyes moisten, glistening, like someone either furious or devastated.

'Told whom exactly?' I ask. 'And why?'

Kristian is so flustered that he is almost out of breath. A fresh throng of children is approaching the train.

'Just some people,' he mumbles, his voice lower now.

I can sense that the pressure inside Kristian is malignant; it's growing. Of course, he's embarrassed, but he is also furious and extremely muscular. At this point I don't need any extra problems. And while I really want to bring this conversation to an end, I am perturbed by almost everything about it: the derailed kiddie train, the thawed chicken leg, Kristian's unwavering desire to become the general manager, all the people who know that Juhani promised him this in the first place and how much they know about the park's internal affairs. Then, as the children approach the train like the walking dead – inexorably yet all the while fumbling for the right direction – I have a thought that might bring at least temporary resolution to the situation. I think of my former boss.

'Kristian, do you think of yourself as an open and emotional leader or a more traditional, hierarchical leader?' I ask.

'What?'

'Have a think about it,' I say. 'Leadership isn't what it used to be. Nowadays leaders need a whole range of different qualities: not just a results-oriented understanding of the internal emotional dynamics of the workforce but also a holistic awareness of our interactive, socio-experiential economy and an appreciation of its primary importance at all levels of an empathy-driven, inter-personal leadership philosophy.'

I could never have imagined hearing myself talk like this, but right this minute I am indebted to my former boss Perttilä for all those years listening to his nonsense. Perttilä's words flow from my lips as though someone has pressed 'play'.

'I want—'

'To be the general manager,' I nod. 'But before that, as the company CEO, I want to be sure you have the necessary internal, external and emotional skill set for the job. I suggest you take part in at least one and, if possible, several training sessions. I want you to draw your own emotional map, find your own treasure trove of positivity that will help teach you to recognise the spectrum of deep emotions both within yourself and in others, and only then will you be able to lead your team all the way to the summit of success.'

Kristian's gaze has wandered to the other side of the park.

'Can you embrace the gift of your team's unique emotional success story?'

'What?'

'It's an essential part of working life these days,' I say and, disconcertingly, I can almost hear Perttilä's voice. 'Your strength might lie in an area where a weaker person might become swept away. That makes you a safe emotional harbour. When strength and weakness combine, a collective synergy emerges from within both, creating successful, empathetic prosperity.'

I can see Kristian doesn't understand a word I'm saying. There's nothing to understand. Even I don't know what I'm talking about.

The children are all around us. The train will soon start moving.

'It's probably best if you look at some different training options, then together we can choose the most suitable. Remember: at least two different courses.'

With that, I walk off. I glance over my shoulder and see Kristian pushing the Komodo Locomotive into motion.

Once back in my office, I do a little more work. It still feels like
Juhani's room, right down to the name on the door. I've asked
Kristian to change the plaque, but he hasn't done it yet. All other
repairs are sorted out quickly, but he still hasn't got around to this
one. I can guess why. I have placed my new laptop on the desk and
replaced Juhani's computer. On the left of the laptop is a pile of
my own paperwork, on the right printouts of Laura Helanto's
murals.

I soon realise I'm doing something I find very peculiar. (The
reality is, everything I do these days feels peculiar.) It seems as
though every time I accomplish a demanding task, I pick up the
printouts of the murals and look at them for a moment. As though
admiring them were a reward for getting my work done. It feels
both entirely logical and, as I have been forced to admit many
times before, utterly insane. I can't find a single concrete, rational
explanation for my behaviour. I look at a series of images and ...
simply enjoy looking at them for their own sake. That's it, that's
all there is to it. But that can't be all there is to it.

I am an actuary.

I know that can't be all there is to it.

7

While sitting on the train I calculate that, assuming the train arrives at Helsinki Central Railway Station on time and I take the most direct route to the Ateneum, I will have – before meeting Laura Helanto in the same place – two and a half minutes for every significant painting and thirty seconds each for all the other works in the standard collection. That should be enough, I think as I gaze out of the window at the autumnal panorama flashing past. It's been a cloudy day and the landscape, which otherwise flickers in front of my eyes like a multicoloured quilt, is now like the patched, dusky surface of something darker. My carriage is almost empty, and all I can hear are the sounds of the train. It makes the waning of the day feel more real, as though large pieces of a puzzle were being moved by a higher, irresistible force.

I am painfully aware that I left my workplace before the end of the working day. It feels neither good nor right. But the murals plague me more with every passing minute. Why do I like them so much? It must surely have something to do with the art itself, which is an area of human behaviour unknown to me. Until now.

I have learned from experience that, if something is bugging me, I first need to isolate its constituent parts, perform a few calculations, then examine the result. I can't imagine that a room full of old paintings will be any different in this regard. I know that most of them represent landscapes and people, mostly depicted in a realistic style. This means they include measurements, perspective and distance, something concrete, well-defined characteristics. I am certain I have performed more complicated calculations in the past.

As I step off the train, small, thin droplets of rain fall from the sky, as though someone upstairs is unsure whether it should rain or not. Rush hour on the platform. I avoid people, walk through the station building booming with the sound of the crowds, cross two streets, then find myself in the Ateneum – which feels pleasantly serene and quiet – for the first time in almost thirty years. I buy a ticket and hire a set of headphones. I ask how long the explanations last, but the ticket vendor, with yellow hair and oblong glasses, is unable to give me a precise idea of this. She starts humming and hawing, estimating the length of the sections at anything from thirty seconds to 'under five minutes, maybe'. I hope she isn't responsible for explaining the actual works of art. Listening to such approximate musings for too long would be painful. I thank her, and I've already reached the steps leading up to the galleries containing the art when the vendor shouts after me. She tells me there's a special exhibition too. That's the term she uses. I ask what's so special about it. Monet, she says, then starts chit-chatting again. This time I instantly cut her short. I tell her firmly, once and for all, that I wish to see every piece of art in the building; that's why I'm here. She gives me a curious look and sells me another ticket, this time, mercifully, without saying a word.

🐇

My plan runs into difficulties almost immediately. From both a temporal and a strategic perspective, the first room proves far more challenging than I had predicted. I can't stick to my target of two and a half minutes per painting, and I'm unable to compile a satisfactory list of bullet points about each individual work. Some of the canvasses fall into logical patterns that open up at first glance (house + crossroads + tree + spring weather = fresh air in a small French village) and provide a sufficiently rational and proportionate explanation of why it is nice to look at them.

Then there are other canvasses that don't initially provide anything concrete to grab hold of (splotches + splashes + lines + colours = experimental use of paint) but in which after a while I can see something different altogether (splotches + splashes + lines + colours = x). What all of these paintings have in common is that I stand looking at them far longer than necessary.

It's the same phenomenon as with the images of the murals, and again I ask myself: why am I looking at something longer than it takes to acquire the information I need? It's as though my brain has switched to a different track. The same happens from one painting to the next. The first room alone takes up almost half of my allotted time. I sigh out loud. There's no way I'll be able to go through all the rooms in the museum before meeting Laura Helanto. Besides, examining works of art isn't foremost in my mind at the moment: far more pressing matters include starting a money-lending business, avoiding the noose and keeping a group of professional criminals happy for however long our undesirable collaboration lasts.

But right now, here I am.

I glance around and resist the temptation to revisit some of the paintings that, for some reason, I liked more than the others. At the same time, I look at the other people in the room. There are only three of them. A couple at the far end of the room, a woman in the middle. I realise that the woman has stood in approximately the same place the whole time I've been in the room. It seems I'm not the only one for whom the fine arts caused problems.

I make a quick decision and head for the special exhibition. The name sounds promising. I need a special solution.

Monet, I think. So be it.

The exhibition gets off to a good start. There are fewer paintings, they are larger, and they contain clear patterns and forms. With a view to working things out, this looks very promising. I am approaching the first painting, my eyes firmly focussed on it, so firmly in fact that I only sense and hear the footsteps moving in the same direction once they are right next to me. I turn my head.

Laura Helanto.

At the moment I see her, something warm shimmers through me, an inexplicable wave of joy, excitement and tingling. I don't understand it. The last time I saw her was in the adventure park, and that was only a few hours ago. I consider this reflex a distinct over-reaction.

'Hi,' she whispers.

'Hi,' I reply, only to realise you're supposed to speak in hushed tones in here.

'You made it,' says Laura Helanto. 'So, how do you like it?'

I quickly look up at the first painting. It is about three metres wide and two metres tall. It seems to show blurry flowers and waterlilies in some kind of pond. Still, there are pleasingly few elements in the painting.

'I like the size of these paintings,' I say. 'And I like that they portray one thing at a time. I like being able to concentrate.'

'Monet painted dozens of canvasses at the same little pond.'

'Ah,' I say. 'One painting per waterlily.'

Laura Helanto splutters with laughter and holds a hand across her mouth. I don't think I said anything amusing, I was simply commenting on the most logical and probable scenario: how many waterlilies, let alone waterlily flowers, can fit into one and the same pond? We both look at Monet's painting, silent for a moment.

'Don't get me wrong,' says Laura. 'But I didn't put you down as an art gallery kind of man. I didn't think you'd be all that interested.'

'I am very interested in art,' I say, perfectly sincerely. 'But I still haven't seen anything as good as your murals.'

From the corner of my eye I see, or rather I can feel on my right cheek, how Laura turns to glance at me. We stand quietly in front of the painting until Laura breaks the silence.

'Would you like to look at them in peace? It's my second time at this exhibition. And I've seen these paintings before.'

'Then you might be able to tell me what each of them is about,' I say.

'Gladly. I know a thing or two. I can tell you what I know. Then you can listen to the commentary and tell me which bits I got right.'

'I doubt we'll have time to check your answers. The museum will be closing soon.'

Laura smiles, almost laughs.

'You've got a good sense of humour,' she says, and I'm not entirely sure what she's referring to.

We walk around two large rooms and stand in front of several paintings for varying lengths of time. To my surprise, we sometimes pass a larger painting with barely a few words, then stop to examine a much smaller painting for a relatively long time. Laura is an excellent guide, though I don't understand everything she says. At no point does she provide an explanation for what I have come here to find out. And I don't mind. Laura's company, her voice, the mere presence of the canvasses. Right now, that feels more important. It *is* more important, I think, then straight away: what exactly is the matter with me?

The tour ends in front of the largest painting in the exhibition. In fact, the painting consists of three paintings, their frames joined together. The whole piece must measure almost five metres across and two and a half metres from the floor. Monsieur Monet must have painted the pond to scale. I listen to Laura Helanto, who sees lots in the painting besides the waterlilies. I feel as though I am gradually sinking into the murky pond. The water feels warm and pleasant. It smells of Laura's hair and…

'The museum will be closing in ten minutes.'

The caretaker's voice on the tannoy brings me back to the here and now.

Laura is smiling. 'Now you won't have the chance to see if I got it right.'

'I don't think that's necessary,' I say. 'Do you have a moment to talk about art a while longer?'

Laura lets out a short chuckle. Then her face turns serious.

'I must say, nobody has ever asked me out like that before.'

'Like what?' I ask.

'Do I have a moment ... It's alright. My daughter is spending half term with her cousin. I'd love to. Let's talk about art a while longer.'

8

'I'd already decided I was going to become a famous artist, that much was clear, but I hadn't found my own style yet,' says Laura. 'After all, I was only eighteen. I mean, I hadn't even worked out what my own style might be or where I might find it. Then I was in London and I saw an exhibition by Helen Frankenthaler. That opened a door. But it really helped that on the same trip I saw the classics with my own eyes, works that are important to me in their own unique ways. Cassatt, Turner, Pissarro, Sisley, Degas, and Monet, of course. Everyone always says Monet, even you – and it's true. I think Pissarro is my personal favourite. Who has captured light in the same way, at a single moment in time, turned a trivial moment into something eternal and beautiful? Then at the Tate Modern and Tate Britain I saw Pollock, Hockney, Rothko, and then there was the Frankenthaler exhibition. Later, on the same trip, I visited the Galerie Belvedere in Vienna, a museum full of famous Klimts. Even *The Kiss*.'

I'm not entirely sure what Laura Helanto is talking about, but I enjoy listening to her. Of course I realise she's talking about art, but the names mean nothing to me. We are sitting in a pub in Kaisaniemi. It was dark when we left the Ateneum. At first the rain was nothing but a drizzle, but as we walked down the front steps to the street it grew stronger. Now the pavement beyond the window is dancing with thousands of droplets, the space between earth and sky is filled with water. Streaks of lightning illuminate the air like the flash of an enormous camera. The thunderstorm is directly above us. A candle burns on our table. I realise that normally I would think this unnecessary, both with regard to the light and the overall functionality of the space, that it is a standard element of the interior decoration of so many pubs, something whose only purpose is to increase ambience and augment sales figures. Now I think its soft, flickering light is perfectly suited to Laura Helanto's exuberant, attractive presence, her wild hair and blue-green eyes. I like the way the flame is sometimes reflected in her glasses, the way it flickers warmly in her eyes.

'What about you?'

'I'm a beginner when it comes to art,' I say. 'I'll freely admit it.'

'I mean in general,' Laura smiles. 'What made you become a … what was the word again?'

'An actuary,' I say and briefly explain how I became fascinated by mathematics, why I believed and still believe that practising mathematics is my most important responsibility, and why I left my job. I mention my chaotic childhood, the comfort and salvation offered by mathematics, and the unfairness of my constructive dismissal.

Laura looks out at the rain, then turns back to me.

'You're very open,' she says.

'That's what happened,' I say.

'Yes, right. I mean, most people wouldn't talk about such personal things on the first … the first time they meet.'

'I don't know about that,' I say. 'I very rarely find myself in situations like this. On the whole, other people don't interest me. But you interest me. I listened to every word back in the museum, I could have listened to you for hours. Your murals, your paintings – or sketches, as we should call them at the moment – I could stare at them for hours at a time. I think you are extraordinary.'

I realise straight away that I've spoken longer than I intended, said more than I planned. The candlelight, Laura's eyes, her scent, Monet, the other paintings. My thoughts are running in directions that feel strange and new, yet at the same time rather pleasant. And I realise I'm thinking exactly the way I just described, as though I've jumped into the water first, and only then decided to go swimming.

Laura Helanto looks as though she is smiling, then almost immediately as though she has remembered something. Her expression turns serious, almost saddened.

'I don't know about that,' she says. 'But it's kind of you to say so. Thank you.'

Then she falls silent. We drink our beer, and the air flashes again. We both look up at the sky. My eyes return to Laura. Yes, there's something despondent about her.

'Is something worrying you?'

Laura snaps back to earth. She shakes her head, then smiles.

'I can be frank with you, yes?'

'I believe it's for the best,' I say. 'Some people say it can be rude, but I think the benefits far outweigh the possible drawbacks. I'm not sure of the exact ratio, but in my experience I can say that the probability of causing offence can't be higher than ten percent. That gives being frank around a ninety-percent chance of success. Those are exceptionally good odds.'

'You ... you really have your own style,' she says, perhaps with a little smile.

'Is that a good or a bad thing?' I ask, genuinely interested.

'It's a good thing,' says Laura.

I say nothing because I sense that Laura wants to continue. She props her elbows on the table.

'You seem honest and trustworthy, and I like that,' she says. 'You say what you think, you keep your word. I don't know if you realise how rare that is. You are what you say you are.'

'I am an—'

'An actuary,' she says. 'Yes, I know. I mean in general. You're not like other people – which is a good thing, too. And it doesn't matter that you look quite amusing, in your own quirky way. That's a plus. Always in a suit and tie, even in the museum. Excellent. But I've said too much, far too much. It's been a long day. An early start, then Monet and now this beer. I was so thirsty I think I drank it a bit too quickly. I don't know. I'm a bit...'

Laura doesn't continue her sentence, though it is clearly unfinished. I wait for a moment.

'Something is bothering you,' I say.

Laura leans back in her chair. 'You won't let it go.'

'No, I won't.'

Laura shakes her head. She smiles. The smile is different from before. This time it isn't so enthusiastic.

'It's the murals,' she says eventually.

'We agreed on a budget and a timetable. All you need to do is paint.'

The sky flashes again. I thought the rain couldn't possibly get any heavier, but that is what seems to happen.

'That's just it,' she says. 'The painting. I haven't ... I haven't been able to do anything. I've produced sketches and plans, sometimes very fully developed ones. I'm excited, keen to get started. But then, when I have to pick up the brush and start, somehow, I just can't ... I put off starting again and again, until I have a new idea and make new plans and sketches that excite me and ... I haven't talked to anyone about this before.'

This is clearly a difficult subject for her. I can see it from her expression, her body language. Her glass is almost empty.

'Would you like me to get you another beer?' I ask.

'Do you think that will help?' she asks. 'I should drink myself into getting started?'

'What I meant was—'

'I know what you meant,' she smiles. To me, the smile could almost be described as melancholy. 'No, thank you. I think I'm good.'

'I have problems too,' I say.

Laura looks at me but doesn't say anything.

'I think everybody does,' I continue. 'But maybe that's a conversation for another time. I solve my problems with mathematics.'

'All your problems?'

'Yes.'

'That's ... an interesting way of thinking. But I don't know what maths has to do with me staring at that wall in the adventure park and just ... staring at it. I look at it, and it's so demoralising.'

'Because you're looking at it as a wall,' I say. 'It's an unknown variable. The wall is x.'

'The wall is x?'

I nod.

'At this point, I would take a step back. I'd look at what information I have available at the moment, what conditions have been proposed. I would consider whether I have encountered the same problem before, or the same problem in a different form. If I can't solve the whole problem in one go, can I solve part of it? Does the solution to the partial problem give me a clue, a key to solving the next part of the problem?'

Laura says nothing, but it looks like she's listening.

'I would choose the sketch I think will be the easiest to realise,' I continue. 'Then I would look at the sketch and choose the part of it that is easiest to realise. Then I would draw up the simplest plan of how to go about realising the sketch, examine the plan, then carry it out without giving it too much thought. In that way, I would have at least one new tool before trying to solve the larger problem.'

'In a way, I know all this,' she says.

'But do you actually do it?'

'No,' she says with a shake of the head.

'Mathematics can help us here too. Just follow the plan.'

'And I'll find out what x is?'

'I can't promise you that,' I tell her honestly. 'But based on the factors that I know and feel, especially the extra-mathematical ones, I think it's possible, even probable. Like I said, you're extraordinary.'

We sit in silence.

'What do you do when you discover you're interested in someone?' Laura asks. 'Do you think of them as x too?'

9

The train seems to be floating. The lights of the houses and office buildings twinkle, flash and flicker in the dark autumn night as though someone were throwing them around, trying to hit the train. But the train is flying, and nothing can strike it. It is quarter past eleven at night, my cheeks simultaneously warm and shivering. Laura Helanto's peck on the cheek travels with me in the train at light speed.

Strangely, I can't seem to recall our conversation in any semblance of a logical order. My mind is a confusion of short, technicolour, kaleidoscopic fragments, some of which rewind to the beginning and repeat themselves again and again, generally overlapping with other short fragments. I even feel slightly out of breath, though I'm sitting still. I'm not sure of all the things I talked about. Particularly hazy is the bit when, as we were saying goodbye outside the train station, Laura moved close to me, thanked me for the evening, which she said had been very nice in a good way, then kissed me on the cheek as if we were somewhere in central Europe. I have a vague recollection that, after the kiss, I said something about how the probability of the murals being a success was around a 120 percent. I don't know where the words came from. That doesn't sound like me; it sounds more like something my former boss Perttilä would say, but I believe I really did say something to that effect. I don't even remember walking to the platform or stepping on this commuter train weightlessly flying through the night.

I can still hear Laura in my ears when I recognise the familiar station name shining in blue and white as the train pulls in. We have reached Kannelmäki. I jump up and barely make it out of the train before the doors slide shut. I walk down the stairs, all the while perplexed at my dreamy mood. I almost missed my stop. When has something like that ever happened before? Never, is the answer. It's almost as though I am walking just above the ground. Just like the train a moment ago, it feels like I'm floating.

The night is chilled, but there's no wind. Autumnal nights have a distinctive smell. The first fallen leaves, wrinkled in the frost, the moist earth, the air, pure from the rain. I look diagonally across the street to where an illuminated letter H glows above the door to my stairwell, and I can already envisage Schopenhauer's protests at my late arrival and try to think of a way to make it up to him. I walk out onto the pedestrian crossing when I hear a car behind me and see someone exiting the pool of light emanating from the letter H. I say exiting, because I realise the person must have been standing there for a while and only now moved. I recognise him at the moment the car's bonnet and its blinding headlights stop so close to me that I could lean over slightly and test the temperature of the hood. I stand on the pedestrian crossing between AK and the SUV.

🐇

Again the air inside the SUV bears the strong reek of aftershave. The air conditioning blows frozen air at my feet just like last time. AK isn't holding me by the hand, but this time he's placed his forearm along the back of my seat so that it runs behind my head. It's an unpleasant feeling, as though at any moment his fist might strike my neck like a snake, grab it, bite and squeeze. Lizard Man is driving. The nocturnal streets and roads are empty, and he's not sticking to the speed limit as scrupulously as before.

One thing is clear: Lizard Man and AK are devoting a lot of their waking hours to me, which leads me to think that either they consider me a priority or they simply don't have anywhere else to go. I'm not about to debate this aloud. Right now, there are more urgent matters to deal with.

'If this is about getting the bank started...'

'It isn't,' Lizard Man replies.

'Then can I ask what this is about?'

'Any guesses?'

'I don't like guessing things,' I say. 'Especially not in situations like this where I don't have the faintest idea how many variables my guess would be based on.'

Lizard Man shakes his head. I can see his eyes in the mirror. He is smiling. The smile is anything but friendly. He remains silent. I think of the two previous occasions on which I've found myself sitting in this SUV. First the trip to the shores of the lake, then to the barn. I don't have pleasant memories of either excursion. Soon we will be somewhere in the back of beyond in Vantaa, I don't know where.

The houses disappear behind us, those up ahead are industrial buildings. It's almost midnight, so most of them are dark. First we pass a couple of larger buildings bearing neon logos of companies that I recognise from vacuum cleaners, drinks bottles and running shoes. After that the names become more descriptive. The dominant format seems to be surname plus some defining feature: tyres, machinery, painting and decorating. Beyond that the names disappear altogether. Now there are just unmarked buildings: some completely dark, some lit in a dim, yellow night-time glow. Eventually we slow down, drive in through a gate in a wire fence and stop at the end of a long row of cars. The motor is switched off. AK walks round the car and opens the door for me.

The building in front of us is on two storeys. Loud music is blaring inside; I can hear the thump of the bass. Upon closer inspection, the cars in the car park appear to be at the pricier end of the scale. There is no indication on the wall of this building that it's a place where people buy and sell cars. And the cars don't look as though they have been parked on the forecourt for months.

Lizard Man beckons me towards him. When we arrive at the door, he waves a hand. For a moment I wonder if he is greeting the door, but then I see a small camera set into the wall. A loud buzzer sounds, and the lock clicks. Lizard Man pulls the door open and gestures to me to follow him inside.

Right behind the door there are two sets of thick, heavy curtains. As I pull one of them back, the volume increases. When I pull the other one, the music resonates through my chest. I find myself standing in a tall room. A disco ball hanging from the ceiling sends thousands of sparkling lights hurtling around the room, and bright, colourful spotlights wash across the room at regular intervals. I can smell cigars and cigarettes, alcohol and perfume. And there's something else too, something sweet and slightly stale. On the left there is a bar, on the right groups of sofas, armchairs and tables. The tables are covered in glasses and bottles, and the chairs are occupied with different-sized clusters of people, presumably the owners of the cars parked outside. I count around thirty people in the space. The lighting is so problematic that it's hard to say anything about these people's appearance.

Right in front of me is a raised platform where two women are dancing. Apart from skimpy underwear and high-heeled shoes, they are naked. I don't have a very good sense of rhythm – this is one area of human behaviour to which I have never paid much attention – but I can tell that the women's dancing fits the flow of the bass-heavy music very well indeed.

'What are you drinking?' Lizard Man shouts in my ear.

'Can I go home?' I ask.

'No.'

AK remains standing next to me as Lizard Man heads to the bar. He soon returns, presses a bottle of foreign beer into my hand and nods at AK, who grabs me by the arm, squeezes painfully, then proceeds to lead me deeper into the dingy nightclub. At the far end of the room is another set of curtains, this time running the entire length of the wall. The curtains are open at the left-hand side, and

we head towards that opening. Beyond the curtains is a more private
version of the sofas and chairs in the main room. In the middle of
the space is a low table, surrounded by a semi-circular sofa. The
lighting is blood-red. AK shoves me in the back and indicates that
I am expected to sit down. I sit on the sofa and place the bottle of
beer on the table. I don't want beer. AK stares at me for a moment,
then pulls the curtains shut. He remains on the other side of the
curtains, and I find myself sitting in the red booth alone.

The thick, black curtain efficiently muffles the noise of the
music. I look around. In the corner of the room stands a mirror,
and I catch sight of myself. There is also a shelf with a roll of toilet
paper and a bowl that I can't see inside. There is something
profoundly odd about the space.

I am about to stand up and leave the building when the curtain
is pulled back and one of the women I just saw dancing on the
stage steps inside. Now she isn't even wearing underwear though
the high heels are still on her feet. She has long blonde hair, lots
of make-up on her face and eyes that seem to look at me, past me
or simply through me all at once.

'Somebody ordered a blowjob,' she says.

'I beg your pardon? I never ordered anything of the sort. This
is utter madness.'

The woman stops. But only for the blink of an eye.

Before I can add that this must be an unfortunate misunderstanding, the woman has sat herself down in my lap, facing
towards me. Her lips find my own and glue themselves tight across
my mouth like a magnet on metal. She tastes of lipstick and
cigarettes. She grips my left hand and places it on her backside,
and with her fingers on top of my fingers she squeezes her buttock.
More precisely, I squeeze her buttock with her help. She removes
her lips from my lips and presses her breast into my mouth. I try
to turn my head, but it's a big breast, it's hard, and by now it is so
far inside my mouth and she is pressing my head so tightly against
her body that trying to let go hurts my cheeks.

The woman pulls my hair as though we are wrestling. I have to lean my head backwards and end up sliding onto my back. With my right hand, I try to prise her fingers out of my hair, but her fist is rock solid. Then she moves my hand, the one that was squeezing her backside, and slips it between her legs. I'm not entirely sure where our fingers, still conjoined, end up. By this point I am lying on the sofa on my back and hollering in pain as the woman continues to wrench my hair.

Everything happens so quickly, it only takes a few seconds, and it's all so bewildering that I simply can't function the way I want to: sensibly. Besides, I am half paralysed, taken completely by surprise. The woman's every move feels adept and calculated. As though she has done this before, many times.

She bounces on top of me, yanks me by the hair even more forcefully than before, then with astonishing strength and agility, she slides a metre forwards and sits on my face as she would a chair. I'm not sure where my mouth is, but I can taste a mixture of sea salt and vanilla custard. She pulls my hair to the right, the left, back and forth, now with unprecedented power, as though she were scrubbing an old rag rug within an inch of its life. With my free hand – the one whose fingers the woman isn't twisting with her exceptionally painful technique – I try to grip her buttocks in an attempt to remove them from my cheeks. Just as I get a good grip, she climbs off me as quickly as she flew on top of me. She backs up towards the curtains, pulls back the right-hand one and disappears. On her way back to the stage she passes a few centimetres in front of AK, but neither so much as glances at the other.

Finally I manage to clamber up from the sofa. It feels as though I've lost half my hair, my scalp is on fire. I stand up and feel my trousers sliding down to my ankles. The woman managed to open my fly and unbutton my trousers. I see the phone in AK's hand as he snaps a picture of me.

Later on, I realise that the picture AK took was only for his own amusement. They didn't need that photograph because they already had dozens of other ones. This I learned on the drive back to the city. For thirty seconds, I was able to flick through a selection of images on an iPad that AK thrust into my lap. The photos give the impression that I was engaged in some particularly heated activity with the naked woman. They give the impression that I did everything of my own free will, to feed my insatiable lust. They give the impression that I was a man bellowing with pleasure, a man with lecherous hands that I couldn't keep to myself.

'Now listen carefully, you fucking dimwit,' Lizard Man says from the front seat. 'The big man that you met – and whose money you're using – doesn't like his employees doing things like that. It shows they can't be trusted. And you remember what he does to people that can't be trusted. He strings them up. If he's in a good mood. You, you fucking shit-for-brains robot, have been pissing me off from the very first time I had to listen to you and your smart-ass comments. I should have let AK break your neck. Now you've managed to hoodwink the boss with all that one-plus-one stuff, but believe me, that can all disappear. Fast. All I have to do is show him these pictures, and you'll be hanging from the rafters in that barn. *Capiche*, moron?'

I say nothing. Lizard Man's eyes flash in the mirror.

'Fine, then,' he says. 'Let me explain it a bit more simply, so you understand. We've got these pictures of you now. If you don't do what I tell you, I'll send them to the boss and your wife or girlfriend, or whatever, I don't care if you're screwing a fucking goat, mate. And there'll be an explanation with the pictures. *Summa summarum*, as I'm sure you'd bloody well put it, you work for me now. I own you.'

I would never say something like *summa summarum*, but I don't tell Lizard Man this.

'I reckon you enjoyed that,' he says. 'Iira is hot stuff.'

'Iira?'

'I knew you were keen.'

'Why did she ... accost me like that?'

'Because I told her to.'

'You tell naked people to sit in the laps of complete strangers?'

Lizard Man laughs. It's the same laugh as in the barn, scornful, spiteful.

'She can do far worse than that,' he says.

'At your orders?'

'Yes, at my orders. I think you're finally getting the message. It's that simple. I own her. And I own you.'

Inside the car, everything is quiet for a few seconds. Then I catch sight of those cold, reptilian eyes in the rear-view mirror and hear his voice, lower now than before.

'It's one plus one, Einstein,' he says.

10

I don't sleep a single minute. I sit on the sofa until morning. My tie done up, a book in my hand. Twice Schopenhauer visits and asks why I'm not in bed asleep. Both times I stroke and scratch him until he has had enough and goes to sleep himself. I can't even bring myself to tell him what kind of thoughts I am thinking or how agitated I am.

The early hours I spend trying to calm myself down. I realise that this is vital – quite literally. Though I can't work out the precise probability that my affairs would become this complicated in such a short period of time, I still have to find a rational way to examine the overall situation in which I find myself. This requires a cool head, and cooling my head takes time.

Lizard Man. Laura. AK. The clandestine nightclub. The body in the freezer. Iira, the naked lap-dancer. The big man. The bank. The money-laundering. The hanged man. Perttilä and his emotional leadership.

I try to arrange everything in my mind, to make sense of it. Eventually I have a semblance of a plan for every name, place and item. Except for Laura Helanto, for whom I can't draw up a plan. When I try to do that, I end up hoping that the constituent parts of my other plans don't prevent us visiting the Kiasma museum to acquaint ourselves with contemporary art. This, of course, feels more than a little crazy, to be frank. The idea that, after all this, after all that's happened in recent weeks, the thing that worries me most is not being able to share an evening of art with Laura Helanto. It's hard to explain why contemporary sculpture, and Laura's explanations and interpretations of it, feel so important after having my hair pulled, a nipple shoved in my mouth and my life threatened, or after having started – temporarily – laundering money or using a giant rabbit's ear to beat to death a man who tried to kill me.

The letter in my hand is from the regional state administrative agency. It arrived with yesterday's post. The letter tells me that I, or rather the company I have set up alongside the adventure park, now have the legal right to operate as a money-lending service. Meanwhile, Heiskanen the lawyer has filled my inbox with various documents and notifications. He has worked quickly and has followed my instructions. His bill, the first of many documents attached to his email, is substantial. Additionally, he rather redundantly tells me that his nephew, a student of information technology, can help me – not surprisingly – with matters relating to the bank's information technology.

Everything is ready.

I can award my first loan.

By half past six, it is light. Not necessarily bright, but there is enough light that we can say a new day has dawned. I stand up from the sofa, take a shower, pull on some clean clothes. I have breakfast with Schopenhauer, check my tie and leave for the adventure park, and so, I hope, will many others.

11

Minttu K is ready to start immediately. This time, she doesn't try to challenge me. Maybe she can see I'm serious. I was serious before, too, but now I realise I am moving and speaking in a different way, more directly, as though there are no alternatives. Which, of course, is true. There aren't.

True to form, Minttu K smells of gin and cigarettes, and it's only 9:00 a.m. Either that or the smell is ingrained into the walls and furniture and the numerous items of clothing hanging in her office wardrobe. It's like sitting in a bar in the mid-1990s. Minttu K is dressed in a tight white top and black blazer, and her tan seems so intense that she's more bronzed than the average Swedish tourist.

'Honey,' she says, and her voice is like two pieces of sandpaper rubbing together. 'I'll get my favourite graphics guy to work on this. We'll have the sketches ready by this afternoon.'

I leave her to order the posters, leaflets and flyers – jargon I have learned during the course of our conversation – and return to my office, where Heiskanen's gangly nephew is sitting at my laptop. His fingers dance across the keyboard. Soon afterwards, he tells me he is finished. I thank him and he stands up from the chair like an animated matchstick: his movements angular, his limbs scrawny. I take two hundred euros from my wallet and hand it to him. The boy looks at the four fifty-euro notes as though he has just wiped his hand in something unpleasant. I tell him this represents an hourly rate of almost three hundred euros. Two hundred and eighty-nine euros and seventy cents, to be precise, he replies. We look at each other for a moment, then I take another fifty-euro note from my wallet and hand it to him. In a strange way, it feels almost like looking in the mirror, a mirror that distorts time, as though I were that young man and my middle-aged self all at the same time. I think of Einstein and his theory of the curvature of time and space, how time passes more quickly in some places than others.

Then I look at my terrestrial watch, realising that time and space waits for no man, and head to the entrance to relieve Kristian from behind the counter. I have timed this hand-over so that there will already be enough customers queuing up for tickets that Kristian won't be able to start another conversation about becoming the general manager. Oddly, he looks as though he doesn't want to talk about it. We can only hope that our conversation, in which I channelled Perttilä the snake-oil salesman as though I had taken leave of my own body and handed it over to my former boss to use as he pleased, frightened Kristian just as much as it frightened me. Kristian says nothing but flexes his muscles more than usual as he gathers up his things – his keys, phone, wallet, protein shake – and does it as though he is showing off his biceps to me. I'll admit, they are impressive biceps. As he leaves, he appears to spread out his back muscles and raise his shoulders. For a moment, it feels as though we have landed in the middle of the jungle and fallen a few rungs back down the evolutionary ladder.

Then it happens. I award my first loan.

It isn't very difficult. There are three children, all at the age when they are more than capable of whingeing until they get what they want, and the father barely has enough money to cover the entrance tickets. I comment in passing that his financial situation looks quite precarious. He says he is aware of that, then lowers his voice and from beneath his thick, dark eyebrows asks me what 'the flying fuck' it's got to do with me. Of course, it's none of my business, I reply, how could it be? But I can award him a small loan right away. After a brief conversation, he types a few lines of details into the iPad on the counter, a flexi-loan account opens up in his name and the money is deposited in his account.

Minttu K arrives to tell me the material she has ordered will be delivered tomorrow, so for the time being I will have to tell people verbally about the possibility of a loan. I have never done direct marketing like this before, but I quickly learn the most effective way to offer people our new service. I make a comment, insinuating that they look more or less penniless, and say I'd like to help them. Things quickly start to take off. Just as I'd imagined, many people need small amounts of money, just a hundred or two hundred euros to help them out. But a surprising number of people opt to take out the maximum amount of two thousand euros right away. This takes me by surprise, especially as the adventure park's pricelist is displayed at the counter, so it only requires a simple calculation to work out how much tickets and a trip to the café will cost. Besides, prices seem to lose their meaning the minute I press 'enter' to indicate that the loan has been approved. But most surprising of all is the fact that people don't seem to pay the slightest attention to the one thing I've put most thought into: our more than fair rate of interest. The question of interest is something people don't even want to hear about. As the number of loans begins to grow, the matter perplexes me all the more. All I have to do is mention the possibility of money, and people close their ears to everything else.

I've hardly been able to develop the thought further when I notice that a man has been standing just inside the doorway, facing me, for some time. At first he looks like one of many mothers and fathers in my peripheral vision, people waiting, either coming or going, and who then disappear into the park (having borrowed some money) or the car park (having spent the money they borrowed).

At some point, however, I realise that this man isn't waiting for the start or end of a day of fun and games in the park. Instead, he seems to be waiting for the foyer to empty so that we will be alone. When that happens, once the final shrill cries disappear into the melee inside the park, he approaches the counter.

The man is heavy-set, but his gait is resolute. He is wearing a pavement-grey blazer, a blue-and-white checked shirt, blue flannel trousers and a pair of black leather shoes. What is left of his blond hair is combed tightly back over his scalp. His face is large and angular, his eyebrows look almost worn away. He is both stocky and has a belly. His light-blue eyes look here and there with a sense of careful purpose before coming to rest on me.

'Pentti Osmala, Helsinki Police. Afternoon.'

'Good afternoon,' I say, trying not to stiffen completely. Perhaps I've been expecting this would happen at some point, subconsciously preparing myself for the inevitable. Still, the fact that I am now face to face with an actual policeman sends a chill the length of my spine.

'I'd like to talk to the manager, Juhani Koskinen.'

'He passed away, unfortunately,' I say, baffled at my choice of words. Of course, Juhani's passing *was* unfortunate – that's exactly what it was – but is it unfortunate right now, in this particular context? Perhaps the reason for the policeman's visit only concerns Juhani, in which case it wouldn't be unfortunate in the least.

Osmala waves his right hand. He is carrying a small briefcase, which looks more like a box of some description. He opens it, and with his left hand he pulls out a sheet of paper. He looks at the document.

'Who is in charge of operations here?'

'I am,' I say.

'And you are...?'

'Henri Koskinen.'

'I see,' he nods. 'That makes sense.'

Osmala puts the document back where it came from and remains silent. He doesn't look as though he is about to tell me exactly what makes sense.

'I wonder if we could talk for a moment,' he says. It's more a statement than a question. 'I quite fancy a coffee and maybe something sweet.'

🐇

I escort him to the Curly Cake Café. The place is swarming with people, fewer than half of them adults. The noise is dizzying. The café smells of the dish of the day, Mum's Meatballs and Bouncy the Mashed Potato. The policeman and I silently stand in line. Once it's our turn, Osmala takes the Very Vanilla cake and I have Grandma's Best Blueberry Pie. As she pours the coffee, Johanna watches the coffee, the officer and me.

There is only one free table, set suitably far away from the others, next to the kitchen door. The children's table is low and small, but the chairs are the café's regular, adult-sized chairs, meaning we have to lean over to place our coffee and cake on the miniature table. Osmala seems unfazed by this, and it doesn't bother me either. What bothers me far more, causing a certain sense of restlessness, is what I can see through the rectangular window of the swinging doors leading into the kitchen. The freezer-cum-coffin stands, grand and gleaming, only four and a half metres away.

'I'm sorry about your brother's passing,' Osmala says before he has even taken a bite. He sounds as though he has uttered more or less the same words many times before. I still don't know how to answer. Thanking him feels unnecessary: Osmala isn't really sorry, any more than I can be grateful for his insincere words.

'Did it come out of the blue?' he asks.

'Juhani had a congenital heart defect,' I reply. 'Why? Are the police ... I mean, you, Officer...?'

'Call me Pentti,' says Osmala. 'No, the police are not investigating Juhani Koskinen's death.'

So, I surmise, his name is Pentti and he is investigating something else. My appetite for blueberry pie has suddenly disappeared.

'Actually, it's a more unfortunate matter, one that inevitably concerns your brother too. We have reason to believe that he had dealings with some criminal elements.'

Osmala bites off a chunk of cake and looks at me across the oozing vanilla filling.

'Criminal elements?'

Osmala nods. It takes a gulp of coffee to restore his ability to speak. After placing the cup back on the table – he is forced to double over as though he were tying his shoelace – he opens his box-shaped briefcase, removes some coloured printouts and places them next to my coffee cup. The photograph is a standard mugshot. The man looks more tanned in the photo than in my freezer. Otherwise, this is unquestionably the same person.

'We suspect that this man and your brother had some form of financial dealings. This man is a professional criminal. He has a long rap sheet featuring everything imaginable, right up to manslaughter. An extremely dangerous character. And it seems he has disappeared. He might have left the country, though personally I don't think that's very likely, or he might be in hiding, either of his own will or ... otherwise. In his circles, it's not uncommon for people to simply disappear. Between us, it wouldn't surprise me if someone had lost their temper with him and given him a little helping hand into hiding, if you get my drift. The guy wasn't exactly up for the Nobel Peace Prize.'

I keep my eyes on the photograph.

'Have you ever seen him in your brother's company?'

'No,' I answer, truthfully.

'And do you know him at all?'

'I can't say I do.'

Osmala slides the photo back to his side of the table, then puts it back in the briefcase along with his other papers.

'So you own the amusement park now, is that right?'

'Yes,' I reply and explain that it is an adventure park, not an amusement park. This I do at considerable length, mostly because it gives me time to prepare for what I assume will happen next. As I guessed, Osmala isn't interested in the difference between the two types of park.

'Perhaps it's the wrong time to ask something like this, but did you and your brother ever talk about the running of the park?'

'He sometimes told me about new acquisitions, the Komodo Locomotive, for instance, I remember him telling me about that.'

'What did he say?'

'That the train resembles a long, shiny Komodo dragon and that the creature's smiling head, complete with a long forked tongue, is the engine, that the ride can carry forty children at once and that, depending on how fast you pedal, the circuit takes about five and a half minutes.'

'I mean, did he ever talk to you about how he financed these acquisitions, where the money came from and where it went? Did he mention any business partners?'

'No,' I say, again perfectly truthfully. 'We never talked about money. And I never had any idea of what kind of people he associated himself with. Or persons, such as the man in that photograph.'

'A very dangerous man,' Osmala nods.

'Certainly looks like it,' I admit.

'How is the park doing?'

Osmala's question has the same intonation, the same tone of voice as everything else he says, soft, almost like a passing comment. I realise he does this on purpose. Osmala looks as though he is pondering something.

'We're in a transitional phase,' I say. 'I must admit, I haven't worked in the adventure-park sector before, and it has taken me by complete surprise. Everything is new. The park's footfall seems to be increasing, sales figures are up and our balance sheet is strong. It's our intention to expand...'

'What about the staff? Are they the same as during your brother's tenure?'

'Yes, every one of them.'

'Would you mind if I showed them this photograph and asked if any of them has seen him?'

'By all means.'

Osmala stuffs a piece of cake the size of a tennis ball into his mouth, leaving vanilla filling smeared across his face. He wipes his lips as his giant jaw chews the sticky mass. We don't speak for the duration of this process. I have nothing to say, and Osmala's tongue is weighed down by half a kilo of dough. I'm beginning to realise that everything Osmala says is some kind of fishing expedition in which every word has at least one extra meaning. The children around us run, shout and whinge, the adults wipe their little faces and ask them to sit nicely. This doesn't have the slightest impact. Osmala finally manages to swallow his mouthful. Even amid the ruckus, I'm sure I can hear the cake squelch on its way down his wide gullet.

'Do you like this?' he asks.

'The cake?'

'The adventure park,' he says and nods towards the hall.

'I haven't thought about whether I like it or not. I inherited it. People rarely get to choose what they inherit.'

'What did you do before this?'

'I am an actuary.'

I briefly explain to Osmala how everything happened. Then I make my apologies and say I really should be getting back to work, if that's alright. Osmala replies that it's more than alright. We stand up, and we have taken about a step and a half when Osmala stops in his tracks, and he does it so forcefully that I have to stop too.

'Would you like me to leave the photograph I showed you?'

With that question, something about Osmala's face changes. Though his voice is low and soft, and though again he asks the question almost in passing, there's something else to his expression. I am suitably alert. If anything useful has come of recent events, I'd say that right now it's much harder to take me by surprise than, for instance, when I was in Perttilä's office for what was to be the last time.

'There's no need,' I say, fully sincere. 'At least, not for my sake. I'm sure I wouldn't forget a face like that.'

Osmala glances at my uneaten blueberry pie.

'You're not going to leave that, are you?'

'Of course not. There are plenty of happy, hard-working little cake-mice in a place like this.'

I have no idea where those words came from. Maybe it's the influence of the Curly Cake Café: all those peculiar product names and weird and wonderful pictures used to promote the food. Osmala is still staring at my pie, then raises his light-blue eyes to look at me.

'You could always freeze it,' he says in that same low, soft voice.

12

The week passes quickly. It's only on Friday, at the hardware store, that I finally relax. Well, maybe it's not exactly relaxation, but my problems seem to fade slightly, to move further away. When Laura asked, I promised there and then to go with her. It's evening and the adventure park has closed its doors. All week I have been granting loans. And I've spent many days thinking about the policeman's visit. All week I've been trying to solve my problems, but so far I haven't found many speedy solutions.

There's a surprise for me at the hardware store too. This surprise is similar in nature to many of the other surprises I've experienced these last few weeks; it feels like suddenly coming round, as though one of my senses has been asleep and is only now shaken awake. I've never felt at home in places like this, but now ... now there's something deeply relaxing about the smell of the hardware store. Here there's a feeling that we're dealing with something profound and fundamental. Here people build floors, walls and ceilings. They buy stone, wood and steel. They grip handles, tools and rods. Their actions make their own loud, distinctive sounds. Their work can be felt throughout the body, and you can see progress with the naked eye. You can smell the wood, touch the chill of metal. Everything here is concrete, tangible: work progresses one nail, one screw at a time.

Such are my thoughts. They're not especially realistic because I know what home renovations are really like. They cost twice as much as the original quote and take twice as long as was originally intended. But my reverie has more to do with the person I am accompanying to the store. Whether I like it or not, something always happens when I am in Laura Helanto's company. I can feel a certain élan flicker inside me, a combination of physical tingling, the images flooding my imagination and an incomprehensible need to start talking and – as I have come to realise – it usually involves something completely unplanned happening.

'Let's head straight to the paint section,' says Laura once we have approached the long chain of trolleys and tugged one free. 'Let's try and be quick.'

I tell her I'm in no hurry, so long as I'm at work tomorrow morning. Laura chuckles. I am serious. I push the empty trolley; it makes that familiar trolley sound, something between a low-pitched rattle and a high-pitched squeak. Laura's fragrance mixes with the smell of the hardware store, and I begin to forget the events of the day. Laura looks up at me, gives a short smile, her glasses catch the light. I could easily push this trolley for a thousand kilometres, I think, as long as she is by my side. At the same time, it occurs to me that we didn't speak much on the drive out here. And that after asking me to help her carry things this morning, she has only allowed me to catch her eye in passing.

We arrive at the paint section, manage to flag down a sales assistant, who initially tries to walk right past us, as though we weren't standing right in front of him and didn't have a physical form at all. Laura begins the process of picking out the paints. She has a selection of samples with her, she shows the assistant the sketches and drafts on her iPad, lists colour codes. The assistant is a young man with gleaming blond hair, who looks like he doesn't have enough muscle to lift the heavier pots of paint. Nonetheless, he manages to mix the colours according to Laura's specifications. The trolley fills up, one pot at a time. The assistant is mixing a shade of green for the O'Keeffe wall when I hear a man's voice at my side.

'Laura. Hi.'

I turn my head and see a man approximately my own age. That's where the similarities end. He is short and athletic, his muscles clearly visible beneath his black T-shirt. He has intense eyes, a deep shade of brown, and short, dark hair.

'Kimmo,' says Laura. 'Hi.'

After this, we all turn our heads a number of times. Standing next to the man named Kimmo is a much younger woman, her hair dyed pitch-black, clearly pregnant and clearly embarrassed. She is shorter than Kimmo, and so small and thin that her baby bump is like some kind of impossible optical illusion. Each of us looks at least once at everybody else standing at the four corners of the very geometrically precise square we seem to have formed, then our eyes return to what we were looking at in the first place.

'So, buying paints,' Kimmo says to Laura. 'Exhibition coming up?'

'No,' Laura replies. 'Yes. Sort of.'

'This is Susa,' says Kimmo, and points at Susa's stomach.

'I'm Henri,' I introduce myself.

Kimmo glances at me, says nothing, then turns his attention back to Laura.

'I must have missed the news about your exhibitions.'

'I haven't had any,' she says. 'I've been spending my time on ... other things.'

'Right,' says Kimmo. 'How's Viivi doing?'

'Her name is Tuuli,' says Laura, the temperature of her voice now below freezing. 'Tuuli is doing fine.'

'My big opening is next month,' says Kimmo. 'I'm looking for barbed wire, some metal poles and wire fencing. This new work is a critique of globalisation, the way it controls us and will ultimately destroy everything, crushing everything under its weight. Nature, people, art. The way it forces us all into a stable to eat, shit, spend money and die. Only money has any meaning now. Money, money, money. Consume, consume, consume. I totally reject that. It's still half finished. You know me.'

Laura says nothing. Perhaps she doesn't know Kimmo the way he thinks she does.

'I want to show how claustrophobic it feels in this police state, this infernal, market-oriented living hell that has become our new normal,' Kimmo continues, and it seems to me as though he hasn't even noticed whether Laura answered him or not. 'The way we're all being constantly oppressed. One of my works was sold to a gallery in London – the one we visited together – then another one went to Malaysia, another to Toronto.'

Kimmo glances over at Susa.

'We just moved in together, a bigger flat downtown. We needed the space, what with the little one on the way. Susa won't mind me saying it's a boy, Kimmo Junior.'

I don't know Kimmo and I'm not sure whether this kind of chit-chat comes naturally to him. But I do know he ought to think about the words he uses, because at the moment there's no sense, no logic whatsoever to what he's saying. I wonder for a moment whether I should tell him so. Laura manages to speak before I have a chance.

'We have to get going,' she says, lifts the last of the paint pots from the counter into the trolley and pushes the trolley into motion. I start pushing too.

'Hey,' says Kimmo as we pass him and Susa. 'What's going on with you? I'll send you an invitation to the opening. Do you still live in Munkkivuori?'

🐇

It's only once we've paid for the paints that I ask Laura when she lived in Munkkivuori.

'I've never lived there,' she replies.

'Then why did Kimmo say that?'

'Because he's a self-centred, self-obsessed man who thinks only about himself and who thinks every idea that pops into his head is pure, unadulterated genius that we mere mortals should admire the way parents marvel at their toddler's light-yellow poo – which is what most of his thoughts are when you scratch the surface. Because he was born with a silver spoon in his mouth, which was swapped for a platinum spoon when he held his first exhibition, which was a success just like all his other exhibitions since. Because Kimmo is a fake, he's spoiled, privileged, blinkered, lives in his own rancid bubble where he's a big fish in a very small and muddy pond. Because nobody ever says no to him. That's probably why.'

The sliding doors open, we walk out into the car park. The trolley's wheels chatter, the pots clatter.

'How do you know him?' I ask, almost without noticing.

'Does it really...? From my student days.'

Laura pauses for a moment, then sighs more than speaks her next words.

'And we dated for a few years. It didn't go very well. The premise was all wrong.'

At first I think the air temperature must have dropped significantly, that night has fallen surprisingly quickly, then I realise that nothing outside has changed. The September evening is relatively warm, the car park is well lit, and the landscape isn't in any way nocturnal. I don't know where all the levity has gone, the tingling that I felt a moment before. And my imagination is suddenly changed too. Where in the past I saw only Laura, now I see Laura and Kimmo together. It's an extraordinary phenomenon. It feels like someone is running a rake across my guts.

We arrive at Laura's car, she opens the boot, I begin lifting the pots of paint inside. I feel almost nauseous, as though, these days, I don't fully know myself any more.

'I suppose I should ask you something too,' says Laura as I lift the final pot into the boot. 'What did that policeman want today?'

I straighten my posture, press the boot shut. Is this what has been bothering her all day; is this why she was so silent earlier? And how does Laura know about it? I haven't mentioned the policeman's visit to anyone. But I don't want to lie to her.

'He was asking about possible connections between Juhani and a certain man,' I say, and it is the truth.

'The man in the photograph?'

That's right. Detective Inspector Osmala walked around the hall once I'd returned to the entrance.

'Yes.'

'What's it all about?'

We are standing at opposite sides of the car, speaking across the roof.

'The police believe Juhani and that man had some financial differences of opinion.'

'Is everything alright with the park?'

I hesitate for about half a second.

'The transitional phase looks like it's going to eat into our accounts,' I say. 'But I believe everything will work out in the end.'

Laura is silent, then opens the door on her side of the car.

'Good to hear,' she says.

🐇

The atmosphere in the car is somehow different now than it was before, and I guess it can't be because the boot is stacked full of freshly mixed pots of paint. For a moment I'm not sure what it is that's spinning through my mind, until the echo grows stronger one spin at a time. *The premise was all wrong.* That's how Laura described her relationship with Kimmo. I find myself wondering about the nature of that premise, its precise nature, its essence. I don't know why I'm thinking what I'm thinking. I don't know quite what the years-old relationship between Laura and the spoiled contemporary sculptor has to do with me or why the thought conjures up images I'd rather not see. But it seems there's very little I can do about it.

13

Schopenhauer's small, sinewy body is quivering and shivering like a kitchen appliance. He is purring more keenly than he has for a long time. He has eaten his breakfast, surprised that I haven't already left for work, though it's the first workday after the weekend, but am instead sitting on the sofa with my own breakfast. He follows me and sits down next to me. His long, black fur gleams in the morning light as he looks for a suitable spot and a comfortable position to sleep off his breakfast. Most of the sun is still hidden behind the building opposite, but its glow across the cloudless blue sky is so grand, so irresistible, that even a small slice of it is enough to line the living room with warm, bright light.

The lawyer has sent me an email. Accompanied with a link. He asks me to choose Juhani's coffin and let him know my decision.

Schopenhauer has never met my brother Juhani, so to him the whole matter is rather distant. I haven't bothered him with the details. I imagine he has his own worries, his own tasks. And in one of his tasks he has always been exemplary. He has always been a realist. He was like that when he was little too, and that's why I named him as I did. I haven't thought about this for a long time. Schopenhauer is seven years old. If the original Arthur Schopenhauer, the philosopher and my cat's namesake, were still alive, he would have reached the ripe old age of 232. I don't know what the infamous pessimist would make of that.

The choice of coffins is vast. The link expounds at length upon the quality of each casket and the local materials used, both on the outside and the inside. All in all, there are over twenty options to choose from, from a basic, no-frills model to luxury items for those who want to bow out in style. At this point, I think, the wishes of the deceased may differ radically from those of the living. How many people say at the moment of death: take the cheapest coffin you can find, it's only my final journey? And how many would request that funeral guests are offered only a glass of water and that the flowers all should come from your own garden, thank you very much? That would be the cheapest, most sensible solution. But that's all it would be.

I know why thoughts like this are bubbling in my mind.

Schopenhauer. *A Pessimist's Wisdom*. In particular the essay 'On the Vanity and Suffering of Life':

> 'For human existence, far from bearing the character of a gift, has entirely the character of a debt that has been contracted. The calling in of this debt appears in the form of the pressing wants, tormenting desires, and endless misery established through this existence. As a rule, the whole lifetime is devoted to the paying off of this debt; but this only meets the interest. The payment of the capital takes place through death. And when was this debt contracted? At the begetting.'

The first time I read these words I was a young mathematics student. It was a month or so after one of my parents had died. Combined with the rigour of mathematics, Schopenhauer's doctrines seemed like the only possible way of surviving in the world, in this life that in all other respects was utterly mindless.

And for a long time thereafter, the German philosopher's writings felt like a reasonable way of relating to people and things. Schopenhauer seemed to tell the truth about things. Whereas Leibniz claimed that this is the best of all possible worlds, Schopenhauer calmly asserted that it was the worst. He substantiated this statement by saying that 'possible' does not mean what somebody might be able to imagine, but what truly exists and what will endure. Thus, our world is constructed in such a way that it only barely remains afloat: if it were even slightly worse, it would no longer be able to sustain itself. And because a worse world would be unsustainable, it isn't a possible world, *ergo* ours is the worst of all possible worlds.

I realise that, right now, I really should try and think more in the former way. That would be the most logical option, it would be based on the recognition of facts – no matter which way I look at it. I have problems, and finding a solution to those problems is literally a question of life and death. And though I might succeed at the first – in staying alive – I will still have greater problems than ever before. In a situation like this, shouldn't I think that life is terrible, futile and silly, that it only ever leads to even greater suffering?

I flick through the coffin options, my mind still on the events of Friday evening.

We carried the pots of paint from the car into the warehouse at the adventure park. The tension that had built up while we were driving began to relent once we stepped out of the car's claustrophobic interior. We found space for the paints beside the Bogeyman Swing, which has been temporarily taken out of use. Laura began organising the pots, and for some reason my attention was drawn for a moment to the hairy, metre-high bogeyman mask attached to one end of the swing. Still, we spoke about things other than those we had discussed outside the hardware store. Laura told me about her plans, I said I would gladly offer my unprofessional help. This comment amused her too, though again I was only being honest. I have no particular skills when it comes to painting. Once Laura had put the pots in a suitable order, she said she had to go and pick up her daughter from a friend's place. I told her this was fine, I would lock up the park. We walked to the door at the back of the park, stepped out onto the loading bay. The evening was cool and dark, and we stood there next to each other. The roar of traffic carried in from the nearby highway. Laura thanked me and said that despite the awkward encounter it had been a lovely evening. I wasn't sure what I was about to say, but just then Laura leaned forwards and placed a gentle kiss on my right cheek. Then she walked down the metallic steps, strode towards her car and waved as she steered the car towards the other side of the building.

Let Juhani have the very best. I select a coffin that looks more like a five-star hotel suite than a place where no one will ever meet anyone else ever again. I send the lawyer an email and switch off my computer.

14

My phone rings as I am waiting for the train on the platform at Kannelmäki. I'm unsure of the number, unsure whether I remember it from somewhere or whether it reminds me of a number I have seen before. In the past, I've always happily answered calls from unfamiliar numbers. Usually the caller is trying to sell me something that, naturally, I don't buy and wouldn't buy under any circumstances. I want to hear their sales pitch, their offers, which aren't really offers in the truest sense of the word. As we speak, I calculate what their suggested purchases will really cost me, after which I tell them the reasons why their offer is unprofitable, why it doesn't fit the definition of an offer, then I suggest what kind of offer might theoretically interest a hypothetical customer, assuming they were interested in what the company had to offer in the first place. Sometimes the telemarketer tries to end the call before I reach my real point: a discussion of the range of mathematical possibilities that have arisen and how they might best be presented to the potential customer. It is precisely these kinds of everyday mathematical considerations that I believe can be of great help when trying to make life as sensible and practical – in other words, as pleasant – as possible. I have often tried to share this joy with these lost souls who call me and try to sell me something. But all that is in the distant past now. It is in the same place as my superficially secure life in my role as an actuary with a stable monthly salary, back when there was an element of predictability to things, a sense that expectations would always be fulfilled, in a world where A led inexorably to B.

I answer the phone and I'm not especially surprised by what

happens next: barely has the conversation started than Minttu K and I are having an argument.

'What do you mean you don't want to draw too much attention to it?' she asks.

Obviously, I can't tell her about DI Osmala's suspicions, suspicions that I don't want to augment in the slightest. My commuter train glides into the station.

'All I'm suggesting is that right now we try to keep a low profile, especially with regard to the banking operations.'

'Honey, which one of us is the marketing director round here?'

The train stops. I wait for the doors to open. Nobody gets off, and those getting on form a micro-crush around the doorway. I look at my feet as I step on board.

'You are,' I say, and without looking around me head straight for an empty carriage. I don't like listening to other people regaling the entire train with news of their families, their political convictions that have nothing to do with statistical probability, their constipation issues. I find a cluster of seats with nobody sitting nearby. 'This isn't a question of—'

'This is a question of striking while the iron's hot, you've got to grab the seal by the horns while the tide is in, and all that. Juhani agreed with me.'

'I'm not sure about that...'

'He was dynamic and forward-looking. Juhani would've seen things just like I do.'

The sad thing, I think to myself, is that Juhani will soon be in a three-thousand-euro coffin, and I wish he was still running the adventure park, striking the iron with you and whatever else the pair of you come up with.

'I know that,' I say. 'Juhani was...'

'Fun and flexible.'

'Right...'

'Humorous and quick-witted.'

'Right...'

'Spontaneous and amiable.'

'Right...'

I don't fail to notice the flipside of Minttu K's list of attributes, the ones that without saying out loud she implicitly uses to describe me. It doesn't feel particularly nice, but I can't possibly tell her I'm only trying to avoid ending up swinging from a makeshift gallows. Instead I apologise for being a bit reserved.

'And right now our operations are the complete opposite,' Minttu K says. 'I've talked to the others about it.'

Which others, I wonder.

'This is a transitional phase,' I say. 'And now I have opened up the bank, which—'

'Which we're not allowed to tell anyone about,' she says, interrupting me again. 'I've been thinking about running an ad campaign on the radio. In the capital region, maybe even right across southern Finland. There's an offer on my desk, an offer we can't and shouldn't turn down. I've got people lined up to make the ad, bloody funny guys. I can already hear the jingle. They could come up with a few one-liners about the slides and the bank. You remember Scrooge McDuck splashing around in his money pit? "Now slide ride into the bank." Something like that.'

'That sounds funny,' I say and realise my voice is bone-dry and businesslike, though there is something vaguely amusing about the idea. 'But maybe later. At the moment, we are operating solely as an adventure park. That's why we ordered the posters, the flyers and everything else. They are for use inside the park.'

'What are you afraid of?'

I must admit, that question takes me by surprise. I feel like I already know Minttu K a little bit and I'm sure she's just pushing me. Still, there's something about the question that gets me thinking. At the same time, I realise this is neither the time nor the place for a deeper discussion of the matter. I have to do what I have to do. So I can survive. So the adventure park can survive.

'I'm afraid that I'm afraid of humour, fun, spontaneity, quick-wittedness and amiability,' I say and notice I have raised my voice. 'For now, we do what the situation requires. Once the situation changes, we'll rethink things.'

I end the call and glance around. Another golden autumn day: the trees are ablaze with colour, there's a bright chill all around. At first, I sense more than feel that there's someone else sitting at the end of the row of three seats. Then I hear that someone has sat down opposite me too.

'The words of a man who means business,' I hear in that now-familiar voice.

I turn my head. AK is sitting at the end of my row, Lizard Man is on the row opposite. We are the only three passengers in the carriage.

15

The train pulls into the station at Malminkartano. There are a handful of people on the platform. I can't think of many moments quieter than when a train has just stopped. It feels as though everything else stops too and falls silent. Nobody gets into our carriage.

'Someone told me this train goes around in a circle,' says Lizard Man. He looks out of the window at the station walls covered in graffiti. 'Which seems appropriate, given the circumstances. We go round and round in circles, and here we are again, just the three of us.'

I remain silent and realise I should have kept my eyes peeled while I was talking to Minttu K. On the other hand, I know only too well that Lizard Man and his friend would eventually have caught up with me somewhere else. Now the three of us are on a train together, and that isn't even half the problem. The problem is sitting right opposite me.

'But you know what really pisses me off?' Lizard Man asks and looks at me. His pocked face looks a little swollen.

I shake my head to indicate that I don't know.

'Nowadays you can't even buy a ticket without a credit card or a debit card. Try stuffing a fiver into an app on your phone. And right there on the side of the carriage, there's a sign saying there's no ticket vendor on the train. Whatever next? Imagine going into an off-licence and they tell you, yes, everything's just like it was before, only now we don't stock booze, or any other kind of alcohol for that matter, but apart from that nothing has changed a bit, come on in. So now AK and I are on this train without a ticket; every time the train pulls into a station we have to sit here worrying whether the inspectors are going to turn up, fine us and throw us off the train. Do you think it's fair that we're made to live in fear like this?'

Lizard Man's gaze is so intense that I think I'd better give him some kind of response.

'I suppose not,' I say.

'AK over there is shitting bricks.'

I glance at AK. Staring straight ahead with the headphones covering his ears, he looks like he might not even know he's on a train at all.

'I'm sure you have a ticket,' says Lizard Man.

'I have a monthly travel card.'

'Give it to me.'

'What?'

'Give me the card.'

We look at each other. I was right, his face is slightly swollen. What's more, he looks deadly serious. AK doesn't look as though he is following our conversation particularly closely. But I know from experience that his apparent passivity can turn to action at the snap of a finger. I take the travel card from my jacket pocket and hand it to Lizard Man.

'Thank you,' he smirks. His smile is a snake's smile.

I say nothing. Lizard Man slides the travel card into his own pocket, his movements so relaxed and suave that anyone might think it was his card all along. Then he leans his head against the back of the chair.

'That feels much nicer,' he says. 'I must say. Not nearly as pants-wetting as before. What about you?'

I don't reply.

'That's the thing,' he says, now overdoing the pathos. 'One day you jump on a train the way you've always jumped on a train, and you imagine the train is going to judder along just the way it's supposed to, and the journey will be the same calm, lovely journey it was before. But then someone turns up, someone taking the piss, someone who says you can't buy a train ticket on the train any more or some other completely nonsensical bullshit. And after that the train doesn't seem to judder quite the same way ever again. It's just that little bit colder inside.'

I know what this is about. His boss. My bank. The fact that my business suggestion was taken seriously despite Lizard Man's chuckling and chortling.

He taps a finger against AK's knee. AK pulls his phone from the pocket of his black-and-white tracksuit and turns the large screen towards me. On the screen is a photograph in which I have my face pressed deep inside a naked woman's groin. Both my hands are raised into the air, one of them showing something that – by complete coincidence – looks unmistakably like a victory sign. In all probability, someone looking at this image for the first time wouldn't necessarily know it was staged. It would simply look like an image of me at my least glamorous moment. Lizard Man nods to AK, who returns the phone to his pocket and concentrates on his primary job: staring vacantly ahead.

'A small reminder before we start discussing the schedule,' says Lizard Man, then leans towards me and brings his face close to mine. 'What do you say? When can I come and pick up the first fifty grand?'

I can smell his breath. It is a blend of unbrushed teeth and something badly digested.

'I don't have fifty thousand euros,' I say, straight up.

It's true. In one week, I have granted many loans while paying off the park's debts using the money from the increased revenue figures – which was always the plan – to such a degree that, at this moment in time, the park's account is almost empty. Things will start to rectify themselves next week when the first loan repayments start to arrive – with interest.

'When...?' says Lizard Man. 'That was my question. I don't care how many times everything has to go through your fucking system or whether you have to check, double-check and explain every transaction six hundred times. When? I said. You realise that means a point in time? So, get your calendar out, Einstein.'

I say nothing.

'Very well,' he continues. 'Seeing as you're exceptionally hard of thinking today and have no suggestions of your own, I'll tell you when. You can put it in your calendar, yes?'

I do not reply.

'Or do I have to ask AK here to ... pick a bone with you?'

'Yes, I can write it down,' I say.

'I'm going on a little trip, so Monday two weeks from now will do fine. That gives you plenty of time. Twenty-five thousand per week. I'm sure you can do the maths yourself, you're a clever boy. Two weeks.'

Finally, Lizard Man leans back in his seat. It feels as though the temperature in front of my face lowers and the air instantly thins and freshens. The train begins to slow; we have already arrived at Martinlaakso. Lizard Man props a hand on his knee, stands up. He looks down at me, says nothing. Then he turns, heads towards the door. AK only gets up once the train has come to a complete stop. Again I am surprised at how agile he is, how quickly and silently he moves. For an enormous man, he is as furtive as a little fox. He steps down onto the platform, and for a moment I see their backs. Then the train jolts into motion again.

And just then, I hear the same announcement from both ends of the carriage:

'Tickets, please.'

16

Esa is sitting in his large chair in front of a wall of monitors, like a king whose kingdom has disappeared from beneath him. Esa cannot control anything, his job is simply to watch as things happen. Again, you could almost take a pair of scissors and cut the air in the room, which is thick with sulphuric fumes whose specific origin and composition I cannot and will not try to identify in any greater detail, not least for my own wellbeing. The control room has the feel of a claustrophobic studio flat, and the lighting is dim because Esa has switched off the overhead lights, meaning the only light in the room is coming from the monitors. The overall effect is something between a science-fiction film and flashbacks to my army dormitory.

My visit takes him by surprise, I can see as much. He's even more surprised by what I ask him.

'Has something happened?' he asks. 'We have all the videos, but I haven't watched them because I didn't know anything was wrong.'

Esa is clearly confused. It's understandable. I tell him nothing is wrong, there's just something I want to check. I give him the date, the estimated time and the area outside the adventure park that should be covered by the security camera. Esa's fingers dance across his keyboard. In an instant, the familiar SUV appears on one of the monitors. I look at the time code, the exact minute and second, and commit it to memory. With that done, I want to get out as soon as possible. There's something about the noxious air that after a while feels almost numbing. This must be the first time I have ever come close to suggesting someone might consider changing their diet. I decide against it. Instead I thank him and take a step back.

'Is there something I've missed?' he asks and spins 180 degrees in his chair. He's wearing the same US Marine sweatshirt as before.

Perhaps, I think, that your diet seems to consist solely of pea soup and pickled cabbage. I don't say this out loud because Esa's expression is now almost panicked.

He continues his line of questioning: 'Has the park's perimeter been breached? Surely nobody has stolen anything...'

'No, nothing like that,' I say. I need a moment to think. Either way, Esa will make assumptions about why I wanted to see the security tapes. And in any case, he has all the tapes at his disposal, containing thousands and thousands of documented events. I make my decision.

'I just needed to check the time,' I say.

At first Esa looks a bit baffled, then his bafflement melts into a nod, which in turn shifts to a form of collegiality: where before he was standoffish, almost cold towards me, now he looks understanding and empathetic.

'Personal matters,' he says.

'Yes. Very.'

'You want to find the owner of a certain vehicle? I can have a look...'

'There's no need,' I say with a shake of the head. 'I already know.'

We both look at the image on the screen.

The SUV on the screen grows in size. I feel almost like I'm moving inside it, I can feel the cold gust of air conditioning at my feet. But only just. I doubt the slightest breeze has blown through this room in years.

'I think I left my travel card in that car.'

My travel card isn't the primary reason for my interest in this vehicle, but it's certainly one of them. My fine from the train is in my jacket pocket, reminding me of the fact. Three stops on the commuter train ended up costing me eighty euros. In so many ways, it's simply too much. Esa is still thinking about what I just said and runs the fingers of his right hand across his geometrically impeccable goatee.

'If there's any way I can help,' he says eventually. 'I work for the adventure park, and I am ready to serve.'

I say nothing. He sounds at once like a soldier and a teddy bear.

'Thank you for your service,' I say. 'And if something comes up, I'll be sure to let you know.'

I suddenly feel bad for my cruel thoughts about his digestive problems. This strange emotional rollercoaster has been going on for some time now. Naturally, it is strongest in Laura Helanto's company. All weekend I've felt the kiss she placed on my cheek on Friday evening. And now – out of the blue – I find myself thinking that ultimately we are all people, all imperfect, and so what if one of us has a challenging flatulence issue? All it means is that air whiffs a bit when it leaves the body, sometimes unbearably so, but that doesn't make someone a pariah, someone we should run away from.

'And likewise,' I add, 'if I can help, I will.'

🐇

In only a minute I am back in my office. I instinctively open the window and through the narrow gap in the wall I draw cool, fresh air inside me as though gulping down water to quench my thirst. Then I sit down at my desk and begin making a series of calculations using my calculator, a pen and Google Maps, in particular the satellite-imaging function. Every time I have sat in that SUV, we meticulously kept within the speed limits. And I'm sure I can remember all the most important turns and which direction they took. At the same time, I can roughly remember stretches of that journey when we didn't turn or slow down, and I can recall the approximate length of each of those sections. The blindfold across my eyes still allowed me to look down, and I was able to follow how the vehicle behaved in relation to the road. But more importantly, now I have exact departure and arrival times. I calculate measurements and distances, I read the map, zooming in and out dozens of times, and before long I have narrowed the options down to three. I know the direction of travel with moderate certainty, I know the overall distance with some degree of certainty, and I know exactly what kind of building I am looking for with utter, lucid certainty.

Forty minutes later, I have two barns to choose from.

17

The adventure park is turning a handsome profit. Naturally, the bank is not. Yet. The park's sales figures have leapt almost twenty percent from the time of the first loan. The numbers are promising. I will be able to pay the staff's wages and clear the park's tax bill and some of the company's official debts. If sales continue like this and the bank gradually becomes profitable – at first only marginally, then exponentially – then I can start to address Juhani's less-official debts. What I can't do, however, is find an extra fifty thousand euros to hand over to Lizard Man.

And that's only part of the problem.

I don't think it's ever occurred to me, not even for a second, that I will actually ever pay him a cent. I've had enough. The moment he stuffed my travel card in his pocket, the matter was done and dusted. I realise it might have been done and dusted much earlier, and in light of the facts I could have made the decision much sooner, but the travel card sealed the deal. Even without the threat of a fifty-thousand-euro debt – you just don't do that. You do not travel on another man's travel card.

I spend a moment addressing both sets of accounts. I don't forge anything, but I extrapolate two separate reports – both of which are truthful – in such a way that the two sets of accounts eventually merge into one. This requires close attention to detail. I am so immersed in my calculations that I only realise I have beckoned someone into the room once Laura is standing in front of me. She has tied her wild hair in a tight bun at the back of her head and propped her glasses on her brow. For the first time, I see her face in its entirety. There's something about it that I haven't seen before. I can't put my finger on what it is, and I don't have time to think about it because she's asking me something. Or more specifically, she repeats something I said to her before and asks me to follow her.

🐰

The first mural is almost ready. Laura has spent the entire weekend painting. She started with the section of the hall least visible to the guests. This is understandable. That's what I would have done too. This also explains why I didn't notice the wall when I arrived this morning, or when I left Esa's control room and walked to my office. The mere thought of Esa makes me hope that the tropical aroma in the control room hasn't become ingrained in my clothes. I refrain from sniffing my sleeve. Instead, I listen to Laura as we walk and talk.

'I did as you suggested. I started with the easiest bit, the part I knew how to resolve. And I solved it. Quite well, in fact. And now...'

I glance at Laura, see her in profile. At the same time, I catch a glimpse of what I have always instinctively known. There is something hard about her face. By that, I don't mean that her face is worn or angular or in any way harsh. Perhaps the word I am looking for is experience, knowledge, a skill she doesn't want to bring out or share publicly. Something that her glasses and her bushy hair usually soften and hide.

'Here we are,' she says as we turn right after the throwing range, the Furious Flingshot, and the back wall comes into view.

And the view is breath-taking.

The wall clenches me, somewhere between my heart and stomach. The swirls and patterns flow and mingle, constantly changing form. Images appear, only then to disappear and create new images. I realise I look as though I've turned to a pillar of salt.

'Frankenthaler,' Laura explains. 'Adapted, of course. It's my version now, my interpretation. Kind of a graffiti version, I'd say.'

I look at the wall, unable to speak. I don't know what it is I can feel. Suddenly I am unsure of everything. A moment passes. I notice I have been silent for some time. My whole body is reacting to Laura's creation, and I can't do anything about it. I feel the mural in my feet, though at the same time I know that, rationally, such a sensation is impossible.

'Frankenthaler or not,' I say, 'this is the greatest thing I have ever seen.'

I mean what I say. I turn towards her. She has removed the band from the back of her head, letting her hair frame her face again. She looks more familiar now. Still, I have seen the hardness now, I know it exists. But I don't think of that any longer. I feel an irresistible desire to hug Laura, to hold her in my arms. It would be inappropriate, I tell myself. But then something happens. I might have inadvertently made to touch her, I don't know, because right then Laura takes a step forwards and wraps an arm around me.

'Thank you,' she says.

'Frankenthaler or not,' I hear myself repeating.

As Laura Helanto hugs me, as I stand looking at this mural, I feel something I have never felt before. I am myself. The thought intertwines with the feeling, the feeling with the thought, they are one and the same, and everything surges through my mind with such clarity, such certainty that it could form the foundation of an entire skyscraper, the bedrock of a new continent. Laura steps away, I can still feel her warm arm around me, the touch of her hair against my chin and cheek. I don't know what has happened. I just know that something has ... happened.

'So you like it, then?' she asks.

'I love it.'

18

Mere mention of the word 'date' has always caused me a degree of discomfort. Not to mention what I think it is supposed to mean in practice: that, of my own free will, I should meet up with someone whom I either don't know at all or only know slightly. This has never struck me as an especially wise way of behaving under any circumstances. There are many rational arguments against such behaviour, not least the fact that the probability that the meeting will turn out to be worth the effort is vanishingly small. We only have to count the number of interesting people we have met in our lives and relate that number to the total number of people we have met to get an idea of what kind of lottery-ticket odds are in play. As an actuary, I obviously don't buy lottery tickets and I have decided that, if I ever did go on a *date*, I would first have to assure and convince myself of the relevant factors so I could deduce whether my actions would be profitable or not.

That being said, I ended up asking Laura out – without carrying out a single calculation or the most rudimentary probability assessment in advance. You could say it all happened irrespective of me. We were standing in front of the wall she had just painted, and I heard myself saying I wanted to see her as soon as possible. It seems she understood what I meant and immediately started calling our forthcoming meeting a *date*. At that moment, I lost control of all my faculties, all my doubts regarding probability calculations, and experienced in practice the adage about butterflies fluttering their wings in someone's stomach when they are waiting for something exciting to happen.

And as I wait outside the restaurant, I feel that same strange, almost dizzying sensation that I always feel whenever I think about Laura and meeting her.

On this late-September evening, downtown Helsinki is like a theatre set soaked through. The streets gleam, making the rain look black and grey, the buildings are nothing but façades, even those where carefully positioned lamps shine in the windows, the stripes of the zebra crossing glisten nonsensically like an ice rink, and all around is the rush of water, the splash of puddles.

A date, I think and sigh into the rain as I shelter beneath an awning: this doesn't make any sense.

Particularly not now, when I have a barn to look for, a place where debtors are either hanged or where they decide to start up their own bank. In reality, I don't even know what finding the barn will mean. I don't know what it will achieve. I don't have a plan. It is also highly possible that, even if I actually manage to locate the place, I will still be too...

'Late,' says Laura. 'I knew it. Sorry.'

She has hurried beneath the awning from behind me. I assumed she would be coming from the direction of the Kamppi bus station, because that's where her bus would have pulled in. If she is coming from home, that is, and chooses the most direct route from the station to our meeting place. I don't understand why anyone would ever do anything else.

'You haven't been waiting long, I hope?'

'I don't even know what time it is,' I say. Even I am taken aback.

She closes her umbrella, shakes her hair and loosens her scarf. She looks past me and into the restaurant.

'Looks nice,' she says.

I turn and look in the same direction. A waitress in a gleaming-white blouse and a tightly fitting black skirt glides past carrying several bottles of wine. The people sitting at the tables look more like characters in American TV shows than people who might visit an adventure park and borrow money from me.

'I don't know,' I say. 'I've never been here.'

'Why did you choose it, then?'

'Given the average rating review, the distance from our respective bus stops, the prevailing weather, the day of the week, the time of year, your predilection for spicy food, and the fact that the point of a date is to try and make an impression on the other person, this seemed like the optimal choice.'

'Optimal...' Laura says, and smiles as though I've said something amusing. Her smile is like a warm lantern in the rain. 'That sounds romantic.'

'I think so too,' I say.

🐇

We are shown to the table for two reserved in my name, next to the window at the far end of the long room. The window is rather low-set against the street as the restaurant itself is slightly below street-level. We can only see passers-by from the waist down. At times it's impossible to guess what kind of face belongs to which pair of legs. If we were only a pair of legs, it would be easy to disguise ourselves. I don't say this thought out loud. I still feel somewhat dizzy; my mouth and tongue, and my entire jaw, feel oddly stiff, yet at the same time frighteningly ready to open up and blurt out whatever comes to mind. I have to concentrate on looking Laura in the eyes without losing myself in them, so that I both listen to her *and* hear her. Her hair is like a blossoming rose bush, her cheeks are glowing, and there's a special joy and contentment in her eyes. She is wearing a white blouse with black spots, buttoned up to the neck.

A waiter appears and asks whether we would like something to drink while we look at the menu. Laura orders a gin and tonic, I have one too. I don't like gin or tonic, but right now that doesn't really matter. What's more, any drink that might moisten my arid mouth is a small step from the desert towards a welcome oasis. Because that's what it feels like: like suddenly wading through sand. The menu is mercifully short and, to my delight, numerical. There are four different kinds of menu: with five, eight, eleven or sixteen courses. We quickly resolve to take the eight-course menu; we might be celebrating but we don't want to be here all night. Once the waiter has left, I raise my glass.

'Congratulations,' I say. I have thought long and hard about what to say, and this seems by far the most sensible option.

'Thank you.'

We clink our glasses. Laura stops me just as my glass is about to touch my lips.

'Without you ... I don't know ... Shall we toast to mathematics?' she asks with a smile.

Then she drinks, and I drink too.

Our first course is a small pink pouch, approximately the size of a pinecone cut in half, filled with a foamy, salty, fishy, essentially weightless substance. Laura seems to like it. This makes me happy. The same cannot be said of my calculations regarding the difference between the cost of the raw materials, the production costs, and the eventual price. I decide to put such thoughts to one side. But only for a moment.

'I took out a loan too,' says Laura out of the blue.

Perhaps I look as surprised as I really am.

'So has everybody else,' she continues. 'The other staff members. But that wasn't the reason I took one out. Obviously.'

I begin to understand what she is talking about. The adventure park. The bank I have opened.

'Everybody?' I ask in genuine bewilderment.

'Yes,' she nods.

'Everybody was suddenly in need of some extra money?'

'You said yourself that borrowing money from our bank is the sensible thing to do.'

'It *is* sensible...' I stammer. It is sensible if you can't get the same sum of money more cheaply somewhere else, I think, which in turns means they don't realise that—

'Exactly,' Laura cuts me off before I can add anything else. 'I really needed that money. Tuuli's school trip to France. I want her to have the kind of opportunities I never had, and besides, travelling is expensive for Tuuli because we have to take all her health issues into account. She's been talking about this trip for a long time, begging me to let her go. I know she's been dreaming about it. All her friends are going, and I felt bad thinking she might not be able to join them. But now she can, and I'm just so happy for her. It's much more important than my wall.'

Just then, the waiter brings our next course to the table. On a large white plate, there are two long, dark strips about half a centimetre high. At the top of the strips is a microscopic bundle of microscopic forest flowers. Around it all is a circle of congealed, bright-red liquid as thin as sewing thread.

'I wouldn't have been granted a loan anywhere else,' Laura continues. 'I've had some ... Well, my wages are spent on living costs, food and ... Let's just say, the final days of the month are always quite the balancing act. And I don't have a penny in savings either. I've never been very good with money, and I've had to learn the hard way.'

Her last words burst out like a gush of water through a crack in a dam. Laura is clearly embarrassed. She has said a lot, and if I had done the same I would be in the extremely uncomfortable position of having to rewind the tape to double-check everything I had said. Then she smiles again. Her smile isn't as breezy as it was before; there's a new shade to it now.

'I don't know why I'm telling you all this now ... Maybe it's the wonderful company, the wonderful environment and wonderful food.'

Again she looks embarrassed. At least, that's what I assume until I realise this is about something else altogether. The realisation is like a flash of light. Mentally I try to put it into words. Perhaps she truly does think of my company in rather the same way as I think of hers: that my company has an impact on her, that it complicates her thoughts and actions in a way that is, at least to some degree, unpredictable. Then there's the thought that she might actually like me – and that affects me in ways that are more than unpredictable. I try not to think about how many love songs, which I used to consider gushing and sickly sweet, suddenly feel like a very concrete consideration of the current state of affairs. Laura praises the dish. All I can taste is a perfectly standard Finnish mushroom and try to avoid thinking about the price per kilo. Right now, I don't care.

The wonderful company.

We eat our way through various gastronomic configurations, each containing around a tablespoon of food. The presentation of the dishes adheres to standard geometrical patterns, and their weight is more or less the weight of the plate. The lightest course – smoked forest hare and archipelago sorrel in an almost invisible form – must weigh no more than a whisker from said forest hare. But Laura likes it, and I like that she likes it. Wine glasses seem to multiply before our eyes as each dish is accompanied by a splash of a particular recommended vintage, but it's hard to drink wine with the food when the food disappears the moment you touch it. And so, each of us now has a row of wine glasses in front of us. The wines don't differ from one another nearly as much as the waiter's lengthy descriptions and background stories might suggest. We are served a slew of adjectives – tart, oaked, complex, toasty, earthy, fleshy, flamboyant and dozens of others – and a hearty dose of highly dubious flimflam about a small organic vineyard in northeast Italy. Still, I realise the point of an overly priced evening like this is not to identify the flaws in the waiters' logic or their attempts to pull the wool over your eyes, but simply to sit opposite each other and to do so over a prolonged period of time.

'It feels like I'm getting my confidence back,' says Laura after we have swallowed a solitary spoonful of crayfish mousse, thus emptying our plates. 'I didn't even realise how blocked I was. And

I didn't know that painting was just the thing to help me – the same thing that caused the block in the first place. I can't believe I'm saying this, but your mathematical model really helps me to think about things from a different angle. It opens up a whole new perspective, in so many different ways.'

Laura's voice is low but enthusiastic, she takes a sip of wine, all the while looking across the rim of the glass and right into my eyes. The soft, dim light cannot hide it: her face, her entire being, combine a new hardness with the happiness and positivity I knew from before. She truly looks like she has turned some kind of corner. Mathematics can work wonders, I know that. But for some reason, I find it hard to imagine that all this is down to the numbers. I don't know why. Maybe my general life experience and the tens of thousands of calculations I have performed tell me that a mathematical awakening like this is a privilege for the few, not the many. I smile because Laura makes me smile. Laura smiles too.

'Things seem to have fallen into place,' she says, leaning forwards slightly. 'All kinds of things.'

By the time dessert number two arrives (three raspberries, a drop of syrup and a minuscule pyramid of vanilla foam), we have started discussing the next wall to be painted. Laura tells me this will be the one inspired by Tove Jansson.

'But it won't be in her style. It will be in my style, but it's so influenced by Tove and her themes that I'm going to place her in the centre and surround her with what she means to me and what her work makes me think of time and again. Freedom, beauty, the sea ... love.'

That last word remains hanging in the air, wedged between us, there above our rows of wine glasses, at the spot where our eyes meet. I've been wondering whether or not to loosen my tie. The notion that the ambient temperature in the restaurant has risen throughout the evening is improbable, but it certainly feels that way. I say what I'm thinking.

'It's going to be amazing. Everything you paint ... touches me. I noticed it in the Ateneum too. I liked the waterlilies in the French pond. I liked the Finnish masters – I had no idea there were so many different ways to paint death, sorrow and misery, and in such an array of melancholy colours. But I didn't love them. But you ... When I saw your work, I mean, your paintings ... I loved ... love ... you.'

I don't think I've had very much to drink, but I feel dizzy, I'm sweating, saying things I don't mean to say, and by now I firmly believe that the substantial financial expenditure for this evening out and all the symptoms of mild ethanol poisoning are infinitely smaller than the joy it has bought me. It feels as though I am lost though I am sitting on the spot.

Perhaps Laura notices this. She props her elbows on the table, and her new face – which I find much harder to read than her previous face – is closer to mine than at any time throughout the evening. When she finally surprises me with a question, there's something new and unrecognisable about her voice too.

'And what were you thinking of doing after dinner?'

19

I've never kissed anyone on the commuter train before. It makes the journey seem much quicker than usual, there's no time to register the stops.

Of course, these are merely superficial observations that I make after the fact, once we are already sauntering through the Kannelmäki night.

In a strange way, my lips feel like they are ablaze; at the same time my body is both light as a feather and taut as an archer's bow. Laura is walking next to me – or, more precisely, she is walking with me. Her shoulder is right up against me. We are on our way to my home. And while I feel the most extraordinary sensations in my mind and body, I still remember to look around.

I'm looking out for an SUV. I look carefully at the parking spaces, the edges of the roads, the driveways. All the while, I spend a second or two examining every person, every figure that walks past. AK would stand out due to his size, I assume, and Lizard Man with his shoulder-less frame. But I can't see an SUV, I don't see the two men or anyone else who might threaten my life, tonight of all nights. With a view to our date, I decide this is a good sign.

I open the front door and we take the stairs in silence. We arrive at my apartment door, I hold it open for Laura and walk in behind her. I help her shrug off her coat, tell her where the bathroom is, then walk into the kitchen and give Schopenhauer his little evening meal. Once I have done that and I hear Laura flushing the toilet, washing her hands and opening the bathroom door, I no longer know what to do. But at this point, my body seems to know on my behalf. We kiss each other in the living room, bathed in moonlight, right in front of Gauss's equations. Naturally, I see the equations, but I don't feel the same steadfast, respectful admiration for and awe at them as before. Now they are only symbols, a moment later not even that.

Once in the bedroom, we undress. For my part, at least, this is a very disorganised affair, as if I didn't know how to remove items of clothing or in what order. Last of all, I take off my tie. The entire process is complicated by the fact that by now I am like the afore-mentioned archer's bow, taut and ready to fire. Undressing and finding a comfortable position on the bed are made all the more difficult because our lips and tongues are so tightly pressed against each other, as though they were glued together, as though we are unable to affect the matter one way or another. Our mouths feel like they are at boiling point, our kisses are a long, wet, molten-hot tongue wrestling match. This isn't as off-putting as it sounds. The sensation is very pleasant indeed. But it is nothing compared to the feel of Laura's bare skin against my own.

The feeling is intoxicating, yet at the same time very liberating. My hands know where they are supposed to go, what they are supposed to locate, how to act under the present circumstances. When our mouths momentarily separate, we let out sounds, the kind of sounds I would prefer not to make during the daytime. Then Laura moves sideways, gently pushes me onto my back. Her wild hair tickles my chest and stomach. The tickling causes shivers to run the length of my spine. After that, Laura's mouth and tongue find something new to wrestle with, and that something makes me forget I ever laid eyes on Gauss's equations. All I can see is my bedroom ceiling, illuminated by the strip of moonlight beaming in from the living room, and I can't even really see that.

The closer we get to black holes, the more time slows down and material condenses. Just as I am about to fall into the chasm beyond the event horizon, ready to experience the fate that awaits me inside the black hole, where I will be crushed into a speck smaller than a pinhead and merge with the endless darkness there,

I realise that I must wrench myself out of this ungovernable state and back towards gravity as we know it.

I tell Laura that I think a certain reciprocity is only right and proper. She might have giggled, I'm not sure. She might have said something too, but I don't understand what because part of me is still attached to her tongue. In any case, we swap roles.

In a way, I wish our waiter were here to witness this. Laura tastes better than any of the dishes or wines we sampled earlier this evening. And judging by the noises she is making, her fragmented half-sentences, I conclude that she too must feel a certain satisfaction that we didn't pick the sixteen-course menu after all; we would still be in the restaurant. Now the cost–benefit ratio is at a level with which both of us can hopefully be much happier.

After this, we press against each other again, and here my archer's bow tension comes into its own. I am able to operate at a satisfactory intensity. I'm not very experienced at what we are doing, but maybe I don't have to be. Laura's volume, the way she pulls me towards her, grips me with her fingers and sinks her nails into my various appendages, strongly indicates there is a significant probability that I am at least partially succeeding in my current task.

We perform a few variations on ways of experiencing each other. The changes are not very big, they seem more like corrective movements, the way you might add decimals to a calculation depending on how exactly you wish to express a number. Laura lets out a long, shrill, profound cry, like a simultaneous show of surrender and victory, while I notice a hitherto unfamiliar grunting emanating from my throat, a sound that for some unexplained physiological reason lasts much longer than the air in my lungs.

I can hear Laura breathing beside me. It feels as though there is something more real about it, more important than anything else right now. I don't know where all these new feelings have come from, these peculiar ideas and observations. At the same time, my skin is beginning to cool. The duvet is in a pile at the foot of the bed. I sit up slightly, find one corner of the duvet and pull it towards us.

'Do you think it's time to roll over and start snoring?' Laura asks.

Her question is perfectly reasonable. It's very late, and there is a direct correlation between an optimal sleeping position and our quality of sleep. But right now, that is of secondary importance. I don't want to catch a chill, I tell her, particularly in view of our business activities.

'That's one I've never heard before,' she says, rolls onto her side and props herself on one elbow. Her face is above mine, so close that again I can feel its glow. She smiles. 'But you don't look like you're about to ask me to stay the night.'

'The commuter trains aren't running at the moment, so you'll save a considerable amount of money if you stay here until morning,' I say, and it all feels wrong. Of course, it's true and it would be the sensible thing to do, but it doesn't express what I'm really feeling or what I want to say. I look at Laura. 'There's nothing I want more right now than for you to stay here next to me, so that I can ... sense you.'

The words come from somewhere unusual. They are the result of neither critical thinking nor computational processes, but all the same these are the words I want to say. It's probably best to say words like this lying on my back, I think suddenly, because they bring about that same dizzying sensation that I have been suffering from of late. Laura smiles, snuggles closer.

'It's just as well I asked Johanna to watch Tuuli tonight,' she whispers. 'I was hoping you'd say something like that.'

20

There isn't a cloud in the sky, the placid air is full of September bite, and the morning sun is atypically generous for the time of year. I can feel the warmth on the left of my face as I walk from the bus stop towards the adventure park. The morning feels flawless in every way, as though it too has experienced something irrevocable, a crucial sea-change from its last attempt. Naturally, today I see everything through some kind of filter; I realise that. It's as though I am slightly outside my own body, and the feeling is both elating and nerve-wracking. It fills my chest with prowess and something I might even call happiness. But at the same time, it feels as though I have laid myself bare, vulnerable to something as yet undefined, as though I have reached a hand into the darkness without knowing what it is I expect to find.

The overall feeling is jubilant nonetheless, as though I have won a secret competition, and the only people who know about it are those who received a secret invitation. Something like that. These thoughts are hard to control or guide. They are different from my normal thoughts; in fact, they are not really thoughts at all, more like peculiar spurts of energy, flashes, gentle bolts of lightning. I walk quickly in long, light steps. I think about how my concept of a date has changed most fundamentally. Though, naturally, only in certain respects. Yes, I want to go on another date, but only with Laura Helanto. Otherwise, my notion of dates remains the same: I wouldn't attempt to recreate the intimacy of last night with just anyone. To me, that still seems like playing with low odds.

I am very late by the time I reach the edge of the adventure-park car park, but it doesn't matter. I have a new-found strength, I'll make up the...

A cold wind whips through my shirt and jacket.

I feel my tie tightening though I haven't touched it. I'm sure that even the blue of the sky loses some of its brightness, that the only cloud locates the sun and purposely obscures it.

Nothing darkens a morning like the sight of a police inspector.

Osmala is standing almost diametrically in the middle of the car park, right at the spot where a large YouMeFun flag would normally be fluttering in the wind. Of course, it isn't fluttering because, to my understanding, it is still in the laundry after the flagpole came down, and the new flagpole hasn't arrived yet. And Osmala has already clocked me. He waves. I wave back and walk towards him.

Standing in the middle of the car park in his grey blazer and badly fitting light jeans, he blends in with the surroundings about as well as the Easter Island statues. By that, I don't mean that nobody knows where he came from or who hewed him in rock, but there's a certain statuesque austerity and mystery about him. The chilly morning has pinched his ears and the end of his nose, leaving them fire-engine red. They make for a surprisingly refreshing detail in his otherwise grey and angular features.

'The flagpole has fallen over,' he states once I am within earshot.

The information is wholly redundant: I am the owner of this adventure park, and Osmala knows it.

'I know,' I reply. 'We've just ordered a new one.'

Osmala stares at what is left of the flagpole, scrutinises it for a long time. Then he slowly turns, running his eyes across the car park, and rotates through 360 degrees.

'It didn't fall over by itself,' he says eventually. 'Look at the break; you can tell from the angle. There's a dent and an impact mark. It would be hard to hit something like this by accident. Even for someone who finds reverse parking a more complicated affair than most.'

'We've chosen a new one and...' I pause.

'Who knocked it over?' Osmala asks.

'I don't know,' I say, honestly.

'Isn't it on the security cameras?'

I tell him this part of the car park is in a blind spot, due to a faulty camera that was badly installed. The journey from the road to this particular spot is right in the middle of the blind spot. Either Osmala looks pensive or he's pretending to look pensive. Judging by the shade of red on his nose and ears, I assume he has been waiting for my arrival for some time.

'Can you think of anyone who might want to knock down your flagpole?' he asks.

'No, I can't.'

'You don't think this is some kind of message?'

'A message?'

'Someone who wants to remind you of something?' he suggests.

I shake my head and look at the metallic stump.

'This doesn't remind me of anything,' I say – and it's true. Like Osmala, I've wondered whether there might be a message implied in the felling of the flagpole, but if there is, I'm unable to read it. Because, ultimately, knocking down a flagpole isn't particularly sensible.

'Do you remember that photo I showed you?' Osmala asks.

I tell him I do.

'Could he have been involved in vandalising the flagpole?'

Only if he climbed out of the freezer, walked into the car park, put his foot on the gas, knocked over the flagpole and returned to the freezer afterwards, I think to myself.

'I don't know,' I say. 'I think it's highly unlikely.'

'What makes you say that?'

'It just … Well, you told me the man's a professional criminal. This looks more like an amateur job to me.'

I hear my own words as if someone else has said them, and I realise that is precisely what has happened. On the one hand, the flagpole was damaged on purpose, but in many ways its demise was something of a DIY job. All of a sudden, the matter is crystal clear.

'But I'm not here because of the flagpole,' he says.

This is Osmala's style, that much I've learned. Rapid changes of tack, trying to catch people off guard. I know how I need to respond.

'Is there any new information about my brother's death?'

'Not to my knowledge,' he says, and doesn't appear the slightest bit confused by my conversational attempt to switch lanes. 'It was a fairly clear-cut case, if you'll pardon the phrase. How well do you know your staff?'

'I've only been at the adventure park since—'

'Of course,' Osmala nods, then continues. 'In such a short time, it's hard to really get to know anyone, to become intimately acquainted with them, if you will.'

I say nothing. Now Osmala is scrutinising me with the same keen interest that a moment ago he reserved for the flagpole stump.

'But did your brother ever speak about the members of staff? Did he ever tell you anything about who he hired, ever comment on how the hiring process worked?'

'No,' I say, again truthfully. 'We didn't speak about that ... either.'

'And what about you?'

'What about me?'

'Have you brought up the matter with them? Have you had, say, performance appraisals with the staff and got to know them that way? This type of leadership approach is very popular, I understand.'

'I really haven't had time ... Perhaps once I've familiarised myself with—'

'Exactly,' Osmala nods. 'Participatory leadership, they call it – boss and employees sitting down together, talking, letting one another speak and be heard, opening up, talking about their lives and needs. So I've heard.'

There's something very odd about Osmala's tone of voice. We're standing in the middle of an enormous car park, there beneath the clear, open sky, and still I feel as though I'm in a very small, badly ventilated room. One with glass walls, perhaps.

'I'm running a bit late,' I say, and take a cautious step towards the entrance to the adventure park. 'If it's all the same...'

'Duty calls.' Osmala nods and waves a hand. 'By all means.'

His gesture looks as though he is showing me the way to the front door.

21

The barn where the man was hanged is red and large and stands clearly apart from the other buildings on the farm. From my perspective, one positive factor is that the forest extends almost right up to the southern side of the barn. Furthermore, due to the location of the sun, the forest is currently shady and protected. I am slightly out of breath after the long, brisk walk, and I'm still not entirely sure what it is I have to do next. A strip of woodland a few metres wide is all that separates me from a stretch of open land; from there, it is about fifteen metres to the end of the barn. Around the corner, in the middle of the building, is a door, left just open enough for a cat or a dog to pass through. Or a young piglet. Or a slim man, his body slightly elongated from the noose. I catch my breath, lean my shoulder against an old spruce and try to gather my thoughts. There are certainly plenty to gather.

The forest smells of autumn.

As contradictory as it sounds, given the circumstances, the last few days have been the happiest of my life. That sleepless night that Laura spent with me lit a fire within me, a fire I didn't even know existed until now. And the fire hasn't confined itself to my inner world. By that, I don't mean I have suddenly turned into the smooth-talking touchy-feely type like Perttilä, or that I am constantly flexing my biceps and back muscles like Kristian. I have simply noticed that I speak in a slightly different way, I move differently. Quite simply, I have more certainty about things. And every time I see Laura, that certainty, that fire – they nurture and warm each other.

Laura has been painting her murals at an increased pace. Every time I walk past the walls she is working on, I am bewildered and

beguiled. And every time, I have to pull myself away. Not that
Laura is keeping me; she is so focussed on her painting that
sometimes she even forgets to respond to my greetings.

I draw the forest fragrance deep into my lungs, bring myself
back to my location behind the barn, to the cool of the autumn
afternoon, to what I am doing, and why.

The adventure park's financial affairs are not what they should
be.

The bank has essentially awarded all the loans that the balance
sheet will allow. The park's revenue is at a decent level, but that's
still not enough. Money is a growing problem.

And naturally it's not the only problem.

I will have to do something about the CCTV footage.
Thankfully, footage over a week old is automatically deleted, and
Esa doesn't routinely go through the tapes without good reason.
The chase and my act of self-defence with the rabbit's ear have long
since disappeared into the ether. To my knowledge, Esa hasn't
watched the videos showing me hiding the body in the freezer
either. I would have noticed this in his behaviour as we sat in the
thick, gaseous environment of the control room and he explained
which cameras cover which areas of the park. He did ask why I
was interested in the tapes. I gave him an honest answer: I am
concerned about the park's security.

Kristian approached me again about the general managership,
but this time his approach had changed. It was no longer as
aggressive or impatient as before. Now there was a smile that,
though it looked forced, was broad and revealed his astonishingly
white teeth. Kristian told me he had found courses that were
fantastic and *mind-blowing*. Moreover, he looked strikingly
different in a smart, light-blue shirt. We didn't have time to get
into details – he told me he would get back to me once he had
talked to his mentor, whatever that meant – because his phone
rang, interrupting us, and besides, I had to continue my discussion
with Minttu K.

The scent of gin, Mynthon pastilles and Pall Malls enveloping Minttu K grows stronger by the day. With the blinds closed, disco music blaring and its bar-like spotlights, her office is like a nightclub. In the mornings, her voice is so rasping that it could sand down a tall spruce tree. Needless to say, she wants to increase the marketing budget again. I wonder – out loud – where our last marketing investment has disappeared to, as only a single, measly box of posters and flyers advertising the park's banking operations has ever materialised. Minttu K says I clearly don't know anything about long-term branding strategies, key target demographics and influencer interaction. This matter, too, is still unresolved.

Another unresolved matter is that of the freezer in the café. Johanna watches over the café as if it were her own. In a way, it *is* hers, and in other circumstances this would be a good thing. Our customers seem more than happy with the quality and quantity of our food and pastries. I too have been very content with the hearty ham-and-cheese sandwiches I've eaten there. But what I saw there last time I picked up a sandwich somewhat complicated matters. Padlocks have appeared on all the freezers. Johanna said it's about ice cream going to waste: in addition to the occasional bit of shoplifting, she says that opening and shutting the freezer lids unnecessarily heats up the contents. Things that are frozen need to stay frozen.

And on top of all this is Lizard Man's demand for fifty thousand euros.

What I need is a time out. And that's why I am here. My decision is based on purely mathematical reasoning.

Whenever I encounter a problem in the later stages of a complicated calculation, I return to what is most important, that is, the original problem. It's pointless trying to solve an individual problem, if the core of the problem is still unresolved and if it is obvious that this core contains the key to the entire problem.

And that is ultimately the reason for arriving under the cover of the trees. I didn't want to take the long path up to the farm only to come face to face with Lizard Man. I can't see the SUV anywhere. He isn't here. But who is here? I haven't seen any signs of movement in the yard. The house is a two-storey prefabricated building, light yellow and built in imitation of a traditional farmhouse. The white door of the garage is closed.

I make my move.

I walk from the forest into the yard, and approach the house and porch, and I'm not entirely sure what it is I can smell in the air. Of course, there is the damp forest, rustling in the north-easterly wind, the fields opening out on the other side, but there's something sweet too. I take the steps up to the porch, see the doorbell on the wall, and just as I am about to press my forefinger against the white, round button, something startles me. I instinctively back away towards the edge of the porch, almost falling over it.

The door starts opening by itself. Things like that don't just happen. I hear a voice from inside.

'Henri, come on in.'

The fresh cinnamon buns smell just the way I remember from cafés and bakeries. We sit down at a sturdy wooden dining table. In the middle of the table is a pile of cinnamon buns, one of them on a plate next to my porcelain coffee cup. Sitting across the table is a man, taller than me, his broad, spade-like face slightly reddened.

'I'm been trying out a new recipe,' he says. 'But I think the biggest difference is that I've started using only organic flour. It really affects the taste. Some people say they can't tell the difference, that it doesn't matter what flour you use, but I vigorously disagree. It's organic flour or nothing. What do you think?'

The big man talks about baking in the same voice with which

he hands out death sentences. There's no point asking how he knew I was walking towards the house or the exact moment I arrived at the door. He knew.

I pick up the bun and take a bite. An idyllic rustic landscape of fields and forest opens up in the window to the side. The bun is soft, warm, it melts in the mouth. I chew under his watchful eye. Once I have swallowed my mouthful, I tell him the buns are a towering success.

'And the organic flour?'

I don't need to think about this for long.

'Organic flour or nothing,' I say.

'A few more little secrets,' he says. 'A slightly shorter baking time and slightly more butter. It takes courage to leave the dough a bit raw in the middle. And the cinnamon should be fresh. Eat, eat, eat.'

I eat. A black pistol in his resting right hand lends a certain added motivation to the big man's request. The cinnamon bun is large; it's a lot of cake. I am about to stop, but the big man indicates with a flick of the wrist and his pistol that I should continue chewing. And so I find myself in a fake farmhouse in the middle of the southern Finnish countryside, stuffing my face at gunpoint with a half-kilo cinnamon bun, the size of two fists.

We don't speak. Of course, I can't speak as my mouth is full and my jaws are chomping, but the big man is silent too. The small black hole in the muzzle of the pistol is pointing right at my chest. All I can hear is the sound of my own eating. After what seems like an eternity, I finally swallow the last morsel of bun and wipe my mouth. We look at each other.

'Well?' he asks.

'Delicious,' I say, thinking I should probably attempt to use the correct terminology. 'Just the right oven temperature, the texture is buttery and creamy, and the organic flour ties everything together perfectly.'

The big man looks at me as he might an old fish.

'I mean, you must want to say something, as you've come all the way out here.'

'Right,' I nod.

That is indeed why I have come. Either I will be taken into the red barn or to Lizard Man's favourite pond, or I will be able to walk the three kilometres back to the bus stop on my own two feet.

'I have a problem with the mid-level staff,' I say, trying to watch the big man's face, to gauge his reaction one way or another. 'It's a problem that has a detrimental impact on what you and I have agreed.'

'By mid-level, you mean…'

'I don't know his name. Last time, I came here in his SUV. His friend, the tyrannosaurus, goes by AK.'

The big man laughs. The laugh is short and is over quickly. His eyes are a shade somewhere between blue and grey; they are like two scratches, as though he has been squinting for years and eventually the squint got the better of him. I take a deep breath. I tell him how I got into the SUV, how my face ended up providing a seat for a naked woman and eventually – and most importantly – how the big man's employee wants fifty thousand euros of the money that by rights belongs to the great baker himself. I leave out the bit about the baker, but other than that I tell him everything just as it happened.

After that, we sit in silence again. I hope the silence doesn't mean I will soon have to eat more cinnamon buns. I can't do it. My stomach is so full of sugar, butter and the aforementioned organic flour that it aches.

'She sat on your face?'

'Technically, it wasn't what I'd call sitting,' I say. 'She just … lowered herself. For a short time. As though she had hopped on a bicycle saddle, but after a few seconds grew tired of it and hopped off again.'

The big man thinks about this for a moment.

'That'll perk you up,' he says. It sounds as though he is speaking more to himself than to me. 'All this baking. Buns, buns, buns. It would make a nice change.'

'I didn't find it particularly stimulating,' I say, keen to steer the conversation back on track. 'And fifty thousand euros is—'

'I got that bit,' the big man interrupts me; he is his old self again. Well, the self that I have previously encountered. He sits up straighter in his chair, pointing the pistol at me all the while.

'Do you have fifty thousand? Extra?'

'What?' I ask. 'Absolutely not.'

'How is the bank doing?'

'It's too early to say precisely,' I reply. 'Where we have exceeded all expectations is in the number of loans granted.'

'So, money is flowing out but it's not coming back in.'

The big man's voice is frightening now, I think. Frightening in the sense that it remains perfectly neutral as he states something that goes against his financial interests.

'At this stage, that is to be expected,' I say, honestly. 'Getting operations under way is—'

'Has anybody paid back their loan?'

There is only one answer to this question.

'No. But I didn't expect them to either. The first repayments are due next week.'

'What about the amusement park?'

'Adventure park. It's in the black. Only just.'

'So, in a nutshell, the parent company is doing quite well, and the bank has got off to a promising start?'

'That's a fair assessment of the current situation,' I say. That's my assessment too.

But there's a tone to this conversation that I don't fully understand, something that doesn't quite fit. In front of me is an investor whose capital is dwindling and whose immediate future involves only more and more risk, but who doesn't look the least bit worried about it. Be that as it may, I don't have time to sit around pondering the matter. I still have to take care of—

'As for the mid-level staff,' he interrupts my train of thought. 'Let's just say, I'll look into it.'

'What does that mean?'

'If you don't have fifty thousand euros, how are you going to pay him fifty thousand euros?'

'I can't.'

'And what happens then?'

'He'll show those photographs to you and...'

I am about to say Laura, but she has nothing to do with the photographs, with this situation or this man.

'...And you've already seen them, in a way,' I continue. 'So there's nothing with which to blackmail me.'

'I intend to tell him that.'

I am astonished. Was everything really this simple? Then it dawns on me.

'What happens then?' I ask.

'*Que sera sera*, what must happen will happen,' he says. 'The stronger man will survive. And as you've learned today, you have to eat what's in front of you.'

🐇

The big man doesn't offer me a lift and I don't ask for one. First I walk one and a half kilometres along the dirt track, then another one and a half along the cracked cycle path running alongside the main road. Evening draws in, darkening the afternoon, the trees have grown tight against the sky. I don't have my phone with me; I deliberately left it at the adventure park. It's a strange feeling, as though contact with the outside world has been severed outright. But right now, that suits me perfectly. I need to think. Or, more to the point – a point I only realise once I am on the bus and the gloomy forests and ever-brightening, intensifying suburbs swirl endlessly behind the window – I think about everything I still need to calculate.

22

Laura is painting her fourth wall on the eastern side of the adventure park. She is moving around in front of the wall like a boxer, stepping back then returning to the wall for another round of jabs and punches. The children are screaming, the smell of paint blends with the scent of meatloaf wafting in from the Curly Cake.

Time passes as I make a variety of plans. Sometimes I try to decide what to do about Lizard Man, other times I try to find a mathematical path to guide me through everything, but I can't seem to find the kind of clarity I need. With one exception. I know Lizard Man is following me, biding his time, waiting for the moment to strike. I know he is near me, though I have no empirical evidence to prove it.

Everything moves as if on fast forward.

Time passes.

Although, time never does anything else. This is a one-way street. In one of the definitions of time that I have read somewhere – the continuous and essentially irrevocable progression of existence and events from the past to the future via the present moment – my attention is drawn to the word 'irrevocable'. For this reason alone, time should come with a warning label.

I find myself getting lost in these kinds of thoughts more and more. And no matter how many calculations I perform, it all feels pointless. Meanwhile, I've noticed there are problems with my calculations. Or, if not problems *per se*, then at least a sense of slowness, a lack of focus and general sluggishness. Such things are new to me and very strange indeed.

I stand behind Laura, but I don't know why I can't bring myself to say anything. She is working on the de Lempicka wall.

'Hi,' I finally stammer.

Laura turns quickly, she looks a little surprised. I try to behave the way we have behaved before: I lean towards her an inkling, ready to hug her and give her a kiss. But she doesn't lean towards me. Our kiss is awkward, a dry peck on the cheek. Even the hug becomes my responsibility, and I realise that one-way hugging is neither natural nor particularly invigorating.

'I've asked the cleaners to give the hall a thorough going-over next week,' she says. 'There was another surprise in Caper Castle, the slides in the Big Dipper smell of stale milk. They'll be scoured thoroughly.'

Her tone is suddenly very matter-of-fact. She looks first at Caper Castle, then the Big Dipper, but doesn't so much as glance at me.

'Good,' I say automatically.

'We'll clean the Doughnut too,' she continues, and I realise she sounds the same as she did on our first day working together. 'The walls are so sticky in places that the children might get stuck.'

'Thank you,' I say, suddenly almost on autopilot. 'Thank you for looking after the park.'

'That's my job,' she says.

'Right,' I say.

Then neither of us speaks for a while. A cold knife slashes my stomach. I feel detached from my body, as though there is nothing holding me down. It's not a very pleasant sensation.

'I wondered if, later on, we might—'

'I'll be here all evening,' says Laura, and by now she has turned fully to face the wall. 'Johanna is taking Tuuli to the cinema. I need to get this section finished.'

'Perhaps after that...'

'And I have an early start tomorrow.'

'Maybe tomorrow...'

'And Tuuli has her aerobics class in the evening.'

And with that she starts painting again. Her movements are

quick and precise; Laura clearly knows what she is doing. I am still standing near her, but it feels as though I am drifting further and further from her, as if sucked away by the sea or into outer space.

'I'm going to have my hands full these next few days...' she says and glances behind her, though not in my direction. I see her face, her lips. When was the last time we kissed? I won't ask her. Laura returns to her painting and I stand on the spot for a moment. It's as though an icy wind is blowing through the hall. My phone rings. I have to go. For some reason, leaving feels physically challenging. But I leave all the same.

'Bye then,' I say.

Laura turns, though she certainly does not spin right round. Her gaze brushes across me.

'Bye,' she says curtly, and it sounds like the same tone of voice someone might use when leaving a supermarket.

🐰

Later that day, after the park has closed its doors, I walk around the hall and look at Laura's paintings. I am alone. I can smell the fresh paint, and there's a strange pain in my gut. At first, I imagine it must be caused by the strong smell of paint, but I soon realise this is not the case. The walls are beautiful, but as I look at them something starts gnawing at my insides, a new, nagging uncertainty that grows with every minute and eventually feels like the cold grip of rats' teeth.

It is so late that the bus I would normally take to the train station has already stopped for the night. I have to walk over a kilometre to the next stop. There is no traffic. It is late, and in this part of town the last shops close at ten o'clock. That was an hour ago. The cycle path is completely empty in both directions. A narrow strip of earth separates the cycle path from the road, and as the landscape is still and deserted, it feels as though I could walk right down the middle of the road. It wouldn't shorten my journey, and it would represent a significant risk with regard to road safety, so obviously this wouldn't be a sensible course of action. But as has happened so often lately, strange thoughts like this fly through my mind, like darting, unknown birds: they appear out of nowhere, flap their wings once or twice, and then they are gone.

The cycle path starts to tilt downwards, and I see a worksite up ahead. An intersection and an underpass beneath the highway are under construction. A lot of earth has been dug out and moved to the side. In some places there are piles of mud, in others potholes filled with water. I am walking beneath a streetlamp, at the brightest point of its fluorescent light, when I hear it. The sound of a motor. I notice it because I hear it differently from the cars on the highway. The sound hits my ears from ever so slightly the wrong direction. I turn and see a car moving at high speed.

The car – now with only one person inside – is driving along the cycle path, and it's heading right towards me.

A lot can happen in a few seconds.

Of course, I can't calculate everything precisely, but I know straight away that if a vehicle weighing a thousand kilograms is travelling at a hundred kilometres an hour, it represents the same scale of risk to humans as a hammer to a mosquito. There is only enough time to move in one direction.

I leap to my right and dive behind a grassy knoll on the embankment. The knoll is in fact part of the construction site. I estimate the height of the knoll at around forty centimetres, at an angle of around forty degrees. That should be enough.

The car follows me to the embankment, its front wheel hits the knoll. The motor howls, the tyre rises up from the ground. I lie flat against the ground, as though trying to burrow my way into the earth. I feel the tyre scrape across my back as the car flies above me. My spine feels as though it might snap in two, the skin on my back as though it will be torn off. The sound is like a jet engine flying directly overhead. And right now, that's all that matters: that the car remains over my head.

Once the car has passed me, I turn my head.

Straight away, I see something has happened to the car. The relation of the tyre to the knoll is in direct correlation to the car's speed and mass. There's no need for any calculations here either; the result is right in front of me.

The car jolts, then flips onto its roof and slides ahead at breakneck speed. It even seems to accelerate. The car glides like an enormous, fantastical sled – all the way to the construction site. And there it comes to a halt with such power and precision, it's as though that's what it was aiming for all along.

The pit fits the car almost exactly.

The roof of the car splashes down into the pit and the car comes to an abrupt halt as though held in place by a giant magnet. I get up – first onto all fours, then my knees, and finally my feet – and try to comprehend what I see. The car's motor has stopped, the lights have gone out. Everything is just as quiet as a moment ago.

In fact, everything is like it was a moment ago.

Except that, fifty metres ahead, is a car parked upside-down, like a giant beetle flipped on its back and pushed down into a puddle.

My back is burning, both inside and out. My heart is beating so frantically that I have to swallow and force myself to breathe. For a moment, all I can do is stand on the spot until, mustering my force of will, I realise I am alive and that the present danger is over. All the while I stare at the car, unable to process what I see.

I run up to the car. It happens instinctively. My legs ache, stiff with the after-effects of the adrenaline. The closer I get to the car, the better I appreciate how perfectly the pit fits the breadth and width of the cabin. There's a roughly twenty-five-centimetre gap on either side, and at the ends there's even less. I approach the edge of the pit and look down. At first, I can't quite work out what it is I see beneath the water, but then I understand.

An arm dressed in a black tracksuit with three stripes along the sleeve is shaking a fist at me.

AK is behind the wheel.

The driver's door won't open, obviously. The pit is deep and narrow, and it is flooding quickly. Water gushes across the sharp edges of the pit. AK is stuck inside the car, the airbag and seatbelt holding him firmly in place. He is still making protestations at me. I think he's been doing it ever since the first time he tried to run me over.

His fist punches through the water one last time.

Then it disappears into the depths of the pit, beyond the reach of the streetlights.

I walk around the car and can't see any other passengers; AK is alone in the BMW. Then I look around. No traffic, not a single person, just a long, wide skid mark, first on the cycle path, then through the gravel, and right at the end of the mark, like the dot above an i, is the upside-down wreckage of the car.

My back hurts so much that I'll either have to lie down or start moving. I consider this for a moment. I don't see how AK, or I, or anyone else would benefit from me lying down next to the pit.

I take a few deep breaths and start walking.

23

'Kid's broken a leg.'

Esa's expression is pained, as though the broken leg belongs to him. He runs up to me and has to catch his breath. His legs seem to be working fine.

In my hand is a broken step from Caper Castle. I place it on the floor and follow him back into the hall. I have just arrived at work – slightly late, again – after a night of barely any sleep, and during the few fragments of sleep I managed to get, my mind was plagued with nightmarish scenarios about being chased by expensive German cars and large angry fists rising up from construction pits filled with water. My back hurts with each step, as though someone were battering it with a club again and again. But, nonetheless, today I have decided to concentrate on physical work, for two reasons. First is the hope that this might focus my thoughts. The second is more practical: our maintenance man Kristian is yet again standing in for Venla at the ticket office and doesn't have time to fix the broken step.

'What happened?' I ask, struggling to keep up with Esa.

'Breakdown of surveillance protocols, I'm afraid,' he replies. 'This little commando climbed on top of the wall with the Trombone Cannons and fell off. Probably trying to eliminate the enemy with superior fire power. Admirable boy-scout prepared-ness, but back-up was AWOL.'

'Have you called an ambulance?'

'Yes,' says Esa. 'But I told them there was no rush.'

I'm sure I must have misheard. The hall is packed with screaming, running customers brimming with the strength of a new morning.

'What?'

Esa repeats himself, and I hear the same thing again.

'Why, for god's sake?'

'I performed a quick field bandage,' he says. 'The casualty's mother and father provided first-aid assistance too.'

After the Banana Mirror, we take a sharp left turn and arrive in the area where parents can wait and relax. We find the correct booth, and I see the child lying on one of the sofas. In light of everything that has happened, the child, a boy, seems perfectly fine – except for the scare and his copious weepy tears. As for the parents...

'Who is responsible for this?' the father bellows as he leaps to his feet. He is around my age with short, gleaming, dark hair combed to the side in an austere right-hand parting. He is wearing a dark-blue sweater with a logo on its chest showing a silhouetted figure playing polo. The child's mother has long blonde hair and a white turtle-necked sweater in which the same silhouetted figure continues the same endless polo stroke. Her face is red, her eyes too. She looks agitated.

'Responsible for what?' I ask sincerely.

'Julius's leg,' says the father, and points at the boy's leg.

Credit where credit's due, Esa has done a good job. The bandages are neatly tied around the leg, and beneath them, serving as a splint, is a straight section of one of the trombone rifles.

'If Julius is a minor – and it looks like he is,' I begin. 'Then I assume his parents are responsible for him and his leg...'

The father shakes his head as though he has just heard the most unfathomable statement ever made.

'I want to see the manager,' he says.

'I am the manager,' I reply.

'And I want the police here too,' he informs me.

'The police just left,' Esa says before I have a chance to respond. I turn around.

'What?' the father and I ask in tandem.

'The detective that was here talking to you before...' says Esa. From the position of his head and his tone of voice, I can tell he is addressing these words to me. I also realise I have to stop him in his tracks. Osmala, I think instantly. He's been here this morning. He must already know about the drowning incident on the cycle path.

'Thank you, Esa,' I say, and turn my attention back to Julius's mother and father. 'What's most important is that Julius is just fine.'

'But he isn't just fine, is he?' his mother shrieks.

'It's only a fracture,' I say.

'How can you say such a thing?' she asks.

'It's a fact,' I say – again sincerely. 'He is not in any mortal danger.'

'Mortal danger?' the father roars. 'You mean Julius might have died?'

'Julius, you, me,' I say, both in reference to my recent experiences and leaning on the principles of actuarial mathematics. 'Anybody could die anywhere. It's more likely in some circumstances than others, but the fact remains that it can happen anywhere to anybody at any time.'

Once I have reached the end of my sentence, three things happen simultaneously. Despite the fact that I know I am completely, unquestionably, factually correct, I feel as though I have said something I shouldn't have. Secondly, the father seems to be trembling, and the ruddiness of the mother's cheeks seems to deepen further. Esa adjusts Julius's bandages. Where is the ambulance? I think. For a moment, nobody says a word, then everything explodes at once.

'This pig wants Julius to die right here in this park,' the father hollers. 'I'm going to sue your ass and take your poxy park to court. I'm calling my lawyer right this minute.'

The father takes out his phone but doesn't call anyone. The mother is kneeling next to Julius, stroking his hair.

'If he's left with any kind of trauma...'

'He only took a hit in the leg, ma'am,' says Esa.

The mother bursts into tears.

'You'll be hearing from us, you con artist,' the father growls.

Now I am beginning to get agitated. That allegation is unfair and wholly unsubstantiated.

'I am not a con artist,' I say.

'Oh yeah?' the father shouts and gestures towards the signage by the entrance. 'Is this what you call fun and games for all the fucking family?'

'We also inform customers about the rules,' I explain. 'And we expressly forbid climbing on top of the rides.'

'Julius is a free spirit, aren't you, darling?' the mother says, her voice bleary with tears.

'You don't get to tell me or my kid what we can and can't do,' says the father. By now his chest is almost touching mine.

'It seems I have to,' I say. 'The rules apply to everyone equally. That's the basic principle of rules. Otherwise we'd have anarchy, and that's a demonstrably worse option.'

The father is about to open his mouth and raise his right hand when I see a group of men dressed in white appear behind him. Without looking at us, they kneel down next to Julius.

Our attention moves to the men in white. They work quickly and precisely. There is nothing about the situation to increase their pulse by so much as an extra beat.

A moment later, Julius is carried out to the ambulance. He looks perfectly calm and happy. His parents huddle on both sides of him, and from their tones of voice I assume they are giving instructions to the paramedics and presumably already accusing them of professional malpractice.

Esa returns to his control room. I decide to forget about repairing the step in Caper Castle for a moment. Osmala's morning visit bothers me, but I don't know what I can do about it. Then I think, the least I can do is make sure he has left the park. Is his car still parked outside? I walk into the foyer, pass Kristian, who is on his phone, and move outside. I take a few steps beneath the cool blue sky and allow my eyes to pan across the car park from one side to the other. I don't think I can see Osmala's relatively new, deathly green Seat anywhere. The late autumn chill quickly works its way beneath my shirt, and the tie on top of my shirt doesn't provide much warmth either. The wind catches the tyre mark on my back. I look around one last time, then turn and walk back indoors.

🐇

Kristian ends his call as I approach the ticket office. He smiles, the collar of his blue uniform shirt like a pair of tectonic plates, large, stiff and magnificent. His cropped hair is spiked with gel.

'Fabulous day, isn't it?' he says.

'Hello,' I reply curtly as I don't have any superlatives to describe this day. 'I see Venla hasn't turned up again.'

I don't know why I am even asking. Maybe it's more about solving a mystery than asking as a concerned employer. I notice Kristian no longer seems embarrassed at the question.

'The key to success as a salesman is true dedication,' he says. 'You're not just selling milkshakes or a hoover or whatever, you're selling yourself. Success is a state of mind.'

Kristian smiles. Again. Perhaps he never stopped smiling. It takes a moment before I realise quite what has happened. My next thought is that I have created a monster. Kristian took me at my word. He really has taken those courses: the path to becoming the general manager is finally opening up.

'And I was thinking,' he continues before I have a chance to respond. 'Why don't we push these loans more aggressively? If I was in charge, it would be ABCD: Always Be Closing the Deal. We should push them, right?'

He gestures at a small stand propped on the end of the counter. The stand invites customers to avail themselves of a short-term pay-day loan at a sensible rate of interest. I take the stand and place it behind the counter, out of sight.

'We are not *pushing* anything right now,' I say. I note that my tone is rather harsh and, when I employ Kristian's jargon, almost mocking. It's hardly surprising. Someone has driven a car over me. Both literally and figuratively.

'Kristian,' I begin, now in a much more conciliatory tone, realising I have only one option left: I need to find my inner Perttilä and let it out, and I need to do this right now. 'The journey to deep, inner success is aligned with the development of positive team synergy, and from there it's only a short leap to optimal success in the mind-body-soul trinity. The solution is often a process of emotional transference, which in turn is symbiotically linked to the interaction frequency we use to bring about the best reciprocal default dynamics. I estimate there's still room for improvement and an element of collective adaptation on your journey towards a fully-fledged, personal awareness of your entre-preneurial self. On the other hand, this gives you a chance to explore other professional opportunities within the field of resource management. Learning about self-relevance isn't just a linear-psychological or a cumulative emotional learning curve, you know.'

We look each other in the eyes. I will not blink first. Eventually Kristian lowers his gaze and starts fidgeting. The front door opens, customers begin flowing into the adventure park and Kristian starts serving them.

24

On the way back to my office, I think about my encounter with Kristian, about what it really means, and I know all too well.

I'm putting everything off, stretching everything out. I know that we can talk about infinity in mathematical terms, but in this world and this reality, everything has a point beyond which it will not go. Everything has a breaking point. I can feel myself approaching that point. The feeling is all the more disconcerting because I can't work out what exactly is going on. Everything from the loans to the rabbit's ear is finely balanced, taut as a violin string, and right now I can't afford for anything to start fraying.

Upon reaching my door, I stop. At first I don't know why. Everything is exactly as I left it yesterday. I have tidied the room up and organised the things Juhani left behind, and I can see that every pile of papers is exactly where it should be. But still: something in this room has been moved, perhaps simply picked up and put back again, but the equilibrium has been disturbed. I've always noticed things like this. In a calculation a page long, if you change even a single number or symbol, the result is completely different. But in the following minute or minute and a half I can't work out what has changed, so I walk behind my desk and sit down.

A moment later, it feels as though I might never stand up again.

I don't know whether it's the fatigue. Maybe the metaphorical sled I am pulling has quite simply started to weigh too much. Maybe the combination of the debts, the struggle to get through them, the body in the freezer, the multiple attempts to murder me, the other body trapped in a car in a pool of rainwater, and my growing uncertainty about almost everything are too much to cope with. Still, I am an actuary, I remind myself, I am used to logic and predictability; in a word, to reason. But the thought is instantly followed by another, that I am an actuary with tyre marks on his back and a death sentence hanging over his head. And I know it was Lizard Man who sent AK to find me.

And though AK is currently revving his BMW along cycle paths in a higher plain of existence, Lizard Man's orders have yet to be carried out. I know he is close at hand. He's probably watching me right now. And for the moment at least I can't think what to do about him. I remember the big man's words all too well: *The stronger man will survive*. Right this minute I don't feel very strong.

But there is one thing that gives me strength. And hope.

Laura.

Maybe I've been misinterpreting her these last few days. Perhaps she just wants to concentrate on her work because, like me, she wants to do her paintings as well as possible, to give them everything she's got. If I'm trying to resolve an especially complicated conditional probability equation, I don't have time for minute-long French kisses either. Afterwards, by all means, as long as the person in question is appropriate and we have reached some form of consensus on the matter.

I can still feel our shared night on my skin. When the memory creeps up on me, the images in my mind are astonishingly physical. And I can't understand the logic of my thought processes in that the less I see of Laura, the more I think of her. It doesn't make sense. At the same time, I hear her saying all those things about me that nobody has ever said before. The phenomenon of remembering our conversations verbatim is not new to me. But now I don't find myself listening to our conversations and rewinding them merely to check particular facts, but to hear everything else that is there besides the words: the softness, the gentleness and something that tells me she sees me just the way I am and that she likes what she sees.

Maybe Laura really is just busy. She has a few walls and a daughter to take care of. All the same, my mind is filled with images of us waking up in the same IKEA bed, buying a shared apartment with a reasonable price tag per square metre and a sensible price-quality-location ratio, jetting off on a last-minute holiday somewhere where the sun burns down on bare rocks and the sea is a cobalt blue, walking hand in hand through the crisp autumn morning from the bus stop to the adventure park.

At the same time, I am reminded of the morning's events.

Schopenhauer appeared in the kitchen and stirred me in a manner I was not expecting.

He stretched the way he has stretched for years: pushed his back legs out as far as he could, arched his back, lowered himself into a forward stretch, then straightened up again and shook his legs. Then he started up a morning conversation the way he always has. And I realised that, just like his namesake, he has remained the same while I am the one who has changed. All I had to do was recall recent events, and I could see quite clearly that I have been behaving in ways in which I have never behaved before, felt things I have never felt before. My life had changed, and I quickly realised it had changed for good. Maybe. Schopenhauer, meanwhile, was still following his old script. I didn't bring the matter up. I stroked him and said I understood him. At the same time I wondered whether perhaps it is our very routines that reveal how much everything has changed.

I adjust my position in my chair, look at the time and make up my mind. I will speak to Laura today.

Perhaps these feelings are reciprocal after all. Amid all the uncertainty and confusion, it is good to have something bright and clear to focus on, like an exact calculation achieved through diligent, concentrated work.

I think of a ship without an anchor, then one with an anchor, and ask myself: when a storm whips up, which is better?

I switch on my computer and resolve to examine the room with fresh eyes later, when I notice movement in the corridor. Samppa is standing at my office door.

'Hiya,' he says.

'Hello,' I say, and I can hear from my own voice that I'm surprised to see him. Samppa has never before tried to strike up conversation with me. I'd assumed it must be because, with his nursery-teacher's education and youthful persona, he probably enjoys the kind of independence that is beyond most of the park's employees. He quickly glances over his shoulder, his silver earrings flash, then returns his eyes to me.

'Have you got five?'

'Yes,' I nod, once I work out what he means. 'Five minutes. Take a seat.'

Samppa sits down and starts organising the bracelets on his wrists. The colourful tattoos along his bare forearms dance here and there; I make out Mickey Mouse, some kind of angel, something resembling a Viking helmet. His name tag has six love hearts, one for each letter. This is the first time Samppa has set foot in my office – in fact, it's the first time the two of us have been alone together. I wait for him to get his bracelets, his jewellery and himself in order and tell me why he's here. But he doesn't say anything. He just sits there looking at me.

'Is everything alright?' he asks eventually.

'What do you mean?' I'm genuinely confused at his question.

'You look kind of stressed out,' he says, and raises his shoulders slightly. 'But I get it. Death shows how fragile we are.'

'Death?' I ask, and wonder how Samppa knows about the car accident at the cycle-path construction site.

'Your brother.'

'Yes, right,' I say, and hope I don't sound like someone whose brother's passing is a trivial event. 'Absolutely. It's been a … surprising and, as you say, fragile time.'

'That's another reason I wanted to wait,' he says, again without continuing his thought.

'And what is it you're waiting for?' I ask.

'I wanted to respect that fact that you've experienced a terrible loss and that it must be quite difficult to adapt to a new job. And I'm not the kind of guy who barges into new situations like a bull in a china shop or who always wants to be first in line for everything. I believe in the virtues of soft power.'

Another pause. This gives me a moment to think about what I know of Samppa's soft power. Very little, is the answer. I know I was relieved that he took care of the children's playgroups, the adventure corner and other activities without feeling he had to tell me about them. With hindsight, I suppose I automatically assumed that he is the only park employee who exclusively does the very thing he is paid to do. I don't know what it would be like to run a business with thousands of staff all wanting to do something other than what they are paid to do, but I know that juggling a business with only a handful of employees is already akin to solving the most complex theoretical mathematical conundrum.

This time I don't intend to help him end the pause. Perhaps Samppa realises this too.

'I've noticed that a lot of the park's staff have been given new opportunities these last few weeks,' he says. 'Which is a good thing. Learning new things gives us confidence, and an increase in self-confidence encourages us to try new things, which in turn leads to learning new skills. It's a positive cycle. You see it in children – and adults too. Esa has started talking about things other than the marine corps; Kristian is taking managerial courses; Laura is painting; Johanna is trying out new recipes. I've been following this development. This is great leadership. You have introduced a fresh new approach, really aired the place out. Everybody has found new facets to their work.'

Samppa pauses briefly.

'Almost everybody.'

Aired the place out. I try to dismiss the thought. I haven't been particularly aware of Esa or Johanna's positive cycles, but gradually I begin to understand what Samppa is saying. He wants something. It's only natural. Everybody seems to want something on top of what they already have.

'What do you have in mind?' I ask.

Samppa looks as though he is mentally weighing things up. The fingers of his right hand fiddle with the bracelets on his left wrist.

'A Kiddies' Day. Here in the park.'

I look at him. 'A Kiddies' Day?'

'Yes. In big letters. Maybe even a Kiddies' Week. But we can start with a day.'

'Isn't that the whole point of the park? That a day spent here is quite literally a Kiddies' Day?'

Samppa shakes his head.

'Immersion,' he says. 'Role reversal.'

Samppa holds another, now-familiar pause.

'I don't follow,' I say. I genuinely don't.

'This will take courage.'

'Very well.'

'You probably don't think of these things, sitting there in your manager's chair all day in peace and quiet, locked away from it all.'

I say nothing.

'Okay,' Samppa nods. 'For one day, or preferably a week, children are adults, adults are children. It's role reversal. And stepping into someone else's role – that's immersion. For one day, or preferably a week, the children get to make the rules, bake cakes, keep watch, even paint the walls if they like, and the grown-ups can play.'

I say nothing.

'Imagine,' he says. 'A child sitting there in your chair, a kid being boss for a day, or preferably a week.'

I take Samppa's advice and try to imagine this scenario. I imagine a child having a meeting with Lizard Man. A child rummaging in the freezer and discovering a frozen grown-up. A child in debt to the big man.

'You see?' he continues. 'The idea gets wilder the more you think about it!'

'True,' I say.

Samppa shifts in his chair, he sits up straighter, and the fingers fidgeting with his bracelets move all the more quickly.

'As far as I'm concerned, we could get this started very quickly. I've already designed some background material both for the kids and the grown-ups. Many adults find it surprisingly difficult to enter into their children's world. They have lost the ability to play. Of course, that's partly because they are frightened of—'

'No,' I say, aware that I'm interrupting him in full flow.

'No, what?'

'No,' I repeat, and pause. I can't tell him anything about what is really going on at the park or behind closed doors.

'No Kiddies' Day, at least not right now,' I say in as conciliatory a tone as I can muster.

There's an instant change in Samppa's body language. After all that enthusiasm, hitting a wall really hurts, I know that. His face starts to redden, and there's a gleam of annoyance in his eyes.

'Why not?'

'It's just ... not possible right now.'

Samppa stares at me as though I have personally offended him. And it seems I have.

'Painting the walls wasn't meant to be possible either,' he says.

'What's that got to do with it?'

'You're afraid of play, but you're not afraid of cavorting with criminals.'

'Excuse me?'

'Like many adults, you're afraid of playing—'

'Yes, I get that bit,' I say quickly. 'But what did you mean by criminals? Did those men turn up here at the park? Did they approach you?'

Samppa squints, as if to sharpen the image of me that is beginning to take shape.

'What men?' he asks. 'I'm talking about Laura.'

Naturally I don't know what it feels like to have a tower block collapse on top of you, but for a brief moment I get an inkling of the emotions that must engulf the ground floor half a second before everything hits. I say nothing and concentrate instead on staying seated in my chair and maintaining my expression and posture.

'Indeed,' is all I can muster.

'Of course, I don't mean that prison itself makes anyone suspect in some way,' Samppa continues, switches fidgety bracelet and, naturally, fidgety finger too. 'I really believe that people can change. Everybody deserves a second chance. That's why I came here to talk about a Kiddies' Day, or preferably a week, which will open up—'

'Let's return to your colleague,' I say, interrupting him. I know I'm on thin ice. I'm beside myself, but I try as hard as I can to make sure it doesn't show. Samppa clearly assumes I know something that wouldn't have occurred to me in a month of Sundays. 'This is all confidential. I assure you. I only have the best interests of the adventure park at heart.'

This isn't the whole truth, but as statements go, it is true. Samppa looks at me. This is a rematch of the staring competition I had with Kristian earlier. And I don't have any more options now than I did then: I must win. Samppa holds his longest pause thus far.

'Let's talk honestly,' he says eventually. 'There's the fact that when Juhani hired her, she kind of skipped the queue. I know this because I suggested someone for that position – an old college friend who has really great, innovative ideas about art education for children and adults, and he'd just graduated with a PhD in educational science. But then, completely out of the blue, Juhani hired Laura, a fine-arts graduate who, it turned out, had just come out of prison. It wasn't for murder or anything like that, but those were pretty serious financial improprieties, or whatever the term is: defaulting on debts, embezzlement, fraud, tax evasion – I'm not sure of everything but it was something like that. To be perfectly honest, I don't know how that qualifies anyone to work at an adventure park or how Juhani was able to justify the decision. Of course, Laura has a really artistic side, which is now blossoming brilliantly, it's a good, positive example to us all. And that's why I've come to you to talk about a Kiddies' Day, or preferably a week, because all the other staff except me are being allowed to realise their hopes and dreams—'

'Have you discussed this with Laura?' I ask, again interrupting him. I can't help myself: he talks the way a marathon runner runs: kilometre after kilometre, hour after hour at a steady speed, and right now I don't have the patience for it.

'Kiddies' Day?'

'Prison.'

Samppa looks surprised; the surprise looks genuine.

'I don't think I've ever seen a stare as cold or heard a voice as cold as when a man visiting the park with his children went up to Laura and said something like, hey, nice to see you got out. A few colleagues and I were standing nearby when it happened. And what she said to that man ... Wow, I'd rather not repeat it. It was chilling. And I suppose that day we learned that some topics of conversation are best left alone.'

'This man...' I ask, trying to remain interested but neutral, though inside I want to shake Samppa and force him to tell me everything, quickly, right this minute. 'What did he look like?'

'A kind of ... normal guy,' Samppa replies. 'Well, no. Maybe not that normal. At least, he probably wouldn't consider himself normal. He was a bit smug, a bit full of himself.'

After this, Samppa pauses again, and I realise I can't ask any further questions. I think I recognise Kimmo, but I don't know what relevance that might have. Besides, I need to get Samppa out of my office. I can feel the weight of the walls, the quickening crush of the floor and ceiling, my strength seeping away. Now I know the cause of my exhaustion and why it seems to be growing. It washes over me, surges from the darkness that has surrounded me all the while, though at times I've been blinded by the occasional ray of sunshine.

'About Kiddies' Day,' I say. 'I promise I'll give it very favourable consideration.'

'What does that mean?'

'It means I'll try to find a way we can make it happen.'

And I mean it. If I can find a way out of the park's problems, I will be only too happy to temporarily give up the general manager's chair to a six-year-old.

For the first time in our meeting, Samppa smiles.

'Like I said, you've been a breath of fresh air in this park,' he says. 'You've got the Midas touch. Everything you touch starts to bloom.'

25

The screams shatter my eardrums, split my ears. A group of children passes me on both sides. The hall seems more brightly lit than ever. Everything is garish, glaring, over-exposed, and therefore ugly. The children's squeals are like thousands of nails scraping down a blackboard. The smell of oven sausages coming from the café is reminiscent of a dog park when the snow melts. The steel hills of the Big Dipper glow ice cold and the carriages of the Komodo Locomotive, which usually feel as though they are travelling at a snail's pace, now look like a decent express service. The park's general commotion, the incessant sound, the irregular regularity of loud noises – everything has assumed a physical form, like blows coming from all directions, a weight that I feel in every part of my body.

Eventually I have to stop, and I realise this is a good thing. Laura is speaking to someone. The man is about my age, he is gesticulating with great gusto and pointing at Laura's walls. In every respect, he looks like a man who cannot believe his eyes. I understand him. I too am having difficulty believing what I see. I don't know if this is a painting world record, but something of that magnitude has happened.

The walls are finished. And they are astounding.

I step back a little and remain standing in the bridge-like area between the Trombone Cannons and the Doughnut. Several of the parents are leaning on the railings too, looking as though a day at the adventure park is perhaps not the most scintillating thing that has ever happened to them. Laura and the man are talking at length.

The man flits between pointing erratically at the different walls, folding his arms across his chest and nodding at whatever Laura is saying. Eventually she and the man shake hands. The man spins around a few times, his eyes find what they are looking for and he walks off in that direction. It's highly probable that the focus of his gaze is at least one of the infernally shrieking children.

As I approach her, Laura is wiping a white cloth across the indigo left-hand edge of the O'Keeffe wall. She has her back to me, she is dressed in black work trousers and a red T-shirt. Her bramble-bush hair is loose and wild. Perhaps she senses someone approaching, as she turns when I am only a few steps away. Her expression is one of contentment, pride even. But only for a moment. In a split second, everything changes.

'Hi,' she says.

'Hello,' I reply.

She glances first left, then right. She doesn't seem particularly thrilled to see me. Not at all.

'The walls are finished,' I say. 'Congratulations.'

'Just a few touches left. But ... thank you.'

All the kindness, the familiarity that I once heard in Laura's voice, is gone. Not to mention the warmth.

'Someone seemed to like them,' I say, thinking how best to proceed.

'Who?'

'That man ... just now ... the one who...'

'Yes, him, right, of course. A journalist from *Helsingin Sanomat*. He was here with his children and noticed the walls. He's coming back tomorrow to photograph them and do an interview for the paper.'

'That's wonderful.'

'I'll admit, it's a bit of a surprise.'

Laura looks me in the eyes, and I look back. Her face is neutral, expressionless. Though we are quite near each other, it's as though our previous connection is gone. It's hard to imagine that, only relatively recently, we were kissing on a commuter train – of all places.

'Was there something you wanted to ask?'

The question takes me by surprise.

'Actually' – I nod, though now I'm not so sure if there's any point to this conversation; or any conversation, for that matter – 'I don't know.'

'As you're there,' says Laura and glances in both directions as though she is crossing the road. 'Then maybe it's best if I ... There's something I'd like to say.'

The children's yells and the sounds of the adventure park are like a squalling sea behind us, as though we were standing on a wind-swept beach trying to make out what the other is saying.

'This isn't easy,' she begins. She twists the cloth in her fingers. 'I should have ... told you ... earlier.'

I feel a sudden rush of relief. Laura is finally talking about what made me so agitated in the first place. This is for the best; she can tell me in her own way, and I won't have to ask.

'This can't be easy,' I say and give her an encouraging nod. 'I truly understand.'

She seems somewhat surprised at my words. 'No, it's not. It's ... good to know you understand. You and I ... had a nice time.'

'A very nice time,' I add.

'Yes,' says Laura, but she does it in a quick, quiet way, the way you might say something just to get it over and done with. It makes me feel as though I ought to say something too. But now all I can think of is some kind of follow-up to my previous comment, something along the lines of 'a very, very, *very* nice time', but that feels wrong for a variety of reasons.

'But,' she continues. 'Sometimes *nice* just doesn't cut it. How should I put this: you and I ... I think we're on different paths.'

'Obviously,' I reply. 'You're an artist and I'm a mathematician, now managing an adventure—'

'No, that's not what I ... This isn't easy to say.'

There is definitely a new tone in her voice, as though some part of her is hurting, badly, but she doesn't want to show it, and now

I have the feeling I'm riding on a train hurtling towards something collapsed, most likely a tall bridge. The feeling is instinctive; until now I had no idea I was on any kind of train.

'I mean, at this point in my life and in your life,' she says. 'We're going in different directions. That's what I mean.'

She touches her glasses without actually moving them at all.

'Well, I should just spit it out,' she says, faster, her voice now somehow forced. 'What I'm trying to say is that ... what we had is over.'

I look at her. She still looks like the person I knew a minute ago. All I can do is say what I honestly think.

'I don't understand.'

Laura has turned away. I see a tear running down her cheek. 'I'm sorry.'

I feel another tower block come crashing down on top of me, and again the shrieks of the hall are unbearable. My mind does several things at once. I feel I've made an error in my calculations, a critical error. Everything that has happened between us – Monet, the dinner date, our conversations and my interpretation of those conversations, the extensive kissing on the train, a night of very thorough and balanced back-and-forth intimacy – added up to this. No matter which method I pursue, it doesn't seem logical; each time I calculate it, I end up with vastly different results. And most alarmingly, I appear to have lost the ability to proceed in any direction that might have seemed sensible just moments ago. I simply stand on the spot and watch another tear trickle down Laura's cheek.

'Over?' I say, though I'm not sure who to.

Laura nods and says nothing. Her lips and cheeks tremble almost imperceptibly.

I'm not sure how long we stand there opposite each other, but at some point we move at the same time, she turns towards her O'Keeffe, I start walking back to my office. I walk through the blaring hall, careful not to step on any of our clients, and eventually reach the office. I sit in my chair until closing time.

I lock up the park and switch off all the lights. Then I call a taxi to meet me at the front gates. This goes against my principles for two reasons: my monthly travel budget is carefully calculated, and this taxi journey will effectively ruin the figures, and besides, driving from door to door has a detrimental impact on my daily exercise. However, the arguments in favour of this ex tempore trip in a Mercedes Benz are compelling. Something has exploded inside me, leaving a lifeless crater behind.

26

On the morning of the laying of Juhani's urn, I wake before 06:00 a.m.

I have remained at home, but the last two and a half days have been spent in a fog. A thick, asphyxiating fog. What's more, I've noticed that most practical matters can be taken care of from the laptop on my kitchen table or my phone, even the upcoming renovations to the Big Dipper, which I address in back-and-forth emails with Kristian and the machinery retailers, the contractors and subcontractors. Kristian seems to rise to the challenge of the general managership at even the slightest opportunity. He does the right thing, he behaves the way you should when opportunities present themselves: he grabs them with both hands. And it's not his fault if my own prospects aren't all that attractive right now.

I lean against the sink; the kettle is bubbling and gurgling. I look out of the window; it is the time between dark and light, that time of day when you can see shapes in the landscape without knowing whether they are the contours of real, concrete objects or simply the product of your imagination. My laptop lies shut on the far side of the kitchen table as though it is radiating something toxic. It pushes me away, resists when I try to approach, creates a force field around itself, a bubble. This morning, the feeling is particularly strong.

Schopenhauer has eaten, and now he is sitting with his back to me in the space between the kitchen and living room, and washing his face, his front paws diligently wiping at both sides. What if he was right all along, that excess effort is always pointless and that in this life it is always best to focus on what is most important and walk calmly by when someone suggests anything other than eating, sleeping and sporadically keeping watch on the balcony, and that nothing ever ends differently from how it has always ended: with struggle, defeat, loneliness and eventual death.

I cut into the loaf of rye bread, toast two slices, place a few discounted turkey slices on top, pour hot water into a mug and sit down at the table. I open the newspaper and see the picture straight away: Laura posing in front of her Tove Jansson adaptation. I turn the pages and find the article. It is a full, double-page spread with three photographs. The text introduces Laura and her work. No mention of prison. That was mean-spirited of me, I recognise that. But many of my emotions these days are new, and at least to some degree uncontrollable. In the largest of the three photographs, Laura is leaning against the wall, and the mural behind her inspired by Tove Jansson looks as though it continues into infinity. From reading the article, the impression one gets of Laura is that she is a beginner, that this kilometre-long wall is the first that she ever painted. Just seeing her picture hurts me; the fog becomes thicker, condensing around my chest and stomach into its own cold, nagging space, which grows the longer I look at the image. I fold the paper, look out of the window for a moment and chew on the toast. Then I take my mug of tea, move to the other side of the table and switch on my laptop.

And a moment later I have to steady myself against the table so as not to fall off my chair.

The information has been updated.

Nobody who has taken out a loan has paid up, neither the original sum of the loan nor the interest. Not a single one. The bank's profits from its first cycle are zero, no more no less. I stare at the figures, but they don't change. This means that nobody has upheld our very fair and reasonable agreement. Nobody seems to think that a pay-day loan at a very low interest rate is a bilateral agreement. The product, which we named Loan Sense and whose concise, fact-based information leaflet laid out in the simplest possible terms quite how rare such an opportunity really is, has not compelled people to cooperate with the rules. I quickly recall that, when I started the bank, there was always the risk that someone might not repay their loan. But reason – and mathematics – dictated that the majority of people would make the repayments on time, because our terms and conditions are better and our interest rate lower than those of our competitors. This is simple mathematics. It has been proven in practice. And the original capital ... is now in the borrowers' pockets. Or, as I quickly come to realise, it's probably not there either any more. Far more likely, it has been squandered, frittered away, flushed down toilets around the world.

This is wholly irrational.

And yet...

This is the end.

On this gloomy, drizzly afternoon, the cemetery in Malmi is almost devoid of people. That's because everybody is dead, Juhani would quip, I know he would. But Juhani is quiet. He is ash in my arms. The urn, with Juhani inside it, arrived at the cemetery in the funeral home's own black hearse. I carry the urn in the crook of my right arm. It is surprisingly heavy. An employee from the funeral home follows me at a polite distance: a youngish man wearing a hat and sunglasses, despite the weather. The walk is relatively long. The umbrella in my left hand seems more eager to fly off in the wind than to remain in my hand and protect me from the rain.

We make several ninety-degree turns on the way, we stop, then take a few careful steps across the sodden lawn and arrive at a small hole in the ground. The earth around the hole is fresh and muddy. I glance behind me, and the quiet man dressed in black appears beside me almost instantly, I hand him the umbrella and he holds it over me. The urn is attached to a string, which I wind around my right hand. Then I begin to lower the urn. But not quite yet.

I stop, and it feels as though everything else stops too. I look up.

Thousands of graves, the diagonal rain, the tall stone wall, the highway behind it. Tree trunks black from the rain, wreathes heavy from the weight of the water. A solitary candle in a lantern like the last spot of light in the world. Then – because everything is still – I see movement. About thirty metres ahead and to my right, someone in a raincoat moves, turns and remains standing on the spot. The raincoat's hood is pulled over his head. Maybe the man has finally found the grave he was looking for. Or then again...

I have the sudden feeling I am looking at Lizard Man's back. The posture is the same. Further off, I see a group of people walking more or less in my direction. I look up again at the lonely figure; he too appears to notice the arrival of the group. He starts moving, walking away. The briskness of those footsteps reminds me of Lizard Man too. The figure disappears behind the hedgerow before I can be sure. The group of mourners has changed direction. I look at them from the side. One of them is carrying an urn. It's perfectly possible the person they are here to grieve protected me.

The dead save the living.

But I don't give the matter another thought.

The afternoon is dark and grey, my suit is soaked through.

I am here to bury my brother.

The string is taut as the urn calmly descends into the bosom of the earth.

The urn reaches the bottom of the hole, the place from which it shall never return.

I let go of my end of the string. And I let go of something else too. I'm not sure whether I say this out loud or not, but at least mentally I say to Juhani, whom I will never see again in any mortal form: I couldn't do it.

I simply couldn't save the adventure park, I couldn't even save myself. It just wasn't possible. I tell him straight up that I can't think of anything else, I can't bear anything else. And how you ever thought I might be able to pull it off using simple logic, well...

There's just no logic to it.

There's no logic to anything.

And there is no logic anywhere because nobody seems to need such a thing.

Look around you, Juhani – not down there, not at the dark urn or those clayey walls, a bit further up, if you are in another form somewhere or have reached a higher plain of existence – and you'll see that nothing that happens here is profitable in any way, shape or form.

Look at the world.

Schopenhauer was right all along. Only the unborn are happy.

Life isn't a loan; it is a payment fraud. It is a project, lasting on average seventy-five years, whose sole aim is to maximise our own stupidity. And yet, that's exactly what we seem to crave. Look at the choices we make. If we are healthy, we make ourselves ill by smoking cigarettes, drinking alcohol and over-eating. If we want to bring about societal change, we vote for options that make our situation worse. When we should be thinking about what is rational, people start talking about how they feel. The most important thing is making sure that nothing rational accidentally happens. The most successful people are those who talk the least sense and blame everybody else for it. One plus one is not two, Juhani; depending on the day and who is speaking it can be whatever the hell you want it to be.

And I'm supposed to succeed in a world like that – by using logic.

I take a deep breath.

I'm almost sure I haven't been speaking out loud. I stand at the edge of the pit a moment longer, follow the droplets of rain as they disappear into the ground. I have made up my mind. We return to the car park, where the man from the funeral home takes his black hearse and I take a white cab.

🐇

Back home, I slide my damp suit onto a hanger, wipe clean my shoes, make some tea and sit down at my computer. I click open a browser that won't reveal my IP address and an email address that won't reveal my identity. I remember Juhani showing me how to do this, how to operate on the web without leaving a trace. At the time, I thought it was just another fad, one of thousands of things that vied for Juhani's attention. In light of recent events, I wonder whether remaining anonymous online was more than just a hobby for him.

Be that as it may, this message needs to come from someone other than me. It needs to start a chain reaction in which I too will get caught up. The message is ready to go. But I don't press 'send' quite yet. I'll do it in the morning. I want to be there when it happens.

The recipient of the message is one Detective Inspector Pentti Osmala of the Helsinki organised-crime and fraud units. I still have his card. The message states that, rumour has it, one of the freezers in the adventure-park café might contain the body of a person who might be of interest to the police.

27

It is a bright morning and the autumn sun, low on the horizon, blinds my eyes and warms my face as I step out of the taxi, a self-imposed security measure I've now decided to take. The car park is empty, the tarmac smells of the overnight rain. The adventure park looks smaller somehow. Of course, it is still an enormous box that fills my field of vision from north to south, but now it doesn't feel so commanding, so overbearing. It doesn't have the same grip on me; I'm no longer carrying it on my back.

Something, somewhere, has changed.

I think it's probable that that something is me. I check the time on my phone. The message was sent forty minutes ago.

Inside the building, I bump into Kristian almost instantly. He is coming from the direction of the staffroom and is walking towards the entrance hall. Upon seeing me, he smiles straight away. I smile back. His smile is extremely broad. My smile feels light. His smile quickly disappears as he opens his mouth to say something, but I manage to get in first.

'The general managership might be closer than you think,' I say.

Kristian stops. 'Seriously?' he asks.

'Oh, yes.'

In the blink of an eye he seems overwhelmed with emotion.

'Tough love, right?' he says. 'Your methods are harsh, but you know what you're doing. You're a good boss.'

I give him a few taps on the shoulder and see tears welling in his eyes. Then I continue on my way. I don't care to correct his misunderstanding of the situation or to explain that my visionary leadership will likely soon be the subject of police scrutiny.

I step into Esa's control room. The air is almost as thick as jelly and smells so strongly of sulphur that breathing it hurts even the deepest recesses of my brain. Esa spins round in his chair and stands to attention when he sees me.

'Would you like a seat?' he asks.

No, I think instinctively, because if I sit down, I'm unsure whether I'll ever walk again, and regardless of what lies ahead of me, the idea of perishing in a cloud of human gas would feel like something of a ... waste, in so many ways.

'No, thank you. I just wanted to say that I admire and respect what you do. Thank you for all your good work.'

Esa shakes his head.

'I'm the one who should thank you,' he says. 'You've brought new rigour to the park. You take responsibility, you lead by example. First to fight, as they say in the marines. It feels like I can finally relax a bit. I've even started cycling to work. I'm keeping my Škoda here in the car park, is that OK?'

'Of course,' I quickly reply. Parked at the back of the building, Esa's camouflage-painted station wagon is hardly an intrusion. I have a very unpleasant sense that my face is starting to melt. I realise this is factually impossible, but my thirst for oxygen is all the more real. 'Carry on as you are. There's no sense in exhausting yourself. No sense at all.'

I return to the hall and walk through it with a strange sense of melancholy. I could never have imagined looking at these slides or the assault course in Caper Castle and feeling overcome with emotion. I wave to Samppa; he waves back enthusiastically and gives me a thumbs-up with both hands. Kiddies' Day is closer than he realises.

I arrive at the office wing and find Minttu K in her office, her forehead literally against the desk. She is wearing a trouser suit – as usual, black and tight-fitting – and her bronzed hands with all their silver rings are resting next to her head. The room smells of gin, cigarettes and a particularly pungent men's aftershave, which surely can't be emanating from Minttu K.

'Is everything alright?' I ask.

Minttu K bounces upright. At first, she looks like she has just arrived on a new planet, but two seconds later she is her old self again.

'You were right,' she says without a good morning or any other pleasantries and takes a cigarette from the packet on the desk. 'Sometimes old school is the best option. You don't have to reach every single influencer. Anyway, some influencers are just assholes.'

'I meant that because our marketing budget is limited...'

'Honey...' she says, lights the cigarette and points it at me '... exactly. I like your thinking. More bang for your buck. When Juhani was here, things got a bit out of hand. No offence.'

'Right...'

'Honey,' she says, her voice sounding more and more like an antique chainsaw, 'you've got good style, let's go with that. Now if it's all the same, I'm going to make a few calls, secure us a little discount.'

'Of course,' I say. 'Great that everything is in order.'

I genuinely mean it. I have barely walked out of the door when I hear the hiss of a can being cracked open.

🐰

I switch on my computer, and as soon as the relevant programmes are up and running, I get to work fast. My plan is to leave my successor, whoever that may be, a set of book-keeping documents that are as simple and as easy to use as possible – and which will stand up to close scrutiny. The bulk of the work was done last night. Now it's just about the finishing touches, and as I suspected, there is hardly anything to do. From the outset, I have been meticulous – for want of a better word, methodical – so this side of matters is quickly taken care of. I lean back in my chair and look around. Juhani's jacket is still hanging on the coat stand. But even that no longer seems about to fly away on the back of someone leaving the room as the door closes behind them. It is empty, resigned to its fate.

I have tidied the room, gradually putting things in order, so whoever ends up sitting in this chair will be able to look at neat piles of papers and a clear, empty desk. I am ready.

And as if by design, Johanna appears at my office door and, though I have already seen her, she knocks on the doorframe. I gladly stand up. Johanna is the one employee with whom I have spoken least. The Curly Cake Café is a success story, and Johanna runs it like clockwork. If at times I have queried her methods, she has always explained things from a practical point of view. And there is something very practical about her: she never seems to do anything that doesn't have a purpose, even the smallest movement is carefully considered. Her face is furrowed, harsh perhaps, she is strong and muscular.

'You're wanted in the café,' she says. 'Well, the kitchen.'

I walk ahead of her.

'Thank you,' she says as we walk across the southern end of the hall.

I glance over my shoulder. 'For what?'

'The freedom.'

'The Curly Cake Café is a success story,' I say. 'You run it excellently.'

We arrive at the café and continue through into the kitchen.

'I don't mean that. You're the best thing that could ever have happened to this place.'

I don't have time to ask what she means. We enter the kitchen, and I see Detective Inspector Osmala and two uniformed officers wearing light-blue latex gloves.

28

'Morning,' says Osmala and waves a blue hand.

He is standing in the café, his blazer open and his back to the freezer, almost as if he is trying to hide it behind him.

'Good morning,' I reply.

'Mind if we take a look in the freezer?' he asks.

Needless to say, the question is irrelevant. Osmala can look wherever he wants, whenever he wants. That's his job. I am about to turn to Johanna to ask her to remove the padlocks on the freezer doors when I notice they have already disappeared.

'By all means,' I say eventually.

Osmala nods to the officer on his right. They have clearly agreed on the choreography in advance. The officer steps towards the freezer, opens the lid and positions himself next to it. Osmala turns towards the freezer and bends down to look inside. A cold wave surges through the kitchen.

Osmala nods at the other officer, who positions himself next to the detective inspector in front of the freezer. Osmala begins handing items taken from the freezer to the officer, who sorts them into piles on the metallic table.

'They'd better not thaw out,' I hear behind me.

We all turn around. Johanna seems utterly serious. Of course she is. She doesn't know what I have preserved at the bottom of the freezer. I glance at Osmala. He is holding a bag of thirty pre-baked Belgian buns.

'These could have been used in the commission of a crime,' he says, brandishing the pastries at Johanna.

She doesn't look at all convinced. I need to get her out of the kitchen. I decide that what is about to happen here is my responsibility and mine alone.

'Can she go and serve the customers?' I ask Osmala. 'There's quite a queue in the café.'

Osmala is still weighing the pastries in his hands.

'Why not,' he says eventually.

I look at Johanna. Perhaps my expression tells her it's probably best to leave. She glances over at the freezer once more, almost offended, then leaves. Osmala and the officer continue emptying the freezer. I note that the other officer doesn't seem to be watching the freezer, which is motionless, but me – unlike the freezer, I have a pair of legs. He has moved quietly, imperceptibly, and has positioned himself between me and the kitchen door. It's hardly surprising.

The freezer is gradually emptied of its contents. Now the chicken wings are beginning to appear on the counter. After the bags of chicken wings, there is a thick layer of croissants, which I recall only too well. I can't remember the exact number of croissants, but I'm sure the packet Osmala is currently pulling up is one of the last. I am right. He stops. I assume that right now he is looking at the layer of polystyrene panels and white paint, and it will confuse him for a few seconds at most. But he remains in the same position for far longer than I presumed he would, and when he finally moves, he moves in a way that doesn't suggest he has discovered anything out of the ordinary. He begins pulling more bags of chicken wings from the freezer.

I don't know how many packets of wings come out of the freezer because I don't have the strength to count them. There are a lot. The volume of chicken wings building up on the counter represents more or less that of one professional hitman. Osmala leans forwards and his upper body, which is broad and large, disappears inside the freezer. I hear him tapping his knuckles against the walls and bottom of the freezer, running his fingers along the insides. Judging by the noises he is making, he sounds like a man who is disappointed. The anonymous email specified that this was the freezer in question. I should know, because I wrote it myself.

Eventually Osmala reverses out of the freezer. His face has turned a shade somewhere between cherry violet and fire-extinguisher red: he has been dangling, head upside-down in minus twenty degrees for several minutes.

'Let's see the other one,' he says.

'By all means.' I don't know what else to say, to him or myself. To say that this doesn't line up with my calculations would be something of an understatement.

🐇

The other freezer is full of frozen goods too. By that, I mean frozen food. I have not mistaken the freezer.

I repack the freezers in the order that Osmala emptied them and see with my own eyes that the freezer I thought contained something altogether different is exactly like the freezer I once emptied out: it is simply a freezer, no more, no less. By the time I'm finished, my fingers are stiff from the cold. Osmala has sent the uniformed officers on their way, presumably for more pressing cases than those involving frozen Belgian buns and hundreds of chicken wings. He gives the kitchen the once over, looking but not touching anything. I know what he is looking for, but I know it won't be found in any of the cupboards or shelves.

'Do you remember the photograph I showed you?' he asks suddenly.

I tell him I do.

'Have you seen that man since our conversation?'

'No,' I say with a shake of the head.

He takes a few brisk steps towards the kitchen door. Then he turns, tugs the sleeves of his blazer back into place, stretches his back. His face has regained its usual deathly grey hue.

'You never asked what we were looking for.'

'I assumed you knew what you were looking for,' I say, genuinely.

Osmala seems to consider my answer, then accepts it.

'Indeed,' he says. 'Obviously, I can't comment any further.'

Neither can I. I realised that as I was repacking the freezers.

Just then, my phone starts to ring in my trouser pocket. Osmala takes this as a sign, turns, pushes the door open and disappears into the café. Through the chink of the swinging door, I watch as, like a flickering film, he walks heavily and decisively towards the entrance hall and the front door. I take out my phone and look at it. An unknown number, but I decide to answer, thinking it's extremely unlikely I can be taken by such surprise for a second time in one day.

It turns out I might very well be wrong.

29

Esa is no longer in his room, but his car keys are still on his desk. I pick them up, drop them in my pocket and write him a note in which I tell him I'm going to borrow his Škoda for park business for the next few days and, obviously, that I'll reimburse him for the petrol. I hold my breath until I have returned to the hall and started heading towards the back door.

I see the change immediately.

This section of the park was always a strictly children-only zone. Now there are just as many adults too. They are either standing on the spot or slowly walking and pointing at the murals, stopping in front of them, taking a few steps back and moving closer again. More seem to arrive with every passing minute. Small throngs have formed in front of some of the murals. I can't see Laura anywhere, but I notice I'm hoping she can see the crowds of people who have turned up to admire her work. The thought makes me feel both proud and sad. I leave before I start to feel any worse.

I follow the Highway Code to the letter, making sure to check regularly in my rear-view mirror. I'm not being followed. The journey takes thirty-four minutes.

The small industrial building is grey and wine-red; the grey section is made of concrete and the wine-red bits are corrugated iron. On the wall is an illuminated sign that isn't currently switched on. It shows a faded strawberry and some slightly wonky lettering reading *Southern Finland Preserves and Berries*. The name feels somehow ungrammatical, unfinished, as do the surroundings. The road comes to an end just in front of the factory complex. The way it ends inevitably suggests that the original intention was to continue the road, until someone interrupted the act of digging, looked up and realised there wasn't a single good reason to carry on. The embankments on either side of the road leading up to the factory are empty; on the way here I passed forests of various trees, and fields and unkempt clearings. We are not surrounded with the buzz of innovation; this is not the heart of a thriving start-up community.

From the road, I drive a short distance uphill to the forecourt outside the factory, where I see two other vehicles: a relatively new, black Land Rover SUV and a slightly older-looking red Audi, a gas-guzzler from yesteryear. I park Esa's car behind the others, forming an orderly line, and step out of the vehicle. The sun flickers between small yet thick, grey clouds; at times it is bright, at others almost dark. Just then the clouds part, and the effect is like that of a surprise camera flash. The landscape flares up: the birches have already lost half of their leaves, and those left on the branches are yellowed and dry, most of them shrivelled. The light-grey gravel on the ground is streaked from the rain, with larger puddles here and there. The building needs some renovation and a fresh coat of paint.

At the top of a short flight of stairs, a door opens and a familiar man steps onto the landing. This time I doubt he intends to show off his baking skills. The big man is dressed in a green hunting jacket, some kind of hiking trousers and a pair of heavy-duty outdoor shoes. Combined with his expression and the colour of his face, the overall effect is one of someone about to kill an elk, quite possibly with his bare hands. He waits for me at the top of the steps and holds the door open. I step directly into the main hall of the factory.

Tall steel receptacles, like gigantic potato pans, steel piping and some smaller vessels, some form of conveyor belt winding its way out of sight, an abundance of different smaller workstations, each sporting an array of meters and gauges. Steel, aluminium, rubber, plastic. The space smells of chemicals and only very faintly of berries. The name on the side of the building conjures up all the correct associations: this is a place in southern Finland where things are preserved and where something happens to some berries. One of the machines is currently running; I can hear a strong, low-pitched humming sound.

I glance behind me, and the big man points up ahead. I walk towards what I assume must be the middle of the complex, and because the big man says nothing and simply follows me, I presume I am walking in the right direction. The sound of machinery grows stronger.

'We have a problem,' he says.

'What kind of...?'

Now I see the machine making the noise, and I see something else too. The machine is some kind of crusher, like an enormous, automated orange press, the kind many people use every morning. Attached to the machine is a man, his head inside the mechanism. He speaks.

'You came back,' he says from inside the machine. His voice booms as though it is coming from the bottom of a well. 'Good. Like I said, last quarter was only a temporary blip, and once we move into cloudberry and lingonberry season, we'll get the jam operation up and running again – I've got a German buyer lined up for the bilberries, he's visiting next week. Together you and I are going to keep Germany in jam...'

The man is speaking so quickly that the echo makes his words unclear.

'This kind of problem,' says the big man and points at the man taped inside the berry crusher.

I tell him I don't quite follow.

'The scenario here is quite similar to yours. This factory is like a transit lounge for cash. Or, at least, that was the plan. This man here took my money, but the money didn't find its way back into the company. He spent it all himself. And when I sent one of my freelancers to recoup the money, this guy made moose meat of him.'

'All a big misunderstanding,' comes the voice from the crusher. 'Jam is the business of the future. It's all about networking...'

'And on top of this,' the big man continues, 'I've had to let my subordinates go. As you know.'

He looks at me in a way that suggests he knows what's going on and he's well aware of the drowning that occurred on the cycle path. I say nothing.

'And that's not all,' he continues. 'I need some cash. Now.'

I don't plan on telling him I don't understand for a second time. Besides, I *do* understand what he's saying, every word.

'That's why you're here,' he says, and takes a few steps to the side. He grabs the control panel with gloved hands, turns something, pulls something, and the noise from the crusher grows stronger. Then he walks back in front of me.

'I don't understand how—'

'You have money,' he says, looking me in the eyes.

An icy current courses right through me, as though I had opened a freezer lid deep inside me.

'As a matter of fact, the bank—'

'Isn't working,' the big man says.

The crusher is still working though, I can hear its humming sound, but otherwise I am convinced everything has stopped, at least for a few seconds. I say nothing.

'Nobody has paid back the money they borrowed,' he says, and I recognise this tone as the same one he used in his home when he threatened me with a pistol and forced me to eat his cinnamon buns. The voice is similarly neutral, and as such all the worse suited to the situation and the matter at hand. 'I'll be surprised if anyone has even paid the interest. There's no point lying; liars end up in the juicer.'

'This is categorically not a juicer,' says the muffled voice. 'That's a thing of the past. The juicing business is nothing compared to the growth potential in jam...'

The big man turns and kicks the side of the crusher. It's a quick

movement and reveals his irritation, though there is no sign of
this in his body language. The jam entrepreneur seems to take the
hint, and there is no more quibbling from the crusher.

'I have a debt-collection operation up and ready to go,' the big
man says. 'I own part of the company. It buys loans with cash.'

'With a collection agency, interest rates will be many times
higher,' I say.

'I estimate about ten times higher.'

'I'm not sure about the legality of such operations...'

'What were you thinking? All that nonsense about sensible
loans, sensible interest rates.'

The big man's expression remains impassive. I might never have
seen anyone more serious. I remember what Laura told me about
her own financial situation and that of the other park employees.
They have all taken out loans – specifically because of the low
interest rate because they wouldn't be able to cope with higher
rates, let alone a rate ten times higher. And now...

'You will make the transfers within the next two days. The
money will flow through the park and back to me. I know you
can do this, I know you'll find a way. I've been sure of that right
from the start. Make sure everything in the park's finances looks
kosher. We'll be taking out plenty of loans yet against that
capital.'

The last sentence seems to slip from the big man's lips. I'm
convinced of it. He didn't mean to say that out loud – at least, not
at this stage. He turns quickly, looks at the confiture magnate.

'And let this be a cautionary example to you,' he says. 'That's
another reason you're here today.'

'What's going to happen to him?' I ask.

'The same thing that'll happen to you, if you fail to uphold our
agreement.'

I don't remember agreeing to anything, but I get the impression
there's little sense in arguing the point. This meeting appears to
be over. I take a few steps backwards and glance at the door. When

I look back at the big man, he is holding the same pistol he had in his kitchen during our little coffee date.

'Where do you think you're going?'

'Back to work. This isn't a simple matter. There's a lot to think about.'

This is all true.

The big man nods. 'Fair enough.'

I wait a moment longer.

'And I thought,' I say eventually, 'that the meeting had ended.'

'Of course,' he says and moves back to the control panel, the pistol in his hand all the while. 'The official part, that is. Now that I don't have any subordinates, until I can source some effective workers, my own role is much more hands-on. It's refreshing in a way. Salt-of-the-earth stuff.'

Now, I think to myself, he sounds like he did when he was talking about baking. His tone is gentle, almost maternal.

'Speaking of subordinates,' he says. 'I had to relieve our mutual friend of his duties, and in a fit of, shall we say, mild agitation he told me that he knows what you did to his two henchmen. I imagine he feels a bit jealous that I'm doing business with you now.'

We look each other in the eyes. The big man turns his head and the noise from the crusher grows stronger again. I'm not sure whether I've been given permission to leave or not. The big man has turned his back to me, the muzzle of the pistol is pointing at the ground. I cautiously start to turn and take another few steps towards the door. Soon my steps become brisker, my eyes are focussed on the door's square window. I can already see the dusky afternoon beyond it.

'Remember. Two days.'

30

The metallic bench at Malmi cemetery is cold and slightly damp. I don't mind. I'm sitting beneath a large oak tree. I can make out Juhani's headstone and the mound of fresh soil where his urn disappeared into the earth. I haven't brought flowers or anything else because I didn't know I would be coming here. You could say I was merely driving the car that brought me to the cemetery. I don't expect Juhani to have any answers – and I don't know how I would hear them if he did – or what I could find here that might change things. Perhaps I came out here just to be somewhere. And to think.

The missing body isn't my only problem. I was convinced the big man must have been responsible for the dead man's disappearance in one way or another, but now I'm just as convinced that if he really knew something about the body's movements and whereabouts, he would have said something. It's not his style to do people favours out of the goodness of his heart. Which reminds me of his collection agency and the idea of selling on people's debts.

The big man had been planning this all along. I was just a middleman, a conduit. And there isn't a shred of doubt that the collection agency would be a conduit too. I can already envisage the collection agency taking out a loan in order to buy up my loan, and once their own money has flowed through the books, the agency's only capital will be the unpaid loans, and eventually it will go bankrupt. Which was the point all along. Just as the adventure park is intended to go bust once it has been bled dry. The big man must have been so caught up with his fruit crusher and his soaring rhetoric that he inadvertently let that particular cat out of the bag. But I understood what was going on right away and what that might mean for the adventure park: it will eventually fall under the weight of its debts and loans, money that has ended up somewhere altogether different from funding the park's activities. I sigh, my breath steams up in the buzzing glow from a circular bollard light that has just switched itself into life. The big man's business model leaves nothing to the imagination, and he has demonstrated the practical implications of that model both in the barn and most recently at the jam factory.

When the steamroller's brakes malfunctioned, I ended up being crushed. That I can accept. I have made mistakes in the last few months. I have erred and misread things. The fact that I am where I am is logical; it is as just as life ever can be.

But ultimately this isn't about me.

What's at stake is the adventure park and all its staff. Their jobs. They have taken out loans because I told them it was sensible, and they trusted me. I think of Samppa and his Kiddies' Day, Laura and her daughter Tuuli, Kristian and his new-found thirst for study, Esa and his lifestyle changes, Johanna and her dedication to the cafeteria. Every last one of them deserves better than broken promises, bankruptcy and financial ruin. I think of Juhani, his dreams, his wishes, and above all his child-like enthusiasm and indefatigable ingenuity. I don't know if these things have any more or less to do with reality than before, but I want them to thrive all the same. I want the park to thrive. But to do that, it first needs to survive.

I realise something else too. At first the significance of the big man's words eluded me, but only for a moment. He said that Lizard Man knows what I have done to his two partners. That means not only the drowning incident on the cycle path but the freezer too. And there's another reason I am glad I remember his comment. It gives me the germ of a plan.

I sit on the bench for a long time, the evening darkening around me.

Then I set off.

31

I walk around the deserted adventure park in the half-dark. It's just gone eleven o'clock. My walk-around is unnecessary: I already know that the park is empty and the doors locked. For now.

The foyer is lit up, and because it is dark outside I can't see what is on the other side of the door. I flick the manual switch, and the doors slide open. I step outside. The night air is cool, the cloudless sky reaches right up to the stars. The car park is empty, further off I can see the front and rear lights of passing cars.

I head left, turn the corner, continue for a short distance, turn again, walk back all the way to the opposite corner and beyond, I head towards the road and walk almost right to the intersection, then in a sweeping curve return to the doors. I don't know what my evening walk must look like, but I don't care. The point is that, no matter which angle you look from, I will be seen in and around the park. Then I walk through the doors and back inside.

And leave the doors open behind me.

On the dark side of the Big Dipper is a bench that the parents can use. I sit down and wait. I can feel the draught from the front door against my ankles. I am wearing my suit trousers, a shirt and tie. I have taken off my blazer and folded it next to me on the bench. The car's keys are in my pocket.

'You're about as good at setting an ambush as you are at everything else,' says Lizard Man. 'I don't know what the big boss sees in you.'

I see his silhouette. He is standing only about fifteen metres in front of me. He has strolled into the park silently and managed to get this close without my noticing a thing.

'If you want to take someone by surprise,' he continues, 'a word of advice: you need the element of surprise. You understand what I'm saying, Emmental?'

'Einstein,' I say and stand up.

'What?'

'Einstein. He was a physicist. Emmental is a cheese.'

'For fuck's sake,' he shouts. 'I know that. The question is, do you?'

I can only see his outline. Judging by that, he is approaching me and shaking his head.

'Now listen the fuck up.'

I take a few steps, small sideways steps towards the Big Dipper.

We are both moving now. He is approaching me directly, I am slowly inching my way towards the Big Dipper.

'Are you really that thick? Is this your idea of an ambush? This shithole?'

Ten metres. Nine, eight...

A knife. It flashes quickly, then disappears back into the shadows.

'How do you know I'm alone?' I ask.

'Listen, errand boy, I don't know if you've noticed but you opened the doors over an hour ago. It's just you and me in this dump of an amusement park...'

'It's an adventure park,' I say emphatically, and as soon as I've uttered the words I take my first running steps.

I hear Lizard Man doing the same. We both break into a run. He wants to exact his revenge up close and personal. I dash behind the slides, arrive at the opening between Caper Castle and the Big Dipper and sprint towards the entrance. But I'm not heading for the doors. My destination is far closer: when people arrive at the park, it greets them happily and cheerily. Its smile is always broad and sunny, its front teeth are like bright, white oar blades. It waves its front paw so enthusiastically that it compels you to respond, though you know it's only made of metal and plastic.

Lizard Man is gaining on me with almost every step, I don't

have to slow down at all. He is maybe only five metres behind me when I reach the rope. I have to slow down to give the rope a firm yank, then I slightly alter the direction of my run and place my trust in physics and mathematics. Lizard Man and I are only about two metres apart when the giant rabbit starts to topple.

Velocity, the ratio of mass and speed: gravity does its job.

'You fucking shit-for-brains number-crunching freak...'

A hundred and forty kilos of jolly leporid hits Lizard Man squarely in the face. He slams into the rabbit as if it were a wall.

A wall that cracks ever so slightly.

Of course, this is only a figurative wall. In reality, it is only a man and a giant plastic rabbit colliding at speed. The crack is followed by a loud crash, after which there is utter silence.

I stop and I listen.

The silence is like the sea standing perfectly still. From what I observe of the collision between man and rabbit, I conclude it is the man who has been forced to yield. Lizard Man is lying on his back, vacantly staring at the ceiling of the adventure park, far from the angry, cursing, threatening man he was just a moment ago.

The rabbit looks almost the same as before, only now it is missing an ear again.

🐇

With a spot of geometrical adjustment, Lizard Man fits into the boot of the car.

I start the engine, drive slowly to the other side of the building and peer towards the entrance. The doors are shut; Esa's security cameras were switched off a long time ago. The rabbit is upright again with its ear in place. Perhaps my previous experience helped make standing the rabbit upright and clearing up my tracks such a quick operation. Having said that, the ear will not withstand another conflict. Cleaning it, fixing it and gluing it in place took almost as long as everything else put together. But it looks like it is firmly attached to the rabbit's head once again, and at a quick glance I doubt anyone will be able to see any evidence of hand-to-hand combat.

I look at the adventure park a moment longer. Not because I want to make sure of anything in particular, but simply because it is there. I remember my first day at work, the way I wanted to be rid of the park for good, how I considered every minute I spent there a minute wasted. How wrong I was. And how differently I think now. Now I see something that deserves to be protected and must be protected. I know people use the word *love* in all its different forms and in all possible contexts to refer to everything from washing powders to grandmothers, from muesli to holiday destinations, but my heart thumps, my chest pounds and my mind seethes at the thought that someone is trying to threaten my adventure park. I have to say it, if only to myself.

This is my adventure park. I love it and I'm going to do anything it takes to save it.

🐇

The route is familiar by now. The traffic thins out as the number of lanes decreases. The night turns darker, squeezing the car tighter and tighter. The headlights guide me round the darkening turns and bends. On the dirt track, I can finally drive completely alone. I recognise the familiar intersection and slow down on approach. I take the path leading gently uphill, I reach the top of the hill and begin to drive down the other side, I steer the car out of the protection of the forest and before long I can make out the figure of the barn ahead and to the right.

Do I really believe that the big man is out?

That being said, this isn't the first time I have turned up at his extraordinary farmyard unannounced. If he is at home, I can say I have come for a chat. The time of day won't be a problem; his operations don't adhere to standard business practices anyway, and I doubt he cares much for office hours. And there's no reason for me to show him the contents of the car. Lizard Man is in the boot, permanently subdued. He's unlikely to run out into the yard and surprise us.

Ultimately, this is a classic example of the old adage that you first need to rule out the impossible: in this instance, turning back. Then you need to look at what options are left: there is only one direction – full steam ahead. You have to start with what can be resolved, then you can resolve something new in order to move forwards.

I steer the car back to the dirt track.

A moment later, I turn onto the path leading up to the yard, driving at precisely the speed I would if I were arriving for an impromptu visit. The path feels unbearably long. The headlights glide across the house and the yard. I open the window, switch off the engine but leave the lights on. I listen. I can't even hear the wind in the trees, let alone the sound of birdsong. It's so late in the autumn that even the mosquitoes have stopped buzzing. I smell the moist earth, there's a lingering hint of summer, a late blossoming, an after-burn.

And there's something else too.

Cinnamon buns.

In the middle of the night.

I switch off the headlights and wait for a moment. The house is dark and it remains dark, except for a faint light in the left-hand window, which I know to be the kitchen.

It only takes a few seconds to add up what I can see and smell, and I reach the conclusion that there are no alternatives: I will have to go in and eat another gargantuan cinnamon bun in what would normally constitute my sleeping hours – most likely with the big man watching over me while Lizard Man rests in peace in the boot of the car. This outcome is far from optimal, but if an excess of carbohydrates at this unfortunate hour of the day is all that's required in my effort to save the adventure park, I'll do it.

I take a deep breath, step out of the car, walk up to the house, take the steps up to the porch and wait for the door to open. I wait a little longer. Nothing happens. I ring the doorbell which, last time, I didn't even get to touch. The doorbell peals through the dark house. I wait again. Nobody moves inside the house. I look at the door, then try the handle. It turns.

The house smells like a mid-sized bakery. I take one step further inside, then two steps, and, trying to keep my voice as normal as possible, I call out and ask whether this is a good time to pay a visit. There is no answer, so I raise my voice and ask again. And again, nothing. It seems the house is empty. I proceed carefully into the kitchen.

The buns are already in the oven.

I'm no expert when it comes to baking, but I do know this.

The average baking time for cinnamon buns is approximately thirteen to fifteen minutes. When the buns are this big – I can see their size as I peer into the oven – baking time can take up to seventeen or even eighteen minutes. Judging by the current colour of the buns, they must have been in the oven for roughly four to five minutes already.

I see something else on the table: an empty coffee packet next to the coffee maker. There is already fresh water in the coffee maker and a new, clean filter in the top, but then ... the big man has realised he's out of coffee. And you can't have cinnamon buns without coffee.

I remember the map of the area. There is a petrol station in the opposite direction from where I came, perhaps five or six minutes' drive away.

I am used to performing multiple calculations in my head at once. Complicated, challenging ones. I am used to the presence of several simultaneous variables. I am able to compare calculations to one another while working through them. Of all available options, the conclusion I arrive at is the best, the one that will most likely lead to the optimal result, the one that significantly increases the likelihood and probability of the next desired outcome more than any of the other options on the table.

I run.

I return to the car, open the back door and take a flashlight from the footwell. I flick it on and walk towards the barn. It is an old building with a ramp leading up to a wide set of doors. The doors are closed. I walk round to the side of the barn facing the woods from which I stepped out into the yard on my last visit. I find a small door that is unlocked and slip inside. The odour of mould is like a blade cutting through my nostrils. It's so sharp and powerful that I feel as though I can almost see it in noxious clouds in the light of the torch. There is an uneven coating of cement on the floor, and the small, narrow windows remind me of a prison cell. I step over planks of wood, debris, piles of rubbish. After a quick search, I locate the stairs and climb to the upper floor.

The floorboards creak as I move around the tall dust- and mould-smelling space. Each time the flashlight illuminates something, the item seems to leap out at me, to take a step or two forwards out of the darkness. Almost everything is exactly where it was the last time I visited. I walk the length of the barn and emerge at the far end of the main space, just as the big man did at our first meeting. I continue towards the large main doorway and lift the plank placed across the latches to hold it shut. I push the doors open and walk down the steep slope leading out into the yard. Then I reverse the car back up the slope and stop once the vehicle is half inside the barn, then switch off the engine.

I get out of the car, walk round to the boot, open it.

I grip Lizard Man beneath the arms and start hauling him further inside the barn. His armpits are moist and warm. He is heavy but flexible. Finally we are inside. I sit him against a pillar, then walk back towards the steps. The quadbike is where it was before, the rope still connected to its roof rack. I untie the rope, for now. I return to Lizard Man, wrap the rope around his neck and tighten it. I throw the other end of the rope over one of the rafters, sigh, then look away.

I don't do this gladly; in fact, I'd gladly never think about it at all.

I hang a dead man.

The process is more difficult than I'd thought.

Lizard Man weighs about as much as an average adult male, and it's not as if he is putting up much of a fight. The rafter groans, the rope chafes against the wood as I pull. I try to close my ears, try to convince myself that this is inevitable, unavoidable. Eventually, after much exertion on my part, Lizard Man is firmly in the air and the rope is once again attached to the back of the quadbike.

I roll the car down into the yard, close the large doors from the inside, take the flashlight from the floor and walk back to the ground floor without so much as glancing at Lizard Man. At the top of the stairs, three steps from the top, I look over my shoulder after all. A man who hanged others, who used people, threatened and blackmailed them, who was planning to kill me. If I were him, I would say something like one plus one equals two.

But I'm not him; I am me.

And so I say nothing. I simply go through my calculations one more time and leave as fast as I can. The smell of cinnamon buns makes the impenetrable night seem strangely sugary and sweet.

🐰

After driving about eight kilometres, I stop at a remote lay-by. I pull off the latex gloves and remove the protective coverings from my shoes. I do the same with the overall. I took the hairnet from my head earlier. I place everything in a black plastic bag and stuff it in the bin.

I return the car to the adventure park and walk a kilometre in the direction of the airport. Then I hail a taxi and arrive home just after five. My phone is exactly where I left it: on the table in the hallway.

I give Schopenhauer his food, have a shower and make some tea. I don't regale Schopenhauer with the details of the night's events, instead I stroke his head, his smooth back and purring sides before letting him out onto the balcony to watch the sunrise. I drink my cup of tea and eat a slice of rye bread with butter and gravlax. Eating this triggers my hunger. I make another sandwich, then a third, then eat two pots of sour yoghurt with a thick drizzle of honey. I hadn't even noticed how hungry I was. I have been on the move all day and all evening, and the day's events have made paying attention to today's menu something of a challenge.

Finally, once I have brewed another cup of tea, I sit down at the kitchen table and compose another email to Osmala. This time I don't need to think about the tone of voice. It comes to me right away. I believe this will make the message convincing enough, the kind of message that will make Osmala act, despite the previous false, bodiless alarm.

In the message, I explain that I fear for my life and that I am on my way to a particular farmstead in the woods to meet my boss, an infamous criminal, and that if this is my last message, I want the police to know who murdered me. I give coordinates for the barn that are as specific as I believe the putative author of this email would be able to give, then add a description of the barn itself. I tell him that this message will be sent automatically at a specific time unless I can get home in time to disable it. Then I press 'send' and switch off my computer. I stand up, put my plate and Schopenhauer's in the dishwasher and switch it on. I lean against the kitchen counter and listen to the slosh of water. For the first time in a very long while, my mind is calm, emptied of thoughts, and I go out to the balcony to join Schopenhauer.

The morning is still fragile, the sparsely positioned lampposts leave large dark spots across the forecourt. Schopenhauer's eyes are fixed on the ragged, almost leafless birches and the bushes beneath them, which now look thicker than a jungle. I don't see anything out of the ordinary there myself, but I can perfectly understand why Schopenhauer is watching them so intently.

He has decided he will not be taken by surprise.

32

I sleep until midday, shave, get dressed, do up my tie and step outside. The day is bright and windless, the air crisp and refreshingly cold, the sun looks almost white, though it gives no warmth at all, like a winter's day in the middle of autumn.

The train journey is pleasant: no one tries to threaten my life or steal my travel card. I glance at the tabloid headlines on my phone, but I know it's still too early. I prefer not to imagine that my plan hasn't worked. In any case, I will need to be more alert, more vigilant than ever before. Perhaps it's not the worst thing that could happen after all. Before ending up at the adventure park, who did I trust most in the world? Schopenhauer. And who do I still trust? Schopenhauer. Both of them, in fact: the cat and the philosopher.

I enter the adventure park via the back door. I walk through the hallway, and a cursory glance tells me our customer numbers are on the up. There are more children – and adults – in the park than ever. Laura's murals and the attention they have garnered have injected the kind of energy into the park that I had imagined the bank might have done. The bank that will soon no longer exist. I reach my office, sit down at my desk and switch on the computer. As I wait for the system to boot up, I listen to the sounds of the park. My office door is open, and though there are two corners between here and the hall, the noise carries right the way in.

I sign into the bank's management system and see that the account balance is a big fat zero. Because granting a loan can be done in only a few clicks, everyone working at the ticket office has been able to award them. Judging by the log-in history, most of

them were awarded by Kristian, who, to his credit, has demonstrated first-class sales skills. In a single afternoon he managed to
award almost thirty loans to the maximum credit limit. If I'm not
mistaken, this was the afternoon when he first told me about his
courses and showed off his sales techniques.

Yet again, I have to admit that I was both right and wrong: there
is clearly a market for low-interest loans, but though they are fair
for all parties, people feel no more compunction to repay them than
they do exorbitant interest rates. Nobody has paid so much as a first
instalment, not a single client seems interested in paying back on
an interest-only basis. I am about to log out of the management
system and into the accounting system I have created for the bank,
when I see someone walking into my office without knocking.

I know who this new arrival is without raising my eyes. I
recognise the way the steps fall one after the other.

Laura looks astonishingly similar to how she looked the first
time she showed me round the park. Naturally, her bushy hair is
the same, brown and thick, her dark-rimmed glasses are the same,
she has the same bright, inquisitive look in her eyes, and she is
wearing the same clothes too: a yellow hoodie, black jeans, a pair
of colourful trainers. And when I say she looks the same, it's
something more than just her hair and clothes; there's something
about her way of being, the way she moves, the way she stands in
the middle of the room. In a way, it feels like returning to the
moment I first laid eyes on her. Except I can't return to that
moment. I cannot. Not to mention that in reality such a thing is
impossible, but after everything that has happened, given
everything I know about her – I just can't.

'Have you got a minute?'

'Yes,' I say once I am able to form words again. 'Would you like
to sit down?'

'That might be better.'

Laura sits at the other side of the table. I find myself hoping she
will start the conversation – and, I assume, so does she – because

I don't know what to say, let alone how to say it. Because what I see in the figure in front of me is once again the moment when she said that whatever had happened between us was now over. And the memory of that moment is physical, paralysing, as if something were being ripped from me, a part of me that controls my actions, my emotions. It feels as though I am wading through cold concrete, both internally and externally.

'I want to thank you,' she says eventually, and pauses for a moment, perhaps waiting for me to show that I am still involved in this conversation. But I can't bring myself to say anything. 'Without you, these murals would never have come to life. You let me use the walls, you encouraged me in such a ... unique way. I just wanted to ... thank you.'

'By all means,' I hear myself saying.

Then Laura clearly hesitates. She looks me right in the eyes, as she has done many times before, but this time she opens her mouth only to close it again. She makes a second attempt, and this time she manages to speak.

'I've been offered a job,' she says.

I say nothing.

'And I've accepted it.'

Is the noise and clamour of the hall now suddenly more audible? Something in the background din becomes louder; it travels through my ears and spreads through my body.

'I'm handing in my notice,' she says.

We sit in silence, our eyes lowered. I know I have to say something. I even know the right words.

'Congratulations on your new job.'

'Thank you,' she says, pauses for a moment, then continues. 'You haven't asked me what it is.'

I try to open my mouth. My mind is swirling with a thousand and one questions, and none of them necessarily has anything to do with Laura's new job.

'What is it?' I finally manage to ask.

'I'll be painting walls, just like I did here. Eight walls, all roughly the same size. It's a commission, a company that wants the kind of foyer that makes a real impact.'

There's a flicker in Laura's eyes, a smile on her lips that I remember only too well.

'What I mean is, now I'll be able to do the kind of work I've wanted to do all along,' she continues. 'This is my real calling, the profession I've always dreamed about. Finally. Sometimes our dreams ... really can come true.'

She's not smiling any more.

'I want you to know that it's partly thanks to you.'

'Thank you,' I say and try to continue, but I can't quite grab hold of my thoughts.

'As you probably remember, I found painting really difficult for so many years. This was a big turning point for me. Thank you for that too.'

'Of course,' I force myself to say. 'It's a pleasure.'

'What about you?'

The question takes me completely off guard. There's no quick answer, and Laura notices it.

'The park seems to be doing really well,' she says. 'I've never seen this many people here before.'

'Footfall is at an all-time high,' I admit.

'You did it, Henri.'

'What did I do?' I ask before I even realise.

For a moment, Laura avoids eye contact and gently strokes a few wisps of hair.

'If I understood correctly, the park was in a spot of financial difficulty when you took over,' she says. 'But now things look much better, right? There are plenty of customers, and the employees all seem so ... happy and satisfied. You could say, you saved this park. You've done a good job.'

We don't know that yet, I think. It's still hanging in the balance. Well, it's hanging, let's leave it at that.

'It looks like most of the work is done,' I say. 'I truly hope so.'

Laura seems as though she is about to say something, but then clenches her lips tightly together and looks like she is just waiting for the impulse to pass. The change in her face is slight, it lasts only a fraction of a second, but I notice it all the same. Then her eyes begin to glisten. She gives a curt smile.

'I don't want to keep you,' she says quietly.

'It's no trouble,' I say, and the words sound every bit as banal as they are. Because this might not be any trouble, but it's the utmost agony.

The pandemonium coming from the hall is like a sea surging behind us or somewhere to the side. Perhaps both of us listen to the waves for a moment. There's that same numbness in my fingers now as before, an invisible weight pushes down on my diaphragm, and icy stones seem to churn through my guts. I assume our meeting is over. I am preparing myself to say something fitting, such as, I should be getting back to these spreadsheets, or something like that, but Laura speaks first.

'I have one more thing to ask.'

I try to look curious and expectant. I might have succeeded, I'm not sure.

'This business,' she begins. 'The one that has commissioned the murals. They want to proceed quickly. The official opening of their new premises is in a month and a half. And I have to work a month's notice here. I won't have time to finish the murals in only two weeks. I am prepared to forgo my wages for the next month.'

Perhaps I look as though I haven't understood her, though I believe I have. She continues.

'I want to leave right away, so that I can get started on the new murals. Of course, I don't expect you to pay me a month's salary while I'm working for someone else. So I will forgo my—'

'That's not necessary.'

'I *want* to.'

'It's not—'

'It would make me happy.'

Laura certainly doesn't sound very happy. In fact, she sounds more serious than she has for a long while. I don't know what it is about her reaction that surprises me the most. And it makes me move, somehow, though I still feel shackled in a bath of concrete.

'For your daughter's language school or...' I begin without knowing where I am heading. At the same time, Laura lowers her eyes, her hand rises quickly to adjust her glasses. Then she looks up at me again.

'It's all taken care of,' she says, her tone indicating that there is a full stop at the end of the sentence. She pauses.

I tidy some papers on the table that don't need to be tidied. I can't think of anything else to do with my hands. All I can do is remain seated and look directly into Laura's blue-green eyes.

'Of course,' I stammer. 'You can leave right away.'

These are perfectly everyday words, but they hurt my mouth. I don't fully understand why. Laura's eyes gleam, and in a movement as quick as lightning she wipes her temple and cheek with her right hand, then corrects her posture again. She looks as though she is both sitting and standing up at the same time. Eventually she places her hands on the arms of the chair.

'I'll get going,' she says. The words sound as though they are directed at someone other than me, other than herself.

She stands up. For a moment, I think the squall from the park grows stronger, then I realise that the waves are inside me.

'Thank you, Henri.'

33

It takes two days. Then the tabloids have a field day with the news.
'BODY IN THE BARN'
'SHOWDOWN IN THE UNDERWORLD?'

I glance through the news until I find the crucial piece of information I am looking for: 'One suspect has been detained on suspicion of murder. The suspect has a history of involvement with the criminal underworld and is well known to police.'

It seems I have succeeded, I think. It's over. Everything is over.

Or, as I have realised earlier today, almost everything is over.

I lock the back door of the adventure park and take the metal steps down to the forecourt. It is eleven o'clock, the air cold and still. Without electric lighting, the world would be like an immense, dark cellar. I carry a rubbish bag out to the bins, open the lid and dump the bag inside. The lid slams shut and lets out a clang that is just as loud as I'd hoped. One way or another, I want my departure to be noticed. I want to be seen walking away from the adventure park.

After walking around the corner, I set off diagonally across the car park. Once I am far enough away I glance to my right, and against the wall of the building I see the same slender, vertical reflection as before.

I should thank the news headlines for bringing it to my attention.

After reading the headlines earlier this morning, I really needed some fresh air. The news was good, or as good as could be expected, but it triggered a delayed yet massive stress reaction, which in many ways was linked to Laura, to everything being ... over.

I walked around the adventure park. As I was finishing my walk and began to calm down again – my breathing stabilised, I was getting enough oxygen, and my stomach no longer felt as though it was filled with thawing metals – I arrived in front of the big YouMeFun sign on the roof, the clouds in front of the sun parted and something flashed in the corner of my eye.

At first, I couldn't see anything else.

Then I looked more closely at the wall and saw where the flash had come from. Seen from the right angle, the sun was reflected from a thin wire cable running down the length of the building. From where it touched the tarmac, the cable ran along the ground and behind a concrete bollard, where it lay tangled in loops on the ground. Then it ran up the wall and disappeared over the gutter and onto the roof. I went back inside, climbed up to the roof via the indoor access stairs and walked over to the spot where I assumed the cable must be. The other end of the clean, new cable had, it seemed, recently been knotted around the YouMeFun sign.

Now, as I arrive at the side of the car park near the road, I turn right and continue along the cycle path. As usual, I head towards the bus stop. When I arrive at the spot where the cycle path veers off between the rocks and a thin strip of woodland, meaning there is no way of looking back to the road, I leave the path, climb over a small ridge covered in trees and reach the car park of a neighbouring furniture outlet, walk around the furniture store, and before long I am approaching the adventure park from the other direction. I find a suitable place to wait in the shadows of an unlit road-side greasy spoon café. The café has permanently closed its doors, but the smell of last spring's fast food still lingers in the air.

I have been seen leaving the park, I was the last person to leave, and the wire cable is waiting. Everything is ready. The equation is beautiful in its simplicity. I notice I am finally rediscovering my calculus mojo. It comes in fits and starts, still feels as though there is a tiny yet all the more determined grain of sand in the cogs, I just don't know where. The friction is akin to completing a jigsaw only to discover that the final piece is missing; the larger picture feels unsatisfyingly incomplete.

Then, finally, the missing piece of the equation pulls into sight.

A Hyundai slows and seems to hesitate before turning into the adventure park. I see exactly what I expected to see: a bumper guard. I mentally thank Osmala. The vehicle that knocked over the flagpole turns carefully into the car park. It continues diagonally across the asphalt, and now I understand why: the driver wants to scout out the area at the back of the park first. Once the Hyundai disappears from view, I start running.

I have crossed the road and made it into the adventure park complex, and I am sprinting along the building's tall façade when I hear the sound of the truck again. I stop. Just around the corner, the truck approaches, getting closer and closer...

Until it stops.

I peer round the corner. The driver is turning the vehicle, reversing towards the wall. I take out my phone, then a moment later return it to my pocket. The towbar stops a few metres from the wall, then the driver's door opens. The driver jumps out and runs over to the bollard. The driver is wearing a large jacket and a hoodie beneath it, the hood of which is pulled so far over their head that their face remains obscured in the shadows. The driver picks up the wire from behind the bollard and starts attaching it to the towbar.

I take a few brisk strides towards the knot-tier. The truck's engine covers the sound of my steps. The driver finishes tying the knot, stands up straight, and is about to dash back to the vehicle when I reach out a hand and grip the perpetrator by the shoulder.

The driver both turns and lurches backwards. This happens with the sheer momentum of the movement; I neither shove nor hit out. The driver falls back, knocking their head and shoulders against the truck, and gives a yelp. A rather high-pitched yelp. The hood has fallen right in front of the driver's face; the hoodie is about three sizes too big. The driver is clearly disorientated. And only now do I realise how short and small that driver is.

I grip the hood, pull it back and – find myself looking at a young woman.

'Venla?'

'What?' she asks.

It looks as though I've calculated correctly, right down to this final detail. Venla looks a bit shocked and more than a little annoyed. She has very short bleached hair and startlingly angry blue-green eyes.

'First you knocked over my flagpole,' I say. 'Then you pushed a frozen chicken leg under the tracks of the Komodo Locomotive. And now you're trying to pull the sign from my roof.'

'So?'

'So ... the adventure park pays your wages. You don't get a monthly salary to sabotage the park but, in your case, for your customer-service expertise. This isn't at all sensible. The adventure park is suffering. Your father's Hyundai will suffer.'

'How do you know...?'

'I checked the registration number a moment ago,' I say. 'And I doubt your name is Tero. This has to stop.'

Now there's something else to Venla's expression besides frightened irritation. More than anything else, she looks confused.

'Who *are* you?'

I explain who I am, how I ended up doing what I am doing. I tell her about Juhani's untimely death, the park's current state of affairs, the growth in footfall. I also mention that the ticket office is badly in need of another member of staff, particularly one who is already on the payroll.

'Juhani's dead?'

'Yes,' I say. 'Didn't Kristian tell you?'

Venla shakes her head. 'We never talk about anything. I just WhatsApp him and ask if he can stand in for me, and he replies with a heart and thumbs-up emoji.'

'It's highly likely he has a crush on you.'

'How do you know that?'

'I have experience of such things, and it's not exactly hard to see,' I say, eager to change the subject – for a variety of reasons. 'But that's not why we're here this evening. This evening, we are—'

'Look, Juhani promised to produce my album, if I beat my sales record. And I smashed it. But he didn't produce my album. So I thought I'd smash something else too...'

It takes me a moment to work out quite what Venla is talking about. I think of my brother again. Oh, Juhani. What else was I expecting? What else have you left behind for me to clean up? What kind of secrets is the adventure park still hiding? I haven't got the strength to be angry. This is the least of my worries. We've experienced worse in recent weeks.

'Juhani wasn't a record producer,' I say.

'No shit, Sherlock.'

'I mean, I'm sorry if he promised you something like that. He promised people all kinds of things. But he also paid you a monthly wage.'

Venla glances to her left, towards the wall. The wire cable shines in the red glow of the truck's rear lights.

'Are you going to call the cops?'

Calling the police would only bring Osmala out here again, and how many times will he be prepared to visit the park without turning everything upside down? Besides, I don't need any more problems right now. I don't want to prolong the problems we already have. I want solutions, clarity, I need people who keep their word.

'Will you come to work tomorrow at the agreed time and will you undertake to do the work for which you are paid?'

Venla doesn't think about this for long. 'Yes.'

'Nine o'clock?'

'Nine o'clock.'

'Good.'

Venla scrutinises me.

'Really?'

'Really.'

'I can just jump in the car and drive away?'

'I'd untie that cable first.'

'Right, yeah,' she remembers. She walks towards the towbar, unties the cable and shows me the loose end before letting it drop to the ground. She steps past me and gets into the truck. She is about to pull the door shut when she suddenly stops.

'About my sales record...'

'About my flagpole,' I reply.

'See you in the morning.'

Venla steers her father Tero's Hyundai across the car park, then down to the road, and speeds off until the truck eventually disappears from sight.

34

I do the final check before opening the park's doors. I notice I am thinking about the future as something more than just a matter of survival. I haven't done that for a long time. A moment later I seriously consider commissioning a full overhaul of the Big Dipper. It will be a large investment and, as such, carries a certain risk. Children's slides are no laughing matter. And still the thought feels ... good.

I complete my checklist, make the final notes in my papers and close the folder. I look around, and my eyes are drawn towards the Curly Cake Café. I haven't spoken to Johanna about the padlocks on the freezers or asked her why they appeared one moment, then were gone the next. I don't want to say anything that might make her think that the body that rested at the bottom of the freezer – assuming she even noticed it – was brought there by yours truly. There is nothing tying me to the man. I am happy to let Johanna think I was puzzled by the police's visit as the concerned manager of an adventure park, and that's all.

And it really is all, I think, and immediately feel another burden lift. I can even look at Laura's murals again. The thought of her still mauls my guts and clouds my eyes, but in a strange, nostalgic way I am glad I told her what I think of her: that she is extraordinary, that she has awoken something within me that was previously unknown, almost non-existent. I have come to understand that it is in precisely these kinds of situations that people talk about love. I don't know what else might feel quite like this – happy and sad and bright and very, very unclear, all at once.

And I can look at the whole park and confirm that Laura was

right in this respect too. It seems that, despite everything, I have succeeded. At least, I'm pretty close.

I feel a variety of emotions, but foremost among them is a sense of victorious relief as I walk into the foyer to open up the doors to the adventure park. Outside, the piercing early October sun lies low on the horizon. It is dappled and cut into the shapes of the windows, refracted into the foyer in squares and rectangles. Beyond the doors, I can see the outlines of today's customers: this too is a new phenomenon – a queue has formed even before we open the doors.

I use the manual opener on the wall and the doors slide open, I bid everyone good morning and usher them inside. A stocky customer appears, steps out of the silhouettes and into the light. I recognise him, and my relief is suddenly gone.

Osmala is alone. I automatically make a mental note of this and only then understand why. If he was here to arrest me, he would have brought back-up. This must be about something else.

'Not disturbing, am I?' he asks. It's an odd question. I can't imagine anyone who wouldn't be disturbed at an inspector from the Helsinki constabulary regularly visiting them and asking all kinds of awkward questions.

'Not at all,' I reply. I catch the familiar scent of medium roast coming from the Curly Cake. 'Coffee?'

'That would be … You're sure I'm not taking up your time?'

'Let's call it my coffee break,' I say. 'I own this park, after all.'

I hear a note of pride in my voice and I see that Osmala notices it too. The inspector and I walk through to the hall, then he stops. I notice this a step and a half later and turn.

'Is it alright if we don't go to the café?' he asks. 'Let's look at these walls instead. My wife was reading about them in the paper.'

'By all means,' I say.

'But allow me to show you a picture first,' he says, and opens the large folder in his hand. He takes out a sheet of A4 with a colour photograph of the big man. 'Has this man ever visited the park?'

'Not to my knowledge,' I say. 'I think I'd remember if a man like that visited the adventure park. He looks like quite a dangerous character.'

Osmala nods, takes the image and returns it to the folder.

'Extremely dangerous. And you're absolutely sure you haven't seen him, perhaps in your brother's company?'

'I'm absolutely sure. What's his name?'

My question is sincere. I know almost nothing about this man, not even his name. Osmala's light-blue eyes open and close.

'Pekka Koponen,' he says.

'Doesn't ring any bells, I'm afraid.'

Perhaps for the first time in my company, Osmala smiles. Almost. Then he nods. 'I thought as much.'

'Has he, this Koponen, said something regarding the park?'

It's a natural question, it's only to be expected. After all, I *am* the owner and general manager of the adventure park, so I need to know. However, Osmala seems somewhat surprised at my question.

'Has he said something? No. He hasn't said anything. It's no secret that these people prefer not to talk to the police.'

I wait. Osmala has turned slightly and seems to be looking at something behind me.

'How many slides do you have over there?'

'Thirteen,' I say and turn to look at the Big Dipper. Children squeal; gravity is a joyful thing.

'I take it you know that one of your employees has a past conviction for embezzlement?' he asks, then waits.

I remember this tactic. Osmala chats jovially, but it's a diversionary tactic; he bluffs like a striker approaching the six-yard box.

'The matter has come to my attention,' I reply honestly, and realise that I can easily ask the kind of questions that the owner of an adventure park might ask in a situation like this and in which I have an acute interest, for a number of reasons. 'Do the police suspect her of something too?'

Osmala's steps are slow and heavy. I walk alongside him. Osmala looks over at the Komodo Locomotive, which is about to leave the station.

'No, not as far as I know,' he says. 'Should we?'

We arrive in front of the Frankenthaler wall and stop to admire it. I think to myself how I both do and do not know the person who painted it. Once again, I have a chance to be exactly what I am: a concerned adventure-park proprietor.

'I couldn't possibly know about that,' I say. 'But does one of the park's employees have a connection to this Koponen?'

Osmala turns slightly. 'No,' he says. 'I didn't mean that. I meant, have you noticed anything suspicious regarding this particular employee?'

'No.' I shake my head, relieved at this information. I don't know how I would have reacted to the knowledge that the big man and Laura had some form of contact. 'There's one thing I must ask. Off the record, if that's alright. I own this place and I'm trying to make sure everything works as smoothly as...'

'You're worried. I understand.'

'Naturally.'

'The police turn up here asking all sorts, opening up the freezers, and so on.'

'Right.'

Osmala looks at me, clearly taking stock, then starts walking towards the next wall, the Krasner. I follow him.

'I understand,' he says. 'But at this stage in the investigation, I can't go into details. I'm sure you'll appreciate that we've looked into all kinds of connections.'

'But you just said—'

'And you'll appreciate too,' Osmala continues as though he hasn't heard my protestations, 'that I'd be here in a different capacity if we'd found any sort of connection between the two of them.'

We come to a stop.

'I'll be honest,' he says. 'The same goes for you and this painter.' Osmala nods at the Krasner wall.

'This isn't anything you wouldn't have been able to deduce for yourself,' he continues. 'But there's something very interesting about the set-up.'

'What set-up?'

'An inexperienced adventure-park owner turns up from outside the industry. Waiting here is an employee who probably learned a thing or two as the partner of a skilful fraudster and who – rather unjustly, if you ask me – was convicted alongside him. Of course, she did sign those documents, but she was up against a master manipulator. As you can guess, we looked into this connection right away: was this employee trying to trick you or was she in cahoots with Koponen?'

I look at the mural. The colours seem to have become more vivid throughout Osmala's explanation, and they are brightening still. Osmala shrugs his shoulders.

'Like you said, you haven't noticed anything – because there wasn't any contact or connection. Personally...' Osmala takes a deep breath. 'I'm very happy. I think it's great to see people survive, change direction, turn a page. Just look at these murals.'

Krasner, Tanning, de Lempicka, Frankenthaler, O'Keeffe and Jansson. It's as though I am seeing them for the first time. Osmala reaches for his jacket pocket and glances at his phone.

'I have to go,' he says.

'Of course,' I say without looking at him. The murals gleam, now dazzlingly bright.

'Behind a success like this,' he says, 'there's always so much more dedication than we can see with the naked eye.'

My senses are heightened, and, more importantly, for the first time in a long while I can calculate things the way I last did when I worked for the insurance company – so that I know with absolute certainty all the variables in the equation.

'That's true,' I admit.

'I'll be back at the weekend with the missus so we can look at these,' he says, and takes his first emphatic step towards the entrance.

'The door is always open,' I hear myself say.

35

I continue my calculations in my office. I open up the park's consumer-credit loan-management system. At first glance, there is nothing especially noteworthy. Then I move all the information regarding the loans into my own, parallel Excel spreadsheet and begin going through the loans one at a time, and before long I begin to see the tiny discrepancies.

The balance in the consumer-credit account is decreasing faster than the value of the loans ought to entail. At first the discrepancy is small, then significant, and eventually, once the direction of travel becomes clear, the balance all but falls off a cliff. Once I have added the total amount of money loaned and subtracted it from the opening balance, I see that around half of the bank's money, just shy of 125,000 euros, has essentially disappeared into thin air.

But the money hasn't disappeared. It has been neatly transferred out of the account, after which the details of the transfer have been erased from the book-keeping and the balance adjusted accordingly. This is a simple procedure, just a few strokes of the keyboard, a few clicks of the mouse. On the surface it's hard to notice the operation, not least because there are so many loans to itemise and some of them are so small, some as small as fifty euros, that the sheer length and scope of the list tricks the eye, like a rug covering a gaping hole in the floor. From the bank's loan-management system, it is very hard to see where and when these ghost transfers took place.

However, they are relatively easy to spot in the bank's actual bank account, where it is impossible to play with smoke and mirrors, and I can see exactly what has happened to the money: apparently it has been spent on consultancy services. The message field tells me as much. The recipient's account number is always the same too, which helps identify these out-payments.

One hundred and twenty-five thousand euros' worth of consultancy services.

I lean back in my chair.

Someone knew about it. Maybe right from the start, or at least very soon thereafter.

The situations come to my mind in a series of images, as though I have taken ancient photographs and am now looking at them in a frame. The first encounter with Lizard Man, in this very room, the way the employees came into the room one by one, as if to save me, the way glances were exchanged, that moment of recognition. Then, soon after that, my announcement about the opening of the bank, the sudden appearance of the initial invested capital, the money that I disguised as increased sales revenue. Which, naturally, didn't fool the one person who always took care of the daily sales reports. Then: how I quickly organised training for all staff members on how to use the operating system designed to make awarding loans as quick and easy as possible, and how a certain person with previous experience of living in financial grey areas, if only following from the side lines, might see something interesting in my all-too-simple programme. Then, how the decidedly unofficial aspect of my operations would become clear at the very latest upon the discovery of something in the café's freezer that didn't belong there.

At this point, someone who has been closely following events must have drawn the right conclusions. That person knew I wouldn't be calling Osmala in a hurry. That person also knew I would eventually have to quietly wind down the bank's operations, write things off in a creative manner, probably using some form of double-entry book-keeping, something this person also understands very well. And even if she didn't, she must have suspected something along these lines was going on. But ultimately, she knew she was stealing money that had been acquired dishonestly, money that didn't officially exist, and for this reason alone she knew I would keep things to myself later on – even when I finally joined the dots between the missing 125,000 euros and her being gone for good.

I notice that as I've been doing these calculations my heart has started beating harder and louder, that a freezing wind has been moving and gathering speed within me. I look again at the results. Mathematics is incorruptible, it always tells the truth. And the truth is, I have been outcounted. And that's not all. Now it feels as though the truth has sharp, cold, deeply personal nails ready to scratch and tear at me. I keep staring at the numbers, the wind gathers force and the nails grow sharper.

Finally, I give in and let the storm come.

TWO WEEKS LATER

The parking lot fills up at midday. The sheer noise and frantic movement inside the park suggest that this might be our best Sunday – or any day – this year. The number of tickets sold offers solid proof: it is our best day of the year. While this feels rewarding in both personal and financial terms – at this rate we will be back in the clear sooner than I had anticipated – it also means I'm running at great speed from one crisis to the next.

In the last hour alone, there have been incidents ranging from a sprained wrist, counterfeit entrance tickets and a bubble-gum-induced blockage at one of the slides, to a pair of quarrelling mothers who are first escorted outside, then all the way to their respective cars.

I stand by one of the cars on this cloudless, chilly October afternoon, and I can still hear the cursing coming from inside the vehicle when I receive a text message from the Curly Cake Café. The message is short and to the point; from Johanna, I would expect nothing else. The mother in the car twice shows me her extended middle finger: first as she backs out of her parking space and again a second later as she speeds away.

🐇

I find Johanna in the kitchen, which is both spotless and full of action. This in itself is unsurprising. Johanna is dedicated to her café and she keeps it running like clockwork. She sees me and nods. My first impression of her as a fearless Ironman competitor, hard as rock, hasn't changed. I still haven't had an actual conversation with her, a conversation longer than a few words here and there. There's been no need. Even now, everything in the kitchen seems to be running in synchronised harmony: the ovens, the fryers, both dishwashers, the big steel dough kneader the size of a small cement mixer. At a quick glance, I can't see anything that I could help her with. Before I can ask or say anything, she gestures toward one of the tall stools.

'Sit down,' she says. 'We need to talk.'

'Very well.'

'Eight minutes,' she says as she slides a tray of croissants into the oven the way curling players send off the pin, only she does it faster and with even more precision. She closes the oven door and consults her smart watch. 'That should do it.'

I am unsure whether she is referring to the croissants or the estimated length of our conversation, so I remain seated and wait. I realise this is the second time in recent weeks that I've found myself racing against the clock and buns in ovens.

'I'm sure you've noticed something is missing,' she says, and I think I see her nod in the direction of the freezer, but I'm not sure. 'All you need to know is that you don't need to worry about it.'

Now I am absolutely positive, one-hundred-percent certain.

'Thank you,' I say hesitantly. 'For the chicken wings.'

'As I said before, I'm the one who should be thanking you. But there's something else missing too, right?'

This is all going too fast, I think. On the other hand, if Johanna already knows ... If the freezer is anything to go by, she might even know more than I do. A lightning-quick re-evaluation of the situation tells me this must be the case.

'The hundred and twenty-five thousand euros,' I say.

'Any theories?'

Again, this is too fast, but I conclude that since she must already have a grasp of the basics, so to speak, I can safely present a theory of my own. Because that's all I have. A theory.

'She did it,' I say. 'Laura did it. I can only guess when it all started, but I think I know. When those two men visited, she recognised the one I call Lizard Man. Perhaps he was one of her ex's acquaintances, the ex whom she eventually joined in prison. Laura realised the park was in financial difficulty, maybe she noticed something during Juhani's tenure here too. Then you looked in the freezer and discovered the man I had temporarily hidden there. The way she talked about you and the fact that she let you look after her daughter told me you two were close. I think I know where you and she met and when.'

I pause. Johanna remains silent – but she doesn't deny it. So I continue.

'Perhaps one of you recognised the man in the freezer. Then I told Laura about the plans to set up the bank. As someone very familiar with the park's finances, she knew that the park itself didn't have any capital. She knew the money must have come from outside, and because she knew who I was dealing with, she also knew that money would be tainted. Everybody learned how to work the bank's new software. Laura has experience of how certain kinds of transfers can take place under the radar and how everything can be made to look legal as long as those transfers meet certain criteria. She knows I don't think collection agencies charge a fair interest rate and she knew I wouldn't contact Osmala, whom you recognised right away – of that I'm quite sure. She trusted that eventually I would put a stop to it all. The rest was about making sure there was nothing to connect her to the park any more. Laura took the money, and now she's gone.'

Johanna's expression hasn't flinched. She looks at her smart watch, and perhaps there is a slight flicker of something on her face. For the first time in my presence, she looks worried. Perhaps at the thought of the croissants over-heating, I think, but dismiss the idea. This is something else.

'No,' she says.

Her eyes are fixed on mine.

'It's a theory...'

'I don't mean that,' she says.

The machines hum steadily. The only sound in the kitchen is their low purr.

'You're right,' she says. 'She did know where the money was coming from. She also knew the park was in danger – and she knew you were in danger too. She wanted to help the park and to help you, but she had to stay away from both once the detective turned up. The detective I recognised. You were right about that too.'

'But when I said she took the money, you said "no".'

'Because your theory was wrong,' she says. 'She didn't take the money.'

Given all the nonsensical things I've heard lately, this last sentence makes the least sense of all. I'm trying to see any new scenarios, new ways the chain of events could have panned out, but they are scarce. In fact, they are non-existent. Johanna must sense the cogs aimlessly ratcheting in my brain.

'Not for herself,' Johanna says. 'For the park. The money is ready to be used for the park when the time comes. As far as I've understood, certain parties might still show an interest in the park's finances.'

She is, of course, referring to Detective Inspector Osmala. From what I gather, the police are winding up their investigation into the park. But that is not the reason I feel as though the world is fading away, the reason I can no longer hear the noise of the park behind me, the hum of the kitchen, the reason that my ears are now filled with the sound of my own heart and blood.

'Assuming that is what happened…'

'It is.'

'Why would she … go through all that?'

Johanna no longer looks like an Ironman competitor. Now she looks like an Ironman winner, the toughest, the hardiest of them all.

'You're going to make me say it, aren't you?'

'I'm just trying to understand...'
'She loves you.'

The road curves slightly uphill. The evening is dark and the sky is clear. A few stars are already visible. I walk faster and faster and make observations that, even as I register them, I know are only an attempt to distract myself from the matter at hand. As I turn onto the short, crescent-shaped road that leads to the right apartment block, I look at my surroundings and think that this really is a very well-chosen neighbourhood given its location, its proximity to the nature preservation area, the general quality of the housing – all built during the 1950s when functionality rather than fantasy was the main design principle – and the steadily rising market value of the properties.

Indeed, it's a 1950s building I'm looking for, a very well-maintained one, beautifully situated on a slope giving marvellous views of the bay on the other side of the building, most likely with apartments ranging from one to three bedrooms with straightforward layouts that allow for maximum utility. Logical, sensible, beautiful...

And all of a sudden it's as clear as the evening sky that I can't distract myself any longer, not for a single moment. At the same time, it's obvious that being logical and rational alone is no longer enough; now I will have to be something else too. What that something else might be, I don't know exactly, but it feels as though I have to let go of something I've been holding on to, something I've been clinging to with frozen fingers.

I stop in a dimly lit doorway in eastern Helsinki and ring the downstairs doorbell. Sunday evening in the suburbs. The birds have flown south for the winter, there is no wind, and the hum of traffic is far away. I hear a voice in the intercom. A very young voice.

'Who is it?'

'My name is Henri Koskinen.'

There is a pause.

'Who's there?' the young voice asks again.

'Henri Koskinen,' I repeat.

'Why?'

'Why is my name Henri Koskinen?'

'What?'

I find myself at a loss. I'm about to ask who it is I'm negotiating with when the buzzer sounds and the door's lock is released. I grab the handle and step inside. There is no lift, so I take the stairs to the fourth floor. The apartment door is open, and as I climb the final steps I see a small face disappear from view. That must be...

'My daughter,' says Laura Helanto. 'Tuuli.'

Laura is standing in the hallway beneath a ceiling lamp that seems to set her wild hair on fire. Figuratively, of course. Tuuli is half hiding in the doorway to the right. I say hello and she disappears altogether.

'Come in,' says Laura.

I take a few steps and close the door behind me. I turn, and there we are, the two of us standing in Laura Helanto's home. It is warm and cosily lit, and I catch the aroma of lasagne. I find myself thinking that this is what a home should feel and smell like. Laura stands looking at me, and it takes me a moment to realise that she seems to be waiting for me to say something.

'I talked to Johanna today,' I say. 'She told me why you did it.'

Laura looks over her shoulder, then back at me. Light reflects from her glasses like a beam. But I've already understood the situation. I understood it long ago. With Tuuli still within earshot, I won't say aloud that her mother did an excellent job on the bank-fraud front, that she managed to mislead both the police and myself, and to shelter me from further harm while I was involved in hiding a body, learning the ins and outs of hanging techniques, and otherwise dealing with a gallery of unscrupulous criminals with dangerously – and lethally – low levels of self-restraint. But that's all water under the bridge. Now there is only one thing left to do.

'And so,' I continue, 'I wanted to thank you.'

Laura seems unmoved, and I don't know why it takes so long for her to speak.

'You're welcome,' she says eventually.

'That's not all.'

'No?'

'No.'

We stand there for what seems like an eternity, the seconds feel longer than usual, until I manage to prise open the frozen fingers gripping me from the inside.

'From the very first day we met, I've felt extremely uncomfortable in your presence,' I begin. 'It's the best feeling I've ever experienced. I've concluded this is due to at least three separate factors. First, you are the smartest person I have ever met. You fooled me, and nobody has ever been able to fool me. Second, your art makes me feel things I've never felt before. I can't explain it, and actually I don't even want to explain it. Third, you make me forget about mathematics. Not all the time, of course, that wouldn't benefit the business and would probably ruin the promising growth we're experiencing. But you make me see things in a new light; you make me want to live my life differently. Or, at least, you make me want to try and live it with less of a focus on probability calculus. And now I'm starting to feel there was a fourth factor too, but as I said, you make me forget things, and I like that too.'

The words have come out very fast, and most of them are different from the ones I'd been planning to use. Just as surprisingly, I mean every single one of them. At first I think Laura is smiling, then I see a tear roll down her cheek. No. Yes. She is doing both – smiling and crying.

'Henri, I can honestly say that nobody has ever said anything like that to me before.'

'That's not all,' I say.

'No?'

'No.'

I step closer. Just then Tuuli comes out of hiding. She is short and looks very much like her mother.

'You're Henri Koskinen,' she says.

'And you're Tuuli,' I say.

This brings a smile to her face. I smile too. Then I look at Laura Helanto and remember that I still have two things to take care of. The first is something I've been waiting to do since my chat with Johanna.

'I love you, Laura,' I say.

And the second one...

'I love you, Henr—'

I kiss her, she kisses me, we hold each other. And if I could speak, I would tell her what a perfect equation this makes.

SOURCES

The following works have helped and guided me in the process of writing this novel. One way or another, I have employed artistic freedom in interpreting the wisdom contained in these volumes. Thus, all possible mistakes and misunderstandings are solely my own responsibility. Just like the novel itself which, I should reveal right now, I have fabricated from beginning to end.

Gigerenzer, Gerd: *Risk Savvy: How to Make Good Decisions* (Penguin Books, 2014)

Holopainen, Martti: *The Foundations of Mathematical Statistics* (Otava, 1992)*

Laininen, Pertti: *Probability and Its Statistical Application* (Otatieto, 2001)*

Salomaa, J.E.: *Arthur Schopenhauer. Life and Philosophy* (WSOY, 1944)*

Schopenhauer, Arthur: *A Pessimist's Wisdom. Selected Essays from Schopenhauer's Works* (WSOY, 1944)*

Schopenhauer, Arthur: *The Art of Being Right. 38 Ways to Win an Argument* (1831)

Schopenhauer, Arthur: *The World as Will and Representation* (trans. R. B. Haldane & J. Kemp, 1844)

Taleb, Nassim Nicholas: *Fooled by Randomness: The Hidden Role of Chance in Life and the Markets* (Random House, 2001)

Taleb, Nassim Nicholas: *The Black Swan: The Impact of the Highly Improbable* (Random House, 2007)

Tilastokeskus: *Finnish Statistical Yearbook 2017* (Tilastokeskus, 2017)*

* Only available in Finnish

ACKNOWLEDGMENTS

It's a long journey between the writer's finished manuscript and the reader – even when that journey is smooth and fast. But if you add the fact that I write my books in Finnish and publish them first in Finland, we have, I think, something of a miracle here. There are so many things that could go wrong or, obviously, not happen at all. Yet, happily, everything has gone right, the right things have happened, and here we are: you are reading the book in English somewhere in the world, and I'm here in Finland thanking you for it. (Also, planning to go to the sauna later this evening.)

All this, excluding the sauna, has been made possible by several wonderful people.

In Finland, the manuscript was expertly edited by Aleksi Pöyry. Then, David Hackston performed his magic and took the book from Finnish to English in a way that seems seamless. If you know anything about Finnish, that is a thing to behold. David is simply the bee's knees, as I believe you say.

In Stockholm, Sweden, my literary agent, Federico Ambrosini at the Salomonsson Agency, has provided me with invaluable insight and support throughout the years. The same is true for everyone at the agency, and I am deeply grateful to them.

In London, England, the English-language manuscript has been steadfastly and precisely edited by West Camel, who always seems to find the correct linguistic equivalence for my words. And the book has seen the light of day because the fabulous Karen Sullivan has published it. It's a huge joy and a privilege to work with Karen.

Everywhere and anytime, I wish to thank my Faithful First Reader: Anu, I love you.

Finally, from my heart, thank you, the reader, for reading. I don't take it for granted and I do hope to see you somewhere down the road.

And now to the sauna.

An exclusive extract from *THE MOOSE PARADOX* by Antti Tuomainen, book two in The Rabbit Factor Trilogy. Translated by David Hackston and forthcoming from Orenda Books in 2022

NOW

The new budget forecast is ready at half past ten. Because of the rapidly changing circumstances, I have had to cut our expenditure even more radically and cancel a number of investments that we had previously agreed upon; but I have tightened the belt equally, spreading the burden across all our departments. I have lowered my own salary to zero. Separately, I have drawn up a plan to create a financial buffer in case of an emergency, so that a situation like the current one – not to mention the recent threat of wholesale bankruptcy – will never happen again. Building up a buffer like this requires patience and frugality over many years, but the chances of it paying off one day will be greatly increased. The numbers speak for themselves: if we work systematically and trust in the facts, we will survive. This I know from personal experience.

Mathematics has saved my life, both figuratively and literally. This is what mathematics does: it saves us. It brings balance, clarity and peace of mind; it helps us see how things really are, it tells us what we should do in order to reach our goals. Though the current situation at the adventure park is challenging, I still believe that the future is bright, and it's all thanks to mathematics – and a little bit of effort. Of course, my views and feelings about this have adjusted slightly, mostly because I've been able to dedicate myself to the data and have been allowed to calculate things in peace.

The last customers left the park a while ago, and, according to the rota, today Kristian has locked everything up. During the daytime, the background noise in the park is like the rush of crashing waves. Now the sea has calmed, and everything is perfectly still.

I go through the Excel file one more time. The rows flow beautifully, complement one another, and the sums are correct. I notice I'm not so much checking things as going through them one more time, simply for my own pleasure. Perhaps this is just what I need after all the recent twists and turns and surprises: good old-fashioned arithmetic, clarifying and illuminating matters and the relationships between them. I have to remind myself that Schopenhauer needs his supper and maybe even someone to talk to (which, while not entirely unprecedented, is, statistically speaking, a much rarer occurrence), and I click the file shut. I stand up from my chair and blink my dry eyes; I can almost feel how red they are.

The door into the corridor is open, and I can't hear anything coming from Minttu K's room either: neither her rough, ratchety voice on the phone nor the radio, let alone a low-pitched snore infused with cigarettes and gin *lonkero*. My back feels stiff, and again I am reminded that I really ought to take up some kind of exercise, though I have no idea where I would find the time. I'm coming to realise there's no rest for the director of a successful adventure park.

I stare out of the window for a moment and see nothing but the empty, November-grey car park in front of me. Suddenly my attention is drawn to the furthest left-hand edge of the car park. It takes a few seconds for my brain to process what I am seeing. The spot is right between two streetlamps, each pool of light barely touching the metal and the rubber, and this is why it takes a little while to put the shapes and contours together.

A bicycle.

It is propped on its stand, and in every respect it looks like a very average bicycle, parked and waiting for its owner. What seems somewhat out of the ordinary, however, is the bike's location, which cannot be considered remotely sensible: it is far away both from the road and from the main entrance to the park. In fact, it is far away from everything. I look at it a moment longer, unsure what I'm expecting to see. The bicycle is parked in the half-light. Eventually, I come to the obvious conclusion: someone has simply left it there.

I switch off my computer, take my scarf and coat from the stand and pull them on. I switch off the lights in my office and walk across the dusky main hall to the back door. I don't want to use the front door because opening and closing it again would require a complex series of checks and double-checks. The back door is quicker and handier.

I step out onto the loading bay, take the metallic steps down to ground level and set off around the building. I can hear the roar of traffic in the distance, and my own steps sound almost amplified.

The night air has that crisp, late-autumn note to it, and the earth is wet even without the rain. I arrive at the corner of the building, where I have a view of the full length of its left-hand wall and the left side of the car park. This is the narrowest strip of the park's grounds. From the outer wall, it is only about five metres before the asphalt comes to an end and the terrain dips steeply down into a ditch, then rises up just as steeply at the edge of a small stretch of tangled woodland on the other side. I walk alongside the wall, and the strip feels more narrow and corridor-like with every step, as though the adjoining woodland were a united front, growing in strength and tightening its grip on the building with small, inexorable steps. Of course, this isn't literally true. What is true, however – though at first I think my eyes must be playing tricks on me – is that the bicycle has now disappeared.

Perhaps someone simply had a spot of acute, late-night business to attend to in the woods. We're all different, as I've come to appreciate on many occasions. If you have something to take care of, something you might not necessarily do elsewhere, here, in a spruce forest in the middle of Vantaa, you can do it to your heart's content – spend a moment of time in your thicket of choice, before continuing on your way, the richer for it. But these thoughts are like matchsticks that won't quite light; they flare up only to go out right away. I'm indulging in wishful thinking, and I know it.

Then I see him.

A man running right towards me.

Like a bowling ball with legs, I think to myself.

And we find ourselves in a bowling alley of sorts. The strip of tarmac is long and narrow, and the bowling ball is hurtling towards me at a ferocious pace, right in the middle of the alley – and I am standing at the end of it. On top of this, the ball seems to be speeding up. I turn as soon as I realise what's happening. I set off running, and at the same moment I see that the corner of the building and the back yard are much further away than I had estimated.

I am still stiff from all the hours sitting at my desk. The bowling ball's speed is quite simply greater than mine, I realise this from the very first step. But I have to run.

I quickly glance over my shoulder. The bowling ball is wearing a dark-blue tracksuit, a black or blue hoodie and a black woolly hat pulled almost right down over its face. Its short little legs look like something out of a cartoon, in which the legs are replaced with a wildly spinning tornado. Arms punctuate its frantic run like a pair of pistons on overdrive. If this were any other situation, I would stand there watching the bowling ball's acceleration out of sheer fascination. Instead, I run as fast as I possibly can, and still I can hear the whirring machine gaining on me.

The corner is just up ahead.

The loading bay is right around the corner. At the other end of the loading bay is a ladder leading up to the roof. I can't think of anything else. If I can just reach the foot of the ladder and start climbing, I'll be able to kick at the fingers of anyone trying to climb up behind me. Naturally, this is a far from optimal solution. It's hard to think of many alternative scenarios, let alone consider which of them is the best choice, as the ball is rolling ever close, and I am the tenpin.

I'm nearing the corner, it's only fifteen metres away. I reach the corner and change course.

I run towards the loading bay, only a few more steps until the steel stairs. I reach the foot of the stairs and start climbing up to the loading bay, one rattling rung at a time. I see the ladder in front of me and think I might just reach the lowest rung and make it up to the roof when...

The bowling ball slams into my back.

The impact knocks me forwards, as though someone has flung me up into the air. I slump face first to the latticed floor of the loading bay. I try to stand up, but I can't. Instead, a horse appears on my back. At least, that's what it feels like, as though rider and ridee have suddenly changed place.

The bowling ball presses down on my back, gripping my head in its hands – I can feel its cold, stubby, but strong, fingers against my temples – then it lifts my head up ... and slams it right down again.

My forehead strikes the steel grille once, twice, thrice. I hear a dull metallic sound ringing in my ears and vibrating through my body. I grip the man's wrists, but they are thick and sturdy as pipes buried in the ground, which means I can't stop their movement. My forehead is battered against the grille over and over. When my head rises again, or, rather, when it is yanked upwards, ahead and to the left I see some wooden planks that I've been using to mend the Strawberry Maze.

I stretch out my arm, elongating my entire upper body, and

manage to grab hold of an L-shaped length of wood. I pull it closer, inch by inch, and eventually clasp my fingers tightly around it. At the same time, my forehead is still being thwacked against the steel floor, and I get the distinct impression that the steel will soon give way under the force of the blows. There isn't much time. I grip the plank as firmly as I can, make a quick assessment of the length of the bowling ball's back and the position of its head, and fling my arm backwards with all the strength I can muster.

As it lands, the sound the plank makes is surprising. It's soft and wet.

The ball's fingers release their grip and the horse on my back wobbles. I push myself up, and the horse staggers again, a little more violently this time, and I manage to crawl out from underneath it. I move my legs, stand up, and my first thought is that I ought to start running again. But that's not what happens. The beating my head has taken causes me considerable dizziness, and I have to move with careful, fumbling steps. I glance over my shoulder. The bowling ball is staring at something in his fingers, then he looks at me and holds up the focus of his attention for me to see. A tooth. It quickly dawns on me exactly where I struck him with my wooden hammer.

Square in the mouth.

The bowling ball throws the tooth from his hand. It arches through the air and disappears into the darkness. He wipes his bloody mouth on the back of his sleeve. Then he lunges at me again. I turn and dash into a sprint. Another mismatched bout of wrestling will be too much for me, I know that. But I run all the same, and it's only ten or so metres to the foot of the ladder. Every step requires the utmost concentration. Maybe that's why I haven't noticed that a third person has appeared on the loading bay.

This new arrival is wearing a balaclava and is approaching me from the dark end of the loading bay. The balaclava first runs towards me then changes tack, and I can see he is trying to pass me.

A lot happens in the next two and a half seconds.

The bowling ball is about to catch up with me again; now he is only an arm's length away. The balaclava is approaching from the opposite direction, from the darkness behind me, so it's likely that the bowling ball hasn't seen him.

As he runs forwards, the balaclava crouches down, snatches up the strawberry, and finally reaches me.

The strawberry in the balaclava's hands is part of the Strawberry Maze. It's a decoration, the same one that I brought out here earlier this afternoon to take it apart and put the pieces in two separate recycling bins, the plastic with the plastic and the metallic parts with the metal. It has a diameter of around sixty centimetres, and I removed it from the park because it is broken and its cracked edges might injure the children.

I try to change direction, but this only makes me stumble and partially turn around. And then I see what happens next.

The balaclava and the bowling ball collide at full pelt. It might be more correct to say that the balaclava strikes the bowling ball with the strawberry, bringing it crashing down on his head. Or, to be even more precise, I should say that the bowling ball merges into the strawberry. The plastic cracks even further, and the bowling ball's head disappears inside the strawberry.

The strawberry becomes lodged around the man's shoulders, it looks like a giant cochineal crown with a tuft of green hair on top. At the same time, the sharp straggles of steel wire cut into the man's neck, specifically his jugular. Which tears open. And the result of all this is...

...a strawberry-headed man staggering to regain his balance on the loading bay with a fountain of blood gushing from his neck.

I feel dizzy, my ears are rushing, and the only way I can remain upright is by gripping my knees for support. I assume there are several reasons for the dizziness: lack of oxygen, the sustained pummelling of my forehead against the steel grille and the sight in front of me. It's as though I'm watching a complex magic trick that has gone wrong somewhere along the line, or perhaps even an attempt at some kind of world record.

The man is clearly bewildered, a little discombobulated – who wouldn't be, after getting lodged inside a plastic strawberry and sustaining a deep laceration to the neck? And his subsequent actions aren't at all sensible. His arms are flailing here and there, and he seems to jump up and down on the spot, though what he really should do is...

The balaclava takes a few steps towards him, says something I can't hear, then approaches the man, his hands outstretched in what I assume is an attempt to help him. Perhaps the man hears the approaching footsteps and fatally misreads the situation. Either that, or something else makes him panic, and he suddenly spins round 180 degrees and bursts into a run.

The strawberry-headed assailant dashes across the loading bay, sputtering blood as he goes, his legs moving like little propellers.

The balaclava runs after him and shouts something again. It looks as though the man is speeding up. Then, only a few steps later, the strawberry starts to sway, and the orbit of the swaying motion increases with every step. The balaclava is about to catch up with him when the final sway makes any kind of assistance virtually impossible. The man dives from the bay into the night.

For a brief moment he flies through the glare of the streetlamps, the strawberry gleams, the blood forms a red rainbow through the air, his legs paddle hard...

Then all the variables change at once.

Gravity has the last word.

EIGHT DAYS EARLIER

1

The adventure park could be seen from afar. It was a brightly coloured, red-yellow-and-orange box, in size somewhere between Stockmann's department store and an average airport terminal. It was almost two hundred metres in length, stood fifteen metres tall, and on its roof in giant lettering was the park's name: YouMeFun. Right now, the wistful, beautiful November sunlight struck the sign, bathing the car park the size of three football pitches in gold and lending a soft sheen to the great mass of tin and steel standing proudly behind it.

I stopped at the traffic lights, looked up at the adventure park across the road and thought once again that something really was different.

Something had changed and changed for good.

This was my park, I thought to myself. The thought gave me strength. I had almost died trying to save this park. I had steered it out from under a mountain of debt, and though it might not be profitable yet, at least, in all probability, it would be a survivor.

Only six months ago I'd been forced to resign from my job as an actuary at a leading insurance company. I was faced with choosing between a change in my job description that would have seen me moving into a broom cupboard to conduct an endless stream of meaningless pseudo-calculations, or taking part in an emotion-oriented, time-dynamic training programme, not to mention group yoga sessions. But only a moment after handing in my resignation, I learned that my brother had passed away and that I had inherited his adventure park. Upon arrival at said adventure park, I learned that I had inherited my brother's considerable debts too, debts that he had taken out with a number of hard-boiled criminals. One thing led to another, and to save my own life, the jobs of the staff and the park itself, I had to resort to some radical acts of self-defence, and as a result of this one of the gangsters had died after finding himself on the receiving end of the kinetic intersection between me and a giant plastic rabbit's ear, I ended up opening a payday-loan operation, then quickly running it down again, I met an artist who aroused feelings I had hitherto never experienced, I had to avoid both the crooks and the police and witness an event that still makes me touch my neck somewhat nervously.

After all this, the park's financial situation was still tough. There was no other word for it.

I'd already resorted to numerous money-saving measures, and I suspected there would be more of them down the line. I'd tried to lead by example in every respect. My salary was already lower than anybody else's, and I paid for my lunch and snacks myself at the park's main eatery, the Curly Cake Café. I didn't want to cut the other employees' salaries, but obviously I'd been forced to take a closer look at budget allocations for each department. This initially met with some resistance, but I defended my solutions with a series of carefully compiled spreadsheets and stressed to the staff at every turn that we had to look at things over a five- to ten-year timeframe. This was greeted with silence. Which, in turn, gave me the chance to outline my money-saving proposals, which ranged from the largescale (energy saving: the ambient temperature in the main hall was now on average one and a half degrees cooler than a month ago. Naturally, the children hadn't noticed the change, and I provided the staff with warm sweatshirts sporting the park's logo) to the smaller scale (I repainted the Loopy Ladder in Caper Castle by myself, which was evident in the splashes of paint on the wall behind it, but the saving was not insignificant).

I crossed the road and walked into the car park. My mood

improved with every step because all the pieces were finally falling into place, both in general and individually, in the long term and on a day-by-day basis. The equation was beginning to take shape. All was well.

This was my life nowadays. And most importantly of all, my life was orderly again.

A series of brisk steps brought me to the main entrance, the sliding doors opened and I stepped into the foyer, which was well lit and decorated in bright colours. This was always the point at which I felt as though I was stepping into another world. Something like that happened now too. Alongside this feeling, there now appeared another, one that I recognised right away. I realised that I felt at home. Was that what all this was about – that this adventure park had become a home from home?

Kristian was standing behind the ticket counter. He was handing a set of tickets to a tired-looking man trying to shepherd three shorter customers, all actively pulling in different directions. The man took his tickets, turned reluctantly, herded his flock, and together they all disappeared inside the main hall.

I bade Kristian good morning. I expected to see that broad, eager smile of his and to hear him give some variation on the theme of how fabulous or magnificent this particular morning was.

'Morning,' he said politely and continued staring at his computer screen.

Kristian was highly effective in his role as sales manager, and on the whole he was extraordinarily enthusiastic. He was in the habit of calling me and sending me messages, even outside of work hours. *Hi Boss, there's a SUPER-AMAZING surprise here waiting for you!!!* he might text, though upon arrival at the park I would learn that this super-amazing surprise was nothing more than the release of a new flavour of ice cream at the self-service counter at the Curly Cake Café. For Kristian, every day was a great day, and he never tired of telling me so. Now, however, he was sullenly clicking his mouse. The clicks sounded like nervous little fillips. I glanced over my shoulder. There was no queue at the counter. By the volume of cars parked outside, I concluded that we had a moderate number of customers right now, just as one would expect on an unremarkable Wednesday morning in November.

'What a fantastic morning,' I heard myself saying and realised that the words came out of my mouth precisely because I hadn't heard them from anyone else.

'What?' asked Kristian. It was only now that he looked at me properly. He made eye contact with me, but his gaze was somehow unfocussed, as though while looking at me he had forbidden himself from seeing me. I was about to ask if there was anything troubling him, something pulling him closer and closer to the screen in front of him – he was stretching his neck in a most unnatural fashion – when I noticed the large clock in the park's foyer.

It was eleven o'clock. I hurried inside and found myself at the start of the Komodo Locomotive. The Komodo Locomotive was one of our oldest rides, a perennial favourite among our younger clientele. It was also one of the safest rides we had, suitable for those who weren't even old enough to ask to get on it. To increase security further, we had decided to install additional airbags in each of the seats. I thought this a bit over the top, but Esa was the park's head of security, and he believed we should prepare for anything. I'd realised some time ago that when Esa said 'anything', he really meant it.

I found Esa behind one of the carriages. He was lying on his stomach, tapping it with a hammer from underneath. As always, the air around him was stale and thick. And even though he was lying flat on the floor, he looked as though he would be ready to leap into action at any moment. The sweatshirts of the US Marine Corps, which he had worn religiously until only a few weeks ago and which listed the bearer's years of service, might have had something to do with it. Though these sweatshirts had recently been replaced with cosy-looking woollen jumpers, complete with colourful animal figures, I saw the same military demeanour and physical readiness that one might expect from a former US Marine.

'Aren't the airbags supposed to be on the inside?' I asked.

The hammer stopped in mid-air. Esa didn't turn or take his eyes from the underside of the carriage.

'All in good time,' he said.

'Meaning?'

'Once we've secured our position.'

I couldn't imagine what Esa was referring to, but this style of communication was typical.

'How long do you think it will take to ... secure our position?'

'Hard to say with our current intel. We're vastly outnumbered and constantly having to make do with inadequate coordinates. And there's no let-up in enemy fire—'

'Quite,' I interrupt him. 'I have to take an important call at eleven-thirty...'

'It'll take longer than that,' said Esa, this time speaking more quickly than ever before, the words spilling from his lips in a single jumble of sounds.

I looked around. Getting the Komodo Locomotive up and running wasn't a matter of life and death. There were still only relatively few customers, and most of them were larger than the median traveller on the Komodo Locomotive, and in all respects it looked as though today would be a fairly quiet day. Just then, Esa very clearly passed a cloud of noxious gases from deep within. I felt a warm puff of air on my face, stopped breathing through my nose so as not to trigger my gag reflex, opened my mouth and instantly felt a burning sensation at the top of my larynx.

'I'll come back later,' I suggested.

The hammer resumed its tapping. Esa said nothing.

I walked off towards the Big Dipper, and once I was sufficiently far away – in Esa's case, I considered a safe distance around fifteen metres – I filled my lungs with pure air once again.

The Curly Cake Café smelt of salmon soup and pastries fresh from the oven. Our shorter clients were often at the louder end of the scale, and that was the case now too. Though the air conditioning had recently been enhanced and optimised, the café was still very warm. Taken together, the cumulative effect of all these factors – the thick, greasy smells, the shrill squeals, the higher-than-usual temperature – made the place feel quite exhausting. I often felt conflicted when visiting the café, my mood a vexing combination of drowsiness and dread.

I walked up to the counter and saw Johanna in the kitchen. I took a butter-and-sugar bun from the glass cabinet and raised my plate so that Johanna could see it. She noticed me, lowered a batch of French fries into the vat of bubbling oil and walked to the other side of the counter. I was about to say I would pay for the bun and take it back to my office when Johanna cut me short.

'This one's on me,' she said. 'Do you want another one?'

I looked at the plate in my hand, the bun sitting on the plate. Then I looked up at Johanna again. The very first time I had met her, several months ago, I'd been struck by the way her face made me think of a former convict training for an iron-man competition. I wasn't wrong. And the café meant everything to her. Here, nothing happened without her say-so, and nobody circumvented the rules, both the written and the unwritten varieties. But more to the point, she never, under any circumstances whatsoever, gave anything away for free. And now she was offering me a second bun.

'I only need one,' I said.

'Just a thought, in case a second one might come in handy.'

'By my initial calculation, one should be enough to raise my blood-sugar levels,' I replied, and in a curious way I felt like a turtle that had been turned upside down: I couldn't move, and even if I could, it would have taken far too long.

'What about lunch?' she then asked.

'Lunch?'

'We have Sailor's Salmon Soup, Cock-a-Noodle-Do, and today's vegan option is Tearaway's Tofu Tart. For dessert there's Spotted Quick and all the grown-ups' favourite, Caramel Cannons. It's my treat.'

'I think I'll be fine with this for now…'

'I meant later on,' she explained.

I was about to say something – I didn't quite know what – when I noticed a queue had formed behind us. Johanna seemed to notice this too. She looked at me and gave a curt nod. I assumed this meant I was excused, for now. I took the opportunity and, once my legs started obeying me again, left.

I walked towards my office, passing by the Strawberry Maze and the usual cries and stampede of footsteps coming from inside it, then I turned right at the noisy, rattling Caper Castle, made my way around the Turtle Trucks, whose loud and over-excited drivers were currently changing seats, and headed towards the corridor, at the end of which was my office. I had only taken a few steps along the corridor and I was about to pass the office belonging to Minttu K, our head of sales and marketing, when she stopped me in my tracks.

'Hi,' she whispered. At least, I thought it was a whisper. The voice was gravelly and demanding, like a serrated saw against a plank of hard wood, but much, much lower. It was morning, but Minttu K's room already exuded the unmistakable aroma of tobacco and gin. She raised her right hand and waved me over, beckoned me inside. 'Let's talk money.'

'The marketing meeting isn't until Thursday,' I said. 'It's probably best if we return to the—'

Minttu K shook her head and raised a well-tanned hand to silence me. Her silver rings sparkled.

'Honey, this Tesla waits for no man. Imagine, a karate sensei. Thirty-five thousand followers on Instagram.'

Minttu K took a sip from her black mug. From her expression, it was hard to tell whether there was coffee in it or something else.

The mug was as black as her blazer, which was at least one size too small for her.

'And why do we need a ... karate sensei?' I asked.

'Karate kids,' she replied. 'There's plenty of them round here. All we need is a slogan.'

Minttu K ruffled her short blonde hair. She seemed utterly convinced of whatever it was she was trying to tell me, which didn't particularly surprise me.

'First, this sounds like it could be a little dangerous, and the park isn't really a martial-arts college...' I began but started to feel a slight wooziness. I had to get to my office. 'We don't have the funds to cover any extra activities. As I've said several times.'

Minttu K twiddled a cigarette in her fingers. It had appeared there without my noticing.

'You're going to let this fish get away?' she asked huskily, and before I could say anything at all, she answered the question herself: 'Fine then. We'll forever be second best.'

I was genuinely taken aback. Usually Minttu K was ready to fight to the bitter end, figuratively speaking. Now, barely seconds after the apparent end of our conversation, she was calmly sipping from her mug again, sucking intensely on the end of her cigarette and tapping her computer keyboard as before, as though she was reprimanding it for doing something naughty.

There was one final corner in the corridor.

The morning's encounters started replaying in my mind. And I realised that the brief wooziness of a moment ago had very concrete origins: it had grown exponentially with each encounter. Now they were all playing through my mind on fast-forward, getting stronger and sharper, taking on depth and life, and I started seeing and hearing things in them that I hadn't registered at the time. Kristian wasn't bursting with enthusiasm, he hadn't suggested any changes or offered to make improvements first thing in the morning, the way he usually did; Esa was in no hurry to shore up the park's security, and instead he was carrying out repairs at a leisurely pace and without any sense of impending disaster; Minttu K caved in quickly and easily; Johanna offered me a second bun in case I needed it. As that last thought came into focus and began echoing more vividly through my mind, I felt the hand holding the plate with my bun begin to tremble.

I turned the final corner, stepped into my office and stopped in my tracks.

The butter-and-sugar bun leapt into the air.

The plate flew from my hand and smashed to smithereens.

The dead had come to life.